"CATES, YOU KNOW WHY I'M HERE, DON'T YOU?"

Of course I do, Cates thought. It's been there all along. I just didn't see it at first.

Aloud he responded, "Yeah, I know."

"How long have you known?"

It depends on what you mean by *know*, Winston. I think I've known it for quite a while, but I just now admitted that I knew it. "Awhile, I guess."

"How'd you know, Cates? How did I give myself away?"

Several things, Cates thought. Things that showed you weren't an FBI agent, at least not in the sense of somebody who investigates crimes. You didn't know what returning a search warrant was. Then, too, you didn't know that the FBI—the real FBI—had already been to DRT before we got there; you'd have known that if you were one of them. For what you were supposed to be, Winston, you were too damn naive in too many aspects of the cop business.

"Oh, no one thing," he responded at last. "Just a few things here and there."

1199

Charles G. Rogers

W💿RLDWIDE.

TORONTO • NEW YORK • LONDON • PARIS
AMSTERDAM • STOCKHOLM • HAMBURG
ATHENS • MILAN • TOKYO • SYDNEY

TO MY WIFE, JULIE,
AND MY DAUGHTER, KATE,
ALL MY LOVE

1199

A Worldwide Library Book/December 1988

ISBN 0-373-97089-7

ACKNOWLEDGMENT

I would like to express my appreciation to the many people who found time to help me with this novel, by way of research or advice or, on some occasions, old-fashioned arm-around-the-shoulder encouragement.

Detective Geary McMurray of the National City Police Department provided that. Ditto for Jim Palmer, a former Deputy Sheriff and now Dean at the San Diego Police Academy, and Harold Phenix, formerly with the San Diego Police Department and the Narcotics Task Force. Lastly, Craig Walker, a former federal agent, helped me through many a sticking point in this book and elsewhere. In many respects the best of Steve Cates is drawn from these men.

To Sheriff John Duffy I would like to express my appreciation for his interest in this undertaking and his permission to use the department's badge for the cover.

To the San Diego Sheriff's Academy, which I like to describe as the cutting edge of law enforcement training, I owe a substantial debt. Under Lieutenant Dennis Kolar and Sergeants Maury Freitas and Earl Wentworth, the S.O. Academy has developed a program of role-playing and scenario training that is second to none. A scene or two in this story are drawn from just such examples. Thanks also to others on the Basic Academy staff: Deputies Mel Roberts, Carey Dressler, Dennis Ferons, Don Crist, Jim Cook, Vince Albini, Al Skogland, Tom Snowden, Jack Strumsky, John DeAngelis, Jock Ogle and the many others who have provided their assistance to this book.

As a prosecutor I worked with Special Agent Marcus Caspar of the Las Vegas Field Office in connection with an organized crime case. The same case involved Sheriff's Sergeant Bill Hammond, one of the leading experts on investigation of illegal bookmaking operations. It was also my privilege to work with Sheriff's Homicide Detectives Craig Henderson and Bob Fulmer and Detective-Sergeant Charles Curtis. The same is true of Lieutenant Dave Bliss and Sergeant Steve Blackwood. These men are fine law enforcement officers, and each provided invaluable assistance in this project.

An even greater debt is to those many who shaped my impressions of the legal process as it is practiced in San Diego, which I suggest is as good as there is anywhere. District Attorney Ed Miller, Chief Deputy District Attorney Brian Michaels and Judges Richard Huffman, Lou Boyle, and Donald Smith each shaped my legal and writing careers in inestimable ways. I worked for Judges Boyle and Huffman when they were with the San Diego District Attorney's Office and each contributed in large measure to my thoughts on the ultimate duty of law enforcement as depicted in Steve Cates's final confrontation.

Thanks also to Gene Fisher, Jean Dickson and to Dan, Dixie, Frost and Phillipson, each of whom contributed to my writing endeavors in important ways. Blair Burkhardt contributed his special skills in connection with the Sheriff's Department badge depicted on the cover. Also, thanks to my editors, Feroze Mohammed and Dianne Moggy, for their unfailing encouragement and efforts in this project as in previous ones.

Charles G. Rogers
February 23, 1988

1

hostage

THE DAY ELIZABETH FISHER disappeared was the same day that Sheriff's Homicide Detective Steve Cates accidentally shot the hostage.

It happened on a bright Friday afternoon in May. It was the kind of afternoon that explained why Cates lived in San Diego. And it was a payday Friday to boot. Robberies and hostages were about the last thing in the world the rangy, powerful deputy wanted to be reminded of, let alone confront.

It never seemed to fail, Cates reflected grimly. In real life, the hostage incidents went down at largely unpredictable and maximally inconvenient times, although there was no really convenient time for some creep to use a woman or kid or other innocent bystander as a shield. Or if need be as a bargaining chip for freedom.

The only thing predictable was that you couldn't predict it.

That was too bad, Cates thought. If you had a crystal ball, you could have the Special Enforcement Detail set up and in place before the incident happened. SED, which was the sheriff's designation for the various specialized emergency units, including SWAT, were specialists in this sort of thing.

In Cates's opinion, a hostage situation—a distraught husband or boyfriend, a drugged-out robber, a psychotic soldier of fortune whose wires had short-circuited or a professional terrorist—called for specialists. Well trained, well equipped, the SED deputies waited for the call-outs while they tried to live normal lives of families, ball games and barbecues.

If the specialists could be there before it happened, he thought, they'd save a few lives, not to mention a hell of a lot of court costs.

Cates had been on SED some years back, when it was still called just plain SWAT. That was also before he decided it personally suited him better to spend his energies finding out who made the dead bodies than making them himself.

His gaze took in the bank building and the frightened citizen who had accosted him in the parking lot, and he wondered if there would still be time to call out SED.

The bank was a one-story affair, a typical suburban branch-bank office. It would be filled with customers and their kids, nice folks depositing their checks or taking some money out for the weekend, innocent bystanders every one. It was, he reflected, a swell setting for a hostage caper.

Cates knew that some hostage situations would keep, at least temporarily.

Under other circumstances, he would have pulled back and waited. Waiting would mean that the patrol deputies, who at least were armed with shotguns in addition to their duty side arms, could arrive and set up a perimeter. Then, if necessary, the specialists in SED could be called out.

But this didn't look like one of those. This was an armed robbery going bad. The suspects didn't want to talk, or deliver a message, or be talked out of it. They would only want to save themselves, using the hostages to do it. That meant that lives, or more lives, depending on what had actually happened so far, could be lost with every passing second.

Or so it looked, anyway.

So "under other circumstances" meant nothing at a time like right now, with frightened citizens standing there outside the bank, and at least two gunmen inside with hostages. It was no-choice time. Rightly or wrongly, the public wouldn't understand why he, Steven Chandler Cates, a Homicide cop, armed with a .357 revolver, hadn't at least done *something*.

And, in a sense, they'd be right.

Still, for just a moment he hesitated, wondering if securing the scene and sitting tight would be the proper thing to do.

It wasn't. It wouldn't—couldn't—be that simple. Besides, getting SED out would mean having the area patrol sergeant buck it up to the field lieutenant, who in turn would need the station commander's approval before SED got the nod.

No time.

Cates had parked his unmarked car, a plain-looking tan Dodge sedan, at the side of the building. The frightened citizen who almost knocked him down as he walked toward the bank building told him what was going on.

"Two guys!" the man gasped out. "Robbing the bank!"

Instinctively, Cates gripped the man's arm and stepped back around the corner so they were no longer in front of the building.

"What did you say?"

"Bank robbery! Don't go in there! We gotta call the cops!"

"I heard that. What's going on?"

"There's two guys in there with guns, robbing the place! They got the teller as hostage!"

The man's face was pale and his eyes looked wild with panic.

Still holding the man's forearm with his right hand, Cates pulled him back toward the D-unit. He unlocked the passenger door and reached in for the microphone clipped under the dashboard. Straightening up, he turned to face the man.

"Run it by me again. Two men, you say?"

"Yeah. Are you a policeman?"

"Sheriff's deputy. What do they look like?"

"Crazy guys. Iranians, it looked like. Rag heads."

"Were they actually wearing—" Cates started to ask, but the man interrupted.

"No. They didn't have turbans on their heads. It's just a figure of speech. You know, kinda white-guy skin, but real black hair, kinky hair. Mustaches."

"What are they wearing?"

"One of 'em's got a kinda tan jacket, military-looking jacket."

"Military? What, like a flak jacket?"

"No. One with those straps on top of the shoulder, the kind that go from here to here." The man put his free hand up to his ear and pointed from there to the point of his shoulder and back up again, several times in rapid succession.

"Firearms," said Cates. "Do you know anything about firearms? Guns? What kind of guns did they have?"

The insinuation that he might be unfamiliar with firearms seemed to pull the man out of his panic a little. "I know my weapons," he said, a little testily. "One of 'em had a mini-assault weapon, an Uzi or a MAC-10. The other one just had a .45, near as I could see."

"Hostage?"

"Huh?"

"You said he had a hostage. What's that about?"

"Oh. The guy with the Uzi or whatever, he's got one of the tellers up there with him. Got her around the neck with one hand while he's got the gun in the other hand. And he got the other tellers over in the far corner. Said he'll blow 'em away if anybody gets cute."

"And the other guy's getting the money?"

"Yeah."

Cates grimaced. All a part of life's rich goddamn pageant. Well, this should stand for a good lesson not to do personal banking on county time, he thought wryly.

He keyed the mike and spoke into it.

"30-Ida-27," he said.

The "30-Ida" designation identified him as a detective unit, and the 27 identified Cates specifically.

"Go ahead, 30-Ida-27," came the emotionless response.

"30-Ida-27, this is emergency traffic."

He paused, and heard the sharp "beep-beep" that indicated he had been placed on emergency frequency, so his message would automatically be put out to all patrol units in the area. Then he continued.

"30-Ida-27, I'm outside the First California Bank at South Miramar, east of Fifteenth. I have a 211 NOW. R/P states at least two male suspects, Caucasian, possibly Iranian, black hair and mustaches, one wearing a tan military-type jacket." Cates hesitated momentarily for a breath. "One is believed to be armed with an Uzi-type assault carbine or pistol. The other with a .45 handgun. Possible hostage or civilian used as a shield."

He glanced down the street, then went on before responses could start coming over the air.

"The bank is about midway between Fifteenth and Sixteenth. Have units respond along South Miramar, from each direction if possible, stopping before they get to the bank. Also a unit to the rear, possibly via alley that exits next to Hill Cleaners on Miramar. Also notify a sergeant for SED call-out in case hostage situation develops."

"Roger, 30-Ida-27," came back the dispatcher's voice. "Other units in the area, do you copy?"

Responses started coming in almost immediately.

"30-Paul-niner," he heard over the speaker. That would be one of the area patrol units. "I'm en route from Black Mountain Road, ETA is four."

"Roger, 30-Paul-niner," acknowledged the dispatcher.

"30-Paul-11. I'm en route from Poway. ETA eight."

"30-Paul-16. ETA twelve."

Cates tossed the microphone back onto the seat of the D-unit. Shit. The nearest patrol unit was four minutes off, even at code 3, red lights and siren. And the next would be two behind that. Four minutes was a lifetime where an unfolding robbery was concerned. Or four lifetimes, he thought grimly.

"What're you going to do?" asked the citizen.

"Stand by, if possible, until cover gets here." Even as he said it, Cates knew it was not going to be possible.

"You can't—" the citizen began.

His words were chopped short by two shots from inside the bank. They were followed by a woman's shriek, though it sounded more like fear than pain.

"Stay here," Cates commanded the citizen. Then, gun in hand, he moved toward the front of the bank.

The waiting was over. Time to move.

No deputy ever stood by while people were getting killed. It was a virtually inviolable rule, though one that was not written down anywhere, least of all in the three-inch-thick binder that held the "Department P and P's," the bible of Policies and Procedures issued to every deputy the first week in the academy. And it was equally imperative—and unwritten—that the suspects not be allowed to get away with a hostage.

Besides, it was not his style to stand by while either of those things happened.

"Just not how I do things," as he normally put it.

Cates had been in on enough of these situations to know that they were always dangerous, always scary, and usually a little depressing. But none of that was a reason not to go in there and kick ass.

The scary part was no sweat. Like most good cops, Cates liked that part, in small doses.

He understood that he had to get scared from time to time in order to appreciate the other things of life. He also had enough street experience to know that almost all people felt the same way, if they would admit it.

It was the scary things—the crises—that happened to people, all people, that they remembered and told their friends about. The visit to the emergency room. The near miss on the freeway. The time Johnnie fell out of the tree and busted his head open and my God you should have seen the blood.

Crises thrown at you, and met head-on, were what it was all about. Calm seas only meant anything if there had been a hell of a storm to compare them to. A good spring was better after a bad winter.

Cates was just lucky his job gave him that. In spades.

He understood that this was part of the attraction of police work. It was part of why he went into it after college ended and pro ball proved to be out of the question.

It wasn't fear that made him wish he could wait for SED. In fact, the scary part drew him, attracted him, in a strange, love/hate sort of way. But there was another aspect to it, too, a depressing component that seemed to always exist on these cases. And it was this part that got to him a little in the long run.

Cates had given it a lot of thought, and was pretty sure he was right.

Most cops he talked to understood it. Fantasies aside, it was what kept them from trying to be John Wayne or Dirty Harry in real life, trying to blow away all the crooks on the street.

The fact of the matter was that when you killed somebody, it really didn't feel great. For a while, there was the exhilaration of having been in a tough spot and survived. There was maybe even some sort of darker atavistic thrill that went with it. But then that wore off, and it was always a little depressing. Taking a life was a big thing, and yet it didn't fix the world. It didn't stop the rising crime rate, and it didn't scare the other crooks into going straight.

It was a letdown of sorts. You felt cheated. You didn't get the benefit of your implied bargain. You killed the creep and the world as a whole didn't get demonstrably better.

Cates knew that if you were lucky, the best that happened was the immediate crisis got handled and maybe somebody's life got saved. Best to keep it in that perspective, all very matter-of-fact. Keep it practical.

For him, this meant two overriding principles.

The first was don't kill anybody if it doesn't look like you have to. And the second was "him or me means him."

It seemed simpler than it was.

It certainly seemed simple as depicted in newspapers and magazines after the hostage caper was over, where neat photos with dotted lines and arrows showed locations and paths of criminals and rescue teams, all done with the benefit of hindsight.

And to just say it made it sound simple, too.

Deceptively simple.

Cates and a few others knew differently. However straightforward it might appear from an objective standard, subjectively it was another ball game entirely, a tricky and dangerous roulette wheel where your own and others' lives were on the line.

First off, the deputies on the outside had no way of knowing where on the inside the crooks would be.

It could be that the man inside had resigned himself to dying, and just wanted to take some cops with him. In that case, he'd be set up and ready to shoot the first thing that came through the door. But he could actually be positioned anywhere inside, off to the left, off to the right, or straight ahead.

One time, when SED took a room in a warehouse, the suspect had been up high, perched atop a massive steel chassis or console that looked as if it had once housed some huge computer or other electronic apparatus.

Inside, from the suspect's perspective, it was exactly the opposite.

The man or men inside knew exactly where the deputy would appear, which could only be through the door or window. They could focus their attention on one or a couple of specific places, whereas the entry team had to perceive and react to a danger that could be anywhere in the room.

The whole thing was sometimes graphically called "the fatal funnel," and it was a real nut-tightener to be the man in the small end of it.

In addition, in most high-risk entries the deputy did not have a "license to kill." This, Cates knew, was because either he didn't want to, or the law wouldn't let him.

It was not as simple as locating the target in the broad part of the funnel and then blasting away.

In almost all cases, the law said you first had to see if he presented "a reasonable threat of imminent death or serious bodily injury to yourself or another person," i.e., if it looked as if he was about to blow your head off, and *then* you could shoot. In other words, did you have to shoot?

On top of all that, having hostages in the picture made the problem a hundred times worse. In such cases, there was a third rule—try not to dump a hostage.

All of these considerations and more went into the situation that confronted Cates as he rounded the corner and sized up the bank.

The doors were made out of heavy safety glass mounted in a metal frame. They could be pushed inward or pulled outward by a curved bar mounted vertically on each one.

He considered then dismissed the possibility of using another entrance. No real chance to improve the odds by doing that.

The glass doors had some sort of automatic closing device on them. The device gave them a certain stiffness or resistance to being pushed inward or outward; a good deal of force was necessary to get them moving. All of this meant that any kind of dramatic kick-the-door/diving-entry approach would not be particularly fruitful, especially with one man doing it.

That didn't leave much choice.

Cates adjusted his grip on his weapon.

Fleetingly, he wished this were his regular gun, the Smith & Wesson short-barreled revolver with the tacky-feeling black rubber grips he had installed in place of the aesthetically pleasing varnished walnut grips that came with the weapon. The rubber ones didn't look as good but made the pistol shoot better. Or more accurately, anyway, because the weapon didn't shift position in the hand with the recoil of each shot, especially when—as now—the palms were sweaty.

But this wasn't his own weapon, it was a substitute he had to use for now, and it had the regular brown wood grips.

But none of that really matters, Cates, he told himself, because you know goddamn well what you have to do, come what may and to hell with what gun you do it with. So get with it.

Nut up and do it.

Gun in his right hand, the arm hanging casually by his side so the pistol was next to his thigh, he pushed open the door to the bank with his left hand and walked inside.

the fourth round

AT LEAST, CATES THOUGHT, he knew the layout of the bank. It wasn't as if he were walking in completely cold.

The tellers' stations were on the left, along a counter that ran from the front toward the back of the bank. In the center, straight ahead of him, were two islands with chest-high writing surfaces, pens and deposit or withdrawal slips. To the far right were the desks of the other employees, the new accounts desk, the loans desk and one that bore the designation Customer Service.

His eyes swept the room.

About midway back, in the space between one of the islands and the loans desk, a small knot of people huddled, their faces frightened. Those would be the bank employees, he knew; somewhere nearby would be one of the gunmen. A sudden movement came from behind him, and a human form in light-colored clothing jerked into view. Behind the form came a vague motion that signified somebody else as well.

Instantly Cates assessed the details of the first person.

It was a man, Caucasian. He wore a lightweight Members Only jacket with zippered pockets on the chest, very dashing, Cates thought incongruously. The jacket was not really tan, more like ivory, almost off-white, in fact. Was it a color that a frightened citizen might call "kinda tan," Cates wondered.

The man had a bushy, dark mustache. What had the citizen said? Iranian types?

The man's gaze, wild and frightened, jerked around the room, then met Cates's.

Cates raised the pistol and fired twice.

He fired one-handed. No standard cop-type two-handed grip on this one. Instead, he simply snapped off two quick shots, not at the man in the light-colored Members Only jacket but at the one behind him.

The second one.

The one who also had a mustache and a light brown coat with epaulets on the shoulders. The one who had the dark shape of a .45 in his hand.

The one who from Cates's vantage point was only three or four feet to the right of the little knot of hostages, and only about the same distance from the man in the ivory-colored Members Only jacket.

The one who had undoubtedly shoved the first man out from behind the rest of the hostages to act as a decoy to Cates.

The one who was the real killer.

Cates hoped.

In some ways it was a risky shot, given the proximity of the hostages. Still, he made the decision instinctively, instantly, based on what had long been his working maxim—when the choice is between slim and none, you go with slim.

Even before the sound of the shots died out—they made loud, sharp cracks in the confined building—it flashed through Cates's mind that the handgun he was using didn't kick much.

He didn't bother to see if or where his shots had hit. They had that feel of being dead on. If they were, there would be time for pride later.

Maybe. And if they weren't, it wouldn't matter anyway.

He crouched slightly and twisted his body to the left, bringing the revolver around and now at last bringing up his left hand to grip the heel of his right in the police combat stance.

"Two men," the civilian had said, "two men."

Cates wasn't betting on it for an instant.

All "two men" meant, from a frightened civilian, was almost certainly more than one, but not necessarily only two. Maybe three. Maybe even four or more, though that wasn't likely. But at the very least, the danger wasn't over yet.

Cates saw the second man there, off to the left, and he had the hostage, a woman, just as the citizen had described. The man's left arm was around her neck.

Bastard.

In his right hand—the left side, from Cates's perspective—
the man held what looked like a heavy automatic pistol. It was
a stubby, squarish affair. It could put out a lot of firepower in
a hurry, usually 9 mm but sometimes .45. The citizen had described it as an Uzi or a MAC-10. Cates saw the frightened
man had made a good call; it was a MAC-10.

He realized all this instantly upon seeing it, his mind working automatically to sift and process the data.

His mind did something else as well; he felt the rage that the
use of innocent persons as shields always evoked. And he felt
an instant of panic, an instinctive "what if I hit the hostage."

What if . . .

But then the training took over, and he didn't really see the
hostage anymore, not as a separate person, a separate shape.
All he saw was the suspect, the robber, with half of his body
behind the frightened human shield. That way, the shot
wouldn't be made more difficult by the fear of hitting the
hostage.

The man swung the heavy assault pistol toward Cates.

"No!"

The word tore from Cates's throat as he swept his own pistol toward the gunman. Not "freeze" or "stop," just the single command "No!" Which he knew the man was not going
to obey.

Twin reports echoed through the building, as the tall detective fired first.

He fired for the shoulder that was exposed and visible, and
tried to give a small margin for error by going a little left of
that, even. Then, because he hadn't been at all confident that
the two men the citizen had described were all there were, Cates
glanced to the area behind the tellers' windows, toward the
vault.

Sure enough, there was a third man, coming around now
with a gun in his hand.

Cates fired twice at him, also. Like the first two, these had
the feel of being good shots, dead on.

Automatically, his mind registered that the pistol would be
empty. He should be going for cover or at least standing side-

ways to present a narrower profile while he swung out the cylinder, dumped the empties and reloaded.

He also knew something else.

He knew that having fired all six rounds, he was five for six in terms of his hits. Only one bad.

Normally, he would consider that very good shooting, considering it was combat. Normally. However, here the bad one was very bad indeed, the worst, because instinctively he knew he had hit the hostage.

It had been the fourth shot.

The third one, which by all rights should have been the toughest because he was still swinging around from the first man, had been perfect. But the fourth round had been too far to the right, and there was simply no way in hell the woman wouldn't be dead or seriously wounded.

A legal concept came from somewhere, something he'd read in the law. ''Force likely to cause death or serious bodily injury,'' ran the phrase. It was the definition of deadly force.

He knew that you didn't shoot women hostages with a .357 Magnum without causing death or serious bodily injury. Chalk up another one, you sorry bastard, he thought.

And now, moving swiftly forward toward the gunman and hostage, Cates saw that there was no mistake.

He'd gotten the robber, all right, about three inches to the side of the sternum, where the shoulder joined the chest. But he'd also gotten the hostage, the woman, dead center in her chest, a more lethal hit even than the robber had taken.

Force likely to cause death or serious bodily injury.

In Homicide he saw all kinds of wounds. He saw them from the outside, when he made the preliminary examination of the body. And he saw them inside, when he attended and in some cases photographed the autopsy, watching as the pathologist traced the lethal path.

It came to him in a jumble that jelled into certainty as he leaped at the gunman.

He knew without seeing it what the Magnum would do to the woman hostage's body. From the outside, there would appear only a neat round hole, bloody red. But beneath it there would be violent, bruising destruction of tissue as foot-pounds of energy from the slug spent themselves in the body, not only the projectile but the hydrostatic pressure from the impact generating a fearful cone of damage and death among the fragile cells.

He must have pulled it, Cates realized, pulled that shot to the right somehow, toward the hostage instead of away.

The same instant, the logical part of his mind tried to clamp the lid on.

Don't sweat it, he thought. Forget it.

So you dumped a hostage, Steve. Tough luck. It's all part of the game. Clearly, his use of deadly force was justified in this, a hostage situation. It was just one of those tragedies that the hostage died. You play quarterback in the NFL, you're going to throw a few interceptions. It's part of the price.

Kind of tough on the hostage who paid it, though.

Don't think about it, he told himself. Think about the others you saved.

The other part of his mind, the emotional part, exploded into fury, hurling away these rational restraints.

He didn't know how he got there, but somehow he was there, on top of the gunman. It all went hazy, a white rage in which everything else seemed to recede into the background. Cates and the robber were alone in a cloud, just the two of them, the robber on his back with Cates crouched over him. He clenched the man's shirt in his fist and jammed his now empty revolver against the side of his head, as if by will and anger trying to undo that fourth round.

The rage grew in his throat.

"You killed him, you bastard!" he heard himself snarling at the robber and jerking his head toward the hostage. "You! Not me, you! Goddamn you, I..."

But then the rational mind reasserted itself.

That's a waste of time, he told himself. It's futile. Save your breath, because it's over already, it's history. You can't undo it, and besides, it is, after all, only a game.

This time.

"Jesus, Steve, lighten up, for Christ's sake! I mean, shit, man, what the hell are you doing?"

The familiar voice of Ron Reynolds, a sergeant assigned to the sheriff's In-Service Training Division, cut through the adrenaline and the anger and the rush of blood in Cates's ears. The white cloud faded, and he felt the heat in his face as he straightened up. The gunman faded, too, and in his place was Jack Kolb, a deputy from SED, on loan to Training.

Jack, Cates noted, looked startled and angry and maybe even a little scared.

Cates straightened up and helped Kolb to his feet. He loosened his grip on the SED man's shirt, and made an awkward token movement toward tugging it back into place.

"Sorry, J.K."

Kolb's face colored. "You fucking ought to be sorry, Cates," he snarled. "It's only a goddamn scenario, asshole!"

"Look, I just got carried away, that's all."

"Asshole!" muttered the erstwhile gunman again.

Cates regarded Jack grimly. He had never liked Kolb or his style of police work. Jack had just a little more of the "knock 'em down first and ask questions later" attitude than Cates cared for. And, though the SED man was well equipped to do that—reportedly a black belt in something or another, and heavily muscled as if he lived at the gym—Cates had him by maybe four inches and twenty pounds.

It would be interesting to have a go at it, he thought. And maybe provide a certain satisfaction as well.

A couple of things said no, don't do it.

First, Cates knew he had overreacted. Kolb would not have been expecting that kind of follow-through—hell, nobody expected it, not even Cates himself. So the SED man's pride had been bruised, especially given the ease with which Cates in his fury had overpowered him, and the fact the onlookers had seen it.

There was something else, as well.

Cates knew it would be impossible to explain why it had happened, not in a way that the others would understand. Best just to play it that he had gotten carried away by the realism of the training scenario, gotten into it too much. He'd eat a little crow, of course, but better that than trying to make them understand what had really happened.

He forced a sheepish grin, which didn't take much forcing under the circumstances.

"Hell, you guys said I should play it for real. I just got into it too much, I guess." He extended his hand to Kolb. "I'm sorry, man, catching you off guard like that."

"You're not wired right, Cates! You're crazy, you know that?" The veins bulged on Kolb's neck in his rage. "Well, fuck you, Cates! You think you're bad, don't you?"

"Not really."

"I could take you, asshole!"

Enough crow, Cates thought. It had been a tough week, and this Pandora's box of a training scenario was the topper. Cates felt his rueful grin vanish.

"Any time, Jackie."

"You're on, Cates!"

Cates made his voice deliberately soft. "Don't let the long walk over here stop you, sonny."

The SED man started toward him, then halted as another voice cut through the tension.

"Hey-hey-hey, you guys!"

Sergeant Reynolds's voice crowded in, calming yet insistent in its authority, stretching out the "heys" and overriding Jack's anticipated rejoinder.

"Save it for the bad guys, for cryin' out loud. Both of you. Knock it off."

Stocky, tough and fit, with his short brown hair and neat mustache, Reynolds had the air of a British commando about him. He'd been with SED for several years himself, before his transfer to Training. Both his authority and his toughness were unquestioned.

He turned to Kolb. "He said he was sorry, Jack. Don't be pissed off just because he saw through your scenario and didn't fall for it."

Kolb didn't respond. Reynolds gave him a hard look, then turned to Cates.

"It's only training, Steve."

Cates nodded.

Reynolds went on. "Let's see how you did, anyway."

"I'm dead," came a voice.

Cates turned and saw Mike Arlo, the deputy who had played the gunman in the tan military jacket, who had shoved out the first hostage as a distractor. With the sharp, sandpaper rip of Velcro fasteners being detached, he unstrapped the brown laser vest that he wore.

The vest was the key element of the elaborate scenario produced by the Sheriff's Training Division.

It appeared to be made of a brown nylon material. Inside was a fine, screenlike mesh of sensors, column upon column of narrow metal strips, as though a sheet of thin steel had been run through a paper shredder. The sensors were part of a system of specially designed photoelectric cells, electronically rigged to record when the beam of light—actually a low-power laser—struck them.

The laser itself was specially fitted into the handgun Cates had been using.

It was a standard department-issue Smith & Wesson Model 66, the stainless steel .357 Magnum revolver issued to all the deputies on the department. When the pistol was fired, a single jolt of high-intensity light instead of a bullet came out. If it hit the vest, the hit was recorded automatically by red LED lights that glowed and stayed glowing until the vest was reprogrammed for the next simulation. The sensors in the vest were further divided into zones to pinpoint more precisely the location of the "hit."

Similar lasers had been installed in the .45 that Arlo was carrying, as well as in the fake MAC-10 held by Kolb and by the third "gunman."

Each of them, as well as Cates, wore one of the laser vests, to record hits. Check the LED lights that glowed and you knew how many hits you made. And, more important, on whom.

The gunshot sound when the pistol was fired came from special nylon cartridge casings, loaded into the cylinder like regular ammunition. Each contained a primer but no powder or shot. The primer, however, made the sharp crack when struck by the firing pin, to simulate the sound of a weapon being fired.

The only thing missing, as Cates had noted, was the recoil that normally accompanied firing such a weapon with actual live ammunition.

"Let's see it," Reynolds directed.

Arlo handed him the vest, indicating the lights that had been activated on the vest to designate the zones where Cates's first two "shots" had struck.

"Looks like you're history, Mike," the sergeant acknowledged. "Been nice knowing you."

"I shoulda listened to my momma," the young deputy said with a grin.

Reynolds turned to the deputy who had been shoved out from behind the hostages, the distractor in the clothing similar to that described to Cates by the civilian witness outside the bank. The "civilian" was also a deputy playing a role.

Reynolds checked the vest worn by the decoy. "You're not hit?"

"That's affirmative. First time today I didn't get dumped. Nice job, Steve."

Cates accepted it with a nod. "Thanks."

Reynolds grinned. "Yeah. It's been a tough day for hostages. A tough week, in fact. Glass, here, has been nailed seven times today alone. Got so bad I started letting him chew on the deputies that 'killed' him, instead of me doing it. He's got quite a routine about listening to details, tan military jacket with epaulets just isn't the same as an off-white Members Only jacket with zippers on the front."

The deputy identified as Glass winked. "Too bad, Cates."

"Why too bad?"

"You spoiled my streak. I was looking forward to a chance to ream out a tough-guy Homicide detective." As an afterthought, he added, "'Course, I shoulda figured you of all people wouldn't fall for it."

Cates didn't respond.

Reynolds checked the third putative gunman. His vest, likewise, recorded two lethal hits. Then he turned his attention to Jack Kolb and the woman who had been playing his hostage, both of whom wore laser vests.

"Let's not give him too big a hand," he remarked with a wink. "Bastards from Homicide are already conceited enough as it is."

A light on Kolb's vest recorded the hit he had taken, probably a lethal one. Reynolds checked it and nodded, then spoke to Cates. "You got Jack, sure. But—" the sergeant shook his head and made a clucking sound in mock disappointment as he examined the woman's vest "—it looks like you dumped a hostage to boot."

He turned to her. "Let's see it, Griff."

The deputy he'd addressed as Griff handed him her vest. The small LED light glowed a dark, ruby red in the center panel of the vest, precisely where Cates had known the fourth round had hit.

Reynolds was speaking again. "Well, Steve, overall, you did the best of anybody so far. You didn't fall for the main distraction, and you got all three of the bad guys. Good work."

Cates only half heard him. He was still staring at the glowing ruby light that meant he had shot the hostage. Now, finally, for the first time, he pulled his gaze away and looked at the role player who had been wearing it.

She was an athletic-looking woman in her twenties, maybe five-seven, he judged. She had medium-brown hair, high elegant cheekbones, a face that was both strong and attractive.

He recognized her vaguely as a deputy in the department, but he couldn't come up with a name. Reynolds had called her Griff, undoubtedly short for Griffin. But what was her first name? Martie? Connie? Something like that. He thought she was assigned to patrol at one of the substations. Maybe she, like some of the SED deputies, had been pulled in to help with the hostage simulations.

Just looking at her, he liked her a little in spite of his other emotions. He made his face into the shape of a smile. "Sorry about that," he said simply.

She grinned. "No sweat. I've been 'killed' a few times, too. Maybe this is just like history repeating itself, except I'm a 'her,' not a 'him.'"

Cates looked at her. There was no malice in her words, he realized. "Yeah," he finally said, wondering how she knew.

IT WAS GOING ON 5:00 p.m. when Cates arrived at the Lemon Grove Substation.

Popularly known as LGS, the substation was located just east of the San Diego city limits. It was one of the sheriff's busiest, and its jurisdiction or area of authority ran the gamut from densely populated urban areas and barrios to ranch country.

Cates had worked LGS a few years earlier as a patrol deputy and later as a detective. He knew the streets, and he knew a lot of the crooks, though new ones were always coming up through the ranks.

By the time the laser shoot was over, it didn't make sense to go all the way back to the Homicide offices in the nondescript building west of downtown out by the San Diego Sports Arena. Depending on the traffic, he would have got there about twenty minutes before quitting time. Instead, he decided to swing by LGS, to see what, if anything, was going on. Besides, it would put him pretty close to home when quitting time came.

He was on call that weekend. By convention if not by written policy, that afforded him a certain leeway between call-outs.

LGS in many ways resembled a fair-size police department unto itself.

Some eighty to ninety deputies, or "sworn personnel" as they were called, worked there. More than half were assigned to uniformed patrol; most of the rest were detectives. For years, the station had been packed into hopelessly small quarters adjacent to a Winchel's Do-nut shop, thus triggering even more cops-and-doughnut references for the overworked deputies to contend with than would ordinarily be the case. As of some eighteen months before, the substation had moved to remodeled premises that were, for the time being, almost adequate.

When Cates arrived that afternoon, the lobby of LGS was empty except for a woman talking to the uniformed deputy on duty behind the counter.

As Cates crossed the lobby toward the door marked Law Enforcement Personnel Only, the deputy glanced in his direction. Following his look, the woman turned toward him, also.

She was, Cates saw, beautiful.

Not beautiful in the classic, Miss America sense. Her features were slightly too strong, somehow, for that. And yet, that fact did nothing to detract from her femininity; if anything, the air of vitality enhanced it. She had dark brown, almost black hair, and a good tan, especially for May.

Yes, beautiful, he amended again. Beautiful in a strong, vital way.

She looked intense, agitated about something. Cates wondered what her problem was. He figured it probably didn't concern Homicide; their cases usually didn't come to their attention like that. Beautiful women just didn't walk into the station and say they had a problem with a murder and they'd like to talk to somebody about it, as they did if their cars were stolen.

Too bad, he reflected ruefully as the deputy buzzed him in. Because if she did have a Homicide problem, he wouldn't have minded listening. The noblest motive, after all, was the public good.

Besides, he liked how she looked.

3

Joyce Kennedy and Beth Fisher

IT HAD TAKEN HER three tries, and she still hadn't found the right street.

The exasperating thing was that she knew it was her own fault, because she should have written down the directions better. Only she had been in a hurry, and she hadn't really been too keen on going to this thing, anyway. In fact, she probably wouldn't have been going at all if it weren't that Beth Fisher, who was new to the company, had asked her to go so she would know somebody there.

Not that Beth could reasonably have been worried about being ignored, Joyce thought, and then regretted the thought.

The regret—admittedly mild, more of a sense of chagrin— came from two sources. The first, she knew, was simple human—she refused to say feminine—resentment at somebody so good-looking. And the second was irritation that she of all people should have such feelings, especially about physical appearance. Even in her bleakest moments, Joyce knew she herself was an attractive, successful young business professional.

Still, some emotions die hard.

Joyce glanced at the slip of paper where she had jotted Beth's address, or what was supposed to be Beth's address.

The paper came from her notepad at work, "from the desk of joyce kennedy, accounting systems division." Everything was in lower-case letters. Very trendy, she thought, because at DRT—Data Research and Technology—we are all very trendy, as trendy as a leading-edge, high-tech R and D firm in the Golden Triangle, San Diego's answer to Silicon Valley, can possibly be.

"4515 MarVista," it read. And below that, "# 13."

Beth's apartment was located somewhere on the eastern edge of the San Diego city limits.

When Joyce had finally agreed to go to the party, she had offered to give Beth a ride. Joyce would pick her up at three that afternoon so the two of them could go to the party together. And leave together, when they wanted to leave.

Though Joyce considered herself pretty easygoing about most things, especially those over which she had no control, right now even the name of the streets exasperated her.

"MarVista," she muttered aloud. What the hell kind of name was that, some sort of cutesy concoction intended to signify that you could see the ocean? And to add a pseudo-Spanish flair, as well?

Damn.

Above the address she had scribbled the names of the other streets that were supposed to somehow get her to MarVista: Massachusetts, Sweetwater and Troy. But when Beth had called, that jerk Bob Meanley had been standing there, fidgeting with the preliminaries on one of the contracts and leering at her at the same time, so she hadn't gotten all the details.

Damn *him*.

The problem, as Joyce was discovering the hard way, turned out to be that there was more than one MarVista in these parts. There were three of them, in fact.

No, she amended, make that *at least* three of them.

First, there was a MarVista Street and a MarVista Way, and neither of them had been the one. Joyce knew that because she'd spent the past fifteen minutes driving up and down each one, and neither of them had numbers even close to the four thousands. So now she had to look for another MarVista. MarVista Court? Or MarVista Road, perhaps, or Avenue, or God only knew what else.

Or maybe she had copied the number down wrong.

"Damn!"

This time she said it aloud. She gave the steering wheel a semiserious smack of frustration with the palm of her hand, as though it were somehow at fault. "Damn, damn, damn, damn!"

She tried to recall the telephone conversation in which Beth had given her the directions. Tried to pull it up again in her mind, replay the tapes, to remember what designation Beth had used.

No luck. And because Beth was new to the company, it wouldn't do any good to check the address in the directory of employees Joyce had kicking around somewhere in the car.

She could stop and telephone, of course, because Beth had given the phone number along with the address. Still, Joyce knew the right MarVista had to be nearby somewhere, and finding a phone would probably take longer than finally stumbling onto the street. Besides, she didn't want to phone, damn it.

She drove on, scanning the streets and wishing she hadn't been such a Good Samaritan to the new woman in the office. Or so curious about the woman.

The company, Data Research and Technology—or Dirt, as it was inevitably called by loyal and disloyal employees alike—did research for the United States government. The type of research it did depended largely on who was president or, more generally, whether he happened to be a Republican or a Democrat.

Joyce had once described DRT to her mother as "one of those places you read about in slick business magazines, the ones that use words like *think tank*, *high tech* and *fast track*."

"That's nice, dear, but what do they make?" her mother had responded.

"What do you mean?"

"Well, companies have to make something, don't they? Something to sell. Like, oh, stoves or refrigerators. Or computers," she added brightly, in an effort to relate to her daughter.

"It's not like that, Mom. DRT doesn't make anything, in the sense of a product."

"How can it be a company if it doesn't make things? What does it do? What does it sell?"

"It does research. 'Research and development,' it's called. R and D, is how they say it."

"Research on what? You're not making atomic bombs, are you, Joycie dear? Or working on that Star Wars thing, are you? I wouldn't like to think my daughter was using all that education to help build all these bombs and warheads."

Joyce laughed. "No, no bombs. We do mainly computer things."

"What kind of things?"

"We make what are called simulations—models—using computers, and then try to predict what will happen. We test things and try to come up with new ideas."

"Who buys the ideas?"

"The government."

Joyce had discreetly omitted the fact that the government meant the Department of Defense, or D.O.D., as insiders referred to it, and the models and things and ideas, while not atomic bombs, exactly, nonetheless consisted mainly of military applications of technology.

Actually, Mom, she thought, we're part of what used to be called the military-industrial complex, and we design and test and evaluate weapons systems and guidance systems and things like that.

To Joyce, the senior executives who had founded DRT were a tough and slightly scary breed. They were the men with the hard, icelike eyes, and, she suspected, souls that matched. Most were refugees from the "beltway bandits," a term derived from the highway that circled the hub of government contracting in and around Washington, D.C. The "bandits" referred to the group of civilian contractors who pursued the most lucrative of the Defense Department contracts. Many had previously worked for D.O.D., and thus possessed a commodity far more valuable than skill or experience.

Contacts.

People who knew. People who knew other people, the ones who counted. People who got things done, who started wars and stopped them again, who decided what research should be done and which contracts to award. At times Joyce found them disturbing, these men and a few women at DRT and the others in similar companies everywhere, people who formed a shadowy infragovernment that shaped the present and the future for years to come.

For that matter, the research that DRT conducted disturbed her a little. She wished their efforts were directed somewhere besides weapons systems. High-tech hospital equipment, or medical research, maybe. Something that didn't require everybody to have top-security clearances, and didn't have mysterious federal investigators lurking in the background all the time.

Yet, despite these misgivings, she stayed there.

Face it, Joycie, she told herself, you're a sellout. You aren't thrilled with what your company does, but you give them your services and take their substantial paychecks.

Apart from the company executive corps, most of the professionals at DRT were relatively young and far more numerous. A good many were right out of college or graduate school. They were the scientists, programmers, technicians, management and support staff of the company. Though she was one of them herself, Joyce generally regarded them as very bright, often neurotic and altogether "with it."

They were paid well. They drove nice cars. They bought their clothes at Nordstom's and Banana Republic, and to Joyce they seemed to represent classic Southern California yuppiedom. Even the company itself seemed to be a part of that scene, located a few miles from the Pacific Ocean, just outside prestigious La Jolla in the Golden Triangle.

They also tended to be well tanned, and they spent a lot of effort and money trying to look casual and disaffected.

Lots of them were runners, and a fair number did marathons. They talked of carbo-loading and electrolyte replacement and how many miles they put in each week. They owned expensive bicycles, and they expected an acceptable number of orgasms—given and received—with an acceptable number and variety of partners.

Trendy.

No strings, no real commitments, but a lot of the new etiquette, things like "you're very *special*," and "that was nice last night."

And, Joyce knew, for many of them there existed another ever-present factor that permeated the entire social ecosystem.

Drugs. Mainly cocaine.

Most of it was social. The DRT people threw a lot of parties, largely informal. At some of these, coke was used openly. Nose candy. Fun stuff. Do a couple of lines and cut loose. Recreational drugs.

Joyce knew that for some, though, the coke had a darker side. It was more than social. An occasional grim toot helped them to face the day, or make a tough presentation, or get this report or that proposal out by a deadline.

At first glance, Joyce might have fit the DRT mold.

When she entered the room, heads turned. Expressions—in varying degrees of explicitness—of appreciation of her figure and features were frequently communicated *sotto voce* among the men present. In some cases, the *voce* was not so *sotto*, and was often embarrassing.

She was a runner and she worked out at a gym three nights a week. Apart from occasional culinary and alcoholic excesses, she followed the more moderate dietary trends. She had thick, dark hair that she wore long, and an olive complexion that tanned dark in the summer.

In other respects, however, Joyce differed from the mainstream DRT young-professional profile.

It wasn't that she necessarily regarded the parties and the casual liaisons and the coke as the root of all evil. But she wasn't committed to the pursuit of the great god Fun in the way the DRT fast-laners were. As a result, she was considered aloof and standoffish by a lot of them, a fact that bothered her not in the slightest.

Or so she said, anyway.

She liked the physical surroundings of the DRT facility, and she liked the salary. And, during the summer the company gave them every other Friday afternoon off. Today was the last Friday in May and the first half day off of the season, which was how the informal party had happened to be arranged in the first place.

All of this added to her frustration as she drove that afternoon, searching for the right MarVista. If it weren't for her agreement with Beth, she wouldn't have been using her first Friday on summer hours to go to this party at all.

Joyce had met Beth the preceding week, following a noontime run.

DRT occupied its own building in the Golden Triangle. The surrounding area consisted of other similar facilities and expanses of open space, hills and areas ideal for jogging.

A side door, controlled by push-button combination cipher lock, had been provided for the runners. That way, visiting military brass, government bureaucrats and researchers wouldn't have to be confronted in the lobby or in the elevators with what a Marine colonel once termed "sweaty yuppies."

Joyce, breathing hard though she had taken the last half mile slowly to cool down, had come around the corner of the building to find a blond woman in running gear kneeling by the door.

"You work here?" Joyce said between deep breaths, when she got close enough.

Startled, the blonde looked up.

Joyce saw at once that she was beautiful. If Joyce would cause heads to turn, this woman would make them turn and stay turned. She was stunning.

She flashed a smile and nodded. "As Sister used to say, I'm the new girl in the room."

Something about the way she said it struck Joyce as discordant. There was a note of hardness, perhaps a trace of bitterness, to the voice that could not be completely masked by the smile. It was as if beneath the brilliance lay old and angry secrets.

Then Joyce dismissed the thought—probably the woman was merely shy, though with looks like that she certainly couldn't be lonely.

She had thick hair and a golden tan. A good guess would be that she, or her ancestors, had come from northern Italy, and that she was a product of that genetic quirk that sometimes produces fair-haired Italians. As if in confirmation of this, her nose had the hint of a Roman curve to it, lending an air of sophistication to her features.

She looked short and compact, though it was difficult to tell as she was kneeling. Her bare legs and arms were smooth and tan, and she projected a certain bouncy, cheerleader quality. Joyce could imagine the inevitable Golden Triangle quips that would be made about this woman.

"Sounds like you went to parochial schools, too," she said lightly, to play the conversational ball and allowing the smile as part of her statement.

"Yeah." The kneeling woman retrieved a sodden slip of white card from her sock and read off the digits. "Four, three-five and one," she said aloud. "See? I told you I worked here." She stepped forward and punched the numbers into the cipher lock that controlled the door.

Joyce laughed. "I never doubted it." Then she extended her hand. "I'm Joyce Kennedy. I'm a systems analyst."

The woman stood up. "Beth Fisher. I just started in computers. This is only my third week."

Joyce looked puzzled. "Have you been running every day? I've never seen you before."

Beth shook her head. "No. This is the first time. Usually I run at night. I just thought I'd give this a try, to see how it goes."

The following day, the two women ran together, and the day after that, as well.

Beth proved to be something of an enigma to Joyce. The new woman's looks and her demeanor suggested she would be one of the "party hearty" types, yet she stayed separate from that crowd. Underlying her aloofness, however, there seemed to be a sort of grimness, a determination, as if her reserve were somehow forced rather than simply being the way she wanted to be. It was so much so that Joyce was actually surprised when Beth suggested they go to the party that Friday afternoon.

Joyce knew that part of the reason she had agreed to go was so she could try to learn more about that seemingly contradictory facade.

And now, Joyce thought grimly, here I am, trying to find which in the hell MarVista Beth's could be and kicking myself for not taking down better directions.

She peered ahead, looking for the street sign. Ahead, at the next corner, an ambulance entered the street she was on and came toward her, driving slowly.

Maybe he's lost, too, she thought wryly.

Then she saw it, the very next street, in fact. The sign was largely hidden by a tree on the corner. And her first guess had been right, it was a court. MarVista Court.

The first house on the right was 4504.

Good, Joyce thought exultantly. The numbers are in the same range. To the left was 4507, then 4509. She glanced up ahead, and beyond a vacant lot with a sign that proclaimed Prime View Lot For Sale, she saw the apartment building that had to be it, 4515.

It was.

The complex had two stories and contained about thirty units, she estimated. If was fairly new, and looked as if it would be moderately plush, if one didn't mind a pseudo-Spanish style, white with red tile roofs. Dark brown lettering angled up the side of one of the units facing the street, announcing the complex as Casa MarVista.

The apartments formed a sort of squared-off U, one end and two sides of a rectangle.

The bottom of the U faced the street. A passageway protected by a wrought-iron gate went through the center of it where one of the downstairs units would otherwise have been. The gate was propped open. As she slowed her car in front of it, Joyce caught a glimpse of bright blue from the swimming pool inside the courtyard. Beyond it, the other end of the rectangle lay open to the west, presumably to afford a view of the ocean some fifteen miles away.

The only available parking seemed to be in front of the vacant lot she had just passed.

Joyce made a U-turn and came back past the complex to park. Beyond the vacant lot lay a canyon, then a fifteen-mile blanket of homes. And sure enough, the ocean made a flat gray plate in the distance.

Beth's apartment was number 13, Joyce recalled. Assuming, of course, she had managed to copy that part down correctly.

Through the gates and to your left, on the side next to the vacant lot, Joyce remembered Beth saying. Upper floor, and the stairs are in the corner.

She glanced at her watch. 3:12. So she was only ten minutes behind schedule, after all. A good lesson not to get all wrought up over these things, she thought, because in the end it usually proved to be no big deal anyway.

Joyce rang the doorbell. She could hear music from inside the apartment, a rock song that was followed by the voice of an announcer from one of the local radio stations.

While she waited, Joyce surveyed the complex.

She estimated that if it had been located closer to the coast, say in Encinitas or Leucadia where about half the DRT people seemed to live, Beth probably couldn't have afforded it on her salary alone. Here, though, it would be affordable.

From off to her left, at the end of the building that housed Beth's unit, came the sound of a clothes dryer, a whooshing noise punctuated with a regular clink as of a metal button against the drum. Through a hall window she could see, below, a slightly overweight woman in her twenties lying on her back on a lounge chair by the pool, taking in the afternoon sun, which was still warm but beginning to weaken. Black headphones covered her ears, connected by a thin black line to a Walkman radio or cassette player; at that distance Joyce couldn't tell which.

Apart from the dryer being in use, and the woman by the pool, there was no sign of other occupants of the complex.

Joyce turned and rang Beth's doorbell again, then turned back and surveyed the canyon to the west. She leaned against the railing, looking out and listening for the door to open behind her.

It occurred to her that Beth might be in the laundry room.
After all, she thought, on occasion I've had to throw in a quick
load before going somewhere. She looked down the walkway
to where the dryer sounds came from. Nobody was visible.
With a shrug, she walked toward it, all the time alert for the
sound of Beth's door opening.

The laundry room had a cement floor and a warm, dusty
detergent smell. It contained three washers and two dryers, a
table and a yellow plastic wastebasket. And no Beth, or anybody else.

Joyce glanced at her watch. 3:25.

She strode back to number 13 and pushed the doorbell
again, listening carefully to make sure it worked. From inside
came a muffled *bing, bong*.

Nothing.

Irritated, she jabbed the doorbell twice in quick succession.

She waited expectantly, certain that at any moment she
would hear the vague sounds of somebody moving. Joyce
found herself already pushing a smile, concealing her irritation.

Still nothing.

"Damn."

She'd gotten the address wrong, after all. Or the wrong unit
number. Or something.

That had to be it. Joyce glanced at her watch again. 3:29.
Now she was hopelessly late, and she hated being late, just as
a matter of principle. Not that this was any big deal, of course,
not a business meeting or even a date.

Still, it irritated her.

She looked up and down the walkway, hoping Beth would
emerge from somewhere and show that Joyce hadn't gotten the
wrong address after all.

No Beth.

Joyce opened her purse to get the paper with Beth's address. At least she had the phone number; she could find
somebody home in this place, or wake up the woman by the
pool and borrow a phone and what a pain, this was the last
time she'd let herself get talked into something like this.

The paper wasn't there. Then she remembered tossing it in the footwell of her car when she found the building.

She gave the doorbell a last, irritated jab. She turned and strode back down the walkway to the stairs. Heels clicking, she clipped down the steps and hurried through the entryway in the front of the complex.

Belatedly, it occurred to her that she had just passed the mailboxes and a directory of tenants. At first, certain she had the wrong 4515 on the wrong MarVista, Joyce had only cast a glance at the directory.

The name and number leaped into sharp focus.

Fisher. 13.

She stopped, then strode over to the mailboxes, mounted in a row along the wall. Sure enough, on number 13 a small red label had been affixed with the name Fisher in raised white letters. And on the directory above it, the name Fisher, E. opposite apartment thirteen.

Relief came over her. And with it, irritation, but a different and somehow better irritation than she had earlier felt.

At least now if they didn't hook up, it was Beth's fault, not hers. Joyce had gotten there, to the right place, and only ten minutes late. Well, twelve. Beth must have had to run a last-minute errand, or been held up somehow. Maybe she just forgot about it. Hopefully, it would be the latter; Joyce would wait another few minutes, then take off, leaving a note perhaps, and she'd have an excuse not to go to the party.

The radio.

She frowned. The radio had been on in Beth's apartment.

Okay. That was easy. So she ran to the store. She needed something and had to run out and she'd be back any minute.

Her car. Was her car there?

Joyce strode outside. Parking was reserved. And in space number 13 was the dark gray-blue Celica that she knew Beth drove.

Suddenly concerned, Joyce turned and hurried back into the complex, through the entryway and up the steps. She rang the doorbell again, but without waiting for the tones she tried the doorknob.

It turned in her hand.

She hesitated a moment, then pushed it open partway. The music from the radio sounded suddenly louder.

"Beth?"

The name came out thin and weak, timid. She cleared her throat and tried again.

"Beth? Are you here? It's me. Joyce."

Though it was louder this time, her voice still sounded somehow unnatural, out of place, almost as if the apartment itself were rejecting it. Like something out of *The Exorcist* or an old *Twilight Zone*, she thought.

She heard another sound, the muffled hiss of the shower.

"Beth!"

This time Joyce shouted it, embarrassed but also angry at her feelings of trespassing. She moved to the entrance of the short hallway. "Beth!" she demanded again. "It's Joyce!"

No reply. No sound other than the radio and the rushing water. She strode rapidly to the bathroom door and knocked, three loud, hollow-sounding knocks that cut through the hiss of the shower. "Beth! Are you okay, Beth?"

Nothing. Angry and a little frightened, Joyce turned the knob and pushed the door open.

"Beth?"

The air inside felt wet and clammy, heavy with moisture but not particularly steamy. Later—much later—the sheriff's detective, Cates, would attribute that to the length of time the shower had been running; the hottest water had been used up, and the mixture was now only lukewarm. But that would come later; for now, she had expected clouds of steam and Beth standing in the shower.

To the right stood a small vanity and sink. Then came the toilet, and beyond it, running the width of the small room, a tub and shower exclosed by sliding doors of opaque frosted glass.

The cover was down over the toilet seat; on top of it was a light blue towel. A box of electric curlers rested on the vanity. The cord was plugged in, and a light glowed orange on the box, signifying they were turned on. A small pile of clothes—

jeans with panties inside them, as though both had been peeled off at once—were crumpled on the floor. On top of them was a tank top of thin ribbed cotton material.

"Beth!" Joyce demanded, knowing there would be no answer.

Swiftly, she took two steps forward and slid the shower door to one side to look inside. Heavy, wet air enveloped her in a cloud.

The tub was empty.

No Beth. Nobody. No body, which Joyce had by then steeled herself to find. And no blood, either. Nothing. Just a shower running, radio playing, curlers warming, a pile of clothes on the floor, and a fresh towel. All the necessities, all laid out and ready for the person who wasn't there.

4

two men on a mule

IT WASN'T UNTIL MUCH LATER that Cates would realize how many things had happened that same bright Friday afternoon in May.

By then the reports would be an inch thick, with more to follow. When he finally saw how it all tied together, Cates would realize once again how in large part police work is a matter of luck. And he would remark, as he had done on many previous occasions, that the information is usually out there if you only knew who had it, and if you could pry it out of whoever that was.

At about the same time that Elizabeth Fisher disappeared and Cates was shooting the hostage, two narcs pulled up the plants and arrested the outlaw biker types. And in the process garnered what would later prove to be one of the key pieces of evidence in the Fisher investigation.

The two bikers turned out to be a three-time loser named Clarence Stuart and his buddy, Jack McKeon. The narcs were a pair of veteran San Diego sheriff's deputies named Dave Karchut and Larry English.

English and Karchut were assigned to the new Street Narcotics Team. Even if it was sheer luck that dumped Stuart and McKeon in their laps, they didn't mind. They'd been around long enough to know that a lot of what went down as good police work was hunch on top of luck, anyway.

The Street Team was designed to go after the street-level dealers, the "retail outlets" of the drug trade. As such, it was supposed to fill the gap that existed between San Diego's major drug enforcement units and the individual patrol deputies.

The major units in the drug war included the U.S. Drug Enforcement Administration and, more recently, the FBI. Both of these targeted the big dealers and the importers. The only time the DEA or the FBI got involved with street dealers was to recruit "confidential informants," or CIs as they were known.

It was a familiar pattern, made necessary by the fact that the drug trade was notoriously difficult to penetrate. Narcotics dealing was blatant, but not that blatant. A cop couldn't just go around and find the big dealers unless he had people inside the commercial machinery, reconnaissance people—spies—to act as his eyes and ears.

That meant CIs. Snitches. Informants. Rats, as they were known to the people they informed on.

The problem was that people usually didn't snitch on their friends out of the goodness of their hearts, or civic duty. It had to be made worth their while to do it. Usually, that meant letting them turn informant in return for a break on one or more of their cases, letting them "work off the beef," as it was known.

Crooks like Stuart, one of the bikers arrested by Karchut and English, knew this from experience. With the Feds, you could probably cut a deal, whereas the locals—the sheriff's office and the various PDs around the country—tended to just throw your ass in county jail and go on to the next case.

In the jargon of these local cops, it was called "hook 'em and book 'em."

San Diego County had also been a pilot in a highly successful narcotics enforcement effort called the Narcotics Task Force. Its complete title was San Diego County Integrated Narcotics Task Force, but the cops and the crooks called it simply NTF.

NTF was a combined state-federal strike force.

It operated under the auspices of the DEA, but was separate from the mainline of that agency. Under NTF, local peace officers were cross-sworn as federal agents with full powers to go along with their authority as local cops.

The idea was to make teams that consisted of both locals, and full-time Feds who were regular DEA agents. And it worked well in a symbiotic sort of way.

The local cops had the informants and the street knowledge, which the Feds generally didn't. And the Feds had the resources, both in terms of equipment and access to the vastly superior federal legal machinery. This was particularly true in California, where the liberal state Supreme Court had utterly emasculated the state grand jury powers and had created the most restrictive search and seizure laws in the country.

It was common knowledge among prosecutors. You want to be in any kind of organized, ongoing criminal enterprise—such as fraud or narcotics—California was your best bet.

Initially, NTF was designed to fill the gap between the individual users and the major-shipment dealers investigated by the DEA and the FBI. But as the so-called recreational usage of drugs grew, the distribution chains expanded and became more complex to meet the burgeoning demand. As a result, NTF found itself up to its peace-officer ears in cases that a few years previously would have been major cases even for the DEA.

And, once again, the street dealers were neglected. They lived in a vacuum of sorts, virtually free to operate in the uneasy no-man's-land that existed beneath the level of cases NTF was now working.

All the street dealer had to do was dodge the patrol deputies.

That wasn't particularly difficult. They just didn't deal to anybody wearing a uniform with a badge and gun and driving a marked green-and-white sheriff's car. Since even a brain-fried junkie or a high-wired meth monster generally retained the cognitive ability to follow this rule, they could deal with relative impunity.

The Street Team was therefore destined to be a success right from its inception.

It was staffed with experienced deputies, like English and Karchut, carefully chosen from the eleven hundred or so members of the Sheriff's Department. Most of the team, especially the men, had gone through both patrol and detective assignments. They knew street policing, and they knew how to be investigators as well. And, because CIs are important in other areas besides dope, most of them already had developed a number of contacts inside the criminal culture.

Thus, though the eight-person team—actually nine, counting the sergeant in charge of the unit—found itself spread pretty thin in a county the size of San Diego, the results had been impressive from the very first week. The men grew long hair and beards and wore grubby clothing, while the women affected a combination of sleaze and sex calculated to fit into the dope culture at the street level.

So it was on that morning in May when Mrs. Angie Miles telephoned the department to report that some dope fiends were growing marijuana in the canyon below her son's house. The report ultimately landed in the lap of the grubbed-out Larry English of the Street Team.

The call had come in to the Sheriff's Communications Center on the 911 emergency line.

Mrs. Miles was a large, heavily perfumed widow in her sixties. She was an ardent watcher of *Miami Vice*, as well as a reader of police procedural stories and an attender of Neighborhood Watch and crime prevention seminars. She sprinkled her conversation with words like "crime in progress," "suspects," "perpetrators" and, in more emotional moments, "dope fiends" and "hopheads."

At the ultramodern Sheriff's Communications Center, which vaguely resembled the control panels of the starship *Enterprise*, one of the civilian operators took the call.

"Emergency Services. Is this an emergency?"

"Yes. I need to report a crime in progress," announced Mrs. Miles proudly.

"Go ahead, please." As she spoke, the dispatcher scanned the computer display on the desk in front of her.

Even as the call first came through, the computers had been at work, tracing and backtracking it. Now they were scrolling out the phone number the call was being made from and the address where the phone was located. This information would show which law enforcement agency had jurisdiction over the address, and could ultimately be correlated with the specific beat if necessary. Depending on the emergency, the dispatcher could have a unit rolling within seconds of receiving the information over the phone. Assuming any units were available, of course.

"Some dope fiends are cultivating cannabis in a canyon near my son's house."

Mrs. Miles made the announcement and then waited expectantly. She had heard the term "cultivating cannabis" at a Crime Awareness Program sponsored by the San Diego Police Department. She thought the operator would recognize her as a knowledgeable witness because she used that term.

The keynote speaker at the CAP function had been Captain Wallace Philbin of the San Diego Police Department. Captain Wally hadn't made an arrest of his own or been along on a search warrant for fifteen years. He hadn't even talked to a real narc, let alone a suspect, for ten. He was, however, a good speaker. To the Mrs. Mileses of the world, he looked like a tough veteran cop—stocky, with startlingly white hair over a young-looking face. He always managed to stand with his coat open just enough to reveal the gleaming badge clipped to his belt and even provide occasional glimpses of the unfired .45 Gold Cup automatic he wore in a shoulder holster.

Apart from the Valium and diet pills he regularly filched from his wife's prescriptions, Captain Wally had no personal contact with the illicit furnishing of drugs. However, he looked good on camera and thus frequently acted as the police department spokesman. As a result, he often was called on to read the investigative reports of major drug seizures.

Because of those reports, he actually thought narcs talked the way their reports read, using phrases like "cultivating cannabis" instead of "growing weed" or "growing pot" or, in more articulate moments, "sprouting some herb" or some equivalent description.

If the expression was good enough for a real cop like Captain Philbin, it was good enough for Mrs. Miles.

The operator stopped reading the scrolled information. Growing weed was not the sort of thing the 911 line was designed for. "Are you in immediate danger?" she inquired, her voice formal and polite.

"Not immediate," conceded Mrs. Miles. "However—"

"Please stand by while I transfer you to Street Narcotics."

The switching was accomplished automatically. The call bounced some twenty miles across the county to the sheriff's Street Team offices in Santee, a suburb just east of the San Diego city boundaries.

Mrs. Miles repeated her statement to Sonni Robbins, the Street Team secretary, this time substituting "suspects" for "dope fiends."

"Hold, please," said Sonni crisply. She pressed the hold button, and glanced around the office to see who was available to take the call.

Four of the desks were vacant, and the occupants of three of the others were on the telephone.

The fourth deputy, a muscular, bull-like man in his thirties, was dictating a report from his notes. He wore faded jeans and a black T-shirt with an orange Harley-Davidson logo emblazoned on it. Behind his head, the hair hung down to the middle of his back in a ponytail.

"Citizen call-in, Larry," Sonni intoned. "Lady wants to report quote some suspects cultivating cannabis unquote."

The burly deputy, deep in the intricacies of his report, looked up vaguely. "Huh?"

Sonni shrugged. "That's what she said."

English sighed. He was an energetic and hardworking cop, normally the last deputy to complain about his caseload. His attitude was you bought the ticket, don't bitch about the ride. But today was Friday, and he had a date that evening and reports on three multiple-suspect search warrants to get out before the end of the day.

"Sure," he said resignedly. "Sure. Put her down here."

He set aside the notes he was using to prepare the report. The button on line 5 began to blink, and he lifted the receiver.

"Street Narcotics. Deputy English speaking."

Mrs. Miles repeated her announcement for yet a third time, this time with the noun "hopheads."

English rolled his eyes at the ceiling. "How did you find out about this, ma'am?"

"My son told me."

"He's seen it, then?"

"Yes. He witnessed it personally." It struck Mrs. Miles as odd that a law enforcement officer wouldn't use the more legalistic verb "witnessed," as both she and Captain Philbin did. But then, maybe it was part of his cover, she surmised.

"How many plants did your son see?"

Mrs. Miles hesitated a moment. In fact, her son had told her there were nine plants. Well, she reasoned, nine was right next to ten, and ten was close to twelve.

"Approximately a dozen or so. Twelve to fifteen, possibly," she responded at last. Well, it was *possible*, she thought defensively. Besides, that many plants would surely secure an immediate response.

"Are they inside a yard, somebody's yard?"

"No, Detective. It's a kind of steep canyon with brush and things in it. The cultivation is down below all the houses, near the bottom of the canyon."

"How big?"

"What?"

"How big—tall—are the plants?"

She hesitated again. "The plants are about, oh—" here Mrs. Miles exaggerated by approximately the same twenty-five percent factor as she had in the number of plants "—six feet tall."

"Have you seen them yourself, ma'am?"

"No, Detective. I told you my son has. He reported it to me, and I'm reporting it to you."

English shrugged his meaty shoulders and looked at the notes for his unfinished reports.

He could already visualize the situation. Some dirtbag was growing his own pot at the bottom of the canyon. It was probably steep enough that most people wouldn't go down there, with the possible exception of kids playing. The underbrush that was indigenous to the semiarid San Diego climate would help conceal the plants.

And, though in California simple possession of marijuana for personal use only was legally classified as an infraction—a cite-and-release offense like a traffic ticket, punishable by a fine only—cultivation of even a few plants was a felony.

Of course, English knew he would probably need a search warrant to prosecute the case in court.

The search warrant would have to be written out in longhand. The draft would have to be approved by somebody in the D.A.'s office. Then it would have to be typed and signed by a judge before they could go grab the plants.

English calculated that if he was lucky, he could get it done in about six hours.

The warrant would let him be sure he could seize the plants legally. Of course, he would still have to figure out somehow whose they were. Find out whom to arrest. Who done it, in other words. Unless the dopers had put up a sign identifying themselves, or dropped their wallets or something, that could be quite a problem. The best way to handle it would be to surveil the site until somebody showed up to water the plants, or harvest a little.

Sure thing. Right on. No way would a stakeout be justified for a dozen goddamn plants.

Moreover, English knew that the felony of cultivation was rarely actually punished, even though it was indeed a felony. This was because the law allowed most cultivators to obtain a dismissal of the charges provided they attended drug education class.

Most people who attended the classes provided very positive feedback about them. They described the program as an excellent place to make new contacts, both buyers and sellers, in the drug trade. Also, since the classes usually included a talk by an attorney, the attendees got free helpful advice on how to hide their stashes, when to invoke their Miranda rights and other legal techniques useful to the continued success of a narcotics enterprise.

Six hours for a nothin'-burger case.

1199

Small wonder that half the high school kids went around stoned during many of their waking hours. Smoke was easier for most of them to come by than beer.

There was one other option, however, English knew.

He could simply go over there and yank the goddamn plants out of the ground, impound them and let it go at that. And PR Mrs. Miles a little in the process. That way, the whole thing might take an hour or so, max. Technically it might be a violation of somebody's rights, but that didn't seem so bad, especially when he didn't know who the somebody was. At least the unknown grower would lose his plants.

English spoke into the phone again. "We certainly appreciate you reporting this, ma'am. Now if you'll give me the address, we'll get right on it."

It turned out the plants weren't even in the jurisdiction of the sheriff's office. They were in the city rather than the county.

The second largest in California, San Diego County held the city of San Diego, a handful of smaller cities around it and an unincorporated area that ranged from densely populated urban sprawl to horse-and-cow country, to various Indian reservations—each was usually referred to as "the rez"—to open desert.

The city of San Diego and a few of the smaller cities had their own PDs. Any area outside these cities' boundaries was policed by the sheriff's office. In addition, some of the small cities elected to contract with the S.O. rather than maintain their own police departments.

However, both by operation of law and by a letter of agreement with the chiefs of police of the various cities who did maintain their own departments, including San Diego, the sheriff's eleven hundred or so sworn deputies could legally act anywhere in the entire county. That included inside the city limits as well. Established procedure generally dictated that the location of primary importance to the case determined who worked it.

There were some exceptions, of course—if somebody were killed, say, in the city but the body dumped in the unincorporated area, the S.O. personnel would normally work the case. This would be so even though the site of the killing—once it was determined—might be in some ways more important than the place the body was found. Likewise, a body found inside the city would be worked by SDPD, even if the person had been killed in the county area.

Certainly, though, the location of the growing plants in a cultivation caper would normally dictate who handled the case.

In this instance, Mrs. Miles had said they were at her son's house, which, it ultimately developed, was in the city of San Diego. But she had made the call from her own house, which was in the sheriff's area, and, of course, the 911 computers could only trace and display the number she was calling from.

Per custom, English called up the P.D. and offered it to them.

"Are you kidding me?" the sergeant of the P.D. Narcotics Team demanded. "Twelve plants? Half my guys are off sick or injured, and most of the others are in court. You guys got the call. It's all yours, pal."

So the stocky deputy rounded up Dave Karchut and the two of them headed out to bring in the sheaves, so to speak.

It was shortly after 3:00 p.m. when they arrived at Mrs. Miles's son's house. The house was near the city limits, just on the San Diego side of the line that separated it from the city of Lemon Grove. The latter, though an incorporated city, was policed by the sheriff's office.

Hell, it's almost S.O. jurisdiction anyway, English told himself, thinking about the reports he wasn't getting done.

The house sat on the south edge of a canyon, such that the backyard faced generally north. To the west—the left, if one were looking out from the backyard—the view stretched all the way to the Pacific Ocean, some fifteen miles away. To the east lay a vast blanket of homes and businesses that made up Lemon Grove and the unincorporated areas beyond it.

The two deputies clambered and slid down the steep canyon. About halfway to the bottom, they found the nine four-foot plants.

"Looks like we're shy a couple," observed English dryly, thinking again of his unfinished paperwork.

They surveyed the little garden, well tended, each plant with its own dike around it to hold the water somebody had to be carrying down for them. The plants had been sexed, which meant the male plants had been removed, leaving only the females, which had a higher THC content.

And not a sign of who the cultivator was.

"Jesus," muttered English disgustedly.

"Hey, man, it's a felony in progress, remember," rejoined Karchut good-naturedly. He was tall and lugubrious, a lanky, six-foot basset hound, but he had a quick, dry wit that he exercised frequently. With his straggly beard and lived-in clothing, Dave looked even grubbier than English.

"Jesus," English muttered again.

"Yes sirree, boy, it do appear to be a felony in progress," intoned his partner. "There's one good thing about it, though."

"What's that?"

"At least we didn't get a warrant."

English shrugged. "There is that," he admitted. Shaking his head, he looked around the area.

A few feet away was a clear spot, devoid of brush. He walked over and sat down, partly to catch his breath and partly just for the hell of it.

The afternoon sun shone warm and bright. The canyon was filled with bird and small-animal sounds. Gradually, these seemed to stand out over the faraway background roar of the city. Above them, a jet was making its final descent westward, into the sun, toward Lindbergh Field.

Though English would never have described himself as particularly poetic, he could feel what might be called a hypnotic quality of the place. The hell with the reports, he thought, he'd take just a few minutes and enjoy himself. Stop and smell the roses, so to speak, though in this case it was marijuana plants.

In tacit agreement, Karchut hunkered down on his heels and began flipping pebbles down the sandy slopes.

English relaxed and felt the warm sun heating his black Harley-Davidson shirt. Apart from the houses above them, including Mrs. Miles's son's house, the nearest home was maybe a couple of hundred yards or so away, across the canyon in Lemon Grove.

Karchut's voice came to him as if through a haze. "You okay, Lar?"

"Yeah. Fine."

"Somethin' on your mind, pal?"

The burly narc shook his head. "Not really. Sun just feels good. Wish I could just snooze here for a while is all."

"Yeah, I know what you mean."

English gazed out over the canyon, the downtown sky-scrapers off to the left, and beyond them, the ocean. Cars like toys moved along Interstate 8 as a million people went about their individual lives, some living, some dying, some happy, some heartbroken.

Off to the right, across the canyon and somewhat above them, a red light blinked. No siren, just the winking light.

Idly, he watched as an ambulance pulled into a vacant lot adjacent to a white apartment complex located on the opposite rim. From that distance, he could recognize the logo on the ambulance, though he couldn't read the name.

Caro's Emergency Care, a private ambulance company.

Somebody stricken, hurt or dead in that house, English thought. Idly, he watched.

Two tiny figures trundled a collapsible gurney from the vehicle. The top sheet on the gurney blazed a brilliant white as it reflected the afternoon sun. Then the two men disappeared from sight as they went around to what would be the front of the complex. Within minutes, they emerged again, this time with the white sheet distorted by the human shape it covered. Into the ambulance, doors closed, and then it was pulling slowly away. No red lights this time, and no siren. Either the person was not yet critical, or had gone past it.

Either way, there would be no hurry....

Karchut's voice interrupted his thoughts. "Come on, man. You're the brawn of this operation. Gimme a hand with these."

He sighed and rolled to his feet, fighting off the torporific warmth of the sunshine. Karchut was pulling up the plants, which was no real task given the sandy soil. English grabbed the last couple, then picked up three of the ones that his partner had already uprooted.

Karchut began a good-natured incantation, as though dictating the report one of them would have to prepare later.

"'Whereupon once Deputy English got up off his lazy ass we impounded what appeared to be nine open parenthesis digit nine close parenthesis growing marijuana plants, each approximately four feet in height....'" He let his voice trail off, and turned to begin the climb back up the canyon.

English ignored him and cast a final glance around the peaceful area. Across the rim, the ambulance was gone from view, but the birds still twittered and the sun still felt good.

"Hey, you son of a bitch!" a man's voice roared down at them.

"Jesus!" Larry expostulated, rudely yanked from his reverie by the angry bellow. The shock was made worse by the fleeting thought that by being so complacent about the whole thing he had been violating a cardinal rule of officer survival. It's the harmless-looking ones where you get killed.

Together, the grubby narcs looked up the hill.

Two men who looked like Hell's Angels' rejects were charging headlong down the steep canyon. One was tall and hulking, with the wasting appearance of an addict of some sort, probably methamphetamine. The other was shorter and stockier, a toadlike specimen with a full beard and long, shaggy hair. Both wore filthy denims and leather vests, their arms heavily tattooed.

Sunlight glinted off something in the tall man's hand.

With a start, the narcs realized he was waving a machete over his head as he came leaping down the hill. It looked like a cheap, war-surplus store implement, but capable of chopping a righteous hunk out of somebody nonetheless. His stocky companion gripped something that looked like an ax handle, about two or three feet of very efficient billy club.

"Hold it right there, you assholes!" roared the stocky one.

He was a thick, ugly toadlike brute, whose shirt and vest stopped about six inches short of his greasy jeans. The strip of exposed belly was stark white, fat but "hard fat" that looked strong and solid. Wiry black hairs dotted the exposed flesh. With the ax handle in his hands, the man looked to be a formidable specimen indeed.

English sensed Karchut was about to go for his gun. "Not yet!" he whispered.

"You sons of bitches!" snarled the toad again. "What the fuck are you doin'? Those are our plants, you assholes!"

English stared at him, suppressing the urge to laugh out loud in spite of the club and the machete. Instead he dropped the plants and backed away, trying to look nervous. He found it wasn't altogether difficult to do that, given the weapons in the hands of the agitated bikers.

Karchut came in as if on cue. "Hey, man," he protested, ducking his head apologetically. "We didn't know—"

The two men had drawn up to them. "Well, you know now, asshole!" the stocky one snarled. "That's our stuff. Drop 'em and beat it!"

"Jesus. I mean, okay, man," said the taller narc. "Sorry. Jesus. I mean, how could we know? It's not like there's a sign or nothin'—"

"You fuckin' knew you didn't plant them! You think you got the right to just go around, rippin' off any fuckin' thing you like, just 'cause there ain't no sign saying you can't?"

English regarded the man closely. Nice to be lectured on morality by a biker doper, he thought. But there was something else. The man looked hyper. Speeded out. Wired up. Meth, probably, he thought. The guy's wired on methamphetamine, which accounted in part for his being so aggressive and talkative. Well, if that were the case, maybe he'd like to talk some more.

"Just a goddamn minute," snarled the heavyset narc, his face ugly, the thick muscles of his neck and trapezius bulging. Turning to Karchut, he went on. "How the fuck do we know who these guys are? Or if it's their herb? I ain't believin' it just 'cause he says it!"

Karchut appeared to consider it. "You got a point—" he began.

English interrupted his partner. "Besides, to hell with these guys anyway! We can take 'em, man!"

The taller of the two wild men spoke for the first time. It was evident he didn't relish the prospect of taking on the two dirt-bags stealing his plants, even if he and his buddy had weapons and they didn't.

"See that house up there?" He pointed up to the top of the hill above them, about six houses beyond Mrs. Miles's son's house.

"The yellow one?" responded English.

"Yeah. The fuckin' yellow one."

"Yeah. I see it. What about it?"

"We live there, man."

English spit onto the coarse sand. "Big deal. You live in the yellow house. My ass bleeds for you. So what?"

The tall one made a jab with the machete. "We been comin' down here every day to water these goddamn plants. They are our plants, man."

English glanced at Karchut. The tall narc put on a look of uncertainty, and hesitated. Finally, English shrugged his heavy shoulders. "That so?" he asked the burly biker at last.

"Yeah, that's so, asshole. But it don't matter anyway, 'cause I got the stick and you got shit, Jack, so take a hike before I bust you up. You already ruined our plants, anyway, cock-sucker." He took a threatening step forward and brandished the club menacingly.

The two deputies took another quick step backward.

"Hold on!" snapped Karchut urgently, his hands still clutching the plant stalk. "Lemme show you somethin'."

"I'll do it," interrupted English.

"Let him show you somethin', then," Karchut immediately rejoined.

Before the two bikers could react, English reached behind his back with both hands. The left one found the badge and case in his back pocket. The right one closed around the grips of the .45-caliber pistol—the standard Government Model

Colt semiautomatic—that was tucked into the waistband of his jeans, holsterless, in the small of his back.

"See?" he said in a conversational tone, producing both. Then his voice turned abruptly harsh. "Sheriff's Department! You're both under arrest! Now drop those goddamn weapons or I'll blow your goddamn heads off!"

The two bikers gaped without comprehension.

Karchut, meanwhile, dropped the plants he was holding and produced his own weapon. He moved quickly sideways so the two suspects were at the apex of a triangle, the other corners of which were the two deputies. "Move it!" he roared.

The machete and ax handle dropped to the sand.

As the two deputies cuffed the still-stunned suspects, Karchut was jubilant. "Well, well, well, the yellow house, huh? Thanks for the tip. I do believe it's search warrant time. Yes sirree, I surely do. Wouldn't you say so, Lar?"

English nodded and mentally kissed goodbye to his unfinished reports as well as the date with a young court reporter he had recently met.

By eight that night, the search was over. The two biker rejects were in custody for a variety of charges—some meth had been found in the house, along with several stolen motorcycle casings—in addition to the cultivation and assault with a deadly weapon counts.

The whole affair ultimately became known as "The Two-Asshole Caper." The title was based on a cartoon that English and Karchut included in the reports that went over to the D.A.'s office the following Tuesday.

The cartoon had three frames to it.

The first showed two decidedly stupid-looking specimens—labeled by one of the narcs as Stuart and McKeon, the names of the bikers—riding, one behind the other, on a mule. The second frame had a bystander looking on and saying to another bystander, "Hey, get a load of the two assholes on that mule." In the third frame, the two riders had dismounted and were searching beneath the mule's tail in obedience to the statement.

It seemed to fit the level of smarts displayed by the bikers.

Somehow, the cartoon found its way into the hands of the
defense attorneys, who sought to make a big deal out of it in
court. The judge wasn't particularly distressed over it, however. When the case was finally over, he handed out his usual
stiff sentence to ex-felon bikers who waved weapons at cops
and trafficked in narcotics. That is to say, he lectured them
sternly when he placed them on probation with six months in
jail.

At first the narcs weren't too happy about that. But then it
turned out The Two-Asshole Caper gave Cates a major break
in a tough homicide, so it didn't seem so bad, after all. After
all, it was all hunch on top of luck, anyway.

5

Cates

As he made his way through the detectives' area at LGS, Cates felt a foul mood overtake him. It had to do with all the old garbage dredged up by the hostage scenario he had just completed. It also had to do with killing people, even bad guys, and with the fact that nobody outside the business could ever really understand it.

He also wondered if it had to do with burnout, and hoped it didn't.

One time he started to explain the mood to somebody who wasn't a cop, to see if it made sense to anybody outside the job. The person he had explained it to was Bonnie Kingsley, mother of Kimberly Kingsley, and Cates realized then that the feeling was something that could never be explained.

Kimberly was a runaway teenage girl who had ended up as the victim of a 187, which is how California cops refer to dead-people cases. The 187 comes from the penal code section that defines homicide.

The family from which Kimberly had fled lived in one of the most luxurious houses Cates had ever seen. Perched on a bluff in Del Mar, just north of San Diego, it faced almost due west and provided a panoramic view of the Pacific Ocean beyond the beach less than a mile away. An eminent design architect had created it, all glass and white plaster and oak. Though no expert in such matters, Cates figured it had to be worth a couple of mil at least.

Kimberly Kingsley, age seventeen, had been found strangled to death in a remote area of north San Diego County. Cates and Ben Grummon, his partner then and now, had gone to the Kingsley house to talk to Kimberly's mother.

"What the hell kind of a mother names her kid Kimberly Kingsley?" muttered Grummon as Cates guided the Plymouth into the cement drive.

In his mid-forties, Grummon was a few years older than Cates. He was stocky and cynical, a man for whom the word *taciturn* would seem almost lighthearted. He was also one of the most astute homicide men in the business. And, even though Cates had a college education and wasn't exactly a kid, he was one of the few younger deputies that Grummon liked, largely because he was big and a man and was also astute.

"Not like the usual runts and morons the department's mainly hiring these days," Grummon once praised him. "You just think too much, that's all. Get over that, you just might make it in Homicide."

Cates had figured no response was necessary, so he hadn't made one.

"'Course, you got something else going for you, too."

This called for a response. "What's that?"

"You got me to teach you."

Both men had taken an immediate dislike to the ostentatious and impersonal materialism exemplified by the Kingsley home.

Cates didn't have an answer for his partner's question about what kind of woman names a kid Kimberly Kingsley. Not right then, anyway. Later, after he saw the house—in no sense the home—where Kimberly had existed during her childhood years, the only answer came to him.

The architect had done his job beautifully, exquisitely, and the Kingsley parents had thereafter done their best to prevent any footprint of individuality or humanity or warmth from detracting from the design. The slick magazines displayed about the house were never read; the furniture never relaxed upon.

But it sure looked nice.

Bonnie Kingsley, Cates discovered, was in her early forties. She was blond and athletic and attractive in that taut, fit way a pampered fortyish woman with lots of money can look if she works at it. She had good legs, a lithe, bouncy step, breasts just large enough and firm enough that he couldn't really decide if nature had been surgically enhanced, and faint lines around her eyes and forehead, lines that somehow did not manage to add any particular sense of character to her face. Later, he guessed, those lines would be joined by the fainter marks of facial surgery.

Or maybe they already had.

Mrs. Kingsley expressed her grief as if reciting a part in a play. Kimberly was "my baby, my beautiful, darling baby. She was a cheerleader and in gymnastics and trying out for the debate team, and we had just given her a new car for her birthday, I just don't know where she got the energy for all that."

And probably very popular, too, Cates observed when Bonnie Kingsley paused.

Grummon's eyes flickered as he shot a sideways glance at Cates, indicating that he, at least, had caught the irony in his voice. But Kimberly's mother didn't seem to hear it, or if she did, she ignored it. She continued her recital of Kimberly's accomplishments as if they were her own, all the time conducting a detached review of herself and her grief.

Finally, Grummon had nodded and grunted out a barely civil "Yeah, well, it's tough growing up these days. Lotta pressure on the kids."

Then, while Mrs. Kingsley went to retrieve some telephone bills and some of Kimberly's personal effects, he told Cates he'd just wait in the car.

"Where's Mr., uh...?" she began to inquire when she came back into the room.

"Grummon." Cates was gazing out the broad window at the shimmering blue-gray of the Pacific. Without turning he told her that Grummon had gone outside to monitor the radio.

"He seems so..." Mrs. Kingsley bit her lip and sighed. "I don't know, so hostile."

"He's like that."

"Why is he like that?"

"It would take too long to tell you," Cates replied. "It's hard to explain."

"I see."

He suddenly became aware that Bonnie Kingsley was standing next to him, slightly in front and off to one side. She was holding a bunch of bills and a pink vinyl-covered address book in her hands, and she was examining him with the same bright, detached look of appraisal he had seen her direct at herself when she was discussing her daughter.

He glanced quickly down at her.

She stood closer than even friends stand when they talk to each other. Cates could see the clean white of her scalp beneath the blond hair. She smelled clean and fresh and expensive like a Palm Springs sunrise, and he could feel the warmth radiating from her body.

"How tall are you, Steve—I can call you Steve, can't I?" The words came out as a purr, not breathy, exactly, but not exactly formal, either.

He ignored the second question. "Six-three."

"Do you work out?"

"Yes."

"Lift weights? Run?"

"Both."

"You must weigh close to two hundred pounds."

"Two-twenty right now. More if I'm lifting weights more than I'm running. Less if it's vice versa."

"Two-twenty?"

"Yes."

Bonnie Kingsley considered that a moment. "You don't look like you weigh that much. Two hundred pounds—that's one thing. But two-twenty sounds like a fat man, or a football lineman, or a muscle head. But you're not any of those, are you?"

She spoke with the frankness that only a sexy, rich woman in her forties can speak with, an intrusiveness that is either admirable candor or plain rudeness, depending on the perspective. To Cates, it tended toward the latter.

Her question wasn't really a question, he figured, so he let it pass. She continued speaking.

"You look strong, but you almost look kind of rangy. Big muscles, but lean. Like a timber wolf instead of a buffalo." She hesitated. "Do you carry a gun, Steve?"

"Yes. It's required on duty."

"What kind of a gun is it?"

"A revolver. Smith & Wesson. It's stainless steel. It doesn't rust or get corroded when I sweat on it."

"What kind of bullets does it shoot?"

"Kind?"

"Size. Caliber. Whatever you call it."

"It's a .357 Magnum, if that helps."

And then she asked it, her eyes shining. He could feel the moist warmth of her breath on his arm as she spoke. "Have you ever killed anybody, Steve?"

Cates turned and walked a few feet away.

Why did they always ask that, he wondered, these rich bitches with their shining eyes and beautiful homes? Were they just so sheltered that they really didn't know? Or was it some kink in their psyches, maybe that they had become so bored and emotionally anesthetized by their have-everything lives that it took this to excite them?

He had played this scene before, and it left him cold.

Her next question would be how did it feel, and of course it didn't feel that great. At the time, maybe it did, a little, because you were filled with adrenaline and you were either scared half to death and in awe about surviving it, or you felt exhilarated because you'd handled a difficult job, and handled it well.

But later, the relief and exhilaration went away. And then, there was nothing very thrilling about it at all.

It wasn't that you felt horribly guilty, Cates knew. You didn't flog yourself or vow never to do it again. What you did feel was a strange sort of nonspecific emptiness, almost a let-down.

Maybe it was because you realized that the only good that came of it was stopping the immediate crisis, if there was one. But outside of that one little arena, that tiny theater where that particular drama of life and death unfolded, it was the same world it had always been.

Outside were the same dirtbags, still preying on each other and on the weak.

Maybe the feeling came down to one of disillusionment. The expectation that some great, society-improving benefit would follow from such a significant act as taking a life had been shattered.

Killing crooks didn't have the effect it somehow had seemed it should have. It really didn't do much good in the big picture, though of course it helped like hell in the particular crisis where it had taken place.

Cates had given all this a lot of thought, and he sort of thought that was what it boiled down to.

And when he tried very simply to explain this to Bonnie Kingsley, she gazed at him with a kind of puzzled look on her face, as if she didn't understand. As, of course, she didn't. And she stepped back away from him a couple of feet and gave him the telephone bills and the address book and told him she hoped he solved his case.

As he walked back to the car where Grummon was leaning, smoking a cigarette and looking out at the ocean, Cates had an answer for his partner's earlier question about the sort of person who would name a kid Kimberly Kingsley.

"A woman like that," he said simply.

Grummon, whose eighteen years of cop work had given him considerable exposure to the results of the human psyche, knew instantly what he was referring to.

"You got that right, partner," he said, which was as close to an expression of outright approval as Grummon ever made.

All that went into why Cates preferred Homicide these days to SED. It also explained part of his funk as he strode through the LGS in search of a cup of coffee and something to do until it was officially quitting time.

He found an empty desk in the main detective area and sat down to leaf through a stack of field interview slips.

An FI was a form not unlike a traffic ticket. Cops routinely filled them out in cases where they contacted or detained a suspicious person in the field, but lacked probable cause for an arrest. The FI recorded the date, the time and the identification of the person, along with a brief statement and the circumstances.

Legally speaking, Cates knew, these situations were called either "contacts" or "detentions," depending on the exact nature of the encounter.

The law recognized three levels of what one judge termed "police-citizen interaction." One was a contact. Contacts were also called consensual encounters by the courts. A contact occurred whenever a deputy talked to somebody other than another cop. This included talking to victims, witnesses and even suspects, provided in the latter case it was low-key and the person was free to leave if he wanted to.

The second level was a detention, or stop. That meant the deputy had some factual basis—"reasonable suspicion"—to believe some criminal activity was under way, but not enough information for probable cause to arrest. The purpose of a detention was to investigate whether something was, in fact, up. To do that, a police officer or deputy could hold or detain the person for up to ten or twenty minutes or possibly even longer, depending on the circumstances.

The third level was an arrest, for which a strong, fact-based suspicion called probable cause was required.

All cops had to know the difference between the various levels. If they blew it, they could be sued. Moreover, if a suspect were detained without adequate "reasonable suspicion" or arrested without adequate "probable cause," any evidence obtained as a result of the detention or arrest was tossed out, no matter how relevant it was.

If the crook went free as a result, so be it. It didn't matter what the crime was; the rule applied equally to dope dealers, rapists, child molesters and murderers.

The result was that most criminal cases had what some cops and prosecutors called the "trial before the trial." This was a hearing in which the adequacy of the reasonable suspicion or probable cause relied on by the officer was determined. If the D.A. won it, the evidence was admissible. If the D.A. lost, the court ruled the evidence inadmissible, no matter how guilty the crook was.

Like most cops and crooks, Cates called this the "Fourth Amendment crap shoot." The term came from the section of the Constitution under whose auspices this fraud on the public was created by the courts.

And, like all cops, Cates had closed a number of cases based on FIs. Writing them was done primarily by uniformed patrol deputies, and Cates had written a ton of them back when he was in uniform. Now that he was a detective, he frequently got his leads from the ones being generated by the current patrol teams.

The pattern was so familiar it became almost routine.

A patrol deputy would see a man coming out of an alley on foot at 2:00 a.m. The man is nervous; the deputy suspicious. He detains him. Still, no obvious crime, no recent report of one, no probable cause, so the deputy FI's the man and lets him go.

The next morning the body is discovered in a house that opens onto that alley a half block away. Or the burglary is discovered, or the rape victim finally gets free and makes a report. Thanks to the FI, the detectives would have a place to start.

Cates was leafing through a stack of FIs from the preceding week. This time, he didn't have any particular crime or suspect in mind. Instead, he was simply following his established habit of gathering intelligence, trying to keep up on who was doing what, or running with whom, in the barrios and streets patrolled by LGS deputies.

The FIs made a sort of "who's who of dirtbags," he reflected. Some of the names were familiar; others he hadn't come across before.

"Spider" Corrales, a Mexican street gangster, was out, Cates noted. A deputy from C Shift had FI'ed him last night in Encanto.

Cates frowned. How could that be? Spider had drawn seven years on a voluntary manslaughter conviction. But that was four years ago, he realized, and seven almost always meant three and a half under California's complex determinate sentencing law.

Tyrone Jones, a.k.a. Sledge, had been stopped running away from the scene of a reported mugging. The victim had refused to identify Tyrone as the assailant. Maybe, Cates thought, that was because Sledge was the wrong guy or maybe the victim just didn't want to. Cates didn't have any doubt which it was.

He knew the area, and he knew Sledge.

Given those facts, it was a good possibility the thing had been a dope rip-off—Tyrone agreeing to sell drugs, then robbing the would-be buyer. Drug buyers who got ripped off frequently didn't go to the cops, and juries didn't tend to believe them when they did.

Somebody who gave the name Cecil Andrews had been contacted by a deputy four days ago based on a citizen report of a suspicious person sitting in a car. It had been 4:00 p.m., broad daylight, and there had been nothing to back up the suspicion other than the citizen call. And yet the deputy had made the contact and filled out the FI.

Cates grinned.

Must be a new deputy, he thought. A court would probably toss the FI in a second, even if it led to something and the man proved guilty as hell. Still, good work by the deputy, anyway.

You don't try, you can't win, he thought. The meek shall not inherit an arrest, let alone a conviction. Or even an FI.

He scanned the form for the deputy's name.

"Griffin, M.," he saw, followed by the badge number, 1074. The name seemed familiar; then he wondered if this were the woman he had "shot" in the role-play, the one Sergeant Reynolds had called Griff. The one with the great legs.

David Benjamin had been detained in a car lot just before midnight. Benjamin had ducked down between cars as the deputy drove around the corner. Quick, but not quick enough, as the FI showed. He proved to be clean, however. Cates knew that Danny Benjamin, David's older brother, was a well-known fence, no merchandise too hot for him, no sirree...

A page came over the loudspeaker, interrupting him.

"Detective Cates, line one, please. Detective Cates, line one."

He reached for the telephone and punched the button. "Cates here."

"This is Abrams at the front desk. I've got a woman here who's got something that just might be a Homicide problem."

JOYCE PARKED HER CAR in front of Casa MarVista for the second time that day. This time she found a space almost directly in front of the apartment. She glanced in the rearview mirror and saw that the detective, Cates, was pulling his tan Dodge into the vacant lot adjacent to the complex, in nearly the same spot as she had parked earlier.

She got out of her car and waited for him.

It had been, she reflected, a frustrating afternoon. First, not having complete directions to Beth's place. Then finding her missing—do you find somebody missing, she wondered, or do you *not* find somebody there? Or does it matter?

This is crazy, she thought. Or I'm crazy. My friend has disappeared into thin air, maybe kidnapped, maybe dead. And here I'm thinking about grammar and sentence structure.

And, on the subject of a frustrating afternoon, the cops.

Thinking she was inside the city, she had called the San Diego Police Department. The cop who answered had not been particularly helpful.

"Sounds like a missing person case."

"Yes. I mean, if you say so. How do I file a report? Can somebody come out here?"

"Can't do that, ma'am."

"I don't understand."

"Can't do it."

Joyce gritted her teeth. "I heard that part. What I don't understand is what to do next. I mean, if it's a missing person, isn't there a missing person report or something that has to be filed?"

"Can't take a missing person's report till they've been gone for forty-eight hours."

"I don't understand. Somebody's disappeared—vanished—and you say you can't take any report for forty-eight hours? What if she's in danger?"

"Ma'am, you said it was a missing person. We can't take a missing person report until they've been missing for forty-eight hours. Department policy."

Joyce was flabbergasted. "*You* said it was a missing person case. *I* didn't say it was a missing person until you told me that was what it was."

"Whatever. Either way—"

"Look. What if she's been kidnapped? What if. . ." She struggled, momentarily at a loss for words. "What if somebody had been killed but the person's body wasn't there? Would you call that a 'missing person case' and wait forty-eight hours?"

"Not if there's signs of violence. If there's signs of violence, we can take a report. Is there any signs of violence?"

"Well—"

"Any blood?"

"No."

"Any ransacking? Forced entry? Anything like that?"

"No, but—"

"Look, ma'am. I know you're upset. But there's very good reasons for the forty-eight-hour rule. The vast majority, 99.9 percent of missing persons, show up inside of forty-eight hours. Same with your friend, there."

Enough is enough. "I'd like to speak with your supervisor, please," she said crisply.

"She'll just tell you the same—"

"I'd like to speak with your supervisor, please. Or—" Joyce hesitated. She didn't want to say she'd call the chief; that sounded too trite and, well, somehow petulant. She was saved by the sharp click in the telephone.

For a single, incredulous moment, Joyce thought the policeman had hung up on her. Then the line clicked again, and a woman's voice came on the line.

"This is Sergeant Sullivan. What can I do for you?" The tone of voice seemed to convey the answer to its own question.

Joyce repeated her request.

"Where is this located?" inquired the sergeant.

"4515 MarVistas. Court," she added hastily.

"Is that in San Diego?"

Before she could respond, Joyce heard the question stated again, only more faintly, as if the sergeant were repeating the question to somebody else rather than into the telephone. Then, in the background, Joyce could hear a man's voice—it sounded like the officer she had first talked to—respond, "Lemon Grove. It's in Lemon Grove."

She also thought she heard something disparaging muttered by the same voice.

Sergeant Sullivan's voice came back on the line, crisp and efficient. "That address is outside our jurisdiction. I suggest you call the Sheriff's Department. Good day."

Joyce had done just that.

This time, however, she had just asked for directions to the closest station and told the deputy that she would come in person to discuss the matter, without specifying what it was. Face-to-face, it would be a lot harder for them to pull some sort of "department policy" brush-off.

The Lemon Grove Substation had been a pleasant surprise. It was a clean, modern-looking facility. The deputy at the counter was a trim, fit young man who looked like her kid brother, Danny. Danny's nineteen, she thought ruefully. I'm getting old.

She glanced at the name plate. D. Abrams. His uniform trousers, so dark green they almost looked charcoal or black in this light, were sharply creased. The shirt was tan khaki, pressed military style with three vertical creases up the back and two in front. The shoulder patches were dark, with the gold star and lettering identifying the sheriff's department.

Joyce glanced around the substation.

No slobs. None of those hats like the Royal Canadian Mounted Police used to wear, or some of the state troopers back east, the hats with the flat brims and the high crown.

No paunches. Nobody who looked remotely likely to say "You're in a heap a' trouble, boy."

Deputy Abrams wore a small pistol in a lightweight black holster on the right side of his waist. The weapon, Joyce noted, was snugged in above his hip, not draping down like some gunslinger's weapon. And though she could tell he was skeptical when she began describing the situation, he had listened attentively.

Still, as she described it, Joyce had fully expected a polite explanation of how department policies said he couldn't do anything.

"Ma'am, that is certainly unusual. Please stand by while I check on something."

Then, when the tall detective in the suit entered, she knew what was going to happen. The young deputy had called his supervisor to tell her about the policy. The man in the suit was going to explain why they couldn't do anything.

Except he didn't.

He'd introduced himself as Detective Cates. He looked tall and powerful in a rangy, wolflike way. His eyes were restless and constantly changing, first concerned and understanding, then flicking abruptly toward the door when somebody else came in, as if alert for danger everywhere.

Detective Cates had asked her some of the same questions about signs of violence as the P.D. officer had. And then he had shrugged and said simply, "Well, let's go take a look."

She watched as he got out of the car now and walked toward her.

He's big, she thought. Bigger than he looks. Not big like some monster football player, but just big. Like somebody took a well-built guy about five-ten, athletic and fit but not a bodybuilder, and then just scaled him up to six-two or whatever Steve Cates is. Just made him proportionately bigger all over.

Bigger *all over*?

Proportionately?

The thought leaped unbidden into her mind, and she was suddenly both embarrassed and amused and maybe even a little ashamed at the lewdness of it. She did not consider herself entirely unacquainted with matters carnal—this is, after all, the liberated eighties, she thought defensively. And yet, though she'd had a few lovers over the years, she had never been able to fully embrace purely casual, unadorned and "feel good" sex.

Sometimes she wished she could.

He had dark, nearly black hair, worn short. No mustache. Strong jaw, a vertical cleft in the chin. Creases fanning out from the corners of his eyes; no gray at the temples. She guessed he was in his late thirties. He didn't look like most men look in suits—which to her mind was somehow soft—yet he wore his well, and he moved with a powerful economy of motion.

"You okay?" he asked as he neared. His speech was economical also, few words, not loud.

"Yes. Of course. Why?"

He smiled. "I don't know. You looked sort of odd for a minute there. Flushed or something."

She felt the heat in her cheeks. "Just nervous, I guess."

"That's understandable. Let's go take a look."

Joyce had half expected Beth to be there, laughing, with some explanation for what had happened. *If she is, I'll kill her,* she thought.

"This it?" Cates asked when they got there.

She nodded.

He acknowledged it with a nod of his own. So casually that at first she didn't realize that he had done it, he moved to one side of the door, so he wasn't in front of it. Then, with a glance at her, he rang the doorbell.

Nothing except the *bing, bong.*

His face expressionless, he turned the knob and pushed the door open. He didn't have his gun out, she noticed, but he did have his coat unbuttoned, and his right arm was casually bent at the elbow so that the hand just happened to be near his waist.

The apartment seemed deathly still.

After a moment, he entered. She followed. It was getting gloomy in the light of the setting sun. Joyce stood, arms folded across her midsection, as Cates made a quick once-over through the small dwelling—dining area and kitchen, bedroom, bathroom, even opening the small walk-in closet off the living room.

Then he turned on the lights. She looked at him hopefully, as if somehow he could explain the disappearance.

He shook his head and walked back toward the bathroom.

"The shower was on, you said?"

"Yes. I turned it off."

"And the radio?"

"I turned it off, too. When I used the phone. Not that it was that loud. It...it was just getting on my nerves, I guess, on top of everything else."

He appeared to think for a moment. "You called from here, then?"

Suddenly, Joyce felt foolish. Here she had been prepared to chew out the entire San Diego Police Department for not taking the situation seriously, and all the time she had been blundering around turning things off and destroying fingerprints or God knows what else.

She felt the heat rise in her cheeks again.

It wasn't as if Cates had asked the question reprovingly. Not critical, not sarcastic, not excessively polite or condescending. Still, the words themselves couldn't help but convey the message. Like, "You were standing on this side when you sawed through the limb?"

Put that way, she had to admit, it did sound like a pretty dumb stunt.

"Yeah. Sorry. I guess I didn't think. Did I destroy any evidence or anything?"

He dismissed it. "Not likely."

Again, she thought, no criticism, expressed or implied. He sounded almost remote, distracted. No judgments, just a thorough, professional absorption in his task.

He took her through it again, from the beginning. The party, her plans to pick up Beth, the fact that she had been a few minutes late. What she had touched. What she knew about Beth.

"Did you see anybody leaving as you arrived?"

Joyce thought back. The laundry room, the woman by the pool. "No. Nobody else," she said at last.

He grunted.

"What do you make of it?" she inquired.

"I don't know."

He glanced at the curlers on the vanity. At least that's one thing I didn't handle, she thought thankfully. Though, of course, an attacker wouldn't be likely to touch that the way he might a phone.

Oh, well.

Cates squatted down and examined the small pile of crumpled clothing. Then he lifted the tank top and looked at it. Apparently finding nothing of interest, he set it to one side and picked up the jeans.

He checked the pockets. In the back pocket, he found a small key.

"Look familiar?"

She shook her head.

He looked inside the pants, and then removed the crumpled panties. The crotch panel was stained a dark red-brown. In spite of herself, Joyce felt embarrassed. The detective, however, seemed utterly oblivious to her and to any embarrassing aspects of the subject matter of his study.

She saw him frown again. Then he glanced into the wastebasket. It was empty except for a couple of tissues. He raised the top from the toilet seat; inside, the water was clear and clean, again with the exception of two tissues.

Fascinated, she watched as he pulled a tissue from the box on the back of the toilet, folded it and carefully blotted it against the stain in the panties. When he removed it, some of the dark red had transferred to the tissue.

Finally, he set the underwear back on the floor and put the tissue next to it. Then he straightened again.

"I think something happened to her," he said at last.

"Me, too," she replied. "But why?"

"Why do I think that?" He gestured at the panties. "That was the clincher. The stain—it's fresh. Relatively, I mean. It fits within the time frame you've given me. She was probably spotting right before she took the shower."

He's so clinical, she thought. So matter-of-fact. It's like a puzzle to him, one that he's serious about solving. Aloud, she said, "What does that prove?"

He shrugged. "Maybe nothing. Except, that box is unopened." He gestured at a box of tampons on the vanity. "She could have had some in her purse, of course. But there are no wrappers in the trash."

Joyce started to speak, then checked herself.

Detective Cates was nodding. "And if you're thinking she could have flushed the wrappers, that's true. But there are still a couple of tissues in the john. It seems unlikely she would have flushed the wrappers and then tossed tissues in. More likely she just decided to shower first. And if that's the case, it's very unlikely she would have left of her own free will without putting in a tampon."

His candor embarrassed her. "It all seems so..." She let the sentence trail off, unfinished.

"Clinical?"

The word surprised her, coming from him. It would be easy to underestimate this man, she realized suddenly. Not because he appeared dull—he certainly didn't—but because he was so perceptive.

"Yes," she said after a moment. "I suppose that's it."

He shrugged. "It's just evidence. I investigated a forcible sodomy case once where the crucial evidence proved to be the victim's blood and fecal matter on the front panel inside the suspect's Jockey shorts. Only one way it could get there."

Joyce felt suddenly queasy. Apparently, he noticed something, because his voice became gentle as he continued.

"If a killer's car dripped oil at the crime scene, we'd try to check it out to see if we could get a match with the suspect's." He gestured at the panties. "This isn't any different."

"I don't like it," she said simply.

He took hold of her elbow and guided her out of the bathroom. Then he walked to the kitchen and washed his hands, drying them with a paper towel from a roll mounted under the cabinet.

Joyce was silent for a moment. "What will you do?" she finally asked.

He shrugged. "I'm not sure. Get the lab out here and have them process the scene."

Scene. The word made her shiver. It sounded like the words used by newscasters. "Scene of the crime." Or "homicide scene."

She swallowed and took a deep breath. "Something's happened to her, hasn't it?"

He nodded. "I think so."

"It seems so vague. Not concrete. Nothing to grasp, to get a hold of. Nothing to go on."

"A lot of them are that way. Unless you get a confession, of course. Or catch the guy in the act. Frequently, it's just adding probability on top of probability until the weight of the evidence leaves only one conclusion. One reasonable conclusion, that is."

Joyce realized her arms were folded across her stomach, the forearms pressing into her body. "I'm afraid for her."

"I'll need to get some information from you. After I radio for the lab van."

"This is real scary."

He looked at her. His eyes were kind, but they also showed he was thinking of something else. "Yes. I suppose it is."

the Santos procedure

LIEUTENANT BEECHAM SLAMMED a copy of the paper onto his desk at eight-twenty Monday morning.

"Shut the door, Cates. And sit down. And tell me what the *hell* is going on here!"

Momentarily taken aback, Cates frowned. "What?"

"This." Beecham gestured angrily at the paper.

"What about it?"

"Haven't you read the paper this morning?"

"No."

"Take a look."

Cates frowned. It had made the front page of the San Diego section of the San Diego County edition of the *Los Angeles Times*. Not a headline on page one of section one, of course, but headlines of section 3 nonetheless.

DISAPPEARANCE PROBED, it proclaimed in large type immediately beneath the banner of the *Times*. Below that, in smaller type, ran the caption, Missing Woman on Secret Government Project. A picture of Beth Fisher was adjacent to the column of type.

Cates scanned the article. It was written, as were most newspaper stories, in inverted pyramid style. That meant the first few sentences conveyed most of the information. It was a style particularly suited to this story, he thought grimly as he read it, because the only real news *was* the first paragraph. The rest looked and felt a lot like padding designed to make the article long enough to justify the shout of the headlines.

Sheriff's homicide detectives are investigating the disappearance of a woman employed by a firm engaged in highly classified research for the Defense Department, the *Times* has learned. The woman, identified as Elizabeth Fisher, 25, apparently disappeared without a trace from her residence in Lemon Grove late Friday afternoon. Foul play is suspected.

The remainder of the article was divided among a description of Data Research and Technology, its company headquarters and its work; a statement that the Sheriff's Department was declining comment; and assertions attributed to a spokesman for the FBI that the Bureau would be undertaking a "parallel investigation." The sequence in which the meager facts were recited suggested that the FBI's involvement was occasioned by the S.O.'s attitude toward the case, as well as the widely held misconception that the FBI could do anything better than anybody else.

"Bastards," he muttered.

"Who?" demanded Beecham. "The Feebies or the *Times*?"

"The *Times*."

To Cates's admittedly prejudiced eye, the information in the article was presented in a sequence calculated to achieve the maximum innuendo of hanky-panky by the Sheriff's Department. At the same time, should it become necessary, the order would allow the *Times*' attorneys to argue, "Well, it's all *true*, isn't it? And even if there's a minor discrepancy here and there, there's no *malice*, just a matter of interpretation. . . ."

"Tell me about it," snapped Beecham.

"There's nothing much to tell," Cates responded. "This woman—" he gestured at Beth's picture in the paper "—simply vanishes. Lights on, radio on, shower running. Somebody where she works discovered it. That person reported it as a citizen walk-in to the desk at LGS. I happened to be out there, so I took a look."

"That's it?"

"Basically, yes. It is intriguing, of course. When the citizen described what had happened, I half expected it to be nothing. A misunderstanding. We'd go there, and she'd be there, just stepped out or playing a joke; that sort of thing. Just PR the citizen and let it go at that."

"So what did you find?"

Cates told him.

"And you called the lab out?"

"Yes."

"And what did they find?"

"Nothing dramatic. Some bits and pieces. Smudges where you'd expect prints, as if somebody with gloves on had been there."

"So, what was your bottom line?"

Cates shrugged. "Hard to tell. The circumstances of the disappearance indicate that whatever happened, happened *to* her. She didn't leave. She was kidnapped. I think the kidnappers knew her—not some random thing. And my guess is they weren't too worried about her comfort or getting her back."

The muscles in Beecham's jaw clenched. "And she worked for a secret government think tank?" he demanded aggressively. "You knew that, Cates?"

"I knew she worked for this Data Research company, sure. But—"

"And you didn't think that her disappearance might be connected to her work?" Beecham screamed. "Jesus, Cates! Where the hell is your brain? The fucking FBI is looking into it, for God's sake!"

"Lieutenant—" Cates began. Beecham cut him off again.

"Not to mention the fact it's all over the Los Angeles goddamn *Times*. But that's all right, isn't it, Cates? Because when the sheriff picked up his morning paper, he knew that at least I would have it under control. Didn't he, Cates?"

It didn't really sound like a question that wanted an answer, so Cates kept silent.

"So, when two of the Bureau's boys—*and* an assistant U.S. attorney, I might add—were waiting at his office at zero-dark-thirty this morning with a whole shit pot of questions, all he had to do was call the trusty lieutenant, me. Harry Beecham. Use the chain of command. Right, Cates? And I'd be able to set him straight. Right, Cates? Isn't that right, Cates!"

Lieutenant Beecham had begun this last diatribe at a level many decibels beneath that at which he had maxed out when speaking moments before about the FBI. However, he gathered both intensity and volume as he went along. By the end of it he had easily eclipsed the earlier high-volume mark.

Unabated, he continued, his voice rising still further.

"Only I couldn't tell him spit! Could I, Cates? Because my goddamn Homicide goddamn investigator hadn't told me! Right, Cates? Am I right?"

He slammed down the flat of his hand on the surface of his desk, a resounding smack that echoed throughout the offices.

Cates felt the heat in his face. He knew without turning to see that the rest of the investigators in the main work area outside the lieutenant's personal office would be finding some reason to drift out of the room, so as not to be witness to the carnage.

Beecham was standing behind his desk. Deliberately he put his hands on the surface and leaned forward. When he spoke again, he had lowered his voice to a mere snarl.

"Is there any reason you didn't see fit to call me about this one, Cates? Anything you'd like to *share* with me about it?"

Cates regarded him grimly.

Lieutenant Beecham was normally an okay sort, a little hot-tempered, given to flare-ups that just as quickly cooled down. Out of respect for the man as well as for the rank, Cates didn't mind those occasional displays of temper.

This, however, was different. This was way out of character. To put it bluntly, this was bullshit.

"Are you through?" he asked levelly.

The lieutenant looked at him incredulously. He held that look for several long moments. Then he tilted his head back and allowed a sardonic half smile.

"Yeah," he said, his voice suddenly conversational, even soft. He gave Cates a look of appraisal. "Yeah, Cates. I'm through. For a minute, anyway. Go ahead."

"I knew she worked for this Data Research outfit. And of course, I knew she was missing under mysterious circumstances. But, frankly, I didn't see any connection between the two."

He paused. He half expected Beecham to interject. "Oh, you didn't, did you," or some similar sarcasm. To his credit, however, the lieutenant didn't speak.

Cates continued. "She'd only been working there a couple of weeks. And it wasn't as if she was some Wernher von Braun, for God's sake. She was an entry-level computer operator, Lieutenant. And we didn't have a body. Hell, we didn't even have any definite indications that an assaultive crime had taken place. Or any crime, for that matter."

"So?"

"So I worked the scene. And got the lab out there, sure. I figured I'd tell you first thing this morning. Assuming she wasn't back. Hell, for all I know she had just been snatched by her sorority sisters or some goddamn thing. It didn't seem like something you had to be called out on."

Cates sighed. His words sounded weak, even to himself.

Beecham spoke at last. "You know she's dead, don't you, Steve?"

Cates looked up quickly. "Did her body show up?"

"No."

"What are you saying, then?"

"I'm not saying anything." Beecham's voice contained no anger, though Cates didn't doubt that it could be brought back at a moment's notice. "You are. You did."

Cates wrinkled his brow, but didn't speak.

"You kept using *was*. Past tense. She was only there two weeks. Was only a computer operator. Wasn't Warner—whoever the hell you said."

"Wernher."

"Wernher, then. Whoever the hell he was."

"Wernher von Braun. He made rockets or something for the Nazis before we won the war and recruited him to our side. I was just using the name as an example of some big-shot defense scientist."

"You think she's dead?" Beecham repeated.

Cates thought about it. "Yeah. I do."

"You screwed up, Cates."

"I know."

"You should have informed me about the case."

"Yeah."

"If it was important enough for you to work it . . ." He left
the sentence unfinished, then gave a quick nod. "Enough said
about that. What we have to do now is cut our losses."

Cates didn't speak.

Beecham continued, his voice thoughtful. "The sheriff
wanted to see us this morning."

"*The* sheriff?"

"Yep. Except I told him you had court and might not be
available until later."

"It was canceled."

"Yeah? Well, he doesn't have to know that. You're probably on standby or something. Right now I'd rather have the
sheriff think I'm lying to him to cover you than not know
what's going on around here."

"Sorry, Lieutenant."

Beecham brushed that away with a wave of his hand.
"Turns out he had to be in a meeting somewhere, anyway.
Told the FBI he'd get back to them." He grinned. "You gotta
hand it to him, the guy's got a set of balls, anyway."

Cates waited for the lieutenant to go on.

"So we gotta meet with Assistant Sheriff Tisdale at ten
o'clock. Assuming you aren't in court, of course."

"I'm not, unfortunately. The case got put over."

"Ten o'clock it is, then."

"I DON'T SUPPOSE," Assistant Sheriff Brian Tisdale said
coldly, "that would be demanding too much."

Actually, Cates thought, to say Tisdale spoke coldly was to
make a significant understatement. With heavy sarcasm might
be more like it.

Tisdale was a tall, lean man with pale eyes and a thin face.
The face usually wore the expression of one who had just eaten
a lemon as if it were an orange. And liked it.

The "that" of which the Assistant Sheriff spoke had to do with explaining the disappearance and possible homicide of Beth Fisher. It was typical, too, that he phrased it "demanding too much" instead of "asking too much" or even "expecting too much," as most people might have put it.

Tisdale never *asked* anything of another person, he demanded. The only exceptions were if the other person happened to be the sheriff himself, the undersheriff or one of the other four assistant sheriffs. Those were people who merited asking about things. The rest of the world were people of whom he made demands.

His relative effusiveness to the favored six was not born of any desire to curry favor. Even Cates had to admit that. Instead, it was simply a quirk of the man's personal protocol. Tisdale didn't suck up to anybody. And, while Cates respected that aspect of the man, it also made him somehow all the more formidable.

Certainly a mere deputy on the department didn't merit courtesy—let alone being "expected of" rather than "demanded of"—even if he happened to be the ablest detective in a highly competitive field.

"No, sir," Cates responded, "it wouldn't."

"In that case, I suggest you proceed."

"What do you want to know?"

The assistant sheriff's eyes were utterly without warmth, about the same washed-out gray that Cates associated with barren glaciers. The voice went along with the eyes.

"Everything."

In spite of himself, Cates felt somewhat unnerved.

He recognized the folly of relying on others' opinions for his self-worth. And even more so, he thought, on others' expressions of such opinions. Better to rely on his own judgments of himself, which was not always easy in a quasi-military bureaucracy such as the S.O.

Still, old habits died hard.

Tisdale reminded him of the headmaster of the boarding school he had been sent to after his parents died. He'd spent the sixth, seventh and eighth grades there, before coming to

California to live with an older brother, who by then had a wife and two small children. Those three years were difficult ones in a young boy's life for nurturing self-reliance in the face of a headmaster's arbitrary exercises of power. Tisdale somehow managed to push the same buttons; his bearing revived the old ways of reacting.

None of the mental games that were supposed to cope with such overbearing displays of authority really worked against Tisdale. The man's will was simply too strong.

Picture them naked, ran one such myth. Cates couldn't recall where he had read it. *Psychology Today*, perhaps. Or maybe *Esquire*. Probably not the *Wall Street Journal*.

That might work with municipal court judges and IRS auditors. It had even worked to a certain extent when the young Steve Cates had tried it on the headmaster. The vision of their out-of-shape bodies, stark white or pudgy pink, and their spindly, hairless legs went a long way toward defeating that sort of overbearing display of power.

With Tisdale, however, it would be utterly ineffective. It was inconceivable, in fact. Not only was the man not pudgy, but Cates couldn't even imagine him in anything but his light blue-and-gray plaid, summer-weight suit.

Remember that you could kick his ass, one cocky young deputy, somebody like Jack Kolb, had suggested.

Well, Cates thought, that's true. I could.

Not to sound vain, but he knew that he could still bench-press 350 any day of the week. With free weights, not some wimpy machine. A legal, nonbounced, hips-on-the-bench bench press. And with proper training, four hundred inside of two or three months, without steroids.

Not great, especially these days where 165-pounders are doing more than four, but not damn bad, either.

He knew some other things, too. He knew he could run a mile in right around six minutes—okay considering his size. He'd played college football, messed around with martial arts and gotten into a few fights in his time as a cop. The bottom line was that if it really came down to it, he could take this lean old bastard in his hands and break him like a dried-up branch.

That might be true, but there was one problem with it.

The problem was that he couldn't visualize this any more than he could visualize Tisdale without any clothes on. The authority projected by the man made it seem impossible. Even if the two of them were the last people left on earth, Tisdale would somehow have something up his sleeve to stop it.

Maybe, thought Cates, his partner, Ben Grummon, was right.

Maybe I think too much. Just let him chew on me and be done with it. Turn off my mind and don't let it get to me.

Anyway, the cocky young deputy who gave that advice after being called on the carpet by Tisdale had been fired three weeks later. It had been one of the relatively few firings upheld by the Civil Service Board, who generally let even those very few deputies who had no business being on the department stay despite the sheriff's best efforts to fire them.

Perhaps the most workable advice had come from prosecutor Jim Santos, back when Cates was an area detective, in his pre-Homicide days.

They had been preparing for a hearing on a vice case in front of Judge Arnold Rabeau. Judge Rabeau was widely regarded as the most capricious, overbearing and conceited jurist on the local bench. And, the deputy D.A. had observed, the one with perhaps the least to be conceited or overbearing about.

"Before the case is over, he's gonna chew us out," announced Santos cheerfully. "The 'Rabeau ream job,' it's called upstairs." "Upstairs" meant the seventh floor of the courthouse building where the D.A.'s trial division was housed.

Cates had frowned. He respected Santos. The man had a quiet yet firm commitment to doing what he thought was right, and to hell with whose toes he trod upon. He, like Cates himself, didn't worry much about "going along with the program." And, it was typical that he approached such episodes with a sardonic good humor.

"Why?" Cates asked at last.

"Why what?"

"Why's the judge going to chew us out? It's a solid case. This guy's a righteous pimp, never mind that he's white and drives a Mercedes and looks like a doctor. We did everything by the book. We got a search warrant, we got his bank records, we've got two of his hookers—excuse me, his escorts—who are willing to testify. It's solid," he repeated.

Santos looked at him. It was the kind of look he might have given if Cates had asked why he persisted in asserting the world was round.

"Why? Because he's an asshole, that's why."

"That's it?" inquired the detective.

"That, and he doesn't like whore cases. Doesn't think it's a crime, never mind the drugs and intimidation and the other bullshit that goes along with it. Even the white-collar pimps like this 'escort service.'"

"Probably runs with whores himself."

"Maybe." Santos's voice sounded indifferent to the possibility, as though why Rabeau acted the way he did was an irrelevance. "He wouldn't be the first judge to do that. I'll tell you how to handle it, though, his chewing us out."

"How?"

"Relax your jaw slightly, so your teeth aren't clenched. Lips shut, of course. Got it?"

"Got it."

"Now, are you ready?"

"Ready."

"Good. Now practice writing 'fuck you' on the roof of your mouth with your tongue."

"Fuck you?"

"Right. It's not as easy as it sounds. The letters are hard to form, so you have to use some concentration and go slowly. You put the letters on the same spot, of course, like one on top of the other. Personally, I prefer doing it in longhand, but some guys swear by printing it in all caps."

Cates nodded in mock seriousness, thinking it over.

The prosecutor went on. "There's something about it that imparts a suitably solemn look to your face. Like having hemorrhoids. It makes you look concerned. As if you're taking it all very seriously."

"I wonder why," Cates mused.

"I figure it's the concentration that's required. And the best part is that the message fits exactly what you're thinking, only they don't know it."

Cates grinned. "It really works, then?"

The deputy D.A. shrugged. "For me it does. Works great with Superior Court judges. Even seems to work with justices at the D.C.A.," he said, referring to the District Court of Appeals, California's intermediate tier of appellate courts. "Haven't tried it with the Supreme Court, though."

Thus armed, they had gone into court with their whore case. Indeed, before the hearing was over, Judge Rabeau had reamed them. And, somewhat to Cates's surprise, the process suggested by Santos had seemed to help. True, it felt awkward forming the letters at first, as though he were trying to write with his left hand. But it helped.

Over the years, he had gotten a lot better at it.

Maybe, he reflected, that came from trying to do what was right instead of going along with the program. That kind of approach guaranteed lots of opportunities for practice, especially in the criminal justice field.

However, he'd never had occasion to employ the technique on such a difficult case as Assistant Sheriff Tisdale.

Still unnerved, Cates determined to give it a try. The Santos procedure, it should be called. Like a medical operation. He'd use the longhand version, he decided—the letters seemed to flow better.

If it didn't work, he could jump up and bench-press the old bastard through the wall.

He relaxed his jaw and began the f.

Even though Tisdale had told him to "proceed," and tell "everything," Cates knew he wouldn't leave it at that. At any moment—usually the moment the hapless deputy began his explanation—Tisdale would interrupt and add some more intimidating directions. So Cates decided he'd simply wait for a moment, begin the Santos procedure and avoid the additional unnerving effect of the interruption. Besides, it would irritate Tisdale a little.

Tisdale didn't let him down.

"You can start by explaining your role in this." The assistant sheriff gestured at the newspaper that lay on his desk.

"Yes, sir." Cates answered between the f and the u, then resumed.

"And then you can explain your involvement in the case. And then perhaps you can explain why neither your captain, nor your lieutenant nor sergeant—" here he interrupted himself "—nor, I gather, even your partner, for that matter, knew about it."

Cates waited. He was on the k.

Tisdale smiled a thin smile. "And maybe you can even come up with some good reasons why you should remain in Homicide."

Actually, Cates reflected later, Homicide Lieutenant Beecham had done him a favor by performing a similar ream job earlier that morning. Admittedly, it hadn't seemed like a favor at the time. Nor felt like it, either. Still, it had served as a dry run for the assistant sheriff.

Odd that the two men should approach the subject in such strikingly similar ways. Unlike Tisdale, Lieutenant Beecham was basically on Cates's side even though he yelled louder. He and the assistant sheriff must have gone to the same school on principles of supervision. Or maybe Tisdale had trained Beecham. Or vice versa.

What the entire flap meant, Cates realized, was that some very heavy pressure had to be coming from somewhere. And it had to do with the Beth Fisher matter. That was odd, because although the case was intriguing in an Agatha Christie way, there was certainly nothing in it to call for this kind of reaction.

Or was there?

Obviously, there was. And that made the case all the more intriguing, especially as fiercely independent as Sheriff DeWilt Ramsey was. By extension from the man, so was the department as a rule.

DeWilt Ramsey normally didn't respond to pressure, political or otherwise. He was even tougher than Tisdale, and he was personable as well.

Ramsey was an elected official, to be sure. But he had already served three terms, and was into his fourth. He had run largely unopposed in most of the elections except the first one. In Cates's opinion, the sheriff was tough and independent and honest.

Also, as a general rule, he seemed to back his deputies. Altogether, he was singularly possessed of leadership characteristics Cates often found lacking in law enforcement administrators. But to be called on the carpet like this—first by Beecham and then by Tisdale—meant that even Ramsey was exercised about something.

Cates put aside the Santos procedure and his thoughts. He described the entire incident, much as he had done for Lieutenant Beecham. Assistant Sheriff Tisdale listened without interrupting.

Cates finished speaking. Tisdale gazed at him with one of his glacierlike stares.

"Anything else?"

That question, Cates would later reflect, was susceptible to a number of interpretations. Did it include, for instance, his theories? His hunches? And how about his rank speculations—which were, in a sense, "ranker than ever" now that the FBI and the press had gotten into the act—did it include those?

Did it include the missing woman's storage locker, the key to which he had impounded?

Did it include the automatic speed-dialing apparatus Beth had plugged her telephone into, and that Cates had also impounded? He thanked the heavens for his foresight in so doing, especially if the FBI were going to be monkeying with the crime scene. The Bureau was notoriously difficult to pry evidence out of, even if it happened to be evidence you furnished to them in the first place.

He decided the assistant sheriff did not need to be graced with these details at this point. The man was clearly busy enough without being bothered by such fanciful evidence, at least until it had been explored more thoroughly by a trained investigator. Such as himself.

"No," he answered simply. "That's about it."

"Any idea how the paper got hold of this?"

"No, sir."

"I'm safe in assuming you haven't been leaking things to friendly reporters in exchange for a little favorable publicity. Or for anything else." It was said as a statement, but Cates knew it was a question. At least, it required a denial.

"If I did, sir, I blew it, didn't I? My name's not mentioned, and any publicity there is isn't exactly what I'd call favorable, is it?"

Cates was aware of Beecham's involuntary reaction, a slight tensing as of one getting ready for fight or flight. The lieutenant was seated to the rear and off to the side, on a couch against one wall of the assistant sheriff's office. He had sat there at Tisdale's direction, thus reserving "front and center" for Cates.

To hell with it, Cates thought. I always swore I'd never cower to any man. And that includes the assistant sheriff. I'm sorry if I got the lieutenant in any heat, but for me—what can the bastard do to me besides fire me? Hell, if he tries that, I'll break him in half with my bare hands.

Suddenly, Cates found himself suppressing a smile. The Santos procedure had worked to the point that he was now thinking about breaking Tisdale in half. Hell, he had been thinking about it for some minutes now. Next thing, the man would be sitting there naked.

"You're wasting my time, Cates." The voice was menacing.

"No, I didn't leak it to the papers. I don't have a clue as to how they found out."

"Any idea how the FBI got involved in it?"

"No, sir. Unless it's some routine inquiry."

"Two agents showing up at 0730, along with an assistant U.S. attorney, hardly sounds routine, does it, Cates?"

"What I meant to say is that maybe there's some obscure P and P—" Cates used the term to refer to "policy and procedure," the sheriff's designation of internal operating guidelines "—that requires them to look into every mysterious death or disappearance of somebody connected with certain government contracts. Or maybe even into every death, mysterious or not. Maybe they have to check it out."

Tisdale said nothing. Cates resumed the Santos procedure. He'd lost his place, so he started over again.

"I want to see your reports," the assistant sheriff said at last.

"There aren't any yet."

"Do them. And get copies down to me as soon as they're completed."

"All right."

"Thank you. I'll expect them on my desk at 4:00 p.m."

"Today?"

"Today."

Lieutenant Beecham spoke up. "Four o'clock it is, sir. We'll have them hand-carried over by four."

Tisdale nodded. "I expect so." He turned to Cates. "Anything you do—anything at all—on that case, Lieutenant Beecham gets told. He will brief me on a daily basis. At his direction, you will prepare or not prepare reports on it. Is that understood?"

"Yes."

"Good. You are not to discuss the case with anybody except Lieutenant Beecham or myself or the sheriff."

"My partner?" Cates inquired.

"Who is that?"

It was Beecham who answered. "Ben Grummon," he said quickly.

Something flickered in Tisdale's expression. Then, just as quickly, it was gone. "No," he said. "You'll work this one by yourself, Cates. That way, we'll know whom to go to for information, won't we?"

And whose head to hand up on a platter if it goes wrong, his eyes added silently.

The meeting was over.

7

Martie Griffin

SUNLIGHT GLINTED off something shiny at the bottom of the canyon.

Martie frowned. This was the third time she'd seen the bright flash since having come over the top of the last range of foothills. Ahead of her eight or ten miles to the west lay the community of Jamul. Beyond that, another twelve miles, were the San Diego city limits.

The city, however, had long since expanded beyond that boundary. Now, to the east, San Diego butted up against the cities of La Mesa and El Cajon, and urban-sprawled its way into vast, densely populated areas of the county. Martie had read somewhere that the next five years would see an uninterrupted blanket of homes and communities from the city limits out past Jamul, the area she was now approaching.

All the more business for the S.O., she thought.

With the exception of La Mesa and El Cajon, the sheriff's office provided the law enforcement for many of the smaller cities as well as for all the unincorporated areas of the county. And she, Deputy Martie Griffin, was one of those providers.

Martie slowed the green-and-white patrol car to a crawl and edged it over to the right shoulder.

The semidesert climate gave the area a curious remoteness. The foothills were largely decomposed granite. A narrow shoulder of the crumbly gravelly stuff bordered the right edge of the road. Beyond that, the ground dropped off steeply to the bottom of the canyon, a quarter of a mile down.

The tires made little popping, crunching sounds as they rolled slowly over the bits of granite that had spilled onto the pavement. Martie sat tall and scanned the slope of the canyon hoping to see the flash of light again.

Nothing. Whatever it was eluded her.

She braked the patrol car to a stop and sat there a moment. With the window down, she could feel the vestiges of the cool morning air, though the sun felt warm on her uniform blouse and dark green trousers. Over the idle of the motor she could hear an occasional faraway bird.

She glanced at her watch—nearly a quarter after ten in the morning. It was moments like this, she thought, that made her glad she had joined the S.O. nearly four years back.

Her parents—no, make that her mother—had had a fit, of course.

First they said that they had hoped she would continue in college, get an MBA, or perhaps even go to law school. Martie responded that she didn't want an MBA, and that three years of law school plus a bar exam seemed at that point a sentence without end. So her mother had argued that the four years of college, a bachelor's degree and Martie's demonstrated intelligence would be shockingly underutilized, not to say wasted completely, in law enforcement.

Martie, who had done some checking in anticipation of the objections, had pointed out that some twenty percent of the deputies on the department had college degrees. Several had doctorates of one form or another, there were several with law degrees, and even more with master's and bachelor's degrees.

Finally, the bottom line had emerged.

"It just seems so . . . so unladylike, honey," her mother had said. "Beneath us," she added.

Stung, Martie stared at her mother.

Then she took a deep breath and prepared to unleash a salvo of observations about how her mother wouldn't know what work was—except that she paid others to do it, how cops helped people in their greatest hour of need, and how there just might be a whole world out there beyond bridge games and the country club.

Her father, however, cut in quickly. "Well, Martie, if that's what you'd like to do, go ahead and give it a try. Might be good experience, anyway."

Good experience for what, he didn't specify.

Her mother, as always, got the last word, calculated to be both patronizing and conducive to maximum guilt.

"Your father's right, honey," she said, making a sigh that blew a plume of cigarette smoke up at a forty-five degree angle from one side of her mouth.

"I—" Martie began, but her mother cut her off.

"Do what you have to do. I was just disappointed, that's all. You get expectations for your children, and then they don't come true. Next thing, you'll be wanting to marry a black man, I suppose."

"If I'm lucky," Martie shot back.

"Well, at the rate you're going, you'll be lucky if you get married at all."

So Martie Griffin had joined the department. She, Martha Elaine Griffin, silver spoon and all, was going to be a deputy sheriff.

At five-seven, she had brown hair and clean, attractive features. She played softball, racquetball and that curious San Diego phenomenon called over-the-line, a three-person base-ball-like game, usually played on the beach and accompanied by much beer.

First came the academy.

In an era when many police agencies had adopted a casual, collegelike format for their recruits, the S.O. had not. The course had been a grueling eighteen weeks of law, defensive tactics, something called "arrest and control"—which meant how to actually take somebody into custody who didn't want to be taken into custody—firearms, driving, patrol methods, death cases and a host of other subjects.

The block on death cases was one she had approached with apprehension.

The trainees whispered nervously about the trip to the morgue, the dead bodies they would first see, then touch and search, and finally the autopsies. But it had gone well, actually, thanks in large part to the quiet, low-key, unsensational teaching methods of the instructor, a longtime homicide investigator named Ring. But she still didn't like dead bodies, and wasn't looking forward to her first one now that she was in the field.

After the academy came a little more than two years in the jail.

All the new deputies had to do jail time before they got out to patrol. Martie had done hers, and now, at last, she was where she wanted to be, behind the wheel of a patrol car. The first six months had been in the company of an FTO, or field training officer, to learn and relearn patrol procedures, radio codes and officer survival skills.

She had been assigned to the Lemon Grove Substation both during the FTO phase, and now that it was over. And, much to her delight, she found she loved it.

The area served by LGS had everything a fair-size city had, and more. It had the densely populated barrios that covered parts of Encanto and Spring Valley. It had the average to upper-middle-class sections, as well as parts of posh and expensive Mount Helix. Beyond it, to the east, where she was now, lay hundreds of square miles of rugged hills, steep canyons and expansive deserts that stretched clear to Mexico.

Oddly, the back country was a haven for crime, especially narcotics. Those with an agricultural bent raised high-grade marijuana—sinsemilla—in the isolated areas. The hills and mountains also concealed many a home-built lab for the manufacture of methamphetamine, known on the street as "meth," or "crystal," or, a few years back, "speed," giving San Diego the dubious distinction of being the meth capital of the country.

In short, San Diego was where it was happening. It was the place to be, as far as police work was concerned. The best. And the S.O., and particularly the LGS, were according to Martie, the best of the best.

That morning, Tuesday, she had been pulled off her normal beat in the Spring Valley barrios and put on a search warrant way out in the back country.

The warrant originated with the Narcotics Task Force, based on marijuana they had seen in a helicopter overflight. Martie and two other patrol units had been dispatched to assist in any prisoner transport that might be needed, and generally to act as backup to the narcs.

The warrant was for a homestead affair tucked back in the mountains, about thirty-five miles to the east of San Diego. The nearest neighbor was five miles away, and might as well have been fifty.

The area was overgrown with a tough, scraggly desert plant variously called manzanita and sagebrush. It made a dense thicket, higher than a person's head. Martie had found that when she tried to make her way through it. The gnarled branches had clutched at her uniform and poked at her flesh like witches' fingers.

A helicopter from the sheriff's ASTREA Division had been brought in to assist in spotting the dope from the air.

In the acreage behind the house the narcs found eleven room-size pockets that had been cut out of the undergrowth. Each clearing was packed wall to wall with thriving marijuana plants watered by a drip system threaded through the brush. The plants had been sexed. They had been trimmed off at about six feet high so they wouldn't stick up above the brush.

The Task Force hit the place early. By a little after nine it was over; two in custody and seven truckloads of plants bound for the DEA incinerators. One of the other units took the prisoners, and now Martie was headed back to her normal beat.

Still no sign of the flash she had seen earlier.

With a sigh, Martie slid the gearshift into drive and eased the patrol car back onto the road. She wondered if it would be worthwhile to drive up the road a ways, to try to find where she had seen it.

Probably not, she concluded. Probably, it was just an old car—the hills were full of them, after all. Still . . .

Less than a minute later she saw it again, a bright gleam of sunlight reflected off something halfway down the canyon.

Martie braked sharply to a halt. Then, glancing over her shoulder to make sure the coast was clear, she backed up the road until she found the spot again. She parked, killed the engine and reached for the microphone.

"30-Paul-14," she said into the mike.

A staticlike burst of compressed air greeted her. Amid the hiss Martie could hear a tiny voice, too faint to make out the words.

She adjusted the radio. "30-Paul-14," she repeated. "Do you copy?"

"Go ahead, 30-Paul-14," came the response.

"30-Paul-14, I'm going to be checking a possible disabled vehicle. I'll be out of my unit for about ten."

"What is your location, 30-Paul?"

Mentally, Martie kicked herself. Giving the location of every stop was mandatory. Nothing like broadcasting to the whole county that you're a goddamn rookie, she thought.

"30-Paul-14, I'm at..." She hesitated for a moment, trying to estimate how far she'd come since the last marker on the road. "I'm on Skyline Truck Trail, approximately two miles west of marker 52."

"Roger, 30-Paul."

Martie replaced the mike and got out of the car, taking her binoculars with her. She stretched and then hitched and settled her leather gear—the wide, basket-weave belt, the compact holster for the four-inch Smith & Wesson service revolver, the speed-loader pouches and the handcuff case—into place above her hips. Then she walked to the edge of the road and gazed down into the canyon.

She found the gleam of reflected sunlight again. Moving to one side so as to be out of the beam, she strained her eyes downward.

Sure enough, it looked like a car, a small rectangle far below.

It was nose down into a clump of the scraggly manzanita, stopped, probably, by the boulders that jutted up beyond the plants. From where Martie stood, some three football fields above it, only the back end, the trunk and part of the roof were visible. They made a tiny patch of startling blue against the tan desert landscape.

It was impossible to tell how badly the car was damaged from that distance, except that it hadn't burned and it didn't look smashed to smithereens. Martie took the field glasses out of the case and sat on the rocky shoulder of the road, resting her elbows on her knees.

The car leaped closer.

Through the glasses, it didn't look damaged at all. The rear window wasn't broken and it hadn't been rolled. It looked new, a Taurus she guessed from the body style. Somebody had wired a yellow plastic flower to the radio antenna, a means, perhaps, of spotting the car in a crowded parking lot. Against the bland fabric of the desert, the flower looked hopelessly artificial. And tacky, she thought.

The hillside was largely coarse sand and pea-size gravel. Now that she saw the car, Martie could also see the faint parallel lines down the hillside, its tracks as it slewed down the slope. By chance, it had missed the bigger rocks and the irregular clumps of sage until it ran into the stuff that stopped it.

Belatedly, Martie realized why the flash had seemed worth checking out.

Sure, there were a lot of abandoned cars up there, but usually they were so rusted, and the glass broken or shot out, that they didn't reflect like this. Maybe her subconscious had realized this. Maybe she could be a good cop, after all.

The morning sun was behind her. By walking about thirty feet down the road to a point more nearly in line with the car's rear window, Martie figured she might be able to see inside it. She sat down again and with the binoculars examined the interior of the sedan.

It was empty.

She let out a sigh of relief. The moment she had realized the car was relatively new, not a rusted-out junker, Martie had also resigned herself to the possibility of somebody inside it, dead or injured. But that didn't seem to be the case here.

Good. She didn't feel like finding a body today.

She looked again to be sure. Back seat, apparently empty. And nobody slumped against the wheel in front.

Then she realized something else. She had to go down to the car to see what it was—to get identifying information, see if it was stolen, or a rental, or what.

With a sigh, she started down the embankment.

Martie found she could half jump, half slide down the steep slope. In places it was so steep she could slide down for six to eight feet at a stretch, her feet cutting furrows in the decomposed granite and filling her shoes with the stuff. It would have been almost fun except for the certainty of a difficult climb back up.

The car was jammed into the tough, wiry brush. The driver's door would be impossible, she realized, as it was crushed against the manzanita, which in turn was squashed against a huge boulder just beyond it. Long, deep gouges ran the length of the car, where the limbs had clutched at the paint and then reluctantly yielded.

Martie moved around the back of the car to the passenger side where there was more clearance.

When she was at about the right rear tire, her feet slipped in the steep, loose surface and she sat down suddenly and involuntarily. Before she could stop, she had slid on her seat several feet down past the car, the holster of her duty weapon gouging the dusty gravel.

"Damn!" She ground out the oath. The grit would do no good at all to her revolver if she didn't clean it. And all this for a lousy abandoned car, probably a stolen one that somebody had dumped off after a joyride.

Shaking her head, Martie rolled over to all fours, then crawled her way back up to the passenger side of the Taurus. Using the car to pull herself to her feet, she shielded her eyes with her left hand and peered inside.

"Oh, God!" The words came out involuntarily.

A dead woman stared back at her.

She lay on the front seat. She was on her right side, as if facing the dash, but with her face turned upward. Her right arm was extended above her head, so her shoulder made a pillow for the side of her face. Her other arm hung forward near her waist.

She was quite dead.

"Oh, God!" Martie repeated fervently, her voice trembling.

She stared at the still form, unable to wrench her gaze away. The woman looked calmly back at her, into her, beyond her, with sightless eyes. Martie felt her mouth get dry as her breath came fast and shallow, and she tried to will the image to disappear.

Then she was in control again, as her rational mind forcibly took over.

There's nothing to fear. A body is just like a house after the family have moved away. Nothing to be afraid of; it's just sad, that's all.

"You're a cop, for Christ's sake," she said aloud. Her voice sounded harsh and discordant in the stillness. "What are you going to do, call a cop? You are the cop."

Then, with a nod, she forced herself into action.

She tried to open the passenger door. It resisted her efforts, though the lock appeared to be in the up position. The physical task gave her something to focus on, she thought, and that was good. Bracing her left foot on the car behind the passenger door, she pulled again, hard.

Suddenly, the door yielded.

The effect was like a spring, and the light car swayed on its shocks. The dead woman's head lolled forward off her shoulder and the odor of death washed out like a wave.

Martie's footing went out from under her again, and she slid down the slope again on her hands and knees. For several long moments, she stayed there, panting like an animal. The car and its lonely occupant waited above, silent and infinitely patient.

Finally, Martie made her way back upward and moved around to the open door. Her mind recorded the details mechanically, starting with the most obvious.

The dead woman was blond.

She looked young.

She wore only a man's dress shirt. Light blue.

Oh, God, Martie thought again.

Then she remembered Investigator Ring's words at the academy. First thing, just don't disturb anything unnecessarily. Take stock of the situation, and see what needs to be done.

And look. Look for... What was it? Visible signs of death. Wounds or trauma. Identification.

First, identification.

She looked inside the car. No purse. No billfold. No papers. And, in the ignition, no key—the ignition had been hot-wired.

"So," Martie said aloud, "I've got a dead body wearing only a man's blue shirt in a new, probably stolen car. And no identification."

What came next?

Wounds. Trauma. Visible signs.

It had to be done.

She had to do it.

Curiously fascinated, knowing she could—and would—do it, Martie steeled herself. She reached in with both hands to lift the woman's head up on her arm, where it had been.

It felt startlingly heavy.

Maybe the looseness of the neck made it seem more so. Surprised that she remembered it, Martie recalled that rigor mortis sets in not long after death. It lasts, however, only from four to twelve hours, depending on the environment. Then it goes away again.

Here, Martie realized, it had come and gone.

The dead woman's eyelids were almost wide open. Beneath them, the eyes were dark and dull. There were no ants or bugs yet, thanks in part to the relatively cool nights, but it wouldn't have been long before there were.

Her face was curiously bisected from chin to hairline by postmortem lividity—when the pump stops the blood settles by force of gravity to the lower regions, in this case the right side of her face. It gave her a divided, two-person look, the right side darkly flushed, the left side pale white. The two sides were held together by the dull, dark pegs of her eyes.

No wounds.

No bullet holes. No knife marks. No ligature around the neck.

The neck. Look at the neck again.

A sort of dusky pallor—a bruising?—around the throat. From strangulation, perhaps?

Hard to tell.

Surprised at her ability to remain calm, Martie laid the head gently down on the upper arm. Then she withdrew from the car, and closed the door.

She scrambled up the slope about fifteen feet, then turned and sat down in the morning stillness.

It was a beautiful morning, Martie thought, cool and clear. The clean air made pungent by the desert undergrowth was a welcome contrast to the death inside the car.

Later on the day would probably be hot.

Martie felt surrounded by quiet. Maybe that was because there were no cars and trucks and other man-made sounds. Soon, though, as her body adjusted to the stillness, the other sounds emerged, the sounds of small animals and insects and birds.

In the midst of all this life was a blue pocket of death, a black hole of silence that drew in the sounds of the living.

Martie felt very small in the vastness of it. Loneliness washed over her like a wave. And guilt. For some strange reason she felt a vague, undefined guilt.

Whoa, there. Steady, Griff, she told herself. Keep thinking like that and the men in white coats will be along. They'll give you a little injection to make you docile and take you someplace where they can keep an eye on you.

But it just didn't seem right, somehow. The blond woman had been young, and beautiful. She shouldn't be dead. It was going to be another wonderful San Diego summer, with new songs on the radio and fun at the beach.

But it had all stopped for the woman in the car.

So what?

A lot of things aren't right. And in the end, we're all dust anyway. We're chips, poker chips. Small ones. White chips in a no-limits game. But you're a cop with a job to do, and it's a great life, and you've already been away from the unit a hell of a lot longer than the ten minutes you said you'd be.

"Move it, Griff," she said aloud.

She rolled to her feet and started the climb to the road high above. It was slow going, and her legs were soon aching even though she was in good shape. But she drove herself onward, partly to give herself something to concentrate on and maybe partly to relieve the guilty feeling for being alive when others weren't.

Halfway up, she turned and looked back.

The patch of bright blue with the hokey yellow flower on the antenna looked smaller now. It didn't look so artificial anymore, though. It just looked sad, unutterably sad.

Like a toy in the sandbox after the child has died.

Martie turned and forced her legs to continue the long climb upward.

system

FIFTY MILES WEST as the crow flies from the desert canyon where Deputy Martie Griffin was finding a dead woman, a man gazed out at the Pacific Ocean.

He was looking out a broad bay window of his home. The house was on the west face of the foothills of La Jolla, a posh area of San Diego's elite. It was a small house by the standards of most expensive homes, but it was solidly constructed. Despite its breathtaking panorama, the steep hillside and winding roads and landscaping afforded it a high degree of privacy. Because of the view and the area, it had cost nearly a million dollars to purchase it eight months before.

The equivalent of a million dollars U.S. in Russian money, through the International Bank of Switzerland, in return for access to top-secret information on American national defense research projects.

Both the house and the means of acquiring it were a far cry from the gritty world of street narcotics and violent death; from the middle-income homes and the barrios, and from the cops engaged in a life-and-death struggle against the rising tide of the former in the environs of the latter.

In more ways than one, it was another world. Like the house and the system that supported it, the man was different.

The view—and the privacy—were what he had been paying for when he bought the house. They opened his mind and broadened his existence. More important, they enabled him to think, to plan, to work through all the possible combinations and permutations of his options.

He was at a crucial juncture, he knew, a deadly crossroads in the most dangerous game in the world. A single misstep, or the unforeseeable intervention of some extrinsic factor or

force, and it would all be for nothing. Worse yet, it could mean
his demise, as well as the downfall of others in the structure.

He settled on his plan for the morning, part of which included an evaluation and assessment of how things now stood.

First, he would meditate.

Part of the meditation would be a detached contemplation
of the events of the past forty-eight—no, make that sixty—
hours. The other part, a more traditional meditation process,
would then free his mind, opening new neural pathways and
enabling him to consider the situation in realms beyond mere
cognition. It would particularly allow him to transcend the
Western obsession with cause and immediate effect.

Post hoc, ergo propter hoc.

He knew this to be the greatest single failing of American
thinking, the failure to understand this fundamental principle. *After this, and therefore because of this.* Simply because
one event happened, and then another thing took place, did
not mean that the first caused or necessarily even influenced
the second.

A faint smile traced his lips. Try to tell an American that.
Particularly try to tell it to an American cop, or attorney or
jury.

It began with the typically Western childlike adherence to the
so-called scientific method. Make a hypothesis, design an experiment and evaluate the results. The method was fueled by
the thirst for instant gratification, and blurred by the effects of
time.

The combined result was that if thing A happened at time 1,
and then thing B was observed at time 2, the Western mind
believed thing A caused or influenced thing B. This was especially so if the interval between time 1 and time 2 were appropriately short.

It worked the other way as well. If the interval were longer,
then no casual connection was seen between the two events,
even if they were in fact joined.

If no thing B were observed within a reasonable time after
thing A, then the former was considered to have no effect, to
have caused nothing. And—of vital importance to him now—

a corollary to the same rule seemed to be in control when the starting point in the inquiry was thing B at time 2. Most people would look back only so far to find thing A. If they didn't find it within a reasonable time 2–time 1 interval, they were baffled.

That would, he knew, be no less true when those doing the looking were the inept American police, and thing B was a dead woman. In fact, given the pressures of their caseloads, it was especially true for them.

All part of the mind-set of the West.

In the sixties he had seen it begin. And now it had blossomed and spread like a cancer in the loose body of the American people. Hey, man, try this groovy new drug. Drop this acid. Instant gratification. And, because in a few hours or days, there were no apparent ill effects, it was thought to mean there would be no ill effects ever.

That mind-set still pervaded the popular culture, of course. Only instead of acid, these days it was cocaine and methamphetamine and designer drugs. Even most of the schoolchildren drifted along half-stoned.

The same idea pervaded Western medical theories as well. Something feel bad? Take this pill. Feel better? The pill fixed it. Pay your bill on time, and pay homage to the miracles of modern medical science as well.

Never mind that you probably would have felt better anyway.

Perhaps less dramatically—but more insidiously in the long run—the mind-set took away the sense of assurance that the people's religion could otherwise furnish.

The man had studied Christianity. So ingrained in the Americans was the cause-and-immediate-effect fallacy—and that of a short time 1–time 2 interval—that they didn't really believe in religion. Prove it, they said in their loftiest *post hoc, ergo propter hoc* conceit.

And, of course, the existence of the supreme being and of the spirit couldn't be proved in a controlled laboratory experiment, conducted according to the scientific method. In the West these concepts had become widely regarded as fable, or at best as a hedge, a sort of insurance that one paid for against the possibility it might be true after all. Even though the chief prophet of Western religion expressly warned against putting their God to the test, the people of the West were forever doing so. When the proper indications did not appear, they concluded no supreme being existed.

It weakened them. They never stopped to think that they might be testing the wrong party, and that they should be testing themselves, instead.

The same weakness pervaded their political thinking as well.

Nikita Khrushchev was regarded and ultimately dismissed as a harmless lunatic when he looked the West in the eye and said, "We will bury you." The braggadocio of a buffoon, it was believed. The rest of the Soviet machine could not possibly think that way. Besides, the Americans would say, it's been twenty years, and we're not buried.

No thing B yet. Therefore, thing A must not be true.

Get to the young, and the press, and the educators, the man believed. Less dramatic than bombs, but surer, even if it took a generation instead of a day or week or month or year. Today, the American mind-set was his greatest ally.

He had to remind himself to take care not to fall prey to the same weaknesses that had beset the West.

After the meditation, he would do his stretching exercises. The exercises were vitally important, especially given the construction of his body. He was on the shorter side of average for a man. His legs were shorter than they should have been, proportionately shorter than normal for a man that size. In many men that would have lent an apelike appearance to the body, especially since he weighed a full two hundred pounds even at that height. But in him, it didn't.

In one sense, it was the legs themselves that prevented this image. In part, this was because they—like the rest of his body except for his armpits, groin, head and face—were utterly hairless.

But by far the more significant difference was the construction of his limbs. Unlike the wiry simian legs of anthropoid apes, his were thick and packed with a massive musculature that seemed to sprout from the base of his torso and curve out in all directions before tapering sharply in at the knees, only to flare out again at the calves.

The rest of his body was built along corresponding lines.

He was massively muscled, though proportioned differently and somehow more ruggedly than the puffed forms of most bodybuilding champions. He had exceptionally thin skin, coppery brown thanks to the Asian blood, and the relative absence of body fat displayed his musculature in sharp definition.

Of the rest of his body, the back most closely paralleled his incredible legs. The spinal erector muscles that ran along each side of his vertebrae were so pronounced that they made a groove nearly two inches deep up the middle of his back. His latissimus dorsi muscles seemed to begin at his waist and flare upward and outward to tie in with the dense meat of his upper back, shoulders and neck.

The front of his body, though thick and muscled, did not possess the same degree of development. His chest was wide and hard, but the pectorals were not particularly overdeveloped. Nor were his arms—long and strong looking, to be sure, with the biceps somewhat more developed than the triceps—those of a bodybuilding champion.

In fact, his physique was not borne of weight lifting at all, at least not in the conventional sense. And the stretching exercises—normally ignored or even shunned by most bodybuilders—he regarded as a vital part of maintaining both his body's physical usefulness and its unity with his mind.

After the meditation and the stretching he would go into an hour of practice in martial arts.

The training varied. Today, he would particularly concentrate on the vital points, the places in the human body where a single, well-delivered stroke would paralyze or kill. And where, in the right circumstances, he could kill without hitting.

He thought of his combative arts simply as *bujutsu*.

In Western terms, *bujutsu* was understood as a generic or categorical term to broadly comprise martial virtues or martial arts. In its fifteenth and sixteenth-century Japanese roots, the word encompassed those meanings, but carried with it the connotation of techniques specifically designed to kill a person rather than merely defend. Usually, these techniques involved weaponry, such as the sword, the spear or the bow and arrow. More important, it also conveyed a sense of mastery, of commitment, of regarding these techniques as indeed an art rather than simply a skill.

Though he did not practice with weapons, *bujutsu* was a very good description of what he did and how he did it.

He scorned the popular concepts of the martial arts. They were, he felt, a poor attempt at mass-producing and prepackaging spurious manhood for the ninety-seven-pound weaklings of the West.

Kung fu, karate, tae kwon do and judo—all were but isolated fragments, bits and pieces taken out of context and significant only because they were flashy and visible to a mechanical society that wanted instant everything. They were to true fighting arts what a petal was to the flower and to the rest of the plant and the earth and universe with which it was one.

The ultimate goal of martial art was self-mastery. Not fancy blows or garb that proclaimed to onlookers, "Look at me, I take karate." The garb was too superfluous for words; even the blows were only a small part of the whole.

Today, then, the vital points.

Intense concentration, the use of that part of the organism called the mind as well as that part called the body. Preserving the unity—the oneness—of the mind/body. Perfecting death.

Bujutsu.

And the fourth part of his plan for the day, after meditation, and stretching and bujutsu, would be to specialize on that amazing body.

This was a special day that came only once every three weeks. It was the day when he pushed his body to the point of failure.

The apparatus he used resembled in design though not construction a massive rowing machine, used to duplicate the movement of crewing, and produce a comparable development in the legs and back and arms and shoulders. The difference was that the resistance increased at preprogrammed stages designed never to be capable of mastery.

He would get onto the machine and begin easily, of course. And then, after a few minutes, even as his muscles began to fatigue, the level of difficulty would increase.

It would continue to build, to become more difficult, until the sweat ran from the pores of his thin, coppery skin and his breath came in great gasping gulps and his heart threatened to explode. And then it would become harder still, the machine driving the man inside his self, and forcing him outside his self, past the point of cramping, past the point of pain, until the point of seize-up, when his screaming muscles became frozen in a lactic-acid-induced paralysis.

Usually it took about forty minutes from the time he first got into the apparatus until that point occurred. And, unlike most forms of weight or resistance exercise, this one required each muscle group to work with the others, integrating rather than fragmenting his strength, the whole greater than the sum of all its parts.

He thought about the young woman.

In retrospect, everything had been so easy that all the planning seemed wasted. And yet, to allow himself to so believe could be a deadly error, because it could cause carelessness. Moreover, he knew that it was actually the very planning, the excruciating attention to detail, that caused such planning to seem unnecessary. The countermoves devised and available but not employed were just as important as the ones that had been used.

It took insight to recognize this paradox—this trap, actually—and discipline not to fall into it.

The result of his planning was that he had been successful. He had salvaged the operation, had righted himself on the high wire. In fact, it now looked as if things were even better off than they had been before.

At first, he had seen it as an event of crisis proportions, the unexpected entry of the woman into a system already more unstable than it should be. But, by swift and meticulous—even if highly dangerous and completely unauthorized—action, he had not only forestalled the crisis, but had tightened up other aspects of the operation as well.

He vowed never to let it get so unstable again.

He knew only the passage of time would determine the success of his activities. Appearances deceived. After all, everything had seemed good to the people of Hiroshima at seven-thirty on the morning of August 6, 1945, too. And at eight. And, with the exception perhaps of the sound of a single B-29 bomber high above the city, at eight-fifteen as well.

The blond woman hadn't known anything. He could be sure of that now.

She hadn't even understood the significance of what she had seen. All she had registered was that she had found a supplier, "somebody she could score off of," as she had put it.

She didn't know anything else about what was going on.

In a way, he reflected, killing her was a waste. If he could have known that by an independent means, she could still be alive. But he couldn't have known it by independent means, especially not with the degree of certainty he needed. And, once he had acquired doubts, she couldn't be let loose. To have done so would be like striking a match to test it.

Besides, she'd been a source of some entertainment to him before she died.

As far as he could tell, nobody had seen them take her. Broad daylight, but for all intents and purposes invisible. Without a trace.

That part amused him.

The self-congratulatory press—newspapers and television media—catering as they did to their own vanity and the balance sheets of their owners, loved that sort of thing. At first, especially after the body was found, the press reports would result in increased pressure on the police to solve the case, to bring somebody to justice. Later, thanks to some perverse mystique, these same forces would make it easier for the public to regard it as insoluble.

An enigma. A mystery. One of those weird cases that never gets closed.

The populace would not feel threatened by it as they would have been by repeated burglaries that couldn't be solved. And, they would be fascinated by it, even eager to make it into a minor legend.

The FBI would investigate, of course.

He had known that, had assumed it as one of the consequences of his action. They would investigate it to death, being, as it was, the killing of somebody working at a company that did secret government work.

But they wouldn't find anything.

She was a new employee, and not placed in a particularly sensitive position. The very depth of their investigation would make them eager to conclude that her death was somehow related to events other than secret business, events out of her past perhaps. And then they would close the books, because their job was not to solve the murder, but only to see that it had no link to national security.

That was exactly what he wanted them to conclude. In fact, if he were really lucky, and if the other one, the one highly placed inside the company, lay low and followed his instructions, it was not impossible his information system would be even more secure than before.

System. A set or arrangement of things so connected or related as to form a unified whole. Information came to him, went from him—through him, in a sense—to them; much money came back; some went on back to the source of the information.

The local authorities were the ones who would be concerned about the murder.

He would check into the background of the detective assigned to the case. Find out a little about him. His friend on the staff of the *Los Angeles Times* said the man's name was Cates. Sheriff's Homicide. Big and strong, no doubt in that undisciplined way of Westerners.

But he already knew what he would find. The man was no threat.

Sheriff.

The word floated lazily across his consciousness.

It floated against a background of dark purple mixed with brown, the colors his mind released when he felt contempt during one of his meditative phases. He recalled the word was a corruption of the term *shire reeve*, the chief executive officer on a local level in England from the time of William the Conqueror. And today, thanks to the gunslinging legacy of the American frontier—as portrayed by movies and books—he was just another breed of cop.

His friend on the *Times* had said that Cates had a good reputation. How had she put it? That he was one of the "big guns"? Yes, that was it.

Big guns.

Well, that fit. A street-sly civil servant, essentially slow-witted but with a modicum of animal cleverness. And he was probably big and maybe good-looking in a Marlboro-man way. Give him a good track record at closing the dreary, trivial cases where husbands killed wives and wives killed husbands, where robbers killed their victims, and drunken peasants killed one another over women.

That would be their "big gun."

Big deal.

Add the impedimenta of the American legal system, the incredible quagmire of rules and exceptions and counterrules in which this so-called big gun had to operate. Add the distraction that the media would provide. Further add the fact that the FBI's involvement would interfere with the sheriff's investigation, especially at the early stages when the two groups would be competing instead of cooperating.

When the Feds closed their file, it would be that much easier for the sheriff's man—this big gun, Cates—to close his.

All in all, the man's own safety and that of his carefully constructed system seemed well protected, indeed.

terra incognita

CATES SAT MOODILY at his desk in the Homicide offices.

Before him lay a letter-size manila folder that contained a green steno pad, some Polaroid photos of the apartment, and a five-by-seven studio portrait of Beth Fisher he had taken from an envelope of photos in the apartment.

She had been an attractive woman, he thought. Nice tan, at least in the photograph. A mane of blond hair, dramatically styled, and a party-girl smile.

The folder was positioned so that the side that opened was to Cates's right. It had a tab along the top third of that edge. Along that tab he had printed in bold pencil strokes, FISHER, E. and the date he had been shown the scene by Joyce Kennedy.

The name on the file tab itself presented a minor irony, he thought sourly.

The courts and prosecutors indexed and identified cases by the name of the suspect, a person as yet unidentified in this case. Homicide cops, however, carried them by the name of the victim. Assuming that Elizabeth Fisher turned out to be a 187, to Cates it would always be the Fisher case, not the Jones case or the Smith case or whatever the suspect's name was.

Maybe, he thought, it's because we're the last ones in the system who care, really care, what happened to the victim. From here on out, it's going to be the suspect who gets center stage. Protecting his rights, examining his psyche, giving him due process.

Kissing his ass.

That is, if we ever get a suspect, he added mentally. Then he spoke aloud, his voice unusually tired-sounding for only a Tuesday. "Suspect, hell. I don't even have a victim yet."

He took out the steno pad. It was spiral bound along the top, the front and back cover made of stiff cardboard. Old-fashioned as it might appear, Cates preferred it to a hand-held recorder or a dictaphone, except in cases where a verbatim transcript of an interview was called for.

The crime lab had taken countless photographs and measurements. Those were the ones that would ultimately be used as evidence if the case went anywhere. The Polaroids were simply to refresh Cates's memory as to the scene for the purpose of preparing the reports.

The main body of the report, of course, would be dictated. However, he believed in sketching at least a brief topical outline—a skeleton, he called it—of the report before beginning the dictation. *Skeleton* was a more descriptive term than outline.

He did it by jotting the general headings of the categories he wanted to cover in the report. Under each heading he listed the points he wanted to include—the "bones"—usually only a word or two each.

Ultimately, when he began to dictate the report using the three-part format required by the department—dividing material into origin, narrative and evidence—Cates would refer back to the notes in his steno pad for the detailed information necessary to flesh out the report. It was the only way he had found to prevent the report from resembling a stream-of-consciousness rambling and to avoid omitting some important detail.

Of course, it was virtually impossible to include every pertinent fact about an investigation in the report.

Otherwise, even a routine contact or detention would end up as several pages of single-spaced narrative. His mind necessarily sifted out and prioritized the details against the constraints of time and space and energy.

That was necessary, but it also had its drawbacks.

Chief among them was the fact that the process contained a built-in mechanism that enabled defense attorneys to blow smoke when the case got to court. Often, that meant implying that the deputy was fabricating if he testified to something that was not contained in the report.

Cates had learned about that the hard way. Not long after he had been put in the field, he had seen an old blue Plymouth sedan nearly take out a pedestrian at an intersection. It was nighttime, and then-Patrol-Deputy Steve Cates had followed the car in its weaving and uncertain path down the roadway. Finally, he had turned on the red and blue lights and made the stop.

The driver turned out to be a hard, bitter slattern of a woman named Iris Mosely. Her daughter, a thirty-year-old carbon copy of Iris, was the only passenger.

Iris had nicotine-stained fingers and teeth. She also had what looked like several mixed drinks spilled down the front of her clothing and God only knew how many in her system. As she got out of the car, she snarled at Cates to leave her the fuck alone, and later, when he placed her under arrest, she urged her daughter to "kick this pig in the balls." At the station, she took a breath test, and her blood alcohol level was determined to be .19, nearly twice the legal level for intoxication.

This case can't go to trial, said the prosecutors with knowing grins. One-nines just don't go in front of a jury, they said. Those defendants always cop a plea somewhere along the way. Sort of wish it would go, actually—it'd be nice to try a strong one for a change.

Through her attorney, Mrs. Mosely pleaded not guilty and requested a jury trial, as California law allowed.

She showed up on the trial date in a sedate yellow dress that she had bought for Easter church services, a fact that the defense attorney later was able to elicit in front of the jury.

In court, Iris wore very little makeup and minimal lipstick. The nicotine stains were gone from her hands and from her teeth. She did not tell the judge and jury to leave her the fuck alone, and she did not exhort her daughter to kick them in the balls. She testified that any weaving had been because of something wrong with the steering mechanism on her car—"the darned Plymouth"—and she blushed and spoke hesitantly when she used that language. Finally, she didn't have booze spilled down the front of her yellow Easter dress.

She'd only had three drinks that evening, Iris testified. Moreover, of the three, one had been sloshed onto her clothing when somebody bumped into her. The defense attorney argued the breath test machine must have been mistaken, never mind that it registered accurate on a known alcohol specimen run two minutes after Iris's test. After all, Iris had testified under oath how much she'd had to drink, hadn't she? What is America coming to—trial *by machine*? What is this? *1984*? *Brave New World*? Thank God we still have a jury who can ignore the machine. . . .

The young Cates's lesson on report writing came when he testified about the arrest.

As one aspect of the prosecution evidence—and a minor aspect at that—the prosecutor from the D.A.'s office asked him if Iris had any apparent difficulty in locating and removing her driver's license from her wallet after the stop and before getting out of the car.

Cates replied that she had.

Would you please describe that? inquired the deputy D.A. Cates responded that his best recollection was that it took nearly two minutes for her to do so. The fact was no big deal standing alone, of course—people who are nervous without being drunk might have the same problem—but at least it was consistent with everything else he observed.

On cross-examination, the defense attorney pursued this thread.

The rules of evidence allowed leading questions for cross, and the defense attorney—a wily veteran of many a jury trial— used them to the fullest effect. He was a medium-size, spare man with an old-fashioned mustache. He wore a navy blue pin-striped suit, and he had a voice that could snap like a whip when he wanted it to.

It happened to be young Deputy Cates's first time on the witness stand.

"Now, Deputy Cates, you testified that it took my client, Mrs. Mosely, nearly *two minutes* to find and remove her license?"

"Yes, sir."

"You're sure about that? No way you could be wrong about it?"

"No, sir. I mean, I'm sure about it."

"You couldn't have this, ah, unfortunate incident confused with another arrest, perhaps?"

"No, sir. I remember Mrs. Mosely specifically. I mean—"

"Just answer the questions yes or no, Deputy," the attorney snapped. "So, it's your testimony that you don't believe you have this case confused with any other, is that correct?"

"I—yes."

"Very well, Deputy. Now, did you prepare a report of this incident?"

"Yes, sir."

The attorney held up a copy of the arrest report, five pages of hand-printing, including a chart to record how Iris had done on the field coordination tests used to detect intoxicated drivers. "And this is your report, is it, Deputy?"

"Yes."

"Five pages, is it?"

"Yes, sir."

"And the purpose of this report is to record the important facts to avoid the possibility of mistaking this incident for another arrest, isn't that true?"

"That's one of the purposes."

"Now, Deputy Cates, you've had training in how to write reports, haven't you?"

The question confused him. What did the man mean by training in how to write reports? "Well, on the format. At the academy we—"

"Just yes or no *if* you please, Deputy."

"I—yes."

"Thank you. And you were taught that a good report is an accurate report, were you not?"

"Yes, I suppose so."

"And an accurate report is a complete one, one that contains all the important facts in it, isn't that true?"

"Basically, yes."

"Do you have a copy of your report of this unfortunate episode with you in court today, Deputy?"

"Yes, sir, I do."

"All five pages?"

"Yes."

"Please hold it up and show it to the jury."

Puzzled, Cates did so.

"And now, Deputy Cates, please examine it and show us where in that report you listed this...this *revelation* that it took Mrs. Iris Mosely more than two minutes to find her driver's license that night."

Face burning, Cates started to explain. It wasn't in the report. He'd omitted it, to be sure. Forgotten to put it in, if you wish. But it was the truth, and the young deputy was certainly not likely to forget Mrs. Mosely, or confuse that arrest with one of his other arrests.

"Well, I—"

"No, no, Deputy," interrupted the attorney. "Do examine your report. Take all the time you need. Mrs. Mosely and the jury certainly don't want any *inaccuracies* to enter into this process."

He left unspoken the implication that Cates, on the other hand, wouldn't mind if inaccuracies were thus used.

"I didn't—it isn't in the report," he said at last. "I—"

"Is that because it was not an important detail to you, or simply because you didn't prepare an accurate report?"

The jury deliberated eight hours before declaring themselves deadlocked. The final score was three for guilty, three for not guilty, and six undecided. When they filed out, one of the not guiltys told the prosecutor that they all thought Mrs. Mosely was probably guilty, but they just didn't have enough evidence. And, he said, they were disappointed in the officer's testimony.

Cates's skeleton format for roughing out his reports was born shortly thereafter. He never made the same mistake twice.

Today, unlike most deputies, he didn't particularly mind doing the reports. In fact, he often used the process as a tool to organize his thoughts and brainstorm a difficult case.

The Fisher case qualified for that, all right, he reflected grimly.

The FBI's law enforcement statistics showed that most people who got killed by other people were acquainted with the killers. It became a scrap of grim humor among the homicide cops that one was more apt to be killed by his friends than by his enemies. While the devil you know was usually preferable to the devil you didn't, you were more apt to be killed by the former than the latter.

Chances were, then, that whatever happened to Beth Fisher happened at the hands of somebody she knew.

Or who knew her, which might or might not be the same thing.

The FBI's interest puzzled him. Initially, he had been inclined to dismiss it as simply a cursory thing, a formality, because Beth had worked for a company that did government work.

But one thing—at least one thing—didn't fit with that theory. If it were indeed only a cursory inquiry, why did two Feebs and an assistant U.S. attorney, no less try to buttonhole the sheriff so quickly?

He frowned. That did not sound like a mere formality.

Could it be that the devil she knew, the one who snatched and undoubtedly killed her, had been connected with her work? Another employee of Data Research and Technology, perhaps?

That would explain the Bureau's interest. It was one thing for an employee of a government think-tank contractor to get herself mysteriously killed. And it was quite another for a fellow employee to do the killing.

Of course, if this theory were true, it meant the FBI already had a suspect, somebody inside the company they were looking at. And, from what little he knew of their approach to the sheriff, Cates somehow doubted that was the case.

He shook his head.

So what was left? Either he'd have to end up postulating some wild, hush-hush, spy-versus-spy crap, something the Bureau would be up to its top-secret ears in, or it would turn out to be what most homicides turned out to be, namely, nothing so exotic.

Shutting his eyes, Cates folded his arms and leaned back in the metal chair. Brainstorm it a little, Stevie, he told himself. Turn loose the old mind. Let it ramble and roam.

An old boyfriend, gone wacko when she broke it off.

An ex-husband, ditto, though she looked young for that.

Or, perhaps the oldest motive of all, the triangle—maybe it was the wife or girlfriend of somebody Beth was dating or messing around with. Maybe it wasn't so sophisticated after all.

Hell, maybe she was gay, or bi. In that case, it could be an old girlfriend, or a new one. Or the husband or boyfriend—or girlfriend—of her new girlfriend.

Somehow, for reasons he couldn't put his finger on, such a scenario held just the faintest degree of plausibility in this case. Why was that? he wondered. Was it possibly due to the bizarre circumstances of the disappearance and presumed death? She who lives by the preternatural life-style dies by the preternatural life-style? Bohemian life, bohemian death?

Then again, maybe it was dope.

He thought that over. Could be dope. So maybe Beth was involved up to her pretty blond little tail in narcotics. Maybe she was the supplier for Data Research.

Or, it could be extortion.

Does she have folks with money? Have they been contacted by whoever did this? Is her old man a big shot with the State Department, maybe, and somebody wants him to cough loose a political prisoner?

Maybe somebody from Mars killed her.

And maybe she isn't even dead. Missing doesn't equal dead. In fact, in the overwhelming majority of cases, missing didn't turn out to be dead; missing was simply missing. And yet, he had been referring to her in the past tense. Of course, he de-

fended himself, she was missing under unusual circumstances.

At that moment Lieutenant Beecham strode from his office, his cowboy boots making sharp clopping sounds on the
floor.

"Cates." It was a summons.

"Yeah."

"How're those reports coming?"

"They're coming."

"Well, put 'em aside."

"What's up?"

"Comm Center just called."

"Yeah?"

"Yeah. We just might have the body."

pouched

IT TOOK CATES nearly an hour to get there. Well before arriving, as the detective car climbed the desert road in the foothills east of Jamul, he spotted the green-and-white sedan of the deputy on the scene.

As his car pulled to a stop, Cates realized the deputy was the same one as in the hostage scenario the preceding Friday. She looked as good in her uniform as she had that day as a "civilian," he couldn't help noticing. More important, however, she looked determined and competent, even if a little pale.

As he walked over to her, Cates glanced at the name tag on her chest opposite the badge. M. Griffin, it read.

"What does the *M* stand for?" he asked by way of greeting.

"Martie."

He extended his hand. "I'm not sure we've been formally introduced. I'm Steve Cates. Homicide."

"Martie Griffin," she responded. "I know who you are. Even before you 'shot me' last week," she added with a smile.

Cates started to toss out a hackneyed "don't believe everything you hear," then thought better of it. Her name rang bells for some other reason, however, though he couldn't identify why it should.

"You work out of the Grove?"

"Yes. For the past six months or so, anyway."

He nodded his understanding, then got down to business. "Where is it?"

She pointed. "Down there."

"You've been down?"

"Yes."

"How? Where?"

She indicated her path. Good job, Cates thought, she had moved over to one side so she didn't obliterate the tracks—if they could be called that; actually, they were more like furrows—made by the car.

"You take any photos?"

"No." After a moment, she added, "Don't you have a partner?"

"No." He didn't volunteer any additional information.

Martie appeared to consider this for several moments, while Cates continued to scan the car's path down the steep canyon. At last she spoke. "I thought they always assigned two detectives to homicides."

"They usually do."

Cates walked to the trunk of his car and took out a heavy, wide briefcase affair commonly referred to as a catalog case. Returning to where she stood, he opened it and removed a Pentax camera in a battered leather cover. He took several photos, broad shots of the area, showing the canyon, the furrowed tracks and, far below, the car. Then he walked twenty or thirty feet up the road and repeated the process before replacing the camera in the case.

"General views of the overall scene," he explained, though she had not asked.

She didn't respond.

"Feel like another hike?"

"I'd sort of planned on it," she replied obliquely.

Cates looked at her for a moment, then shrugged. "No time like the present, I guess."

A short time later, he knelt down beside the open door of the Taurus and looked at the woman, lying on her side, her head resting on her arm. Then, much as Martie had done earlier, he lifted her head to get a better view of the face.

The neck is slack, he noted. Loose but not broken. He'd check the lower limbs later.

He looked at the face.

Beneath the pallor of death, the skin had been tanned. The hair was blond, moderately long, and even in death it looked as if it had been cut in a dramatic, layered fashion. The face was not pretty now, though it was unmarked except for the lividity, but it had once been pretty.

A pretty girl. A party girl. A pretty party girl.

A girl whose five-by-seven studio portrait was at that very moment in a manila folder. Elizabeth Fisher, known to her friends as Beth.

It was she, all right. Without a doubt.

Beth—or what had once been Beth—seemed to look back. At him. Through him. Into him.

Into nowhere.

He felt no great surprise, or relief, or even letdown. He had known all along the body would be Beth's. He'd talked about her as if she were dead. Now, gazing at the dulled eyes, Cates realized he had felt almost to a certainty what the result would be from the point when he first investigated her apartment.

Gently, he set the head down. For nearly a minute he stayed there, crouched on his heels, as he tried to sort out his feelings.

It wasn't as if he'd had some flash of second sight, or a dream or any specific precognition. Cates did not regard himself as particularly attuned to the paranormal. Certainly he didn't think he was possessed of any psychic abilities.

The nature of being a cop, dealing as he did with logic and evidence and proof according to the rules of law, was not conducive to belief in things mystical. Anything that couldn't be seen, heard, touched, smelled or tasted—or for that matter, arrested or impounded as evidence—got pretty short shrift in criminal investigations.

At least, that was the way things appeared to be on the surface.

Like many good investigators, however, Cates did not discount the existence of some things that couldn't be explained by this cut-and-dried legal pragmatism. He had learned that in a surprising number of instances, what had broken a case had been sheer hunch, or even less. Something that had proved to be correct, but that certainly wouldn't be listened to by a court of law.

Lots of things cops did were like that, things that began with hunches, or intuition or insight—the educated guess, in other words.

In most of those cases, however, the hunch was actually a combination of observable fact combined with experience. The mind subconsciously processed the sensory data and came up with a conclusion. Even the deputy himself didn't know why he thought what he thought, so it was called a hunch. Like a quarterback with a seemingly uncanny ability to read the defense, or a linebacker who always seems to know how the offensive play will unfold.

"I don't know how I knew. I just *knew*. You understand?"

That kind of hunch came under the legal rubric of "training and experience." Chalk it up to "cop sense," and forget even trying to make a judge understand what you were talking about.

In Cates's book, however, there also existed another type of insight. This was something altogether different from the subconscious reasoning of training and experience.

He found it easier to describe in terms of what it was not than of what it was.

It was not based on cause and effect at all. As such, it was completely nondiscursive, based entirely on intuition, for want of a better word. When it happened, it did not come in the form of a vision, as with a psychic who professed to be able to actually see something outside of the immediate environment, or to relive an incident. Instead, with Cates, it usually took the form of a feeling, something he just knew or felt.

Sometimes it came so clearly and so startlingly that it could only be described as a flash. More often it simply grew on him, something that gnawed at his subconscious and made him uncomfortable until it either grew strong enough for him to recognize it or it went away.

Over the years he had trained himself to be attuned to the signs.

Things would be going along, seemingly normal. Then he would realize that he had been feeling edgy, or a little disgruntled or vaguely dissatisfied for reasons that he couldn't put his finger on.

That was the signal.

When that happened, he now knew, it was time to consciously take stock of himself, time to determine if it might be "one of his feelings." This required him to relax, to mentally freewheel, to allow himself what others might call a period of meditation. Stir the kettle of the old mind and see what floats to the surface.

Often, his best results came either during or right after running or a workout with the weights, provided he had been by himself. If he tried too hard, he seemed to drive it away, or force it back beneath the surface. "If it doesn't fit, don't force it," became the guiding consideration.

Apart from trying to recognize these feelings, he had begun to do other things as well, things designed to actually cultivate them. At first, he had felt silly about it. Later, and now, he only felt silly if he tried to explain it to other people, so he usually didn't.

On two occasions, when investigations had appeared stalled, he had even consulted a woman believed to possess psychic abilities.

In one of the cases—a then-unsolved mutilation homicide—she had been right on target with her profile of the killer, a profile, incidentally, that was at direct odds with the one dreamed up by a $120-per-hour psychiatrist retained by the department. In the second case, she had also provided a profile. However, that case had never been closed, no suspect arrested, so he didn't know if she had been right or not.

Now, as he knelt by the dead woman, it seemed to Cates he had been in the embryonic stages of one of those feelings.

From the moment he entered Beth Fisher's apartment the preceding Friday, he had been experiencing a curious sense of fate. It had the quality of embarking on a quest, mingled with a curious inevitability and a certain foreboding.

He had known she would be dead. And now it was confirmed. But there was more to the feelings than that; if that were all, the sensations would have gone away, having been in a sense fulfilled when he saw the body.

But the feelings hadn't gone away when he saw the body. If anything, they were stronger. That meant that they weren't solely, or even chiefly, based on the fact of her death. If there was anything to them, it meant that the journey was just beginning.

Cates became aware that Martie was quietly watching him. He didn't know how many moments, or possibly minutes, had passed while he sorted out his thoughts.

Squinting into the sun, he looked up at her.

"What is it?" she inquired.

A little embarrassed, he frowned and shook his head, hoping it would appear that he had been considering and then dismissing with minor irritation some theory or bothersome investigative point.

She spoke again after a few more moments. "Anything I can do to help?"

"Not really. Not yet, anyway."

"What happens now?"

He stood up and dusted off his knees. "I'll take some pictures and do some preliminary looking around. The lab should be along pretty soon, and the coroner's deputy. Once the coroner gets here, we can move the body, and do a more thorough examination."

"Why is it that way?" Martie inquired.

"What way?"

"That you can't even move the body until the coroner gets here? I remember that from the academy, of course, but it doesn't make much sense." She hesitated. "I mean, at the time it was one of those things where I wondered if you really did that, or if it was just a formality you were supposed to do but everybody ignored."

"I really do it," Cates responded.

"So I see."

"Historically, the whole idea of the coroner was to investigate cause of death in violent death cases. Nowadays, every county in the state—let alone every state—has its own way of handling such cases."

He paused and glanced at Martie. She seemed genuinely interested, so he continued.

"In Orange County, for instance, only the next county up from ours, the sheriff's and the coroner's offices are combined. Down here, they're separate. And the prevailing interpretation of the law is literally that nobody moves the body except the coroner's man, period."

"So we wait?"

"We wait. I suspect they'll be along pretty soon. Then we'll get her out of the car and do a cursory visual examination. I'll have her pouched and taken to the morgue."

"Do you put every one into a body bag?" Martie inquired. "I thought that was just for the...oh, the mangled ones, or something."

"Different people do it differently. I like to pouch them immediately, then have them taken to the morgue on a 'hold as is' basis. Then at the morgue we can undress them, photograph them, wash them and do the external examination before the autopsy."

"Why," Martie persisted, "use a body bag for every one?" She gestured toward the Taurus. "Take her, for example. Not messy, not mangled—it just seems kind of crude, somehow, to zip her into a hefty bag like a bunch of garbage."

"Killing her was kind of crude, too, don't you think?"

"That's no answer."

She sounded at once serious and troubled. Cates looked at her with respect. This one, he decided, had some gumption. Maybe even guts. "You're right. It isn't an answer. There's a good legal reason for doing it."

"And that is?"

"Sometimes projectiles, bullets, work their way out during the handling or transporting of the corpse. Sometimes the body or clothing will have fibers or hairs that could help tie it to another location—the murder scene, the suspect's house or car—or even to the suspect himself. Either way, it prevents the possible loss of evidence."

He hesitated, then continued. "It also prevents the body from picking up fibers or substances during the transport, things that could mislead the investigation or be used by a defense attorney to suggest somebody else killed her."

Martie grimaced. "So you bag every one," she affirmed.

"Yes." He allowed a twisted grin, though it did not contain much humor. "Last week anyway. And this week, as far as I know. And next week, and until some idiot pencil pusher for the county—or the Board of Supervisors in approving the next year's budget—decides it's too expensive, and cuts back. So then, instead of spending five or ten dollars for a body bag, we can spend five or ten thousand dollars in extra court time litigating where the fibers went or came from or whatever."

After a few moments, Martie spoke again. "What should I be doing?"

"Well, technically, you can back out and just give me an incident report about finding the body." Cates thought for a moment. "Come to think of it, how did you happen to find the body, anyway?"

She told him.

"All right," he said when she had finished. "I'll need that in a narrative. And that's about all, if you like."

"Steve?" Her voice sounded pensive.

"Yeah?"

"Is there something funny—unusual—about this case?"

"What do you mean?"

"Well, you don't have a partner, for one thing. I know you usually work with Detective Grummon, and he's not here. The Lab's not here, either. And when I called it in, dispatch relayed that Lieutenant Beecham said I shouldn't notify my supervisor, that he'd take care of that himself."

"Go on," said Cates without expression.

"Normally I'd expect my sergeant to stop by the scene of an eleven-forty-four," she continued, using the radio code that designated a coroner's case, "but nobody shows up but you. I have to assume Lieutenant Beecham did what he said he would, contacted my supervisor...."

"But?" Cates prompted.

"But, I don't know, it just seems . . . well, weird."

He smiled faintly. "Yeah," he said at last. "It's weird."

"What's going on?"

"Have you seen the papers today? The L.A. *Times*, anyway?"

She shook her head. "I came on duty too early. I don't usually read the *Times*, anyway."

Cates told her about Beth's disappearance, the article in the paper, the FBI's apparent interest and his meeting with Assistant Sheriff Tisdale, omitting, however, the details of the Santos procedure.

"So," he concluded, "you're right. This is a weird one. I'm working on it alone, reporting directly to the lieutenant and then up to Assistant Sheriff Tisdale personally. Something very cute is going on with this one, and I'm damned if I know what it is."

But I am damn sure going to find out, he added silently.

Martie's features moved in a sort of half smile. "Sounds like a great one for me to get my feet wet with," she said lightly.

He grinned. "If I were you, I'd write my report short and sweet, and then get the hell out of here. Put as much distance between yourself and this investigation—and me—as you can, so you can be in the clear if, or when, it blows up."

"You think it's going to blow up, somehow?"

"It has all the signs of it." He thought for a moment, then made a little wink at her. "Let's put it this way. If you're really smart, you'll include something ambiguously negative about me in your paperwork."

"Why?"

"That way, if things really go down the drain, you can point to it and say you didn't like what I was doing all along. It's called 'go fuck over your buddy.' Be good practice in case you ever want to become an attorney."

Martie grinned back. "No."

"No what?"

"No, if I were you, I wouldn't do any of that, because I don't think you would." She hesitated. "I'd kind of like to stay involved in it," she said at last.

"That's not a good idea."

"So I gather."

Cates looked at her carefully. She should realize it was definitely, strongly, not a good idea for her to be involved. And from his perspective, it would be violating Tisdale's orders.

On the other hand, one of his hunches told him that it might be a good thing to have a witness to what he was doing. Off-the-record and not disclosed in the reports, of course. However, the whole case had enough of a bad odor to it that having a back door of sorts might be advisable.

He still didn't like the idea of violating Tisdale's orders.

Cates felt a strong sense of loyalty to the department. This was due, he suspected, both to indoctrination and to his own nature. And, to give credit where it was due, there was less bureaucratic bullshit in the S.O. than in any large organization he could think of. There was even considerable loyalty running downhill, from the command structure to the working deputies.

All in all—having to do jail time aside—he couldn't think of a better place to be a cop.

No agency, however, was completely immune to pressure from outside sources. This was especially so when it was federal pressure and the case wasn't some normal, garden-variety homicide. And while it would be a shame to involve Martie—whom he didn't really know much about, though his instinct said he could trust her—it also didn't make sense not to cover his own ass.

"You don't know what you're getting into," he said at last.

"Probably not, but neither do you, apparently."

"You have a choice. I don't."

"So I'm choosing," she responded.

"It's your career," he said with a shrug.

"Yes, it is." Martie paused, then gestured toward the body in the car. "It looks like she might have some marks, bruises, on her throat," she observed. "You think that killed her?"

Cates leaned inside the car again. He lifted the head and examined the neck. Then he turned the face upward, and, with his thumbs, pulled down the eyelids, first below and then above the eyes.

"No, I don't think so," he responded, backing out of the car and getting to his feet.

"How can you tell?"

"You're probably thinking of the cartilage in the throat, on either side of the larynx. You crush or break that, and it swells rapidly and cuts off the airways. The victim dies by asphyxiation, like being strangled. Chokes to death, in other words."

"But that didn't happen to her?"

He shook his head. "No petechial hemorrhage."

She frowned. "What's that?"

Cates moved back to the car. "Come over here and take a look." He lifted the dead woman's face again and pulled back the eyelids. "Usually, when somebody is strangled, the blood vessels in the eyes and eyelids will be ruptured."

"You can see that? Just looking at it, I mean?"

"Yes. It looks like a case of maxed-out bloodshot eyes, only more so. It's caused by the severe increase in venous pressure from the strangulation. It's kind of a quick and easy sign that the person was strangled." Cates set the dead woman's head down again, and backed out of the car.

"So what do you think caused her to die?" Martie asked.

"Easy. Her heart stopped." Seeing Martie's look, he hurried on. "Apart from that, though, we won't know until the autopsy."

"When will that be?"

He glanced at his watch. "By the time we get her down to the morgue, it'll be too late for today. So probably first thing in the morning."

"Do you mind if I come down there?"

"To the autopsy?"

"Yes."

"It'll have to be off-the-record. Your involvement, I mean. I can't spring you free from your duty station for it."

"I have Tuesdays and Wednesdays off."

"Can you keep your mouth shut? You're playing with fire, you know."

"I know. I mean, I can and I know, in answer to both questions. When shall I be there?"

What the hell, Cates thought. "Seven-thirty."

And then, Ms Fisher, he added silently, we'll see what you can tell us about how you disappeared and how you were killed. Because killed you certainly were, a criminal homicide, the unlawful killing of one human being by another. And I'll be there when they open you up, and I'll be there to listen to what your body says about it. And then I'll get about finding out who that "other" is that killed you, because it's my job. And, if I may say so, I'm not half bad at doing my job.

The sound of an engine reached them. Cates squinted into the sun and pointed. Martie followed his gaze.

"Coroner," he said simply.

Martie watched as the two vehicles stopped on the road above them. She recognized one as the van belonging to the Sheriff's Crime Lab. The other was the coroner's car. Added to her patrol car and Cates's detective unit, it made quite a little group.

Even though she'd been on the department for going on four years, and had been in the field on patrol for more than six months, she still felt a twinge of pride, of thrill, in fact, at seeing the little group of obviously official vehicles.

To members of the general public, such a cluster of official cars generated a sense of fascination. It indicated that something was going on, a human crisis had taken place, and the cops were on the scene, handling it. It made people slow down, take a look, rubberneck. It made them comment to their friends afterward, "I wonder what happened out there, there were cop cars all over the place, do you think somebody died?"

Martie knew the feeling. She'd had it herself, before joining the department. And now she was one of the cops on the scene, handling it.

Even more of a kick was the fact that the real police vehicle, the marked green-and-white patrol unit, was hers.

Two men got out of the coroner's car and walked to the edge of the road. One had a bulky, stout frame; the other looked taller and youthful. The bulky one peered down at them and gave a big wave. Then he leaned backward, shifting his weight onto his heels, and gave a pull on his trousers, as if lifting them and settling them into place the way stout men sometimes do.

Beside her, Cates groaned audibly. Even as he did so, the bulky man began plunging down the sandy hillside, down the furrows made by the Taurus and so carefully avoided by Cates and Martie.

"Goddamn it," Cates growled.

"What's the matter?" Martie inquired quickly.

"Of all the coroners available, why did we have to get this ghoul?" He glanced at her. "Couldn't you have waited until he was off duty to find the body?" His tone of voice did not sound as facetious as the words.

"Which one are you talking about?"

"The fat one. The guy who's wiping out the tracks."

"Why? Who is he?"

"Name's Dave Slaman. Slime-man is more like it, though. That's what he's called by most of the investigators."

"What's the story on him?"

"He's a goddamn jerk," Cates responded.

"Geez, Steve, don't beat around the bush so much."

"Most of the coroner's people are good guys, your dedicated public-servant type trying to do a not very pleasant job. They're pretty damn considerate of the families and whatnot . . ." He let the sentence trail off.

"And this guy isn't?"

"You'll see."

She watched as Slaman's fleshy form continued its reckless, swaggering path down the steep slope.

He looked short, perhaps five-six or -seven. He had an olive complexion—no, make that sort of an oily brown complexion, she amended—and shiny black hair combed neatly over to one side. Arab? she wondered. Lebanese? Maybe from India?

Slime-man, Cates had called him.

The fleshy features, the man's bluff swagger and stocky frame, and Cates's involuntary groan made it easy to understand the nickname.

"Ho!" he bellowed as he drew near. "Detective Cates! And who is your pretty young assistant today?"

Martie stiffened. "I'm *Deputy* Griffin, if you don't mind."

Cates appeared to ignore both of them. "Nice job you did on the tracks, Slime-man," he observed coldly, his features moving in what didn't even qualify as a token smile.

"What's that?"

Slaman swiveled to look back up the hill, which now appeared as if it had been used for a motocross. He stared for a moment, then made a dismissive wave of his hand. "Ah!" he snorted contemptuously. "You worry too much, Detective Cates. The soil is too loose to take impressions of tires anyway."

"Thank you for your advice in that regard."

"Think nothing of it." Slaman turned to Martie. "And you, pretty lady, *Deputy* Griffin, must have been the one to find the body," he announced. Without waiting for a reply—though, she reflected, none was really called for—he started toward the car, some twelve feet behind them.

Cates put his hand on the man's arm. "Not yet."

Slaman's eyes narrowed. "But I am the coroner. It is my duty to take charge of the deceased."

"Yeah. And that is the lab." Cates pointed to the two sheriff's men, making their way down the slope. "And it is their duty to preserve evidence. And once they've gotten here and done that, then you may take charge of the body."

Martie glanced at Slaman, seeking his reaction.

She saw that her initial impression of his size hadn't been quite right. He wasn't short so much as he was stocky, and her revised estimate was that he stood about five-ten. Moreover, what she had originally regarded as simply a fat man was more accurately a stocky, bull-like man with a layer of fat over his flesh. It somehow gave him a sort of dissolute air, as if he were given to excess in every aspect of his life.

Beneath it, though, his wrists were big and stout. I'd hate to have to fight him, she thought.

Slaman thought for a moment. "I remind you, Cates, that I have primary jurisdiction over the body."

"Which you may exercise when I say so."

Cates's face was grim, and Martie wondered if the two men would come to blows. Then Slaman gave an expansive shrug. "But of course, Cates. If it would make you feel better, for you I will wait."

"Good."

The lab technicians had stopped nearby, as if they sensed the tension between the two men. Cates turned to them. After the greetings, he waved toward the car.

"You guys want to get some general shots and measurements before we take the body out?"

A few minutes later, Cates turned to Slaman. "Shall we?"

The coroner's deputy nodded. "Yes, I think it would be good now." Somehow, thought Martie, his statement managed to convey the thought that it had been his idea all along to wait.

She watched as the body was removed and laid on the sandy ground. They performed a quick visual examination.

"No visible signs of trauma," announced Slaman unnecessarily.

Cates nodded distractedly, still kneeling over the body. Fascinated, Martie watched as he seemed to be attempting to straighten the woman's legs.

He gripped the thigh in one hand and the upper shinbone in the other, and tried without apparent success to work the knee. Then he reached down to the foot, which proved equally unyielding. Finally, he took hold of the dead woman's left arm, and tried the same thing. It moved, stiffly but with relative ease.

"Ah, the most fortunate Detective Cates," announced Slaman, standing behind them. "Today even your victims are beautiful young women. Others get murdered addict whores, the fat Indians, the rotted floaters in the lakes. But you, you are special."

Martie felt a sudden queasy anger at what she regarded as the decidedly unwholesome implication of Slaman's statement, and at herself for picking up on it. The dead woman was obviously clad only in the man's blue dress shirt, and she couldn't help but wonder if Cates's actions had prompted Slime-man's comment.

The big detective, however, appeared to take no notice. He rose to his feet and dusted off his knees. "Let's get her pouched and down to the morgue. I want her held as is, and I'll be down this afternoon for a more thorough inspection."

Slaman, who had begun nodding as soon as Cates started speaking, suddenly began shaking his head. "No pouch," he announced.

"What?"

"No pouch for this one."

Cates gestured. "You brought one down," he said, pointing to the body bag held by the second corner's deputy.

"Ah. Yes. But we did not know what shape the body would be in. Now we do. It doesn't qualify for a bag."

"What do you mean, 'it doesn't qualify'?"

Slaman emitted a heavy sigh. "I would like to, of course, Detective Cates. To oblige you. But under the new guidelines, no pouch in a case like this. Just straight transport."

Martie noted that Cates had become "Detective Cates" again. She wondered if it signified that Slaman felt on pretty firm ground on this particular point, so he could afford to be courteous. He continued speaking.

"The budget is being cut back. The County Board of Assholes—" here Slaman interrupted himself with a hearty man-to-man chuckle "—and the auditor's office have decided we waste too much money. So—" he gave an elaborate shrug "—no pouch on this case, my friend."

Martie watched as Cates turned to Slaman's assistant, a young man about her own age. He looked like a TV-show paramedic, or a fireman, and he plainly didn't like being caught in the middle.

"That true?"

The young man grimaced and spread his arms in a how-do-I-know gesture. Cates wheeled back around. With three quick strides, he came literally face-to-face with Slaman, their bodies only inches apart. Though the latter stood on the uphill side, Cates was enough taller that his face was still an inch or two higher.

The big detective leaned forward, his fists clenched at his sides, his face directly in front of Slaman's.

"Listen, you fat little fucker," he snarled, his features twisted in fury. "I'm not your friend. I'm not fortunate, and I'm not special.

"Now, I'm putting her in that bag. And she's staying in that bag. And you're going to transport her and hold her like that until I get there. And if you mess with me in the least way about it—" Cates paused and the snarl became a deadly, deliberate announcement that Martie found somehow even more frightening "—I will hurt you."

Cates regarded Slaman for several moments with a cold, quiet gaze. Then he turned away and walked over to the lab crew. "When you finish processing the car, impound it as evidence," he said in a conversational tone. "I'm going to follow the body to the morgue."

At the same time, Slaman was remarking to his young assistant, "We'll bag this one, I think."

"Martie." It was Cates.

"Yes?"

"Tomorrow morning. Seven-thirty. Can do?"

"Can do." She watched as he turned and began the climb up the slope.

11

Dr. Hastings and Mr. Cates

"Hmm."

The statement—if it could be called that—came from the pathologist, Dr. Hastings.

In his late forties, with a beard and full head of hair, both gray, he looked like a genial college professor except for his favorite footwear, cowboy boots. The image was not altogether inaccurate, for in addition to being a highly skilled pathologist, he was on the faculty of the medical college at the University of California, San Diego.

As a condition of a research grant given to the university, Dr. Hastings and other members of the faculty performed a given number of autopsies per month for the county. Thus, though the coroner's office had three well-qualified M.D.s as full-time staff members to conduct most of the postmortems, some were done by nonstaffers like Dr. Hastings.

Cates had worked with him on one previous homicide, and considered it extremely fortunate—and a pleasant surprise— that Hastings somehow had been drawn for this one.

"What is it?" Cates inquired.

Before looking where Dr. Hastings was pointing, he shot a glance at Martie. He was gratified to note that she wore a look of determination on her face.

"Take a look at this, will you?"

"Where?"

"There." He indicated something in the interior of the chest of the lifeless form.

She lay on the stainless-steel autopsy table.

Cates leaned forward. Dr. Hastings was pointing at the heart, inside the tough membranelike sac or pericardium that held it in place, suspended between the lungs on either side and the diaphragm below.

The body had been in the cool room for the past sixteen hours or so, from sometime early Monday afternoon. The cool room, which held most of the corpses, was maintained at thirty-eight to forty degrees Fahrenheit, not unlike a cold household refrigerator. Thus, they were not frozen, yet the environment was sufficiently cold to retard decomposition.

"Like your refrigerator keeps steaks," Cates observed to Martie.

The popular conception of a morgue was massive banks of refrigerated drawers where bodies were held one to a drawer like so many batches of files. However, the San Diego facility—like most others that Cates had seen in real life—was not like that. Instead, the main storage unit consisted of a large, walk-in refrigerator, similar to a meat locker. Most of the bodies were simply kept in the cold room on gurneys, pending the autopsy and release to next of kin.

A few weren't, however.

The exceptions were the cases where decomposition had advanced to the point where this was not feasible. These, crudely termed "stinkers," went in a separate cold room. There they were placed on individual trays.

The trays caught the seepage from the liquefying fats and other tissues. The cold not only retarded further decomposition but it slowed down the maggots.

The body in the Fisher 187 had been in normal storage in the regular cold room.

Some cops referred to the body by the name of the deceased. Cates, for some psychological reason, didn't. Instead, it became "the body" or "the body in the Fisher 187" or sometimes even "she." But it would never again be "Beth" or "Beth Fisher" or even "Beth Fisher's body."

Some fifteen minutes earlier, the coroner's staff had removed the body from the cold room and placed it on the autopsy table. There they had taken pictures, examined it, washed it and photographed it again.

As a matter of routine, any visible trauma sites were charted.

In this case, these consisted of an old bruise, mainly yellow, on the right shin; a bluish bruise on the buttocks; and a mark on the point of the left shoulder. Apart from the vague, dusky marks on the throat, the rest of the body including the trunk area—was unmarked. Swabs were taken from the mouth, vagina and anus, following which Dr. Hastings commenced the postmortem.

He began by making a sweeping incision in the shape of a Y. Martie knew from the academy that he would examine the internal organs, take fluid and tissue specimens, track and dissect any wounds, and not only look for affirmative causes of death but also rule out other possible causes.

He would in due course slice through and peel forward the scalp, saw open the skull, remove and examine the brain and then pull the scalp back into place. The brain itself, she knew, would be kept with the body, either inside the abdominal cavity, or in a plastic bag for delivery with the body to the funeral home or mortician. If this procedure was followed, the plastic bag and brain would be put between the legs of the corpse; she remembered her academy instructor commenting dryly that all too often, this was where most people's brains were anyway.

The tips of the Y incision started at the base of the clavicle and met in the vicinity of the sternum. A single cut extended down to the pubis, and the ribs were cut with a no-nonsense implement resembling a pair of heavy pruning shears.

Next, Hastings removed and weighed each lung.

With skillful strokes of a long knife—"I worked my way through med school as a chef in a Japanese steak house," he quipped with a wink at Martie—he dissected each one, inspected it and took several tissue slices for later examination.

Then he turned his attention to the heart.

Cates was no pathologist, but he had seen countless autopsies, the subjects of which had ranged from infants to elderly adults. And to his layman's eye, the heart didn't look right.

Dr. Hastings evidently thought the same thing.

He weighed it and then examined it closely, turning it over in his hands. Then he sliced it cleanly open—sectioned it, in his words—and studied first one section, then the next. Finally, he looked up at Cates and Martie.

"Fascinating," he said at last.

"What is it?" Martie inquired. "What's wrong?"

"The cause of death."

"What is the cause of death, Doctor?" she persisted.

"The heart stopped," Dr. Hastings announced proudly. "The cause of death is that her heart stopped."

Cates suppressed a smirk, aware that Martie—her face a little pale, but otherwise normal—was glancing quickly from himself to Dr. Hastings.

"I didn't tell him to say that," he disclaimed quickly. Then he allowed the grin. "But in the future, maybe you'll realize that when you're hearing it from me, you can put it in the bank and spend it."

Seeing the quizzical look on Dr. Hastings's face, Cates started to explain, but Martie cut him off.

"What he's trying to say, Doctor, is that he rendered the same smartass opinion—well, I took it as smartass—when we first found the body, and I was wondering if he had put you up to saying it now. But I take it you're serious?"

"Dead serious, if you'll pardon the expression."

Cates nudged her. "See? You'll learn."

Dr. Hastings grinned, then grew serious once more. "An infarct—" he began.

"I didn't," Cates interrupted. "Honest. And if you didn't, Doc, then it must have been her." He jerked his head to indicate Martie, then looked at her. "Well? Did you?"

Martie looked confused. "What? Did I what?" Then her face colored suddenly, "Oh. Yeah. I get it. Infarct. Yeah."

"I thought so," said Cates. To Dr. Hastings, he commented, "At least we know who the culprit is."

"Good of you to own up to it," the doctor deadpanned at Martie. "A lot of people would have stuck to their denial."

"But—" Martie tried to protest, but Dr. Hastings had started speaking again.

"At any rate," he continued, preventing her from clearing up the ambiguity in her last statement, "*infarct* is the term for what essentially means the death of a section of the heart tissue. Part of it literally dies, in other words. It can happen quickly, or over a prolonged time.''

"What happens then?'' inquired Martie, apparently resigned to let the other matter ride.

"Depends on how extensive it is. In any event, however, we expect to see some diminution in the heart's contractile force.''

Cates nodded solemnly. "No shit?''

Dr. Hastings nodded back. "No shit.''

Martie said, "Could you say it in English?''

"Surely. The heart can't pump as strongly. It contracts with less force, thereby lessening the force or pressure that it squirts the blood with.''

"The person goes into shock?'' Cates inquired.

"*Very* good.'' Dr. Hastings looked at him approvingly.

"Shock?'' echoed Martie.

"Yes,'' said the doctor. "That's exactly what happens.''

"Why shock?''

"There are devices to sense the pressure—to monitor it, in other words—in the aorta and carotid arteries. They're called baroreceptors, and besides monitoring, they are supposed to initiate corrective responses if the pressure gets out of line. Like a thermostat in your house, only it deals with pressure, not temperature.''

Martie nodded. "I'm with you so far, Doctor.''

"If this were a refrigerator or an automatic pilot device on an aircraft, it would be called a servomechanism, if that helps,'' added the pathologist.

"It doesn't,'' she responded.

"After all, she's a woman,'' Cates reminded Dr. Hastings, and immediately sensed Martie's bristling.

"I'd noticed,'' he responded genially. "But back to the baroreceptors.''

"Thank you,'' Martie said, shooting a withering look at Cates.

"When the contractile force drops, the pressure drops. When the pressure drops, the baroreceptors sense this, and take protective action.''

"Like what?"

"Kick the heart in the ass, so to speak."

"How does it do that?" It was Cates who inquired this time.

"Chiefly, they tell the adrenal gland to squirt some adren-aline into the blood to get things hyped up again. They may send some direct neural messages to the heart as well. The body also closes off the blood supply to nonessential areas, such as the skin, by restricting the arterioles—vessels—leading to those areas, so that what blood volume there is gets to where it's needed."

"Like the brain, I suppose," Cates suggested.

"Yes. And the heart, itself. You've probably heard that in shock cases the skin gets cold? Well, that's true when the shock is caused by this kind of situation—the body has in effect closed off the roads to the skin and rerouted the blood else-where."

Martie frowned. "If all this is true, Doctor, what's the problem? I mean, it sounds like a pretty efficient mechanism. Why does shock kill you?"

"Well, it doesn't always. Frequently, the process works as it's supposed to, things balance out, and the organism re-covers. The boat rights itself again, so to speak."

"But?"

"Remember, these are emergency measures, initiated by those sensors, the baroreceptors. If the heart can't bounce back, and get the pressure and volume of blood back up, other organs and systems start to fail. Or the heart itself can't keep up the emergency pace, and finally gives out."

"And the person dies?"

Dr. Hastings nodded. "The shock is deemed irreversible and the person dies."

Cates thought for several moments. "It sounds as if you're saying she died of shock following a real bad heart attack."

"Yes. That's what it looks like."

"I don't understand," Martie interjected. "How can you just give somebody a heart attack? I thought those were caused by, oh, blocking the arteries to the heart or something."

Cates noticed that her earlier paleness—as well as the embarrassment—had gone, and her color had returned. Good girl, he thought.

"Frequently they are," the pathologist responded. "A blood clot, say, forms elsewhere, then breaks loose and lodges in the coronary artery, blocking the blood that feeds the heart. Or they get blocked by buildup of fats, like you hear about in connection with eating too much cholesterol. Other types of damage to the heart can cause heart attack as well."

Dr. Hastings frowned and shook his head as if mystified.

"Could it be caused by a severe blow to the heart?" asked Cates. "Something that just damages the hell out of it?"

"Yes. Not common, but certainly possible. That's what I'm thinking of here."

To Cates, it made sense. "So what's the problem? Some kind of massive blow to the heart, or even the coronary artery, maybe, that wipes out sections of the tissue. Infarcts, you called it. Pressure drops. Shock. Death. That sound about right?"

"Whoa, there. Steady as she goes. I was thinking the same thing. Massive trauma caused by an external force—a blow— could indeed account for this. I'd want to eliminate all the other possible causes, of course."

"Won't the rest of the examination, and the slides and things—" Cates gestured at the jar that held the tissue specimens from the lungs "—do that?"

"Yes. But there's still something missing." Dr. Hastings looked at him, his blue eyes alive with academic interest. "What is it, Cates? What's not right about that scenario? In this case, anyway."

"You're the doctor. You tell me."

Dr. Hastings gestured with the long knife. "Take a look at her."

Wondering what in hell Dr. Hastings had on his mind, Cates looked.

Dead woman on an autopsy table, cut open. Heart all messed up, possibly from a massive blow. Sounded like enough to call it a homicide, depending on how the blow occurred.

Maybe the steering wheel could have done it. But Beth certainly didn't leave her apartment in the middle of a shower to go for a drive into a canyon in what he would bet was going to turn out to be a stolen car.

"I can't see it," he said at last.

"Come on. You're the trained observer, Sherlock."

Cates shook his head. Suddenly, Martie interjected, excitement in her voice. "The skin."

"What about it?" Cates said, a trifle irritably.

"The skin. The other flesh. It isn't smashed up, too. Is that it, Doctor? If that kind of blow caused the heart to be so damaged, wouldn't there be trauma, bruises, something, in the surrounding area?"

"Bingo." Dr. Hastings said it softly, nodding with approval. "Well done. Think about it. In layman's terms, the heart is a hell of a tough muscle. The vessels, such as the coronary artery, are tough as well."

At last, Cates saw the point with crystal clarity. Though part of his mind wanted to resist any challenge to his newfound understanding of the possible cause of death, another part realized the significance of what the doctor was saying. Mentally, that part took out an imaginary three-by-five card and wrote "no external damage" on it and filed it under Hmm in one of the file drawers of his mind.

Meanwhile, Dr. Hastings continued, his voice intense. "Doesn't it stand to reason that the kind of external blow that would, say, spasm or smash the coronary artery so the heart couldn't get fed, would have to be a hell of a blow? And what about a blow that could kill off the heart cells themselves?" He pointed at the body again. "Where's the rest of the damage? Where's the massive bruising in the area of the sternum? Where's the evidence in the subcutaneous tissues?"

"It isn't there," Martie said needlessly.

"No, it isn't," agreed the pathologist. "How could a blow capable of doing that sort of damage somehow virtually originate inside the body?"

"Electric shock?" Cates hazarded at last.

"Maybe. I'm not sure, but maybe. But I don't see any signs of that, either. Normally, electric shock creates an arrhythmia, a fibrillation, of the heart, rather than the sort of damage we see here."

"So what's the answer?"

Dr. Hastings shook his head noncommittally. "We'll finish the post. Maybe something else will crop up that will help us out."

"If it doesn't?" Cates inquired.

"If it doesn't, I'll take a look at the slides, do some blood tests, see what we can come up with."

Hell, thought Cates disgustedly. Couldn't there be anything normal about this damn case? "Can you at least give me a tentative, Doctor? Something to go on as a working theory, while you do the slides and things?"

Dr. Hastings nodded. "A fair question. And the answer is yes. I'll say tentatively that the cause of death seems to be, oh, how would I dictate it? 'Shock, hypovolemic, due to myocardial infarction, massive, probably caused by severe trauma, possibly resulting from the application of external physical force.' Something like that at this point."

Cates grinned. "It's not going to be written down yet, Doctor. 'Shock from a heart attack maybe caused by some unknown type of blow to the heart' sound about right?"

"Close enough."

"Not self-inflicted?"

"Definitely not."

"Not accidental?"

"Almost definitely—no, damn it, definitely—not."

"So it's a homicide?"

"It's a homicide."

"Thanks, Doctor, you've been a big help."

"Take two aspirin, get plenty of rest and call me in the morning. Oh, and don't forget to leave your insurance information with the receptionist so we can bill you."

"The check's in the mail."

"You can trust me—I'm a doctor."

"Yeah. And I'm with the government, I'm here to help you."

"Jesus," Martie observed at last, "as if there weren't enough comedians already."

As they were leaving, they ran into David Slaman.

12

Slaman

"UH-OH," SAID MARTIE involuntarily, when she recognized Slaman's bulky form.

It was nearly ten o'clock by the time Dr. Hastings concluded the autopsy. And now Martie was anxious to get outside, away from that city hall of death. Earlier, the morning had shown all the makings of a lovely spring day; moreover, she didn't have to work. She wanted to go for a run, at the beach or around the bay, anything to flush the smells of chemicals and putrefaction from her lungs.

Slaman didn't appear to notice them.

They had just emerged from a side hallway into the front reception area of the morgue. It was a small room, perhaps fifteen feet square, with several low, plastic-covered chairs. A Formica-covered counter ran along the back of it behind which sat a bored-looking receptionist.

Martie glanced to the right and saw institutional glass doors equipped with panic bars that marked the way out. The glass had been covered with a dull silvery coating that was starting to peel in places, lending the air of a cheap municipal building.

Slaman, wearing a white laboratory coat over his clothes, was at the counter saying something to the receptionist, a heavy blond woman in her thirties.

Cates followed the direction of Martie's glance. "At least you've got the right reaction to the guy," was all he said in response to her involuntary statement.

Just as she hoped they could get by him, already going out the door and too far ahead for a confrontation, Slaman glanced up. A wide, beaming smile wreathed his fleshy countenance. He looks, thought Martie, like a Libyan bureaucrat welcoming an arms dealer. "Ah, Detective Cates," he gushed. "And your lovely young assistant, the beautiful *Deputy* Griffin."

Cates ignored him and continued walking toward the exit. Uncomfortable in the silence, Martie managed an awkward. "Uh, hi."

Moving with an oily grace Martie would have not thought possible, Slaman managed to glide forward and position himself directly in Cates's path.

"Detective Cates," he said chummily.

"What?"

"Ah, Detective Cates, certainly you are not angry over the trifling matter of the body bag for your poor, lovely young victim yesterday."

"No."

Slaman continued as if he hadn't heard. "I, of course, was merely following the directives of my superiors. And you—you were only trying to do what you thought best for your case. Among men such as ourselves such disagreements will inevitably occur from time to time."

The way he said it, Martie thought, with just a hint of emphasis on the word *men* and a slight pause after it, conveyed the assumption that women had no place in the important matters that might create such disagreements. Slimy bastard, she thought.

"Whose directives?" Cates demanded bluntly. "I want to know who's responsible for such a bullshit policy."

"Why, the directives of my superiors, of course. As I said."

"That hardly narrows the field of suspects for me, does it, Slime-man?"

For an instant, Slaman's eyes glittered dangerously, then he smiled even more broadly than before. "That's a good one, Detective Cates. You shot me down truly with that one." He turned to Martie. "And tell me, my dear lady, are you assigned to assist Detective Cates with this case? How fortunate for a patrol deputy to be involved in such a case."

He might just as well have said "mere patrol deputy," she thought, growing more angry by the moment. Simultaneously, however, a pang of concern flashed through her.

After all, she was not supposed to be involved at all, beyond her happenstance discovery of the body. Nobody was, except Cates. And of all people in the world to be in the know, Slaman would be her last choice, especially given the transparent hostility between him and Cates.

Earlier that morning, Martie had bought a copy of the *Times* to see if any story had been run about the discovery of the body. None had. Certainly, no follow-up article connected the body with the disappearance described in the Sunday edition.

And yet Slaman surely knew the significance of the body. He had said as much, in fact—"such a case," he had called it. She had no doubt that he would find a way to reveal her participation to the right—or wrong—parties within the department, just to get even with the rangy investigator.

Cates's voice cut into her thoughts. It sounded both irritated and casual. "For Pete's sake, Slaman, she's just observing. It's her first homicide, that's all."

Slaman shifted his focus from Cates to Martie. His eyes met hers, then shifted downward so that his gaze lingered momentarily on her chest. When he looked up again, his features wore a look of undisguised lewdness. Martie felt the heat of anger and embarrassment in her face, and Slaman glanced back at Cates.

"Ah, of course," he said patronizingly, "I understand. I understand perfectly."

"Good," said Cates shortly. He brushed past Slaman and moved toward the door.

"So nice to have seen you, Detective Cates," he called after them. "And you, too, *Deputy* Griffin. I'm sure you will learn much from such a man as Mr. Cates."

As he reached his pastel-colored sedan, Cates turned to Martie. She saw that his face was grim.

"Someday," he said deliberately, "I'm going to find out if that fat bastard's head screws off or pops off."

She grinned. "Frankly, I thought you were about to do that yesterday."

Cates grimaced. "I'd like to. But he never really gives me the chance. The bastard knows how to stay just on the safe side of the line. He provokes me but always stops short of giving me the justification for using a little reasonable force on him."

"You came close yesterday."

"Over pouching the body?"

"Yes."

The tall detective's features relaxed into a crooked grin. "Nah," he said, turning and leaning against the sedan, arms folded across his chest. "That was ninety percent bullshit."

"You looked like you wanted to kill him."

"Did I?"

"Did you ever!" Martie said fervently. "One minute you're standing there, all tall and quiet and introspective looking, like some movie concept of the thinking man's cop, reflecting for a moment on the vagaries of life and death after lecturing to me about petechial hemorrhage. And then Slaman—Slimeman, that is—says no to the body bag, and you're in his face like a rabid gorilla." She gave a nervous laugh.

Cates grinned. "That bad, huh?"

"Worse. I was starting to step back so I didn't get hit by the blood spatters."

"Well," he said after a moment, "that's good. It was all an act, you know."

"What were you going to do if he didn't agree to use the body bag?"

"Use the body bag anyway."

"What do you mean?"

"Look. Maybe it isn't entirely accurate to say it was just an act. I knew he had a body bag, and I knew we were going to use it. Period. In my mind, there was never any question that we were going to pouch her. We were. I didn't care if it was the last body bag in existence." Cates grinned. "When you start from that premise, people are more apt to take you seriously."

"But what about the policy?"

"What policy?"

"What Slaman said. The directive, whatever it was, not to use bags except in...messy cases." Martie hesitated. "You didn't really have the power to back up your, well, threat. Your determination," she amended.

"Well, I'm not convinced there is any such policy. But that's not the point."

"What *is* the point?"

He thought for a moment before responding. "Maybe I didn't have the power to back it up, in the sense that I wasn't really going to physically assault him to do it. But maybe I did have the power, too. Slaman thought I had it, anyway, so I did."

Bewildered, Martie shook her head. "I don't follow you."

"Look. Power is the ability to get things done. Slaman believed we were going to use that bag, come hell or high water. He believed it because I made him believe it. So, he let us do it. We used the bag. He thought we had the power to do it, so we had the power to do it."

"Gee, I'm glad I asked."

He grinned. "At the risk of getting all philosophical on you, the appearance of power is, in fact, power."

"On the other hand," Martie responded, "to be the devil's advocate, it also sounds a lot like being a bully."

"Not to mention being a bullshitter," Cates agreed.

"So how do you draw the line?"

"Ah, but that's the crux, isn't it? To us, who wanted to bag the body, I used my power well. From Slaman's view, I'm a volatile thug and a bully."

"How do you draw the line?" Martie repeated.

"At the risk of sounding old-fashioned, it's something each person has to come to himself. I draw my own line, I guess. It's something akin to the idea of chivalry."

"Chivalry!" Martie, still smarting from Slaman's blatant sexism, felt her hackles rise. Cates, however, held up his hand.

"Chivalry. The word is misused these days. You think it means only a virile male rescuing a helpless female. Or macho knuckle-draggers in tin suits knocking each other off horses."

"Basically, yes."

"Actually, chivalry originally embodied such virtues as honor, and truth, and courage, and even pity of the downtrodden, the weak and the poor—the Arthurian legends, after all, were steeped in Christianity."

He paused and gazed into middle distance. Then he continued.

"Hell, the Holy Grail that King Arthur's boys were looking for was supposedly the chalice used by Jesus in the Last Supper. And, according to legend, it was the knights' lack of one or more of these types of virtues that kept them from finding it. And all this predated the height of chivalry."

It was all Martie could do not to gape at him.

This was Steve Cates, tall, rangy, powerful deputy sheriff, a minor legend within certain circles of the S.O., generally regarded as a loner, the man of few words. And here he was, giving a discourse on medieval philosophy. Talking about pity of the downtrodden in the same breath as experimenting on Slaman to see if his head screwed on or popped off or whatever he had said.

It boggled her mind.

"Thanks, professor," she managed at last.

Cates grinned. "Hell, Martie, you're the one using the words like 'introspective looking.'"

"Sorry."

Apparently, he wasn't going to let her off the hook so easily. "So you're younger and obviously educated. Just don't think you've got a corner on the reading market." Still leaning against the car, he tapped her foot with his toe. "Don't be an intellectual snob, for Christ's sake."

"Chivalry," she said, shaking her head.

"Like everything else, the concept degenerated and was corrupted into the jousts and duels and all that bullshit. Hell, that's natural. Do you really think the cowboy was the lean-hipped, gunfighting hero we think of? More likely he was a smelly animal herder with hemorrhoids. Or the private eye— you know what whores a lot of them really are, a far cry from the intrepid defender of right that they're made out to be."

"Whereas we, the cops, the S.O., have the corner on righteousness?" she said sarcastically.

"No."

"Well, thank you for that, at least."

"That's my point," he explained patiently. "No group does. Not cowboys or TV evangelists or private eyes or cops or the Church. And certainly not the law."

"So what do you do?"

"You have to draw your own lines. You can never completely abdicate your thinking to any group. And you have to have guidelines to do it by, and for me a lot of the concepts of chivalry seem to work." He hesitated. "Of course, you pay a price for it."

"What's that?"

"You become a loner. And, to the extent that promotions come from being part of the back-slapping blind loyalists, you have to overcome that."

"How?"

"Either you don't get promoted, or you have to be twice as good to overcome the handicap of not being one of the good old boys. You have to just try to do what's right."

"And what's right is . . . ?" she inquired.

He grinned, then spoke lightly, as if trying to lighten up the tone. "Usually, it seems to be the hardest thing. The thing you want ⎯⎯⎯⎯ 'Charge where the brush is thickest.'"

Martie listened intently. She was attempting to get a clear picture of Cates; even more, however, she was trying to reconcile her own feelings on the same topics. Though she loved being a cop, and doing a cop's job, she had the growing realization that she wasn't overly fond of a lot of the other cops. Didn't dislike them, of course, but didn't really like them, either.

She became aware Cates was looking at her.

"Sorry about the bullshit lecture," he said, a look of embarrassment on his face. "It's kind of a hobby of mine."

"Bullshit lectures are your hobby?" she needled.

He shook his head. "Studying this stuff is. Reading about it. Thinking about it. And, by the way, it happens to apply pretty directly to being a cop, also."

Martie shook her head doubtfully. "I can see what you're saying, of course. But it seems pretty hard to apply on the streets."

"The streets are where you need it most. Hell, it's easy to be...what's the word, virtuous? It's easy to be virtuous—hell, chivalrous, as I'm using the term—when your values aren't put to the test. It's like testing a jeep by driving it around the block; that's no test at all. The challenge is to use it where it's needed, in the trenches."

She didn't respond. Cates continued.

"Look. Frequently the law expects you to do things but doesn't give you the clear-cut legal tools to do it with. In those cases—and even in carrying out other duties that are more clear—you have to rely on your appearance of power."

"Command presence," murmured Martie, using the term she'd heard in the academy.

"Whatever you want to call it. It's that ability to convey to the Slamans of the world that you by God *are* going to use that bag."

Martie found herself intrigued. "How do you get it?"

"Frankly, for us, I think jail time develops it."

"How?"

"Survival. How many deputies are on a given shift at one of the big jails? Eight? Ten? Twelve, if you're lucky. Running a jail containing five or six hundred crooks, from drunks to murderers. Am I right?"

She nodded.

"So, you learn how to walk into a tank of twenty or thirty assholes—just one deputy or two deputies—and break up a fight or settle a dispute. Quiet things down. You're not armed—hell, usually, you can't be. Maybe only two or three or five of them are actually in the fight, but the rest are a powder keg that'll explode sky-high if you fuck it up."

Martie had been one of the first women deputies to work in the men's jail, the last year of her jail term. The women's jail was bad enough, but the men's was ten times worse.

"I know what you mean," she said as she nodded.

"But you handle it, don't you? You get your ass kicked a few times, and you kick ass a few times. And you learn real fast not to go in there like a bully or a thug, or you'll get thumped every time. It all develops that intangible something you call command presence."

Martie thought it over. She had to admit that she was a lot more assertive and less easily intimidated than she had been before she joined the S.O. Maybe part of that came with age, part from what Cates was describing.

"Personally," she said, "I learned something else in there as well."

"What's that?"

"They may be dirtbags, but they're human."

"The assholes?"

She nodded.

"Yeah," Cates agreed after a moment. "They are. Not all of 'em, but most. You come to see most of them as pitiful fuckers who in their own way love their mothers and kids when they aren't abusing them. And you even see a little honor and courage and coping on their part." He looked at her. "You want to know how to apply all this on the streets?"

She started to nod, but he didn't wait for an answer.

"Honor. Be honorable."

"Great," she said with a little laugh. "Do tell me how to do that."

"Easy. Just don't ever punk somebody off, not even a dirtbag."

Punk. Martie had first heard that crude term at the academy and then in the jails. On one level, it signified the forcible sodomizing—raping, actually—of one man by another, usually in jail or prison. On a more general level, as Cates was using it here, it signified a particularly degrading domination and subjugation of the "punk" by the other party.

Cates was speaking again. "You bully somebody, chew him off because you have other cops backing you up, you've punked him. And cops who work over somebody who's handcuffed, just because he ran from them, say—that's punking them off."

"Would you ever hit somebody in cuffs?" Martie asked quickly.

Cates thought for a moment. "Yeah. Maybe. In a limited sense I have, anyway. I'm not sure I'd do it again, but I can see cases where it fits. A guy in cuffs spits on me, I'd smack him. Once. He spits again, and I'd tape his head."

"Would you lie about it?"

"No. I wouldn't volunteer it, but I wouldn't lie about it. But usually you don't have to."

Martie frowned. "Why not?"

"You see, if the dirtbag thinks he has it coming to him, he doesn't feel punked. Nine times out of ten he won't beef you to Internal Affairs. But it has to be reasonable. Reasonable force."

"Whatever that is," she murmured.

"It's honor. Any force you use should be sort of proportional to the crook's force or to whatever threat it looks like you're facing. Proportional but more, of course—it better be, or you'll be getting your ass kicked every night. It just better not be too much more."

Martie started to speak, then stopped. Cates was looking straight at her as he spoke.

"You don't ever have to make it a fair fight, but you can't nuke a guy for just calling you a pig or throwing a beer bottle at you. Just use more but not a whole lot more force back.

"Can you ever shoot a clearly unarmed man?" he asked rhetorically. "Hell, yes, you can."

"When?"

"Say some pro-football linebacker type, or karate expert, is coming at you with blood in his eye, and on PCP, maybe. He isn't listening to you, and your stick bounces off his head without his even feeling it—it's proportional and not dishonorable to shoot him. Put three in the ten ring, and if he's still on his feet, put the other three there, too.

"Can you ever be *not* justified in shooting somebody coming at you with a weapon? Hell, yes. Grannie Goose is tottering at you from across the room with a knife in her hand, saying she's going to cut you. Don't shoot her. I wouldn't, anyway."

"Hold on," Martie interjected. "I've heard of cases where that happened, and it was ruled okay."

"Maybe it was," Cates responded. "But that doesn't mean it was honorable. And we don't know all the facts involved, of course." He grimaced. "But it makes me sick, some of these cops talking about how macho and tough they are, then using the letter of the law to justify blowing away somebody like that." As an afterthought, he added, "And that's a different case from the one where the cop dumps the old lady by accident because he thinks, really thinks, she's somebody else, somebody with a gun, or something."

Martie digested this for several moments, trying to sort out her thoughts.

Cates had the reputation of being the quiet type. She doubted if he had ever spoken this many words at one time to anybody else in the department.

To buy herself some time to think these things through, and to show she'd been listening, Martie commented, "So it all boils down to honor and chivalry."

Cates smiled. "As I said, 'charge where the brush is thickest.'"

"Is that one of your principles of chivalry?"

"In a way, yes. It's just a way of saying don't back off from the tough jobs."

It was easy to underestimate him, Martie thought, to see him as somebody without doubts, always in control. Or even as just a big, muscular cop. And at the same time, it was easy to overestimate him. His clowning around at the autopsy, first with her and then as they were leaving with Dr. Hastings, seemed out of character, both with the strong, silent type and even with his fervent discourse on chivalry and honor.

The man has his demons, too, she suddenly realized. For some reason, that autopsy got to him. And the humor and all the rest were simply his way of trying to control them.

Maybe.

It gave him a sort of human side, she thought, and she liked that. If she were ever again to consider dating another cop... But she wasn't. Remember, Martie, you promised yourself.

Then she remembered what she had been going to ask earlier. "So what's the deal between you and Slaman?" she inquired abruptly.

Cates looked at her, his eyes bleak. "That's another long story," he said at last.

"Does it have to do with the Braxton incident?" she persisted.

There was dead silence for about a three count. "How did you know about that?"

His tone shook her. It was flat and icy and, if not angry, then certainly not friendly. His eyes narrowed, and she could almost hear the emotional door slamming somewhere inside him. No, she thought quickly, don't shut down on me, Steve. She wanted to call back the words, to go back to the Cates of the animated discussion on chivalry and honor.

"I don't know about it," she stammered at last. "I've...just heard things here and there."

Abruptly, he pushed away from the car. He turned and unlocked the door, and she was sure he was going to get in and drive off.

"Don't believe everything you hear," he said coldly.

"Wait," she said, a feeling of desperation overtaking her. The suddenness of his reaction meant she must have made a major faux pas. "Please wait. I ... I didn't mean to pry."

He regarded her grimly, then sighed. "Yeah, I know you didn't. Sorry I overreacted."

Martie looked at him. "No. I am truly sorry to have mentioned it if it's that, well, painful. I had no idea."

"I know that."

"You want to talk about it?" She held her breath as she waited for his response, wondering if she had just blown it again by pushing it.

"Yeah," he said at last. "Yeah, I just might."

13

Braxton

MARTIE WATCHED him carefully.

Whatever the truth of the Braxton incident might be, it was apparent that it continued to deeply trouble this man who moments before had spoken with such assurance about honor and the streets. She wanted to learn it, to learn more about this enigmatic homicide cop. And, she felt a bit ashamed to acknowledge, to learn more than just rumors about the Braxton case itself.

Cates shut the door to his car and let air out of his lungs in a long, slow exhalation. Then he resumed his position of leaning against it while he apparently collected his thoughts.

"Braxton was a Fed," he began.

"FBI?"

He shook his head. "No, DEA. Drug Enforcement Administration. A narc. That was six years ago, before the FBI and the DEA were speaking to each other, let alone working together."

"Is this why you don't like the Feds?" she inquired, recalling his comment at the scene of the discovery of the body about how she could practice being a Fed by saying something negative about him in her report.

"Who said I didn't like Feds?"

Martie shrugged. "Nobody, really. Most local cops don't, that's all. And if Braxton was one, well, it stands to reason you wouldn't be too enamored of the Feds. At least, you'd have a reason."

"Well, I'm not really enamored of the Feds, on the whole." Cates made a wry grin. "But then again, I'm not really enamored of a lot of us locals, either."

That puzzled her. "What do you mean? How can you be a cop—and, from what I've heard, such a good one—if you don't like, aren't enamored of, the police system?"

"Generalizations, Griff."

"Generalizations?"

"Yep. You have to make them—rules of thumb, guidelines, that sort of thing. Inductive reasoning, drawing broad-brush conclusions about the group as a whole from the specific acts and qualities of its members. Generalizations."

Martie frowned. "You have to make generalizations," she pointed out. "Guidelines. Rules of thumb. Don't you?"

"Sure. It's okay to do it as long as you remember that they're accurate and useful only when describing the whole group, the class. But then to try to make deductions back down and apply all those features to each individual in the group, well, that's inaccurate and dangerous."

"Pardon me for asking," Martie said with a faint smile, "but what the hell are you talking about?"

"Some of the generalizations about Feds as a whole are accurate. They're in some respects a wasteful bureaucracy, managed in many cases by bureaucrats who were never cops and never will be, who don't act when they should and who grab glory when they shouldn't.

"But within that bureaucracy are a lot of really fine individual investigators. Competent, dedicated, brave law officers who are as frustrated and hamstrung by their superstructure as we are. The local cops who paint all individual Feds with all the characteristics of collective Fed-dom are making the same mistake the media make when they paint each local cop with the negative characteristics that can be used to describe the whole."

"Wow."

He apparently sensed she was kidding him. "You asked." He shrugged.

She grinned. "Yeah, I guess I did."

"Look. Not all Feds are bureaucrats. Not all local cops are macho or heavy-handed or prisoners of doughnut shops. I don't like being prejudged, and I don't like the pressure to conform to the macho images of the whole. And I especially don't like the rest of the cops who surrender their individuality to act as they think cops are supposed to act.''

''So tell me about Braxton,'' she prodded.

Cates made the wry grin again. ''Does it sound like I'm stalling?''

''A skosh.'' She said it with a long *o*.

''A skosh?''

''A little bit. A tad. A tweak.''

He took another long breath. ''Yeah. Well, Braxton was a Fed. He was one of those good-ol'-boy Texans. In his fifties, I'd say. Reddish complexion, looked low-key, and he'd feed his mother to the sharks if it served his own ends to do it.''

''You don't like him much, I take it?''

Cates paused thoughtfully. ''I gave serious deliberation to simply chucking this job and taking him out into the parking lot and breaking a few ribs.''

Martie worked to keep her face expressionless. She had no doubt from the quiet tone of his voice that Cates meant it.

''What did he do?'' she inquired at last.

''Came within one grand-juror vote of having me indicted.''

''For homicide?''

He nodded grimly. ''You've heard, haven't you?'' It wasn't really a question, and anyway he continued before she could answer. ''For manslaughter, to be accurate.''

''How did it happen?''

Cates shook his head, then gazed first at the ground and then off into middle distance. The focus of his eyes was not on any object but on some place in midair; the focus of his thoughts was on another place and time.

As a young deputy, age twenty-six, with four years on the department, he had been dispatched to meet with some agents from the DEA. The narcs had a search warrant for a house in Lakeside, where methamphetamine was believed to have been dealt.

As was sometimes the practice for such capers, the Feds notified whatever local agency had jurisdiction, so an officer could be present if the agency wanted. It also meant that if some neighbor saw the bunch of armed men sneaking up on the target house and called the local cops, the latter wouldn't send in the calvary and end up in an embarrassing gun battle with the Feds.

Early that morning, Cates had been the one dispatched. And it was when he arrived at the scene—an abandoned gas station that turned out to be actually about three blocks from the scene—that he met Braxton.

"So you're Cates, eh?" the veteran narc commented. He wore tan whipcord slacks with a carved Western belt and a trophy buckle, and he spoke with an easygoing Texas drawl. There were four other narcs there; but this man was clearly in charge.

The young deputy nodded.

"Whoo-eee, boy, you are a big son of a bitch, I'll give you that, for sure." Braxton was a good-sized man himself, Cates noted, maybe six feet and 230, give or take a little.

The 230 looked like a good deal of fat overlying some relatively solid meat, the look of an athlete grown old and made older by too many years of beef and booze.

Given the accent and the size, it wasn't difficult to imagine Braxton playing ball at Texas A & M maybe thirty years back. He'd have been good but not good enough for the pros, the kind of man who often ends up selling cars or insurance, making his quotas and getting his bonuses and occasionally talking about the glory days. He had small eyes, recessed in the fleshy face, and probably a long, zipperlike scar on at least one knee.

At that moment, the young Cates decided he didn't like Braxton very much.

Cates had been on patrol for eight months. In contrast to the more rambunctious, cocky, macho demeanors common to many cops, even then he had a quieter approach to police work.

Combined with the fact that he had been to college, it was an approach that sometimes led the macho boys to regard him as aloof, or stuck on himself. Not a team player, they muttered. In a perverse sort of way, the situation was made worse by his obvious strength and rugged physique, which made it all the more convenient for others who lacked these qualities to see his behavior as elitist or snobbish.

In truth, he was none of those things. He was simply independent, something of a loner, one who didn't like to abdicate the responsibility of decision to others. By definition this was not a popular approach. Equally by definition, that fact didn't bother him much.

Braxton, it turned out, was a longtime agent with the U.S. Drug Enforcement Administration, well respected and with a million contacts.

The DEA had always possessed the reputation for being a "kick doors, kick ass and take names" outfit, and if a few of the more complex permutations of constitutional rights got bent a little in the process, so be it.

Right or wrong, that aspect of the DEA didn't particularly bother Cates. Thoughtful loner he might be—introspective, even—but timid or fainthearted he was not. He regarded many criminal procedure decisions of the Supreme Court in the sixties and seventies, the so-called Warren court, as absurd deviations from reason and dignity, though they professed to be protecting both.

What he did object to about the DEA was a sort of bullyboy, all for one and one for all approach to police work that he too often found. He regarded it as the ultimate in the fraternity syndrome, and he both disliked and distrusted it.

Braxton, for all his affable Texas charm, had it.

"What we got here, son, is a routine search warrant for some crystal freaks. It should be no problem; just take down the place, impound the dope that'll prob'ly be there and take the bodies to jail. You wanna be involved in it, fine. You wanna just stand by, that's fine, too."

"I'll stand by," Cates agreed.

Braxton shot a keen look at him. "How long you been out on patrol, son?"

Cates felt a strange embarrassment. "About a year."

"Kicked many doors?"

"A few."

"Like to do another?"

And, in a move that he had regretted ever since, Cates ignored the little tickle in his subconscious that said no and replied, "Hell, yes, if you need the manpower."

The final plan seemed simple enough. The narcs were shorthanded, anyway—a fact that Cates would later attribute to factors other than just inadequate manpower—so it was agreed Cates would kick the door. A team of two men would make the initial entry, and Cates and Braxton would follow, the other two narcs securing the front and back of the residence.

Initially, Cates now told Martie, it had appeared to go like clockwork.

They drove to the house, a fairly large frame house in Lake side, which even then was gaining a reputation for the number of meth dealers who lived there.

Adrenaline pumping in his veins, Cates slipped quietly into position outside the door. The narcs moved into place as well. To his left and back a few feet was the entry team, each man wearing body armor and holding a workhorse .45 Government Model semiautomatic pistol. Braxton was farther off to one side, armed with a 9 mm Browning and no body armor.

Every narcotics warrant was a dangerous one, Cates knew, never mind that some veteran Fed called it a routine warrant for some crystal freaks.

Meth dealers were among the worst, because most dealers were also users, and prolonged usage of crystal inevitably caused an intense paranoia in the user.

This paranoia and the general dangers associated with being a drug dealer—they feared other crooks as much as they feared cops; robberies of dealers were common because calling the police meant admitting one was a dealer—led them to carry weapons in a high percentage of cases.

And, too, there was the funnel effect. Cates was aware of it even in those days. It was logical and inevitable and dangerous, coming through a door at the narrow end of the funnel and having to locate and react to hostile targets who could be anywhere in the wide end.

Instinctively, he unholstered his service revolver and held it in his right hand. He gripped it muzzle up, arm bent at the elbow and held close to his body so that the weapon was only a few inches from the right side of his face. His left arm came across his body, the hand gripping the heel of his right hand, ready in an instant to thrust the weapon out before him in a stable, two-handed bipod grip.

Cates had kicked a couple of doors since being in the field, and it appalled him how careless most officers allowed themselves to be in doing it. He was determined to do it right. There were enough chills and thrills in the process without unnecessarily gambling with chance.

The doorknob was to the right edge of the door.

By standing on his right leg and kicking with the left the young deputy ensured that most of his body was not in front of the door. Not only would this provide better protection if somebody began shooting through the door, but it would allow maximum room for the entry team to go through.

He rehearsed the scenario in his mind.

Make the first powerful kick, but keep balance so a second and third one can be delivered if necessary. Keep to the right, protected by the doorframe and the wall, and let the entry team in. Then immediately go in after them, scanning the wide end of the funnel, to back up the narcs if needed.

He positioned himself, weight on his right leg, and looked over at Braxton, waiting for the signal.

"Go for it, boy."

In a single powerful motion, he cocked back his left leg and slammed it forward. With a splintery crash, the door exploded inward. Simultaneously, even before he could flatten out to the right, the two-man entry team burst past him.

Cates followed immediately.

He had barely taken the first step when he heard a shouted "Freeze!" followed by multiple gunshots. The blasts from the pistols were deafening in the confines of the house.

Braxton and Cates got inside at the same time.

They were in a living room. Beyond that was an open dining area and probably a kitchen; ahead and to the right was a hallway that led to the rest of the house.

Their attention was immediately drawn to the far end of the room, the far left. Cates could see the sprawled bodies of two men, one still twitching. Blood spattered the wall behind them. The two men of the entry team were kneeling, their guns in hand, then one of them was scurrying forward, toward the fallen men, Cates assumed for the purpose of seeing if either of them had a weapon.

In virtually the same instant, a snarl and a sudden movement came from behind them and to the right, from the hallway.

Cates and Braxton were the only two who could readily respond, as they were in the line of fire between the two members of the entry team and this new threat. Moving like a younger, trimmer man, the narc wheeled and fired twice. Simultaneously, Cates had swiveled and fired as well.

He paused in his narrative to Martie. He didn't speak for several moments.

"What happened?" she finally prodded gently, though she had heard through the rumor mill already.

Two more people died, he told her.

One was an escapee from prison, a man with a long history of violence, including a conviction for assault with a deadly weapon on a police officer. The other was a hostage, being used as a shield by the con, a sixteen-year-old boy with no criminal record and no criminal involvement with the suspects.

"Did you . . ." she began, then hesitated and started again. "Did you shoot the hostage?"

He looked at her, his eyes bleak. "I don't know," he said at last. "I just don't know."

14

blank-out

CATES STIRRED restlessly, pushing himself away from the car and walking a few feet from it. He pinched the fabric of his trousers near the upper thigh of each leg and hitched them upward, then did a couple of deep knee bends. Straightening up, he shook and flexed each leg before looking back in Martie's direction.

"What do you mean, 'you don't know'?" she inquired bluntly.

He shook his head. "Just that. I just don't know."

"Do you think you did? Or may have?"

"Initially, no. At first, I was sure I didn't."

"How could you be sure?" Christ, Martie thought, it sounds as if I'm cross-examining him, as if I don't believe him. "I mean," she amended awkwardly, "how could you say you knew something like that, something so important, when you can't—when you're not sure, or don't know—later?"

He looked at her. "You know what 'calling your shots' is, Griff?"

The question startled her. "I think so. Why?"

"You hear the term used in several ways. 'Calling the shots' as in being in charge, or running the show, like telling you where to shoot. Or 'calling the shots' as in telling you where your last one landed so you can adjust your sighting for the next one."

Martie didn't speak.

Cates continued. "I'm not talking about either of those."

"What are you talking about, then?"

"I'm saying 'calling your shots' in the sense of knowing where they're going to hit, even before you see them hit, or see where they hit, actually. Sometimes even as you're shooting, or a split second before that. It's when you just know—you sense—where it's going to strike."

She nodded. "I know about it. It's happened to me a couple of times. It's almost like ESP."

He looked at her. "You really do know, don't you?"

His reaction pleased her. "Yeah. I read that sometimes athletes get the same thing, sort of a heightened perception of what's going on when they throw a ball or whatever, that they just know it's on the money or it's not." As she finished speaking, Martie saw him looking at her with surprise and respect in his eyes, and that pleased her, too.

"Exactly that." He paused. "Well, in terms of calling my shots, I knew they were dead on, no pun intended."

"You knew you didn't hit the hostage?"

He nodded. "I could feel it to a certainty. Where the bullets were going to hit, and afterward, that they had in fact hit where I felt they would. And where they hit was not the hostage, but the dirtbag. It's not that I'm such a great shot," he added, "though I practice a lot. It's just that on this occasion, I knew where they were going."

"So what's the problem?"

She could feel the hostility in his look. "Look at you," he said intensely. "You want to believe me, don't you? But even you are skeptical. And you know about this sort of thing. Am I right?"

Martie sighed. "You're right," she admitted after a moment.

"You bet I'm right. And the grand jury has precisely zero grasp on concepts like that, well-meaning though they may be."

She started to speak, but he didn't give her the chance.

"In our Western culture, we don't like to trust such seemingly vague concepts as emotion, and sensing things and how it *feels* right. We like things neat and linear. Try to talk about sensing the gestalt of things in a court of law and they'll say you're nuts."

She didn't respond immediately, giving him time for the anger to dissipate.

"So what happened?" she asked at last. "How'd something like that even get to a court of law, anyway?"

"How indeed?" he repeated.

Martie nodded. "I mean, it was clearly justifiable to shoot the convict. It might be a tragedy for the kid to be shot, his relatives might sue the department—and the DEA—but how'd it go to the grand jury?"

Even as she spoke, she recalled his cryptic outburst at the role-playing scenario, the one in which she had been the "hostage" and he had accidentally "killed" her. "You killed *him*," he had said to the deputy playing the bad guy.

Not *her*, but *him*.

Jesus, she wondered, had he been going through some kind of flashback? How callous it now seemed for him to have to role-play a situation that was so close to one he had experienced.

Ditto her own well-intended comment about his batting average, she added ruefully.

"Easy for you to say," he responded.

"That's valid, I guess."

After a moment he spoke again. The anger was gone from his voice. "You're right, of course. It shouldn't matter who hit him; it's so clearly a high-risk, crisis situation, that legally it comes into a sort of 'these things happen' category."

"I'd think so," she agreed. "So what happened?"

"At first it was all buddy-buddy. We were comrades in arms, fellow survivors of a very iffy and potentially nasty little skirmish, even if it was a hell of a long way from a real war."

"It sounds real enough for me," Martie observed.

"Yeah. A real pucker-upper, as Braxton called it." Cates grimaced. "No matter how tough we talk about police work— it's a jungle, a hail of bullets, that bullshit—four dead people in one entry is a shade over the average, wouldn't you say?"

She recognized the question as rhetorical, and made no response.

"Braxton was . . . he was strange."

"How so?"

"At first he was almost euphoric about the way things had gone. Excited. Hyper. 'Bastards had it coming,' he said. Almost gloating. 'The kid's a problem, too bad about him, but you sometimes get a few porpoises in the net.' And he copped out to it."

Martie stared.

Cates nodded. "He admitted he'd probably been the one who dumped the hostage. 'Between you an' me, son, all I saw was movement, an' I shot. It was me that did 'im, but the main thing is we got the asshole,' referring to the convict, of course."

"Nice admission," Martie commented.

"Yes. And undoubtedly true."

"So then what happened?"

"A few things started not adding up. A gun was found by the two guys they wasted by the couch."

A slow sense of uneasiness began to grow over Martie. "A throw-down?" she whispered.

He nodded grimly. "I think so."

"That's hard to believe, Steve."

"I know it is. But the gun was under the couch, right in the middle, between the two men. Not a likely place to keep a gun, and not possible to have been dropped there from their positions when they were hit. Plus, I'm sure—ninety-nine percent sure—it wasn't there when I first got a look at the room."

"Playing the devil's advocate . . ." she began.

"Yes?"

"You didn't have much time to see anything, charging in like that after the first shots. You might have missed it. Overlooked it, I mean."

"True enough," he admitted. "But where it was supposedly found, I probably would have seen it. It would have been pretty visible. And remember, one of the entry men was up there by them when I got distracted by the guys behind us."

"So he was checking to make sure they were dead, or didn't have any guns," she suggested.

"That's possible. But there's more."

She waited.

"You remember how I said Braxton called it a 'routine search warrant'? It turns out he had a tip from a confidential informant that the convict was there."

Martie thought it over. "I don't get it," she confessed at last. "Was there some connection between Braxton and the ex-con?"

He made a thin smile. "Good thinking, Griff. I didn't know about it at the time, but a few days later I found out that he used to be an informant himself."

"The ex-con?"

"The ex-con. And, he supposedly made some major case against some major dealers, only when the case went to court, he pissed backward and changed his story. The case got dismissed and everybody got sued. And you'll never guess who was the case agent who ran that informant. And who got a punitive transfer when things turned to hell on them."

"Braxton," she whispered.

"Bingo."

"Jesus."

"Yes, indeed."

Martie thought for a moment. "When was that case, anyway?"

"About four years earlier. And, because the ex-con, like a lot of CIs, was a dirtbag, he messed up and got sent back to prison on a parole violation soon afterward. And Braxton somehow sucked his way into getting the transfer rescinded. So guess who was still here when the CI got paroled?"

"My God," Martie whispered reverently. "And you think Braxton learned he was at that house, hanging out with these dealers, and went after him? To murder him?"

"Yes."

"Just like that?"

Cates nodded grimly. "Just like that. Which also might account for how there were only five of them there for the search warrant."

"Fewer to be involved," she whispered.

"Right. The Feds usually send twice as many people as they need, surround the house, plus the entry teams, et cetera. Here we had the bare minimum."

"Jesus," she repeated.

"The two supposed dealers turned out to be such little fish that I think there wasn't even any solid evidence they were dealing. They were users, sure, but that's all. Certainly not big enough for the DEA to be involved."

"What did you do?" Martie inquired at last.

"Fronted Braxton off about it."

"What did he say?"

"Said I was crazy. Said that kind of talk could get me in real hot water, or maybe even worse. And the next thing I know he's saying I dumped the hostage, and denying he did."

"Why? What would he gain from that?"

Cates shook his head. "That's not completely clear to me, either. Probably to give me a warning of what he meant about the hot water I could get into. And maybe to discredit me in advance, in case I took my theories to anybody in authority."

"But he admitted it," Martie protested. "He said he probably did it. What about that?"

He gave her a withering look. "Don't be naive, Griff."

"What do you mean?"

"Look. Of the four people in that room—me, Braxton and the two entry guys—how many do you think would testify he said anything of the sort?"

Martie felt the heat in her cheeks. "Yeah. I see what you mean."

He looked away from her for a moment. "Talk about ideals, code of honor, all that sort of thing. It's easy to have all that when the sea's smooth. It's not so easy when it's not." He was speaking almost as if to himself. "But that's when you really need 'em. When you have to stick to them. And maybe later, when it's all over, you realize they helped, after all."

"What did you do?" she inquired after a few moments.

"Voiced my suspicions."

"What happened?"

"Next thing I know, Braxton and the others are testifying in front of the grand jury, which is then considering whether to indict me for manslaughter."

"Manslaughter!" Martie was shocked. "Even in the worst-case scenario—even if they believed Braxton and didn't believe you—surely nobody could think you intended to kill the hostage."

"They didn't have to. The question was involuntary manslaughter. That only requires recklessness—gross negligence. Doing a lawful act—namely trying to shoot a bad guy—in an unlawful or careless manner, so I ended up killing somebody else. Whether I had intent to kill is irrelevant."

"Whose idea was all this?"

"What? The inquiry?"

"Yes. Who was pushing it? The D.A.?"

He shook his head. "No, I don't think so. I think Braxton somehow got the grand jury all hot to trot, and they ran with it. The D.A. knew it was no case."

"So he told *you*, anyway," observed Martie cynically.

"I saw the transcripts. He—the D.A.—was actually holding the grand jury back."

Martie considered the story. It was a nightmare come to life, a combination of chance on top of happenstance on top of luck, and all of it bad.

"So it was your word against his."

"Theirs. The entry team plus Braxton."

"Okay, theirs."

"Yeah. And, to make matters worse . . ."

She waited. He still didn't continue.

"Yes?" she prodded. "To make matters worse?"

His face was troubled. "I blanked out."

"You what?"

"Blanked it out. Forgot. For the life of me, by the time I was called before the grand jury, I'd told it so many times, I could no longer recall it." He drew a ragged breath. "I could . . . It's all crystal clear up to a certain point, and after that it's all a blank."

She had no doubt of his sincerity. She also had to admit that it sounded, well, fishy. Weak. "How did it happen?" she asked softly.

"It's as if I were watching a movie, but the film suddenly breaks. I can see it all up until the point where the crook and the hostage start to fall, and then it ends."

"You can't remember what happened next?"

He shook his head. "It's as if the film snaps, and they splice it together but there's a piece missing. Or like a gap in a tape recording—one of the grand jurors called it, 'our very own Rose Mary Woods's seven-minute gap.'"

"What did you do?"

He grinned wryly. "Developed a lot of sympathy for Rose Mary Woods."

"I mean, what did you do about the blank-out? Wasn't there any way you could get around it?"

"I tried everything. Even hypnosis." He shook his head.

"And?"

"Nothing. I know it's in there, somewhere, buried in some neurons or whatever in my mind, but I'm damned if I can get it out. I used to have dreams about it; I still do, occasionally."

"Dreams about the incident?"

"Yes."

"Can you see it in the dreams?"

Cates shook his head. "Nope. Even in the dreams, it stops short at that precise point."

Martie added it up in her mind. A well-respected, smooth, veteran DEA man versus an inexperienced and—from the grand jury's perspective—nervous young deputy sheriff.

And, if the young deputy tried to voice his suspicions about Braxton, he would no doubt be seen as trying to CYA—cover your ass.

Worse yet, when he tried to testify about the blackout, they would see it at best as a subconscious blocking of a painful memory, thus confirming that he had killed the hostage. And some of them would doubtless interpret it as what was widely regarded as the ultimate cop-out, as an affirmative, out-and-out lie—the old "I don't remember" routine.

The best result he could have hoped for in the face of all this was for the jury to decide he was a well-meaning rookie who got shook in a crisis. But if that meant his actions were reckless, he'd have been indicted for involuntary manslaughter. And if he had even tried to suggest that wasn't true because he could call his shots, they'd have been insulted and would have indicted him for sure.

Meanwhile, Braxton would have walked away scot-free.

"Did you get indicted?" she asked at last.

He shook his head. "Now you see how close it was, though. They came within one vote, actually."

"What about Braxton?"

"Got promoted and transferred. To Miami, I believe. Not punitive, of course."

"Jesus."

Nothing she had heard about the Braxton case before that morning had prepared her for this. Sure, it had been accurate or at least consistent with what Cates was telling her. However, the whispered rumors had been so superficial that they didn't begin to reflect the true depth and complexity of the matter.

Martie understood how important it was for him to formulate and cleave to his principles of honor and of doing the right thing even if it was the hard thing. That must have been what got him through and kept him going.

She wanted him to know that she understood how tough it must have been.

It occurred to her that all this had happened to him at about the same stage in his career as she now was in hers. She wanted to apologize to him for her thoughtless comment about how he was batting a thousand in real hostage cases. Even though she had meant it to be based on what she had heard—namely that he had in fact shot the right guy—she saw now how totally out of place the comment was. And she wished the matter could be solved, could be put right somehow, to vindicate him.

A sudden thought occurred to her. "What about the ballistics?" she asked excitedly.

"What about them?"

"Couldn't a firearms expert recover the slugs from the bodies and tell whose gun they came from? And didn't you say the narcs had .45s? Just looking at the entry wounds ought to tell you if it was his .45 or your .357, shouldn't it?"

He looked at her. "You ought to be in homicide," was all he said.

"Well? Am I right? A .45 should make a hole about a half inch across, and a .357 is only, well, a third of an inch."

"Close but distinguishable," he murmured.

"Well?"

"Not all the DEA guys had .45s. The entry guys had them, but Braxton had a 9 mm. And a 9 mm is almost identical in diameter to a .38 or a .357. You can't tell the difference from the entry wounds."

"What about the ballistics, the firearms comparison, or whatever you call it? Couldn't they determine that from the slugs?"

"Good point."

"Well?"

"They lost the evidence."

"Lost it?"

"Yeah. The slugs out of the body were lost. They lost them."

"They? Who's they?" she demanded. "How could they lose them on a case like this? Who lost them?"

"The coroner's office."

Now, at last, it dawned on her. "The coroner's office?" she repeated weakly.

"Yes."

"And the coroner's officer was . . ."

"You got it. Slaman."

15

Winston Keith

As HE DROVE AWAY from Martie and the morgue, Cates felt possessed by the foulest of moods.

Though he realized the futility, he was filled with old resentments and new angers. Anger at this case. Anger at the press and the FBI for meddling. Anger at the puzzle of how a blow could destroy a young woman's heart but leave no other tissue damaged.

Resentment of Slaman, for the events of yesterday and of the Braxton caper that seemed a lifetime ago. Anger at Martie for having heard about it, even. Of course she would have heard about it; it was one of those legends within the department that seemed to have a life of its own.

Anger at Braxton; anger at himself for still not having completely shaken it off and for telling Martie about it.

Cates also felt a very real anger—an anger at once both vague and specific—that a pretty young woman, in good health, only a few years past twenty, should be dead, her body carved open in the necessary search for evidence, her soul God only knew where.

He glanced at his watch. Eleven-fifteen; it would take a good twenty or twenty-five minutes to get to the offices of the Homicide Division. Then he could kill fifteen minutes and go to lunch.

Right.

It had taken his whole life to learn the principle that denial and resistance only intensified the damage caused by anger. It was akin to being caught in a riptide in the ocean—fight it, and you'll spend far more energy and possibly be taken under. Far better to go with it, let it wash over you and take you where it will. Soon, its force leaves you behind or is dissipated, and then your energy can be used to swim back to shore.

He drove to Mission Bay, a bright azure blue in the spring sunshine. At the public rest rooms he changed into his running gear—trunks and his one indulgence, top-of-the-line New Balance shoes designed for the punishment generated by a 220-pound runner—and for the next thirty minutes did a slow, easy 3½ miles.

He deliberately made it slow.

So slow nobody would fall in beside him. So slow he wouldn't be tempted to fall in beside some serious runner to push himself. So slow he could resist the temptation to speed it up just a little to stay within twelve feet of one of several delightful feminine posteriors whose owners were also running around the bay.

It was meditation more than exercise.

By one o'clock, he was back at Homicide, his emotional turmoil largely gone. He spent the remainder of the afternoon behind his desk, doing the reports he had not done Monday because he had been working with the body. It was slow going, in part because there were so many unanswered questions, so many issues he had to skirt or omit at this point in the case.

He also called Joyce Kennedy at Data Research to find out what approvals he would need to go through Beth's desk, which he planned to do the following day. She seemed glad to hear from him, and agreed to arrange an entry.

And, though it probably wasn't necessary, he drafted a search warrant for the desk and any other facilities used by Beth Fisher at DRT. As Lieutenant Beecham had remarked when Cates mentioned the idea of a search warrant, "Yeah, it probably isn't necessary, except on the remote chance the suspect happens to share the same desk or some such bullshit. But is this the case you wanna chance not doing it?"

Cates had to agree with his logic.

Shortly after four that afternoon, Lieutenant Beecham hailed him. "Cates."

"Lieutenant," he acknowledged.

"I need a briefing."

"You name it."

"My office. Tomorrow morning. 0830."

"Got it."

"Yes, but you're about to get it some more, unless I can change the sheriff's mind." Beecham stomped off, thus preventing any further discussion on the topic.

What in the hell, Cates wondered, had he meant by that?

Usually, the lieutenant backed his men if at all possible. Sometimes, though, the nature of his position caused him to have to do the dirty work for those above him. And, whatever his cryptic remark had referred to, his tone suggested he wasn't entirely happy with it.

Shortly before nine o'clock Wednesday morning, Cates found out why.

He had just finished bringing Beecham up to date on the investigation. They sat across from each other in the lieutenant's office, the desk between them. Beecham, sitting upright in the swivel chair with his arms folded across his chest, listened intently. Apart from an occasional clarifying question, he let Cates tell his story uninterrupted.

"So what do you make of it?" he said when Cates concluded.

"Hard to tell. I'm going to check out where the victim worked, this Data Research place, and go through her stuff there."

"Any idea what you're looking for?"

"Nothing specific. Address books, notes to herself, appointment calendar, maybe. It's remotely possible I'll find something helpful." He thought for a moment. "And there's always the slight chance I'll come across something that ties this in to her job."

"Such as?"

"I don't know. I'll just be looking for whatever's there. You know as well as I do, though, that most of the time these murders turn out to be relatively straightforward, no matter how exotic they appear at first."

"Think so?" the lieutenant said after a few moments.

"Yeah. Apart from the weird circumstances, it'll probably turn out like any other 187."

"Something not related to her work, you mean." Beecham said it as a statement, rather than a question.

Cates shrugged. "Odds say so. Boyfriend, girlfriend, ex, a lover's triangle, something like that. Except for the FBI's interest, the possibility of it being some big spy-versus-spy caper is about nil."

"But?"

"But what, Lieutenant?"

Beecham unfolded his arms and swiveled sideways in the chair. Resting one forearm on the desk, he began rapping his knuckles against the surface distractedly.

"I know what experience says, Steve, but you seem doubtful about it. I can't put my finger on what you're doing to make me feel this way, but this doesn't smell right, somehow."

"I told you—" Cates began, but Beecham interrupted.

"I know what you told me. But I get the impression either you're holding back on me, or you're not sure in your own mind."

"Maybe I'm not sure in my own mind," Cates allowed at last.

"Like how?"

"Like my head tells me one thing, but my gut contradicts it." And, he thought in silent apology, I'm holding back something, but nothing relevant to this.

Lieutenant Beecham nodded and emitted a sigh.

"I'm inclined to agree with you. However—" The buzz of the com line on the telephone cut him short. Glancing at his watch and making a face of irritation, he answered it.

"Beecham."

Cates could hear the voice of the receptionist, though he couldn't make out the words.

The lieutenant spoke again. "Keep him there for two minutes, then send him on back." He slammed the receiver down and glared at Cates.

"Cates."

"Yeah."

"I'm sorry to have to tell you this. You're getting a partner."

So that was it, Cates thought. But there had to be more to it than just that fact.

"Not Grummon, obviously," he observed.

"No. Nobody from Homicide."

"Jesus Christ!" Cates said with a disgusted shake of his head. Not from Homicide could mean...who? Somebody from Internal Affairs, possibly? Somebody handpicked by the sheriff, or Tisdale? An investigator from the D.A.'s office or the attorney general's office, perhaps?

"No," Lieutenant Beecham said in response to Cates's blasphemy. "Not him. Unfortunately."

"Who is it?"

"The worst."

"I.A.?"

"Worse than that."

"What could be worse than that?"

"A Fed."

"A Fed?" Cates's heart sank.

"A Fed."

"Jesus, why me of all guys, Lieutenant?"

"I know, Cates, I know. At least it isn't the DEA." He probably meant it as a heavy-handed attempt to lighten the situation, Cates realized, but it didn't help.

"So it's not the DEA. Who is it? The Feebs? The CIA? The NSA? The Watergate committee? Or is it Sister Sue's Sewing Circle?"

Lieutenant Beecham shook his head. "It's the Feebs. Direct orders from Tisdale. Or from the sheriff, actually, through Tisdale."

Cates was incredulous. "*The sheriff* ordered me to work with the FBI?"

"Yes."

"Why, for Christ's sake?"

"I don't know why." The lieutenant leaned across the desk and lowered his voice. His lips were tight, his voice showing some effort to control it. "Look, Cates. You know the sheriff doesn't like anybody from outside the department shitting in our mess kit. You know that. Whatever it is, there must be some damn good reason for him to do this."

"God*damn* it." Cates sighed wearily.

"Nut up, Cates," snapped Beecham. "You think I like it? Well, I don't, but that's how it is."

"Yeah. You're right," Cates admitted after a moment. "Yeah, sorry, Lieutenant. Didn't mean to turn into a WSM," he said, using the unofficial department abbreviation for whining, sniveling malcontent. "I thought we just agreed there was probably no spy-versus-spy stuff, that's all."

"I don't think there is," Beecham repeated.

"So why exactly am I getting a Fed for a partner?"

"The Feebies are evidently making a routine inquiry into some national security aspects of this—"

"Which they probably won't tell us about," Cates interrupted.

"Which they won't tell us about," Lieutenant Beecham confirmed equably. "They've assigned a man to work on it side by side with you."

"Is he from the local field office?"

"I gather not. He's from some special strike force or task force."

"Great."

"You know how the Feds are, Steve. They create a special force for things that anybody else does as part of the job."

"Yeah."

"If the Feds ran our department, a deputy wouldn't be 'working patrol out of Lemon Grove'—he'd be 'attached to the East County regional street crime suppression and response task force.' Anyway, the sheriff agreed to it. And he did it for reasons only he knows but that we have to believe are valid or he wouldn't have done it."

Cates thought that over, wondering what those reasons could be.

The lieutenant apparently misinterpreted his silence. "Steve, you know he feels as strongly about it as you or I. Now, your orders are to investigate this thing along with this guy. You're the lead investigator, of course, so you control what happens. Dot all the i's and cross all the t's. Investigate the shit out of it. Write good reports, and give a copy to your new partner.''

"No sweat, Lieutenant.''

"Good. As we said, it'll probably turn out to be a routine 187, so the whole thing will end up as just a PR trip for the department. A shining example of federal–state cooperation, that sort of thing. You'll be expected to interact with him just as you would with Grummon or any other real partner.''

"Is he an attorney?''

"Who?''

"My new partner. Seems like most of the Feebies are attorneys or CPAs.''

Lieutenant Beecham nodded. "Now that you mention it, I believe he is.''

Cates allowed himself to backslide into the WSM mode just a little. "Not only a Fed but an attorney.''

"Whatever he is, Cates, you'll treat him like any other partner you ever had. Of course...'' Beecham hesitated.

"Yeah?''

"Of course, if we are incorrect about this case, and you should happen to develop any really exotic theories, far-out ideas that might explain what the hell is going on here, you may wish to share them initially with others inside our department—namely me—rather than with your new federal friend. You get my drift?''

"I get it.''

"Good. 'Orders is orders,' even if we don't like them. 'You point, we march.' You know how it goes, Steve.''

"Yeah. I know how it goes.'' Better to sound morose than to snivel, Cates thought.

"Look at it this way. The sheriff has a lot of faith in you, I figure, or he wouldn't have put this in your lap.''

"Yeah.''

"Well, it's true.'' Beecham shrugged.

"Maybe.'' As an afterthought, Cates added, "Tisdale sure seemed to have a lot of faith in me the other morning.''

"That's Tisdale."

Before the lieutenant could respond further, a large dark shape appeared through the frosted glass on the office door. Moments later there came three quick knocks.

Cates looked at Beecham. "This him?"

"It must be." Raising his voice, the lieutenant responded to the knock. "Come in."

The door opened, and a man stepped inside. "Lieutenant Beecham? I'm Special Agent Winston Keith with the FBI." He looked at the two men. "I go by Winston," he added.

Special Agent Winston Keith looked young, maybe late twenties, Cates estimated. He wore an expensive-looking three-piece blue suit over a light pink shirt with a red-and-gray-striped tie. His shoes were a dark burgundy color Cates used to call oxblood, and were polished to a soft, high gloss. He stood about six-and-a-half feet tall, and he was black.

Real black, as Lieutenant Beecham put it later. Black and cultured and with his head shaved bald and shiny like Lou Gossett.

The lieutenant rose to his feet and extended his hand. "Come in, ah, Winston," he said smoothly. "I'm Lieutenant Beecham." They shook hands, and the lieutenant gestured to Cates, who had also gotten to his feet. "And this is Detective Steve Cates."

The FBI man extended his hand. "Steve," Winston said.

"Winston," Cates said.

"Gentlemen," Lieutenant Beecham said. "Good to have you aboard, Winston. You'll be working with Cates, here, in case you hadn't guessed. I'll leave it to the two of you to work out the details, but make sure you keep me posted as to what's going on. Fair enough?"

Cates nodded.

"Thank you, Lieutenant," said Winston, inclining his head slightly.

Beecham continued. "Very well, then. I'll leave you to your own devices. And good luck."

THE HOMICIDE OFFICES, located in an anonymous building on
a side street near the San Diego Sports Arena, were actually
situated in the middle of the city, even though the sheriff's
primary jurisdiction lay outside the city limits. Cates and
Winston threaded their way through the small and hopelessly
inadequate parking lot toward Cates's sedan.

The gravel made little crunching sounds beneath their feet
as they walked in silence.

"So," Cates said at last, "what makes all you guys so
special, anyway?" He meant the question to come out as more
of a jest, but he could hear the sarcasm in his voice even as he
spoke.

"What do you mean?" Winston's response was made in the
same smooth, rich tone as his initial introduction. If he noticed the sarcasm, his voice didn't reveal it.

"You're all Special Agent this or Special Agent that. Not
just Agent this or that. Is that just some kind of PR thing, or
what?"

Winston moved his features in the shape of a smile. "Actually," he replied, "I've heard that it indicates limited powers, rather than something more or special. In the common
law, a general agent was somebody authorized to do anything
on behalf of his principal, whereas a special agent could act
only in limited areas."

"That so?"

"It's one explanation."

"Huh," Cates grunted noncommittally.

He unlocked the passenger door of the D-unit and then
walked around to his own side. Moments later, they were
wheeling out of the lot.

"Where are we going?" Winston inquired finally.

The area was chiefly wholesale, light industry and commercial services such as contractors' supply houses. A few blocks
over lay Midway Street and, intersecting it so as to form another side of the square, Rosecrans. Beyond that several top-
less bars and nude theaters were scattered, and still farther were
the Naval Training Center and the Marine Corps Recruit De-

pot. Pickup trucks and vans crowded the narrow road. Cates slowed to allow the car ahead to turn into a narrow driveway.

"I don't know how much they told you," he responded. "I'll get you a copy of my reports so far as soon as the typist finishes them. At any rate, the dead woman worked at a place called Data Research and Technology."

"That much I was told. It's outside of La Jolla. The Golden Triangle, as I understand it."

"Yeah. That's where we're going. First, though, we have to go to the D.A.'s office downtown and get a search warrant."

After a moment, Winston asked, "Are they expecting us?"

"Who? The D.A.'s office or DRT?"

"Both."

Cates shrugged. "I've already got the warrant and affidavit written out and typed. The D.A. just has to approve it, which shouldn't be any problem. Then we find a judge to sign it, that's all."

"And the people at Data Research?"

"Yesterday I called the woman who first found the victim was missing. She was supposed to clear the way for me." He looked at Winston. "Of course, that was before I knew you'd be working with me. But surely your federal strike force status and FBI credentials ought to open any doors we need open."

"Task force," Winston corrected.

"What's the difference?"

The tall black agent grinned. "Strike forces strike, and task forces do tasks, I suppose." He sighed. "Strike sounds more impressive somehow, doesn't it?"

Cates didn't respond immediately. They rode along in silence for a few moments before he spoke again.

"Winston."

"Yes?"

"Just what is your interest in this caper?"

"My instructions are to assist you in the homicide investigation."

"Yeah, but why? And to hell with your instructions. Feds don't investigate homicides. Especially strike fo—task forces.

Us locals investigate homicides. Unless they occur in federal enclaves, of course, which this one didn't.''

"True."

Cates took a breath. "So, what's the deal? Are you looking into some supersecret, hush-hush national security angle? Or are you just here to see that I do it right, look over the shoulder of the inept locals? Make sure I don't miss something."

Or make sure that I do, it suddenly occurred to him for some reason. Why the Feds would want to steer him away from some aspect of the case, however, remained a mystery. Still, even as the thought surfaced, he mentally jotted it onto another imaginary three-by-five card and filed it under Hmm.

"A fair question," Winston acknowledged.

"Thank you."

In his peripheral vision, Cates was aware that Winston's eyes widened slightly. From anger, probably, or at least irritation, because there wasn't anything else to cause it.

Finally, Winston spoke in his smooth, cultured voice. "Certain persons within the Bureau felt that the disappearance and subsequent death of a computer operator at a company whose primary business is research and development for the defense department merited looking into. As a representative of the Defense Security Task Force, I was tapped to do the looking."

"Anybody ever tell you you sound like a Harvard lawyer?"

"I should hope so. That's where I went to law school."

"Are you serious?"

"Completely."

"Jesus. Harvard law grad, you could write your ticket with any major law firm in town. Probably in the country. Why the FBI?"

"It's what I wanted."

"The best reason there is," Cates admitted after a moment.

Winston went on with his explanation. "Those same persons knew, of course, that the Sheriff's Department would be conducting its homicide investigation. And, you may be gratified to know, when your name was revealed as the detective, at least a couple of them professed respect for your reportedly considerable abilities.''

Cates didn't say anything.

"On the other hand, there were also allusions to your personality that were less complimentary.''

"Oh, yeah?"

"Something about being hardheaded. I believe the word *intractable* was used at least once.'' Winston's teeth made a brilliant white slash in his gleaming black face.

"Intractable, huh. What's that mean?''

Winston chuckled faintly. "I think you know exactly what *intractable* means. Try hardheaded. Stubborn. Rebellious. Difficult to control, among other choices.''

"Well, that's something," Cates said approvingly. "Tell me, were you sent here to make me more tractable?''

"Who knows? I might add that other terms were employed to describe other aspects of your character, as well.''

"Yeah?"

"Yes. The term *goddamn chameleon* was one such. As you might have guessed, that was not the same person who called you intractable.'' Winston grinned and continued. "In fact, I don't think that individual knows what *intractable* means.''

"Chameleon?" Cates wrinkled his brow. "Like a lizard, or whatever it is?"

With disarming candor, Winston looked over at him. "I was told not to take you at face value. That you could switch from a dumb cop to an executive-suite smoothie to a bass-fishin' good ol' boy, one right after the other and all convincingly. Not to underestimate you, in other words.''

"Pity."

"What is?"

"That you're not going to underestimate me.''

"Ah," said Winston significantly, "a response calculated to assist me in doing precisely that.''

Cates turned his head and looked at Winston. By then they were on the freeway, Interstate 5 southbound, toward San

Diego, and the traffic was relatively light. Finally, he spoke again.

"What makes 'those persons' within the Bureau believe this might be anything but a routine homicide? That it bears looking into, in other words? Surely the mighty F. B. of I. and your task force don't investigate every time a security-cleared person dies under strange circumstances."

"That's correct. But these are extraordinarily strange circumstances, you must admit."

"What? You think she was questioned or tortured or something after she was snatched but before she was killed?"

"The possibility was raised."

"What would she know? Or have access to? As I understand it, she was a relatively new employee. The security clearances weren't even in the mill, yet, let alone out of it."

"Good point. Those facts were mentioned, by me, in fact."

"And?"

"And there was still some concern she might have been, ah, talked to, before her death."

"Well," Cates said, "she wasn't. I saw the body, and I attended the autopsy. I didn't see any signs she was worked over."

"Nor did we," agreed Winston smoothly. "Although it's always possible drugs were used, so there wouldn't necessarily be any marks. We'll know better after the toxicology tests are completed."

With a certain effort, Cates controlled the impulse to gape at the tall black FBI man. Instead, he spoke casually, as if the same thoughts had occurred to him. Best not to show his amazement that the Bureau had been in on the case from the outset. Not to mention, he thought ruefully, that they, at least, had been taking seriously what his gut had told him, that the case might not be a routine murder.

"What? You're thinking scopolamine or sodium Amytal or something like that?"

"Those, or some of the newer ones that I gather exist."

"I wondered about Dr. Hastings," Cates said at last.

"An excellent doctor, apparently. Well respected and, incidentally, highly cleared."

"Did the FBI set it up so that he did the post?"

"I was given to understand that," Winston replied. "He, or his staff, have to do a few anyway as part of a contract. It was a relatively simple matter to steer this one to him."

Cates considered all this in silence.

Obviously, the forces at work here were considerably larger in scope than he had originally suspected. He had been approaching the case as an ordinary homicide, one with fairly simple and predictable parameters. In fact, it now appeared he had only been dealing with one small segment of a much larger machine—there were wheels and gears turning that he had not even suspected and had no knowledge of.

His first reaction was a sort of childish, self-righteous anger, a "by God what gives *them* the right to do this" emotion. Simultaneously, however, he realized the futility of so feeling; things were as they were, period. It would do just as much good to bitch about the weather not being the way he wanted it.

A more constructive and immediate task would be to find out just what was involved. More specifically, to find out who "those persons" was.

He could think of a couple of ways to do that.

Sometimes, he thought, you meet force head-on with greater force. The frontal assault. "Charge where the brush is thickest."

Sometimes, though, Cates had found that a more flexible approach produced better results.

Beginning a couple of years ago, Cates had studied the Chinese martial art t'ai chi ch'uan.

He had learned that t'ai chi was developed from the ancient Taoist beliefs that the soft and the yielding would ultimately prevail over the hard and the rigid. This led to its sometimes being called a soft martial form, as opposed to the so-called hard martial arts like karate. While the latter frequently involved meeting one blow with another, the Taoists believed this collision of energies would often result in damage to both.

In t'ai chi, then, the philosophy was to avoid and deflect a direct physical attack, then turn the attacker's own force back against him, enhanced, perhaps, by one's own internal energy or *chi*. Cates still practiced the t'ai chi form—a series of stylized motions representing combative techniques—on a relatively regular basis.

As he considered what Winston had revealed, Cates was initially tempted to get a little aggressive about the whole thing.

Make a stink.

Protest the fact that the FBI had apparently assumed an active role, albeit a hidden one, a shadow role, in the investigation from the outset. Demand an explanation, blunder about and incidentally see what he could learn from the reactions.

Charge where the brush was thickest, in other words. Dynamite the mountain and see what comes out.

Something told him not to, however. His gut said that low-key would be better. Be soft. T'ai-chi it, so to speak. Keep centered, keep his own balance, and see if the other guy gets off balance. And, Stevie, he said to himself, you can always make a frontal assault later, if need be.

"Well," he said offhandedly, "you went first class, anyway. Hastings is the best there is."

Winston did not respond.

"Anyway," Cates continued, "apart from the suspicious circumstances of Beth Fisher's demise, what made the FBI so interested? Is there something, some inside information, an informant, maybe, that makes them suspect this isn't routine?"

"I would suspect so," replied Winston in a forthright tone. "However, they haven't told me if there is."

Cates noted the apparent frankness of the special agent's response. It inspired confidence, a certain comradeship, "us two together in the trenches." Moreover, it made it easy to underestimate Winston himself.

Might as well do what he could to turn it around. "Thanks for the candor," he said.

"You're welcome."

They rode in silence. What in the hell is going on? Cates
wondered.

Lieutenant Beecham was right about one thing. More accurately, he was right about several things.

Sheriff Ramsey was as independent as they came when it
came to the workings of his department. For him to have
agreed to allow an FBI agent to second-chair the investigation
meant that he had a very good reason for doing it. And the
reason had to be more than simply the pressure from the
newspaper article; the sheriff was no stranger to ill-founded
negative publicity in the media.

Maybe it was a PR thing, after all. Show how well the department would cooperate with the Feds. And, in the process,
build up an IOU from the FBI, something he could call in at
some future time if he needed it.

Or maybe there was something to the national security aspect, after all, though he doubted it.

Still, the lieutenant had made it plain that Cates was to report anything along those lines ASAP, so anything was possible. Maybe the sheriff was friends with somebody at Data
Research and Technology, and therefore wanted an independent agency like the Bureau present to avoid even the slightest
innuendo that the department had shaded the investigation in
any way.

Whatever it was, Cates was willing to bet that Ramsey had
done it for reasons of his own, and not simply because of
pressure—from the FBI or anybody else.

Moreover, though Cates instinctively disliked the arrangement, he had been pleasantly surprised by Winston Keith.

First, he ruefully had to admit, he had been taken aback that
the man was black. More important, however, he had to admit the man seemed likable, even in the brief exchange in
Lieutenant Beecham's office.

He had expected some self-important preppie twerp with a
fifteen-inch neck and absolutely no street experience. Instead, Winston looked like the type of guy who, if he met him
at the gym, he could like as a friend. And, he looked as if he
knew what a gym was.

But he was still a Fed, notwithstanding his cultured voice and apparent candor. And it would do for Cates not to forget that, no matter how well the two might get along otherwise.

He recalled what some prosecutor—Jim Santos, probably—had once said about defense attorneys.

A whole lot of them were sleazeballs and anarchists, but some were honorable, nice guys, just doing their jobs. "They're simply the other side of the same criminal justice coin, no more, no less," Santos had said. "Prosecutors are just a little taller, a little better-looking on the whole," he had quipped.

But then he had become serious. Even the good defense attorneys, the ones whom you can basically trust on a professional basis, you shouldn't get too chummy with. You can like them, have a drink with them, swap stories, but always remember that their interests are not your interests.

Don't trust them, in other words.

Good advice, thought Cates, in this setting as well. Whatever Special Agent Winston Keith's interests were, they were not Steve Cates's—or the sheriff's—interests, even if Winston turned out to the the most likable guy in the world.

That was how he'd play it, then. He would work with Winston, try to get along with him, even like him. But not trust him. Most of all, not trust the agency he worked for.

Cates decided to be disarming a little, to try to make it appear as if he'd been taken in by Winston's burst of candor.

"Sorry if I sounded hostile," he said. "This case is just getting on my nerves is all."

"No sweat." The FBI man was all agreeable.

"I mean, it's a weird one to begin with. And then the press somehow gets the jump on it. I've got the sheriff breathing down my neck, watching my every move."

"A handle-with-care package," Winston observed sympathetically.

"Yeah." Cates winked and shook his head. "And then I find out I gotta be doin' some goddamn ebony and ivory number, playin' hush-hush 'I spy' with some seven-foot super-spook, if you'll pardon the pun." He grinned what he hoped was his most folksy grin.

"Let's not get racist, white boy," responded Winston, grinning even more broadly than Cates had.

Cates couldn't tell if Winston had swallowed any of his act or not. "So," he said at last, "how the hell tall are you, anyway?"

"Not seven feet." Winston chuckled in his deep, rich voice. "Six-six. How about you?"

"Six-three."

"What's your body weight?" Winston inquired in the peculiar, somehow formal phrasing that for some reason was common to weight lifters, rather than a more casual "How much do you weigh?" Well, that figured, thought Cates. The guy looked like a jock.

"Two-twenty."

"Same here."

"Skinny bastard, aren't you?" Cates said with his wide, easy grin.

"Lean," Winston corrected him. "Lean and fit is what I am." His black face split into a smile. "Hell, man, aren't you going to ask me if I played basketball?"

"I figured you did," Cates responded with a wink. He took the off ramp from the freeway, then rolled to a stop at the bottom of it. "Tall black dude, you must have. But I know how sensitive you people are about being stereotyped. So naturally I wasn't going to ask."

"You haven't exactly been too concerned about my feelings so far," Winston pointed out. "And you came right out and asked me about my height. What's next? You going to say something about whether I have a big dick?"

The contrast between the crudity of the question and the cultured voice that delivered it made Cates suddenly laugh out loud. "Funny how that's the one stereotype I never hear a black dude objecting to," he observed.

Winston chuckled. "You got that right."

By the time they found a vacant red No Parking zone to park in at the county courthouse, Cates realized he didn't know any more about the case than he had earlier. And that was essentially nothing. The case was a bucket of worms.

On the other hand, he now knew it was a lot more complex than he had initially imagined. And, he mentally amended, I now know that I have to be very, very careful. And that was progress of sorts.

"Winston?" he said at last.

"Yes?"

"I'm not intractable."

"No?"

"No. Firm of purpose, yes. Intractable, no."

"I see."

"You'd better see." Cates winked at him. "Or I'll kick your ass."

16

The Bush

JOYCE DIDN'T WANT to admit it, but she had been looking forward to seeing Cates again.

He had been so professional, efficient yet understanding, the preceding Friday at Beth's apartment. And he had called her Monday afternoon to let her know that Beth's body had been found. "Don't run out and tell the papers, they'll get it soon enough," he had said. "But I didn't want you to hear about it first from the papers."

When he called again, this time to request her assistance in getting him into the company to go through Beth's desk, Joyce had initially half expected that he would trot out some sort of macho come-on to her.

She had expected it, and she had hoped it wouldn't occur.

If it happened it happened, of course, but it would spoil it for her. And, if it happened, she was fully prepared to put a major squelch on him.

However, to her delight he had turned out to be just as professional then as earlier. He sounded tired, but also so formal as to be almost proper, in fact. She finally decided her concerns had actually been insurance of sorts, a hedge, a warning to herself not to be too attracted, that the grapes were probably sour, anyway.

Accordingly, she had been only too happy to arrange the clearances necessary for him to get in to do whatever he had to do with respect to Beth's stuff. Frankly, she found herself attracted to the rangy, powerful-looking detective.

She called Security to find out what was required to get access for Cates to the classified area of DRT. The security officer, a stolid type named Mike Stevens, had said hold on a moment, he'd have to check. In fact, it had taken more like three or four minutes, and then he'd come back on the line and told her to see Pam Hotch.

"Pam Hotch?" Joyce exclaimed in dismay. "Why Pam?"

Pam was the Executive Secretary—both words capitalized, thought Joyce sourly—to Dr. Frank Umbeck, head of the Technical Applications Division. She was also cordially detested by virtually everybody who came into contact with her, including Joyce.

"The Fisher woman worked in that division," the security man responded.

"So?"

"So they have to clear the search. I can give him the pass to get into the facility. And where her desk was located is in only a minimally secured area, so I can get him up there."

"I don't see the problem," Joyce said.

"The problem is that because the Fisher woman worked for Technical Applications, the final access to her desk has to be under their supervision. And Pam Hotch is the one with all the tickets to do that, apart from Dr. Umbeck, of course."

"Damn."

"You know how it is, Joyce," he said sympathetically. "I can't change it."

She considered it grimly. He was right, of course. There didn't seem to be any way around it. Finally, she shrugged, forgetting he couldn't see her over the telephone.

"All right, Mike," she said with a sigh. "I know how it is. If you'd arrange initial access, to get him into the facility, I'll talk to Pam about the rest."

"No problem."

Joyce hung up the telephone. For several moments she stubbornly tried to think of some way to avoid going through Pam. Then, with yet another audible sigh, she reached for the receiver and punched the numbers for Pam's extension.

Pam Hotch, age thirty-four, was the quintessential bitch of Data Research and Technology.

No, thought Joyce, "bitch" somehow didn't say it. Even "quintessential bitch" failed, somehow, to capture Pam's character. "Consummate bitch" was more like it.

Might as well call a spade a spade. Pam was a cunt.

Joyce hated that word. She despised its sexual—and sexist—connotations. In her mind, it was a degrading, shameful, disgusting term of opprobrium.

It conveyed every conceivable negative quality that could be associated with the female gender. It described a person who was conniving. Complaining. It conveyed sullenness. Being spoiled. It communicated bitch-ness, a word distinct from bitch*i*ness, which in her view was something more superficial, associated with behavior rather than character, and something that men were equally capable of being.

But the worst aspect of being a cunt as far as Joyce was concerned, was that the term suggested cheating, getting by with things that others couldn't, perpetuating the unequal treatment of women by exploiting the fact that they were women.

Yes, Joyce hated the term. And yes, Pam Hotch was one.

Pam had that unique ability to arouse instant, reflexive desire to support the opposite viewpoint from hers. It didn't matter what the subject was; if Pam said *X*, one automatically saw merit in "not-*X*." A militant feminist herself, Pam could have made even Gloria Steinem crusade against the women's movement.

Pam was tall and lean. She had aquiline, hawklike features and thick hair, dark brown but not black, that she wore, as one of the programmers described it, in "natural kink."

Though she apparently bathed regularly—she didn't have BO, anyway—Pam didn't shave under her arms, and frequently allowed her legs the same leeway. Apart from her grooming, however, she was arrogant, pushy and rude. She behaved in that fashion not simply to persons below her own rank within the company, but to all who fell below Dr. Umbeck's rank. Since he was one of the senior VPs, that afforded considerable latitude for her rudeness.

In startling contrast to his executive secretary, Dr. Frank Umbeck, the head of the Technical Applications Division, was a kindly, professorial type.

He was short and bow-legged and had pink cheeks and thinning white hair. One of the original founders of DRT, he was brilliant on the technical side of things. On management issues, Joyce had heard, he was living proof of the Peter Principle that one will rise to his level of incompetence.

To put it bluntly, she thought, he was too nice a guy and too absentminded to head a division. She suspected that if he hadn't held some of the early key patents, and hadn't worked seventy hours a week trying to be both researcher and manager, he'd have been knifed in the back by one of the DRT sharks long ago.

He was, she thought sourly, the perfect boss for Pam, from the latter's perspective.

To Dr. Umbeck, Pam was both mother and adoring daughter. In many things, she was ingratiatingly, worshipfully servile, and treated him with the utmost consideration. In other areas, she looked out for him and protected him.

She ran interference for him within the company. She screened his calls with efficiency. On another front, she remembered the birthdays of his family members and supplied him with cards for his signature. These qualities, coupled with the fact that she was ruthlessly competent at the thousand and one administrative duties the executive secretary had to perform, allowed her to survive despite her attitude toward others.

It also enabled her to virtually run the Technical Applications Division.

When reports of her behavior to others reached Dr. Umbeck, either directly or indirectly, he seemingly didn't understand or didn't care. On the outside, he was wont to affect a vague absentmindedness that swallowed up the criticism in a cloud of kindly tolerance.

"That Hotch female," Joyce once heard one of the other VPs remark to Dr. Umbeck, "why on earth do you keep her around, Frank?"

"Eh? What do you mean?"

"She's so rude."

"Rude?" It was as if he'd heard the term before, but never heard it applied in this setting.

"Haven't you seen that yourself? Why, Frank, she's the rudest person I've ever met."

"Rude?" Dr. Umbeck repeated, as though still struggling to grasp the concept. "Was she rude to you? I'm terribly sorry, my dear fellow. Terribly sorry. What did she do?"

"Well, not to me. But to some of my people. Talk to anybody, Frank. They all detest her."

"Detest? Ah, well. I'll have to speak to her about it. Don't worry, I'll have a chat with her."

"But why do you keep her?"

"Why? She's efficient, of course. Runs a tight ship on the administrative side of things. Couldn't get along without her, in fact. I can put up with a little discourtesy as long as she keeps the machine tuned and the bottles washed." And Dr. Umbeck had chuckled, his mind probably elsewhere on some technical problem a million miles away from administrative issues.

Well, Joyce thought grimly, to give the devil her due, there was merit in Dr. Umbeck's point. Pam was efficient. She kept the machine tuned, all right.

Joyce often wondered what had caused Pam to work for a company like DRT in the first place.

Philosophically speaking, the Sierra Club or Greenpeace or some kind of radical environmental or ban-the-bomb company would seem more suited to her than a defense contractor.

Still, Pam had been with the company for twelve years, much longer than Joyce. And, as an executive secretary, she had been thoroughly investigated by all the security agencies, and held both a top-secret clearance and special individual security clearances for several different projects.

These clearances—known in the jargon of the trade as tickets—were authorized on a strict need-to-know basis. Joyce had only two, relating to a couple of projects deemed so sensitive even she, as essentially a nontechnical administrative person, had to be cleared.

It was not the case that everybody in Technical Applications Division knew what everybody else was doing, like some undefined, giant think tank. In fact, quite the opposite was true. Only the personnel actually involved in each project, without whom the research could not occur, were entitled to be issued a ticket for that project.

Pam and Dr. Umbeck were the exceptions. For administrative reasons, they were cleared for all projects. This made Pam all the more indispensable, enabling her to be all the more secure in her unpleasantness. Her reputation was legend.

First, though, she had other nicknames. She was typically referred to as Pam Crotch. At one point, somebody placed an anonymous order for "from the desk of" notepads under that name, complete with a stylized pudendum drawn in the center of the pad.

Pam was not amused. Though the full story was never revealed, it was rumored that she extorted substantial concessions in return for not filing a sexual harassment claim against the company.

Her personal habits formed the basis for similar legends, not to mention monikers. In the summertime, it was common for a number of the DRT employees who didn't run or jog to eat lunch outside. The Data Research building shared an open, parklike area with the adjoining facility, complete with picnic tables and a well-tended lawn. On sunny days, it was accepted that anybody who desired could put on a swimsuit and sunbathe.

Pam was not a runner, but she liked to take the sun. During all but the hottest part of the summer, she would spend the lunch hour tanning, her lean body sheathed in a French-cut one-piece black swimsuit.

It was therefore impossible for even the haziest scientist or preoccupied administrative type to miss the fact that Pam's apparent distaste for sharp edges such as razor blades in the area of her armpits also existed for other regions of her body as well. The result was that she gained another nickname—akin to Crotch—in tribute to her ample endowment of pubic hair, copious quantities of which extended in kinky, wirelike tangles beyond the narrow borders of her swimsuit. She became known as The Bush.

Though there was no real reason why it should do so, in a strange, vicarious way, this embarrassed Joyce.

Her feelings in this regard were aptly expressed by one of the ladies who worked in the mail room. Hilda—Joyce didn't even know her last name—was one of those spare, thin old women who had been a loyal employee of the company for a million years and who would probably keep working—and working productively—until she dropped dead at age ninety-five.

Though she usually kept her thoughts to herself, even Hilda was moved to make comment upon beholding The Bush in all her hirsute splendor.

It happened one lunchtime as they rode down the crowded elevator. When the doors opened, Pam proceeded to parade through the lobby—as she had to do to get to the picnic area—wearing nothing but her swimsuit and a short, terry-cloth top.

"For God's sake," came Hilda's disgusted mutter, directed at nobody in particular, "can't she at least edge that damn thing?"

In the next few weeks, advertisements for a variety of garden trimming tools appeared on bulletin boards throughout the company. These included hedge trimmers, lawn edgers and that peculiarly efficient tool sometimes called a weed eater or weed whacker that spins a heavy nylon cord at high speeds in a five-inch radius to slice through stalks and stems. This sudden interest in garden implements came to a halt only when a sternly worded memorandum on the subject of sexual harassment was issued and circulated by the legal department two weeks later.

Today, as she waited for the phone to be answered, Joyce reluctantly had to concede that *bitch* just didn't say it. The woman was a cunt. Period.

The Bush answered it on the fifth ring. "Technical Applications Division—Pam."

"Pam, this is Joyce Kennedy."

"Yes, Joyce." Pam's voice contained that mixture of efficiency and impatience that never failed to make Joyce feel somehow awkward and defensive, as if she were some sort of under-par nuisance.

"Pam, I need—Mike Stevens says I should talk to you about getting a clearance for the police—sheriffs actually—to go through Beth Fisher's desk."

"Oh, God, another one of those?"

"What do you mean?"

"The FBI was already here. What's the sheriff got to do with it?"

"I guess—I don't know. But the detective who's handling the case called and says he needs to go through Beth's desk and things."

"Shit. So now some goddamn you're-in-a-heap-of-trouble-boy Neanderthal type with a big gut and a wide ass wants to poke through our affairs. Who's next, the fucking dog-catcher?"

If it is, Pammie, baby, you better watch out, thought Joyce. She struggled to keep her voice even as she responded aloud. "Look, Pam, I don't know about any of that. But the guy says he has to go through the stuff as part of his investigation. I'm just trying to arrange it, that's all. If you don't want to let him, I'll tell him, and he can do whatever he has to do."

"He have a search warrant?"

"He said he was getting one," Joyce responded, wondering how Pam knew about search warrants.

There was a silence on the other end of the line. "All right," Pam snapped at last. "When's he coming?"

"Tomorrow."

"Well, send him and his search warrant on up when he gets here. If everything is okay, I'll see if he can have a go at it."

"All right. That's how we'll do it. Thanks, Pam."

"Goodbye."

The line clicked dead. Why, thought Joyce as she hung up the telephone, did I say thanks to that bitch?

THE FOLLOWING DAY, shortly before two in the afternoon, Cates and Winston arrived at DRT.

Getting the search warrant had taken longer than Cates anticipated. First they had to wait for a deputy D.A. to spring free to review the search warrant. The prosecutor had initially been skeptical as to whether a warrant was necessary; having been convinced that one was at least advisable, he had found Cates's draft wanting in several particulars.

The three of them had haggled about it, then finally settled on an addendum to the affidavit. Cates wrote it out, the D.D.A. made a couple of minor changes, and sent them off to find somebody to type it before the whole thing could be presented to a judge for signature.

At DRT, Mike Stevens had given them visitors' passes and escorted them to the area occupied by Technical Applications.

Joyce, much to her chagrin, had been required to attend a meeting at one-thirty. The content of the meeting justified ten minutes; the format and the particular person chairing it meant it took nearly three-quarters of an hour. When she got back to her desk at ten after two, there was a message from Mike that Cates and an FBI agent had already been shown the way up to Technical.

"Damn!" she muttered.

She wanted to see Cates, and she felt a little embarrassed that she felt that way. She signed out to the fifth floor, then walked briskly toward the elevator, wondering if she were going to feel even more foolish when she got there than she felt now.

As Joyce stepped off the elevator and made a sharp left to go to Technical, she ran into Janis Gorder, one of the division's young secretaries. Janis wore a look of embarrassed amusement. In response to Joyce's unspoken inquiry, she grinned.

"What is it?" Joyce asked.

"The Bush."

Oh, God, thought Joyce. Was Pam in one of her moods? "What about her?"

"A couple of cops came to look at Beth's stuff," Janis explained. "Some black dude about seven feet tall in a suit and a gorgeous hunky white guy."

"And?" Joyce demanded impatiently. I know what he looks like, she thought, just tell me what's happening, damn it.

"Well, The Bush is giving them the third degree."

"Why? What's her problem?"

"What's ever her problem?" asked Janis rhetorically. "She doesn't need a problem—she's The Bush."

"What's she doing?"

"Just having a fit, that's what."

"A fit?"

"Yup. A genuine, psycho, PMS shit-fit. I mean, they have a search warrant and everything. But she's got her feminist cape on. And now she's yelling at them about national security and their warrant quote isn't shit unquote, and why don't they go oppress some women minorities somewhere. All the stuff she does when she gets that way."

"Oh, God," Joyce said aloud.

"Yeah. To hear Pam, those two poor cops are responsible for putting down every woman throughout history."

"Actually," she added, "it's kind of a sight to see. I just have to go pick up a visitor, or I'd stay and watch."

Joyce brushed past her and rounded the corner.

The room was twenty by thirty feet. An assortment of desks and worktables, most of them containing a CRT—a computer terminal consisting of a display monitor and a keyboard—crowded into the area. Pam stood with Beth's desk behind her, as if she were somehow defending it. Cates was facing her, and off to one side stood the seven-foot black guy in a suit.

Perhaps ten or twelve of the DRT researchers, programmers and secretaries stood or sat at desks around the room, beholding the spectacle before them. Several looked openly amused—Pam was not popular, but on general principle to most of them, neither were cops—and a few others simply looked embarrassed.

The black guy, Joyce noticed, was looking on impassively, his ebony features expressionless. Cates, on the other hand, looked both angry and out of place.

It struck Joyce that he seemed oddly out of his element, almost awkward.

She felt suddenly sorry for him, confronted as he was by The Bush in this setting of artificial yuppiedom, far from the streets and murder scenes where he would be so quietly confident and in control. A pang of sympathy shot through her, matched by anger toward Pam. And embarrassment—for Cates, receiving Pam's tirade, and for herself at seeing him now, apparently so, well, vulnerable. She didn't want to see him like that.

Cates was speaking. "Look, Miss Hotch—"

"*Ms* Hotch," she interrupted.

Joyce saw the muscles in his jaw clench slightly. "Look, Ms Hotch, if you'll just give me a reason—"

"The reason is I said no," The Bush snapped.

"I'm afraid that's not enough—not a good enough reason." His voice sounded patient. "The warrant gives us the authority to search, and unless there's some legal basis not to, I'm afraid I have to look."

Pam moved quickly around the desk, to the side where Beth had sat. She leaned forward over it, her thighs pressing the middle drawer, and snarled, "Not without my say-so, you aren't, buster."

One of the programmers snickered audibly; several others grinned.

Cates moved forward to face her across the desk.

"Ms Hotch," he said awkwardly, his face red with embarrassment, "if you've got a problem with this, take it up in court. Tell it to the judge. Now, I've got a warrant, and I probably didn't even need one to begin with. And I'm going to search that desk. It's—"

"Oh, you are, are you? I wouldn't put all my money on that, if I were you, boy-o."

He continued. "It's a crime to interfere with an officer in the performance of a duty, and frankly I've already put up with way more—"

"'It's a crime to interfere,'" The Bush mimicked, her voice mincingly sarcastic. "Shit. What are you going to do? Arrest me? Take me to jail? Handcuff me?"

Cates spoke again. To Joyce, his voice had a deadly quiet tone to it. "I hope it doesn't come to that, but it is always one way to resolve this."

"Oh, it is, is it?" Pam snarled.

"Look. Why are you being this way? All I want to do is my job, and then I'll be out of your hair."

A ripple of snickering ran through the onlookers, and a couple of them laughed out loud. Joyce groaned inwardly at his choice of words, realizing that he had no way of knowing about the source of Pam's nickname.

Pam, however, had ignored his last response. "That figures. If you're wrong, just use force and do it anyway. Typical Neanderthal male response. Typical Neanderthal male *cop* response. Another tool to control women with. And what are you going to do if I don't want to be arrested? Beat me up?"

Cates opened his mouth to say something, but she cut him off.

"Well, go ahead. Do it, you badge-heavy caveman. It's what you'd do to a man, isn't it? If I were a man, you'd beat me up, you and your little playmate, Super-Fly, there. What's the matter? You afraid of a woman?"

"Miss—Ms Hotch—"

Her voice became shrill and strident. "'Ms Hotch,' nothing! I'm choosing you off, buster. Treat me like you would another man. Arrest me or take your warrant and drag your asses out of here!"

"Like a man?"

Joyce felt her face turn red with vicarious embarrassment for Cates.

Pam, you bitch, she thought, you total bitch. Don't give in, Steve, she silently begged him. Don't retreat, not to The Bush, that bitch. I know you can't really arrest her, but please, *please* don't back down. Do something.

The Bush evidently sensed his hesitation, his apparent lack of confidence, and it added fuel to her anger. "I demand to be treated like a man!" she proclaimed passionately.

"Like a man," Cates repeated.

The Bush pointed imperiously toward the exit. "Or get the hell out of here!" she ordered.

Cates smiled. To Joyce's surprise, it looked like a genuine, happy, pleased smile.

He reached across the desk with both arms and took hold of the fabric of The Bush's blouse on either side of the throat. With a single, effortless motion, he hauled her across the desk, knocking the telephone and a set of five plastic paper-size trays mounted one over the other onto the floor.

The phone struck with a crash; papers flew in all directions as the trays hit with a brittle plastic sound and went to pieces.

Joyce gaped.

It all seemed to happen in a single, coordinated, fluid motion. No wasted moves, no hesitation, no urgency, no fumbles or rough spots.

Cates swung his adversary around to face the desk and bent her forward over it, facing away from him. He crossed her wrists together behind her back, then held them with his left hand while he reached under his coat for handcuffs with the right.

The cuffs went on with a soft ratcheting sound, and then he turned her gently but firmly away from the desk. The seven-foot black guy had somehow latched onto and smoothly rolled into position a swivel chair, and in what seemed a single, choreographed maneuver, Cates swung The Bush into it.

Joyce stared in amazement. The other onlookers did likewise.

Nobody was chuckling now; the balance of power in the room had been turned a one-eighty in the space of about three seconds.

Cates stood before The Bush.

He didn't look angry, he just looked...in control. Of everything. Then he bent forward, his hands on the tops of his thighs, just above the knees. He spoke softly, a benign smile suffusing his features, his face only inches from hers.

"Miss Hotch," he said, his voice mild, kindly, even. He spoke as if explaining something to a child. "Miss Hotch," he repeated. "We go through our lives being known by numbers, don't we? Numbers are a way of life in modern society.

"Your driver's license number. Your social security number. Your age. Your date of birth. And, in your case, you now get to be known by two more numbers.

"One is ten-sixteen. That's the radio code for prisoner, or an 'in custody,' if you prefer. You're now a ten-sixteen. Congratulations." He paused, and his smile became even more kindly than before.

"The other number will be your booking number at Las Colinas. That's the women's jail, in case you didn't know. You see, you're under arrest for interfering with an officer."

He started to stand up, then leaned down again.

"Oh, yes. One more thing. You do have rights, as you are likely about to tell me. Specifically, you have the right to remain silent. And, in your case, I earnestly—strongly—suggest you exercise that right."

He looked over at Winston, then turned back to The Bush and gave her a smile and an encouraging nod.

"I really do."

bindles

BY NATURE, Cates was not the kind of cop who overreacted. More to the point, he was confident he had not overreacted in arresting Pam Hotch for interfering. She had gone well beyond the limits of what he regarded as "acceptable interference."

That aside, however, on a sort of intuitive, gestalt level it had seemed like the right thing to do. Remedial action had been indicated. A statement had needed to be made, not only to her but to the amused bystanders, and he had made it. Priorities had been clarified, so to speak.

All in all, he felt with some degree of satisfaction, a salutary effect had been achieved.

He knew, of course, that she was technically guilty of a 148—as it was known in the trade—long before he made the arrest. The offense for which he had arrested her, section 148 of the penal code, only required that she willfully resist, obstruct or delay an officer in the performance of a lawful duty. Accordingly, the letter of the law had been violated as soon as she refused him access to the desk upon being shown the search warrant. From a legal point of view, he could have arrested her at that moment.

Cates, however, had never been one to go strictly by the letter of the law, and this was true in more ways than one.

On one hand, if the truth be known, on occasion he was not above taking a liberal interpretation of the rules of search and seizure, even stretching them perhaps, or ignoring a meaningless formality if necessary in the course of an investigation. In appropriate situations, then, he had done things such as searching trash cans of suspected bookmakers or narcotics dealers.

No big deal, really.

The cans would be on the street waiting for pickup. And it might come to pass that Cates was interested in seeing if, say, records of illegal gambling had been discarded, or if narcotic debris or other evidence of crime was present.

Technically, of course, the California Supreme Court held that a search warrant was necessary to go through the contents of even a trash can set out for pickup by the garbageman.

However, Cates rationalized that he was doing it just for "background information," not evidence to be introduced in court. Moreover, though he didn't go around volunteering what he had done, if confronted he would simply admit it and let the chips fall as they might.

Besides, it was common knowledge that the system was choking to death on its own paperwork. This was in a sense his own personal version of the Paperwork Reduction Act.

Right.

By contrast, in the context of arrests, he generally went substantially beyond what the law required in terms of protecting individual liberties.

What that meant was that he didn't make an arrest in many cases when he theoretically could have made one. His own personal code required that the spirit as well as the letter of the law be violated before he took any enforcement action.

"Don't sweat the trivial shit," as Ben Grummon put it, the corollary to which was in Cates's book that ninety-five percent of life's hassles, both as a cop and otherwise, were just that, trivial shit.

As a patrol deputy, he had never written CSTs—chicken shit tickets—to motorists. Moreover, now as well as then, he didn't make arrests for crimes like section 148 just because the person had technically "resisted, obstructed or delayed." The person involved had to really earn his 148.

Pam Hotch, however, had managed to do just that.

To Cates's substantial surprise and complete approval, Winston had reacted with smooth efficiency to his sudden display of enforcement action. It was as if they had rehearsed it, or had been partners for years instead of hours.

In his peripheral vision, Cates had seen the tall black man take an easy step backward and hook a nearby swivel chair with one of his long arms. The chair was on casters, and Winston had swung it gracefully into position in a long, lazy loop. He had done it in perfect timing with Cates's equally smooth handcuffing of the woman, such that it was the logical and simple place to sit her down.

Very impressive.

How had Winston known, or thought, or guessed—Cates didn't know which term most aptly described it—to get the chair?

On reflection, Cates realized that even he had not consciously thought of sitting her down after he cuffed her, or where he was going to do it, when he reached over the desk to put the *habeas grabbus* on Pam. And Winston could not consciously have known Cates would react the way he did and use the chair to put her in. Yet somehow, perhaps subconsciously, both men had been so much in sync that he was sure it must have looked rehearsed to the onlookers.

Teamwork.

For a moment, Cates had the urge to slap Winston's palm in a jubilant gimme-five gesture of mutual congratulation.

Instead, he stood up from where he had been leaning forward, speaking to his 10-16. Impassively, he looked around the room.

Things had changed.

The feel of the room was altered, the texture of the crowd of grinning yuppies entirely different.

He turned his head slowly, running his gaze over the crowd. Calmly. No macho display, no "hardassing" them, just making a calm assessment of the impact of his bombshell.

Be cool.

Keep them off balance, Stevie, he thought. They expect you to exhibit the clumsy, authoritarian force that they associate in their narrow, biased little minds with all police officers. So don't do that. Win their hearts and minds first; you can always kick them in the balls later, if it comes to that. Don't look challenging or aggressive; the act of arresting this bitch was all the challenging they needed. Look calm, the calmer the better.

Don't appear intractable.

He let the silence hang, then finally spoke, his voice soft and easy. "I'm Detective Steve Cates of the San Diego Sheriff's Office," he remarked offhandedly, speaking to no particular individual. "This is Special Agent Winston Keith of the Federal Bureau of Investigation. We're investigating the death of Elizabeth Fisher, who used to work here."

He paused. Nobody interrupted him. Nobody spoke at all, in fact.

"Miss Hotch—" he gestured in her direction "—is under arrest for interfering with an officer, section 148 of the penal code.

"She'll be booked into Las Colinas Women's Facility—the women's jail—and allowed to post bail within six or eight hours, I expect, unless there's some problem such as outstanding warrants or something like that. Somebody should notify her supervisor so he can take whatever action he wants with respect to her arrest or getting a temporary replacement or whatever. Any questions?"

Nobody had any questions.

Cates continued, his voice still mild. "I'm sorry it came to this, of course, but in a sense, I didn't put her in jail—she put herself in jail. Now, is there a telephone I can use?"

A woman pointed. Cates walked over and picked up the receiver. "Do I have to dial 9 or anything for an outside line?"

The woman shook her head. Cates punched the buttons for the Comm Center. The phone was answered immediately by one of the dispatchers.

"Dispatcher 22."

"This is Cates, 30-Ida-27. I need a uniformed unit to eleven-forty-eight a female prisoner."

The code 11-48 meant simply "transport," and normally he would have worded it "eleven-forty-eight a female ten-sixteen." This time, however, he thought it would be appropriate for the audience to have Pam referred to in plain English, and just let the usage of 11-48 be enough police jargon for the sentence.

He gave the location and Pam's name, spelling the surname but resisting the temptation to do it phonetically, "Harry–Ocean–Tom–Charles–Harry." It was, after all, the telephone rather than the radio, and the voice came over loud and clear.

The dispatcher's voice came back crisply and it was audible, he was certain, to at least the closest onlookers.

"Stand by, 30-Ida."

Cates could visualize the process. The dispatcher would have recorded the request, in code, on a dispatch card. "10-87 31-Ida-27 11-48 a 10-16." The card would go via conveyor belt to another dispatcher working the main console, who in turn would identify an available unit and put out the broadcast.

The dispatcher's voice came on the line again. "Roger, 30-Ida. We have 41-Paul-6 en route from Encinitas. ETA is ten to fifteen."

"Is that a female unit?" Cates inquired.

"That's affirmative."

"Very good. Thank you." He hung up and turned to Winston. "Let's do it."

He started to move toward the desk, then caught sight of Joyce. "Hello," he said.

She smiled awkwardly. "Uh, hi."

Cates didn't want to embarrass her in front of her friends or co-workers by appearing too friendly. "Thanks for making the arrangements with Security," he said formally.

"You're welcome. Sorry I wasn't here when you got there."

Apparently, he realized, she wasn't embarrassed, or didn't care what they thought. "No problem." He grinned. "Sorry I had to arrest one of your people. Joyce, this is FBI Agent Winston Keith. Winston, Joyce Kennedy."

She extended her hand. "Pleased to meet you."

Winston smiled. "Likewise, of course."

Joyce looked puzzled. "FBI? Wasn't there somebody from the FBI out here already?"

Instantly, Cates was on full alert.

He felt a pang of anger and disappointment, though he tried not to show either. The former was born of the FBI's apparently upstaging him again; the latter because he had unconsciously begun liking Winston—perhaps too much—as a result of even such an apparently minor thing as their synchronicity in the arrest.

He glanced at the tall black man. "That so?"

Winston looked puzzled. "It's news to me."

Cates gazed at him sharply. Objectively, it seemed unlikely that Winston didn't know about it, if indeed it had taken place, and if indeed it had been the FBI. On a subjective level, however, the agent's surprise seemed genuine.

Joyce looked confused. "I'm sure that's what Mike said."

"Mike?"

"Mike Stevens, the security man. He told me the FBI had already been here and gone through her desk." She turned to one of the other programmers, who was nodding. "You know anything about that, Liam?"

The man she had addressed nodded. "Two guys from the FBI were here yesterday," he confirmed. "Not him," he added, indicating Winston. "Two other guys."

Joyce looked at Cates. Cates looked at Winston. Winston shrugged. "It's news to me," he repeated.

Cates considered the matter for a moment longer, then dismissed it. "Let's take a look," he said, indicating the desk.

Keeping an eye on Pam, the two men made a quick but careful inventory of the items in the desk.

Apart from office supplies and aspirin and tampons and miscellaneous items, all he found was a spiral-bound calendar and address book, a paperback novel entitled *Miami Crush*, a pad with some doodles and notations on it and an expanding file folder for keeping bills and receipts. Cates glanced inside the folder and saw that it contained personal papers and bills related to Beth's residence on Mar Vista; she must have brought it to work to pay her bills, he reasoned. They impounded the calendar-address book, the pad and the file.

"Not much here," Winston observed.

"No, there isn't." Cates turned to Joyce and produced a key from his pocket. "You said she had a locker somewhere. Something to do with her running."

Joyce nodded. "It's on the basement level. I'll take you there if you like."

Cates glanced at Pam, who was still sitting handcuffed in the chair. She looked strangely pale and worried, but at least she was silent. "Let's get her down to the entrance and wait for the transport unit," he suggested. "Once she's off our hands, we'll take a look."

He walked over to Pam's desk a few feet away. A tan Gucci purse lay next to it. He held it up toward her. "This yours?"

Pam didn't speak. He shrugged and opened it. The wallet contained her driver's license. The ownership thus confirmed, he began a routine inventory of the contents of the purse, knowing a court might well rule the search illegal if he found anything.

In the bill container of the wallet he found something. Six somethings, to be exact.

The somethings were small squares of paper, each folded in a configuration immediately recognizable to narcs, users and dealers as a bindle, a makeshift container for powdered drugs such as cocaine and methamphetamine.

He opened one and saw that it contained a small quantity of white powder. Seeing Winston's questioning look, Cates nodded in affirmation.

Winston grinned. "Looks like she may be in longer than six or eight hours," he observed.

"I wish," Cates responded.

"How so?"

"She'll be out probably just as fast, but the bail will be higher. Assuming she's got a friend to bail her out, of course. Come on. Let's get her out of here, down to the transport unit." He grimaced. "And then we'll take a look at that locker."

death touch

It was after three by the time Cates and Winston left the Data Research facility.

A feeling of tiredness beset Cates, and they made most of the drive in silence. He hadn't really known what to expect at DRT, but he had expected something. And as a result he was disappointed.

Apart from the arrest of The Bush—Joyce had explained something of Pam's background after the patrol deputy had taken her away—it seemed the only "something" he had gotten was that he would have to look elsewhere—or dig deeper—for the answer.

Answer, hell, he thought—he'd settle for even a lead. Forget about finding the smoking gun, just give some clue as to what the hell was going on.

On the bright side, of course, was Joyce.

She was an attractive woman, and he liked her. Moreover, she had been pleasantly, delightedly, overjoyed by his arrest of Pam Hotch. She had never seen anybody arrested, she explained. And for it to be The Bush...

"She got arrested. You arrested her. I can't believe it; I just can't believe it," she repeated.

"No big deal," he said offhandedly, trying to ignore Winston's amused expression. After all, it wasn't as if she had been one of the FBI's ten most wanted.

But she said it so many times that—though he was greatly complimented by her reaction in general and specifically the resulting attention it brought him—Cates finally was moved to declare, "All right, already! It's a nothing case. Now you're starting to embarrass me." And all the while Winston stood there with a twinkle in his eye, pretending he wasn't amused

and whistling softly through his teeth a fair approximation of
Pomp and Circumstance.

Joyce had nodded vigorously. "I know, I know. I don't
mean to embarrass you." And she added, almost to herself, "I
just can't believe it."

On a personal level, then, the trip hadn't been a complete
waste of time.

In addition, despite his feelings of discontent, he had to admit, however grudgingly, they had indeed learned a little more
about Beth Fisher. Specifically, another bindle, similar to those
taken off The Bush, had been found in her locker, the key to
which he had impounded from her apartment.

"Looks like our victim was no stranger to nose candy herself," Cates remarked dryly when he found it.

It also occurred to him that the FBI agents—assuming that
was what they were—who had searched Beth's desk had not
known about her locker. It was, after all, not something inevitably furnished each employee; rather, it was a sort of extra
fringe benefit.

Winston had shrugged but hadn't spoken. Joyce, however,
had frowned.

Cates looked at her. "That surprise you?"

"In one sense, yes," she responded. "But maybe in another sense, not so much."

"What do you mean?"

"Well, I'm surprised in that she never said anything about
it. No wise remarks or anything like that. So I hadn't specifically associated her with it. Yet . . . well, she looked the type."

"Who doesn't?" Cates muttered, more to himself than to
her.

"Around here, not very many people," she responded.

"You mean that?"

Joyce nodded. "Yes. It's all ov— I can tell you this, can't I?
I mean, you can't do anything about it, right? Like arrest me,
or search the whole place, or something?"

Cates allowed a wry grin. "Obviously, we can't do much
about it. If we could, the stuff wouldn't be all over this place,
would it?"

She looked embarrassed. "I just thought... Look. It's a fact of life around here. Dope's everywhere. I mean everywhere." She said it with heavy emphasis on the *every*.

"Mainly coke?"

"Yes."

Mentally, Cates wrote "drugs" on a file card and tossed it in with other data in the Hmm tray in his mind. Aloud he spoke to Joyce.

"She give you any reason to believe she was involved as more than a casual user?"

"You mean like a dealer?"

"Yes. Or the retail outlet for other people here. Or even a mule—courier—for somebody else. Anything of the sort."

Joyce appeared to consider it. "I'd say not. I've no real reason to say that, of course. But I'd still say not."

"How about Pam? Could she be dealing?"

"The Bush? You've got to be kidding."

"Why? She had several bindles on her. That's consistent with personal use, sure, but it's also consistent with dealing. Even if they were just for personal use, normally one doesn't carry the entire stash around all day."

"Maybe she just bought it."

"True. And if it was just for herself, why buy it in separate bindles? Why not just get it in one? Look. I'm not saying it's conclusive, but you don't have to be a major class 1 violator to be a dealer. All you have to do is distribute to your friends."

"The Bush doesn't have any friends," Joyce interjected. "Not around here, anyway."

Cates, however, was not about to let her off so easily. "You know what I mean. Friends, acquaintances, that sort of thing. Hell, the whole enterprise depends on the little guy at the end of the distribution chain supplying other little guys, usually friends and acquaintances. Friends of friends, even. It can go on forever."

"What do you mean?"

"Hell, you're not naive. You've heard it before. Somebody like The Bush uses. She likes it. Pretty soon she can't afford what she likes to use. That doesn't mean she's a raving addict, but even fifty or a hundred bucks' worth per week... How long could you live with a $200 to $400 reduction in your net income a month? And that's still recreational usage. So, what does she do?''

"She deals," Joyce admitted.

Cates nodded. "She buys more than she needs and starts furnishing it to people she knows. Co-workers, that sort of thing."

"I've seen it," Joyce agreed.

"Sure. Most people have. And while she does it, she rationalizes. 'I'm not really a dealer—they'd be getting it from somebody, anyway.' Am I right?"

Joyce didn't respond.

Cates continued. "At the risk of sounding all moralistic, it's the consummate self-delusion. 'I'm not really a dealer—I'm not making a profit, only paying for my own.' And it has the benefit of mitigating one's own guilt by spreading the vice to others. If a whole lot of people are doing it, it can't be that wrong. Correct?"

"Yeah. I guess so."

"In some ways, in fact, I find the hypocrisy more offensive than using the drug. Though hypocrisy doesn't normally wreck people's lives in the same way."

"I wonder," Winston murmured, but didn't elaborate.

Joyce looked at him, then shot a keen glance at Cates. "Do you use drugs?"

"No."

"Have you ever?"

"Yes. A couple of times. Not coke or meth, though."

"Grass?"

"Yes."

She shook her head. "That's not even considered a drug, really, not in the overall scheme of things."

He shrugged.

"Were you a cop when you did it?"

"No. Before then. College."

"Why'd you quit?"

He considered it. "A couple of reasons, actually. One is that I didn't feel too easy about it, even at the time, and even though it was only grass. But I don't mind saying that becoming a cop was a big reason for me stopping."

Joyce said reflectively, "I've heard of cops who use drugs."

"Yeah. Me, too. I also know a hell of a lot of them who don't, and quite a few who never have."

"So why didn't you continue? Why should being a cop stop you?"

"I don't honestly know. Maybe because it seems dishonest, more so than for the ordinary citizen who isn't sworn to uphold the law. And, of course, hypocritical."

"Do you speed?"

"Speed?"

"Drive too fast, even though you're a cop? Or would that seem dishonest and hypocritical, too?"

Cates was aware of Winston looking on in amusement. He grinned at her. "Touché. And yes, I speed sometimes, even though I suppose I'm sworn to uphold traffic laws as well. And what's the difference?" he concluded rhetorically.

"Yeah. What's the difference?"

"I don't know, exactly. Speeding is probably in a technical sense the same thing. Maybe the only difference is a matter of degree. But that matter of degree is significant." He winked at the tall black agent. "I also sometimes don't signal when I change lanes. Winston does though. He's a Fed, like Eliot Ness, and therefore incorruptible."

"But not, however, untouchable," Winston deadpanned.

"Anyway," Cates said, taking a deep breath, "all of this begs the issue. Which is that this multibindle stash that Pam, The Bush, had in her purse is at least consistent with being a distributor. Is she, in your opinion?"

"A dealer, you mean?"

He nodded.

Joyce appeared to think it over, then shook her head. "No," she said firmly. "Not Pam. No way. I mean, not because she's above it, or anything like that. But people around here detest her. And if she were dealing, they'd all be talking about it."

"Why so?"

"You know how it is—everybody would still score their
dope from her, but they'd slam her about it behind her back.
No. Not The Bush. I'm surprised about her having those bindles, even. Especially in view of all her security clearances."

Cates decided not to correct her grammar. Hell, as an occasional speeder and nonsignaling lane changer, maybe he'd
better clean his own house before he corrected her English.
Besides... "So how do you explain them?" he inquired simply.

"I can't, unless she was holding them for somebody else.
Though she's got so few friends, that doesn't seem likely."

"Huh," Cates said noncommittally. After a moment, he
spoke again. "To change the subject..." he began.

"Yes?"

"You married?"

Joyce looked startled. "No.'

"Seeing anybody? Boyfriends?"

"None presently active." She said it guardedly, as if she were
talking about volcanoes or lines of credit or social diseases.
Briefly, he wondered which one it signified to her.

"Would you like to have dinner sometime? Friday night,
maybe?"

She hesitated for a moment, and for a moment longer as
well.

Oh, well, thought Cates, time to retreat to ride tiger, so to
speak—to disengage and dissimulate—as gracefully as possible.

His face warm, he stepped back and made a casually ambiguous wave of his hand. "Well, I guess not. No sweat. Sorry
I put you on the spot."

"It's not that," she said quickly. "I just—oh, to hell with
it. I'd like to. Only, can we make it Saturday instead of Friday?"

Puzzled, he looked at her. "Sure. Saturday's fine. Seven
okay?"

"Yes. No."

Cates frowned and looked at Winston. "Maybe it's a variation of the ancient Chinese water torture or something?"

Winston shrugged, his eyes glinting with amusement.

Joyce continued hurriedly. "I'm supposed to help somebody—a friend—who's moving on Saturday. Can we make it a little later in the evening? Say eight?"

"Sure. Eight it is."

Briefly, Cates wondered if the friend were male or female. He decided it was probably the former, sixty-forty odds, because if it had been a girlfriend she probably would have said so.

It was a sort of sociological truism, valid more often than not. Like the mothers of girls he had dated who, when needing or wanting to refer to their daughters' old boyfriends—as, for example, when a group picture of their family with the jerk in it was shown—called the guy "Mary's *friend.*"

He didn't give a rat's ass that Mary had had a previous boyfriend or several—he would have been surprised if it were otherwise—or even that they had slept together, or balled each other's brains out, in fact. But the studied neutrality of the word—especially when Mom evidently felt her daughter's taste in *friends* was on the decline—tempted him to make up some bland response like, "oh, you mean lover, don't you?" or "is this the one who had the good dope?" Except that would put the daughter in a bad spot and it was all a waste of energy anyway.

Joyce was speaking again. She wore a look of uncertainty. "Look," she said. "I didn't mean to get all coy when you first asked me. I'd like to go out. I was just wondering—I mean, since you arrested Pam, it just occurred to me that—"

"That this might prejudice the case in some way, and you'd be the subject of some lurid headlines?" He grinned. "Don't worry, it won't be anything like that."

She hesitated again, just long enough to make him wonder if there were something else, then nodded. "Saturday's great for me, too."

"Eight then?"

"Eight's fine."

He smiled. "Great. Anything you can't stand to eat?"

"No. You call it."

"Good. I will," Cates concluded, pleased, but trying to ignore the amused indifference of Winston, who had wandered a few feet away and appeared to be engrossed in surveilling the door to the locker area or something.

Apart from the date with Joyce, however, and the discovery that Beth had used coke—or meth, or whatever drug the powder proved to be—Cates felt singularly let down at the negative results of the trip.

Then he remembered something else.

Now, as he guided the sedan down the Midway–Rosecrans off ramp, Cates spoke to Winston. "You really don't know anything about somebody from the FBI already searching her stuff?"

Winston shook his head, a curiously tight expression on his features. "No."

Cates wondered whether to believe him. Then, for no reason, he found himself deciding that he did. "You mind checking it out?" he said casually.

"Not at all." Winston hesitated. "What's the next step, in your view?"

"Well, tomorrow we have to return the search warrant."

"Return it?"

"Take it back to the judge. We have to lodge it with the court and file a Receipt and Inventory form, listing the stuff we took." He looked at the black man. "Don't you guys do the same thing with a federal search warrant? Or haven't you done one before?"

Winston's voice sounded smooth and easy. "We do the same thing, but your second point is well-taken. The strike force to which I'm attached has legal specialists who handle that."

"Huh."

"What time will we return it?"

"First thing in the morning is usually best."

"And after that? Any ideas?"

Cates shook his head and allowed a crooked grin. "Beats the hell out of me, partner."

THAT AFTERNOON, when he got off work, Cates stopped by the gym for what was fast becoming his weekly workout.

Normally, he liked to work out with the weights three times a week, and do a slow, conservative run a couple of other times. Given his schedule recently, the weights sessions had fallen off to about one every three or four or sometimes five days.

Of course, that wasn't all bad, in that it actually had the curious effect of increasing his strength, in the sense of the maximum he could lift for a single repetition.

Most people overtrained themselves.

They worked out too long and too hard, at least as far as power was concerned. Developing maximum strength—in the sense of ultimate, one-rep, gut-busting power—took a careful balance between training and rest. Some gyms he had seen were literally packed with young men doing marathon high-rep, burnout, pump-up training programs. And these same young men asked one another—or anybody big, for that matter—why they didn't gain any weight or why their bench presses hadn't increased in the past three months.

Those workouts might be okay for building conditioning along with some measure of strength and toughness. They might even help develop some mental staying power for football or wrestling, though Cates had his own reservations about that, too. They certainly helped take off body weight and gain muscle definition—the striations and curvatures that helped set one muscle off from the next one—but they didn't increase power.

Cates knew.

He had done it himself as a younger man. He could write a fairly long book, he was confident, about programs that didn't work, at least not for what the trainee was using them for.

For heavy power training, then, the three days' rest between workouts was not necessarily all bad.

The drawback for Cates was that he wasn't doing heavy power training anymore. He was doing what was sometimes called maintaining, which to him meant finally admitting—mainly to himself—that he wasn't going to set any power records but wanted to hang in there, to some minimal extent at least.

Accordingly, based on a lot of trial and error, he had eased his way into a two- to three-times-a-week program that he could do in an hour and fifteen minutes each session, if the gym wasn't crowded. He prevented overtraining by doing only one or two sets of each exercise, after warming up, and by keeping the weights moderate.

The gym was an old power gym of the kind that can be found in a lot of cities if, in Cates's experience, you asked around and you avoided any place that ran sexy ads for "fitness specials" on a regular basis.

It did not offer courtesy hair dryers for its members. It had no Jacuzzi or steam rooms. It had no carpets on the floor. It had a couple of exercise bicycles that nobody used. Members didn't get reduced rates at racquetball because the place didn't have any racquetball courts.

It did have sets of dumbbells that ranged from ten pounds each—Cates thought they made good paperweights except they tended to roll—up to 160 each, 320 for the pair. It had flat benches, fifteen-degree benches, thirty-degree benches, sixty-degree benches and eighty-five-degree benches.

The benches themselves were massive welded steel affairs, thickly padded on the surface, and it took a strong person just to lift them. It had equally massive bench-press racks, a lifting platform and power racks and five Olympic bars and weights. It had driving rails and pulley-cam leg machines and some heavy cable apparatuses, and it didn't have any Nautilus machines.

It also wasn't coeducational.

Well, it probably was, Cates supposed; the law only allowed women's gyms to be noncoed. However, only a handful of women—college athletes or bodybuilders—ventured into it. Most of the members weren't the type of people most women liked to have around when they did tummy tighteners or bottom lifters or whatever women did in gyms.

Hence, the membership was essentially an eclectic group of males.

A few off-season professional and college athletes trained there, along with a few old power lifters and bodybuilders. There were a few up-and-coming power lifters and bodybuilders, a very few cops, a couple of SEALs from Coronado, one guy who was mainly into martial arts and several men who had done a significant portion of their power training inside penal institutions.

Nobody wore cute little lifting gloves in this place because none of them worried too much if their hands got callused.

If the calluses got too thick, the top layers could be sliced off with a razor blade. If you didn't do this, Cates knew, they tended to tear off during the really heavy pulling movements like dead lifts. Since Cates wasn't doing dead lifts these days, he didn't worry about it much.

When articles appeared in magazines and newspapers about how gyms and health clubs were becoming the new singles' bars of the eighties, they weren't talking about this place.

Cates liked it.

Oddly, there were only three other men in there that evening, unusual for a weeknight. The Padres were off to a less than completely auspicious start, but at least a hell of a lot better than last year's start, so maybe a lot of people were at a ball game. Or more likely, knowing this crowd, watching a ball game at some bar.

Cates was wearing a pair of black trunks and a white T-shirt with a colorful emblem on the back. The emblem featured a picture of the gym owner doing a double-biceps pose while standing on the mutilated body of Khaddafi, all superimposed on a background of the American flag.

He warmed up with a little stretching, a handful or so of twists with a bar behind his shoulders, some movements in all directions and all natural aspects of the major lifting joints like shoulder, elbows, back, waist and knees. Then he moved over to the bench-press rack.

Those who knew Cates could have seen that he was an entirely different man inside the gym than outside.

He was still quiet, even more so, actually.

To the uninitiated he might have been thought casual or laid-back, not serious. But that was only because he didn't shout or grunt or make a big production about huffing and puffing while he worked out. The keen observer, however, would have noted an almost deadly intensity about him.

He waited and watched for a couple of minutes while George Endicott did his last bench, a single repetition at 405.

405 meant four forty-five-pound plates on each end of the Olympic bar, which itself weighed forty-five pounds. If the collars were added on each end of the bar, it would be 415, but George didn't use collars.

He did a single rep with it. Down, pause for an instant, then drive it off his chest. It slowed at the sticking point, but he drove it through anyway with a little to spare. He got up off the bench, rotating his left shoulder and grousing about how he used to be able to do at least three reps with 405 easy, back when he was competing. However, since George was fifty-six years old, Cates knew that was a while ago, and said he shouldn't worry about it.

Let me help you get all this heavy shit off the bar, George offered. Cates said okay. They left one forty-five-pound plate on each end, and Cates lay on the bench and did ten reps.

He did them the way George did, not arching his back with his hips way off the bench and bouncing the bar off his chest in what somebody once observed wasn't really a bench *press* but was a bench any-way-you-can. Instead, he kept his hips in contact with the bench and paused the bar for an instant on the chest before driving it upward. Then they put a second forty-five-pound plate on each end, making it 225, and he did a few more reps. Then he was ready for his one-set bench-press workout.

They put a third plate on each end, making it 315, and Cates got ready to do it.

This part took a little concentration, so he spent a couple of minutes of visualizing, doing the entire set, all eleven reps, in his mind. Then he lay down and did the eleven reps. The last two dragged some, but he made them unassisted.

George, who had hung around to spot in the event Cates got stuck, commented that it looked a little heavy, to which Cates rejoined that there was evidently a lot of gravity tonight. George agreed, but said having such long arms as Cates had didn't help much, either.

Cates then went over to the dumbbells and did a set of eleven with the 120s on a forty-five-degree bench. So much for the chest workout. He switched to back next, doing some heavy seated cable rows. Then he did shoulders—presses behind the neck and dumbbell shrugs, one heavy set each after the warm-up sets—and one set of squats each at 135, 225 and 315. He did some lat pull-downs to stretch-finish the back workout and stretch out his spine after the squats and the shoulder work. He did a couple of sets of curls and triceps presses, and was out of there in just over an hour.

As he was leaving, he ran into Henry Chan, the martial arts man.

He was not Oriental in the least, though he had straight black hair, a thin-skinned, tanned complexion and just a hint of Eurasian cast to his features. He was about five-nine and well built, though not excessively muscular. Cates somehow thought of a candle flame when he saw Henry move—he had a peculiar grace that conveyed perfect balance, his energy centered on a vertical axis to which it would inevitably return regardless of what forces would momentarily distort it.

One time in the course of his official duties, Cates had had occasion to run Henry up on the DMV and the criminal history computers. Henry didn't have any real criminal history—no felonies, anyway—at that time, though he was about to acquire one. However, through these official sources Cates had learned that Henry's real name was Henry Chandler, and he had just sort of unofficially dropped the last four letters.

Later, Henry had been arrested and ultimately served nine months in custody on a plea bargain in a robbery case.

He and a friend had robbed a narcotics dealer of twenty thousand dollars. The money was never recovered. After he was caught, Henry had invoked his constitutional rights and refused to talk. Off-the-record, however, he had told then-

Patrol Deputy Cates that he didn't think it was against the law
to take money from dope dealers, and if it was, it shouldn't be.

Cates was inclined to agree there was at least a little merit to
the position.

Henry's friend, who was black and had a significant prior
felony record, went to prison, where he was stabbed to death
by a member of a white supremacy prison gang affiliated with
the Aryan Brotherhood. Henry drew a year "local time,"
which meant serving it in the county jail. While the case was
still going on, he was offered a complete pass—no time, no
fine—if he would testify against his friend. Henry said no
thanks, he'd rather do the year.

After his release, Henry had dropped out of sight.

When he reappeared six years later, it developed he had
spent the time divided between Okinawa and Hawaii, studying martial arts.

These days, in his early thirties, Henry had a small studio in
which he taught t'ai chi ch'uan and a sort of bastardized martial art he let the students call tae kwon do because it drew
heavily on both Chinese and Japanese arts. He didn't have
many students, but he was able to make a go at it, in part because he didn't burden the IRS with details regarding his
business.

In Cates's opinion, Henry had probably indeed spent the six
years studying martial arts. And he was good at them.

Those who made a lifetime pursuit of the physical and
metaphysical aspects of the fighting ways were undoubtedly
more skilled. Still, Henry was the best Cates had ever seen, and
possessed skills that were orders of magnitude beyond those he
imparted to his students.

Though they would never be all-around fast friends, the two
men held genuine respect for each other. Moreover, within the
context of Henry's own unique, personally tailored code of
ethics, Cates doubted that a more honest man existed, and
trusted him completely.

Henry's face lit up as the two men saw each other, just outside the side door of the unpretentious gym building.

"Yo, Steve-san," he hailed. Henry had never said anybody-san until the movie *The Karate Kid* came out, and Cates suspected that few people realized he was being facetious when he said it now.

"Henry," Cates responded simply. "What's going on?"

"Nada." He used the Spanish word for nothing. "Not a damn thing, in fact."

Something was nagging at Cates's mind. It was something to do with the Fisher case. Mentally, he reviewed the imaginary scraps of paper in the Hmm tray.

And then he had it. "Henry, you got a moment?"

"For you, Steve-san, anything. What's on your mind?"

"I want to talk about hitting people."

Henry shrugged. "Bad idea, usually. Unless you hit them with a stick or a bullet."

Cates spoke carefully. "Is there any way, Henry, to strike a blow that will hurt somebody inside but not on the outside?"

The martial arts expert looked interested. "What do you mean, Steve-san? Can you explain?"

"Suppose we had a dead guy, right? And we, you and I, did an autopsy on him. And when we looked at his heart it showed massive injury, from some incredible force applied to it. Like the guy got hit by a sledgehammer in the chest. You with me?"

"I'm with you."

"Only when we look at the chest from the outside—on the skin—there's no mark. Nothing. No bruise, nothing like would have to be there if a sledgehammer had, in fact, struck him. And," he added, "there's no bruising to the sternum and the flesh between the skin and the heart. If you saw all that, what would you say happened?"

Henry grinned. "I'd say the guy got clobbered by somebody *I* never want to go up against, that's what."

"What do you mean?"

He thought for several moments, then approached the subject obliquely. "You take t'ai chi, don't you, Steve?"

"Here and there. Nothing too advanced, though. I do the form and some push-hands." Push-hands was the basic combative practice, in which two persons stood and exerted force on each other, for the purpose of developing the ability to sense and avoid and counterattack.

"You know what the *chi* is, though, don't you?"

"Yes. It's the energy that circulates through the body. Sort of an inner force."

Henry nodded. "That's basically correct. *Chi* is sometimes called the life force or life energy. It circulates throughout the body, along certain well-defined meridians or pathways. A comparable term in Japanese martial arts is *ki*."

"And these pathways it circulates along don't necessarily coincide with visible nerves or channels or bones or things like that?"

"No, they don't."

Henry looked speculative. For an instant Cates got the feeling that it was easy to underestimate this man, to chalk him up as essentially a quiet, likable ordinary Joe who had learned a little karate and hustled a living from it. In that glimpse, however, Cates realized nothing could be farther from the truth. Whatever training Henry had been through in his years since jail, it was very real indeed.

Henry continued speaking. "That bothers a lot of people in the Western culture. We tend to look for cause-and-effect answers and mechanical solutions. If you can't see a nerve or some visible channel to move the *chi*, you don't believe the *chi* exists." He made a wry smile. "These same skeptics forget all about things like waves, of course."

"Waves?"

"Radio waves. Microwaves. Even electricity. I'm not saying that's what *chi* is, of course. But hell, those are examples of things that move without mechanical tracks. And we believe in those, right?"

Cates nodded. "Sure. But that's science, man. Technology. That's different. Right."

"That's what they say."

"I know. I used to have convictions—sorry about using that term, Henry—along those lines myself."

"Most people do. It's okay for computers and scientific instruments and things, but say it's inside the body and you must be talking about some kind of weird gook mystical shit."

"Yeah."

The martial arts expert paused, then continued. "You do acupuncture, and what you're doing is stimulating, rerouting or finding the *chi*. And in a lot of martial arts, especially the soft arts of China, developing and using the *chi* is an important part of the training. In some ways, it is the ultimate purpose of the training, in fact."

Cates waited for him to continue.

"If I wish to attack you, I could strike you with a physical blow. My fist would hit your body, and the energy would be transmitted by the impact. Like physics, I guess, except I don't really know about physics.

"On the other hand, some people claim that energy in the nature of *chi* can be transmitted without actual physical contact. The *chi* can be projected from the body and hit the other person without any fist-to-body striking."

Frowning, Cates considered this. Then he spoke carefully. "I know about *chi*, of course. I know it exists, and I've felt it inside myself on occasion. But are you saying it might be possible to actually project it without hitting the person?"

Henry didn't respond directly. "Have you ever been struck when the blow seems to hurt a lot more than the physical punch looked like it was going to or should have?"

"Yes."

"What do you think caused that?"

"I assumed I had underestimated the force of the blow."

"Maybe," Henry allowed. "And maybe not. It could be that what you felt was the *chi*, added to the physical blow."

Cates was skeptical. "A couple of times the person who hit me wasn't advanced in martial arts," he protested mildly.

"So? Martial arts strive to maximize the *chi*, and to harness it. But no art or form has an exclusive claim to it. What's to prevent an amateur—such as yourself—or even somebody with no training, from releasing it if the conditions are right?"

"Like a young woman who somehow picks up a car and lifts it off her child?"

Henry shrugged. "It's happened."

"Maybe."

"It has. And sometimes when you're doing push-hands, you might get uprooted and sent flying off your feet, even with a relatively unskilled opponent, if everything by chance comes together just right for him. Maybe that's because you're caught off guard, and maybe it's because he let loose the *chi*."

"All right," agreed Cates after a few moments. "I'll buy it." He thought some more. "Hell, I do buy it. I'm just having an attack of the Western skepticism, that's all. Now, take it on down the line for me. Follow it out. What are you telling me?"

Henry got serious. "It stands to reason that if you can project the *chi* out from your body, and affect an object without touching it, that you might be able to do this through a medium other than air."

Cates frowned. "I don't follow."

"Look. We're agreed the *chi* can be added to a physical blow. And I think we agree that it can also be transmitted without the necessity of a physical blow. Through the air, so to speak. For very short distances, of course, say inches or a foot or two. Okay so far?"

"Okay."

"It goes through the air without affecting it, and for some reason is only realized or actualized or made to have an effect on the ultimate target. Right?"

"Right."

"So, why can't it be transmitted through something besides air—some other medium—without affecting it, and still only be actualized on the ultimate target?"

"Like what?"

"Like skin and flesh."

"Oh, come on," Cates said skeptically. "Are you suggesting a person could project his *chi* into the heart itself, without damaging the external tissues?"

Henry nodded slowly. "I'm suggesting exactly that. And why not? It follows, doesn't it?"

Cates's first reaction was a disgusted "no way in hell." It would be fun to think so, of course, in a sort of Walter Mitty/ Charles Atlas/Superman sort of way. But that was the stuff of books and novels, not real life.

Then he realized his emotions already sort of believed it, and as Henry had explained it, logic couldn't refute it. So, as a last line of defense, he fell back to the weakest of all arguments.

"You've never heard of this actually happening, have you?"

Henry smiled faintly. "Well, as a matter of fact, I have."

Cates stared at him. Henry continued.

"It's sometimes called *noi cun*. It means a sort of highly concentrated internal power. Loosely speaking, *noi cun* refers to generating and focusing inner power—like *chi*—that is so strong it can strike or kill a person without actually touching him. And, in most cases, without leaving any visible mark on the person's skin."

"Bullshit."

"No bullshit. This is real shit. In street talk—street talk by those who know about it—it's sometimes called the death touch. And it's real."

"Bullshit."

Henry shrugged. "Have it your way. You asked; I told you."

Cates spoke again. "Look, Henry. I don't mean to be rude. It's just so..."

"Unbelievable?"

"Yes. Well, hard to believe, anyway."

Henry shook his head. "Not hard to believe, actually. Just hard to allow yourself to believe, white boy."

"Yeah. Maybe that's it."

Henry turned to go into the gym, then stopped. "Cates."

"Yeah?"

"You know, for a cop, you aren't such a bad guy."

"Thanks, Henry. You're a real nice felon, too."

"This *noi cun* stuff—it's real. It exists. But it's extremely hard to do."

"Can you do it, Henry?"

"No." He hesitated. "What I'm trying to say is that if that's what you're up against, you're up against some serious danger, you know?"

Cates shrugged.

"I mean it. This is some serious, heavy-duty shit. Don't try to take the dude by yourself. In fact, don't try to take him at all. If he won't go with you, shoot him."

He could see the concern on his friend's face. And despite his skepticism, for an instant Cates felt a cold knot of fear in his insides. Then it receded, and he affected disdain.

"Hell, Henry, I just bench-pressed three-fifteen for eleven reps, and I haven't even been training that hard. This guy'll be easy."

Henry made a sound that sounded like a snort.

"They were strict reps, too," Cates continued, his face deadpan. "No bridging, no bouncing, good pause."

"Well, not to plant negative thoughts in your mind, but if there's a guy out there with these abilities, he'll kill you if you go after him unarmed, one on one."

"So I won't try to take him unarmed."

Henry nodded, his face troubled. "That's the only way you'd have a chance."

He didn't say it like a gibe or a joke.

19

cross-examine

IN FACT, IT TURNED out to be a couple of days later—a dismal, gloomy Friday, especially for May—before Cates and Winston could return the warrant to the court. Thursday was spent doing the reports, both on the homicide and on the arrest of Pam Hotch, a.k.a. The Bush.

They also took the dope over to the lab to be analyzed. This included a determination of the narcotic quality of the bindles taken from The Bush as well as the one taken from Beth's locker. By a combination of kidding, cajoling and promising to buy lunch for one of the chemists, an attractive Japanese-American woman named Gina Takahashi, she promised to squeeze it to the front of the line, and to call him when it was ready.

Cates also addressed the issue of the speed dialer he had impounded from Beth's apartment, and that neither his superiors in rank nor the FBI knew about.

The speed dialer was an electronic device that could be pre-programmed with certain telephone numbers to automatically dial if that number were triggered. A veteran gambling investigator from Vice had alerted him to the possible evidentiary benefit of such devices.

The problem, of course, was how to decode the speed dialer. The sheriff's lab did not have the electronic ability to do it, so the usual approach was to plug the thing in to one's own phone and start using it, recording and trying to see who answered.

Rather than do that Cates invoked Winston's assistance.

It was a calculated gamble. The FBI was already conducting its own investigation, part of which Winston knew about and part of which he said he didn't. Cates believed him. Fi-

nally, Cates made the decision to reveal the existence of the
speed dialer to the tall black agent, on the theory that it was
better to get the results himself even if that meant that the FBI
would get them, too, than not to get them at all.

Winston registered no apparent surprise at the disclosure.
He also stated that he was confident the FBI labs had electronic equipment capable of decoding it, and undertook to
have that done ASAP.

The reports on Pam's arrest and on the progress of the investigation took the rest of the day on Thursday.

Due to the sensitivity of the case, Cates labored over the
phrasing, and even had Winston read his drafts for form and
content. While Cates was occupied with this, the FBI man
studied the earlier reports. At one point he used Lieutenant
Beecham's office to make a long telephone call—more than
forty minutes, Cates noted.

The Bush had been released on her own recognizance—at
8:50 p.m. on Wednesday night, the same day as her arrest.

When Winston raised a questioning eyebrow at this, Cates
shrugged fatalistically. "She's presumed innocent until proved
guilty, right, Counselor? Keeping them in custody isn't to
punish them—can't do that until she's convicted. Right now,
she's as innocent as you and I, and entitled to an OR release
unless it looks like she'll flee. In this case, she's got cast-iron
ties to the community, which show she won't run. Hence, she's
out zappo."

"Did I say anything?" Winston asked.

"Or unless she's a multiple ax-murderer, or something. In
which case the Supreme Court now finally lets bail be denied
in a few, limited situations—very limited situations—for the
protection of the public."

"Multiple axes or multiple murders?"

"Go to hell. You're the one who expressed surprise at the
fact she was released so soon. And you're the Fed, and the
Harvard law grad, not me, so you should believe in all this
stuff."

After a moment the black man sighed. "Yeah, I guess so. I
remember it all from law school, of course, but all the fancy

rhetoric that sounds great in speeches and case opinions sometimes doesn't look so good in the cold light of the real world. Especially when factually she's so clearly guilty."

"Yeah, but I'm sure you see it, or the same thing, anyway, every day on the federal level as well."

Winston grimaced and went back to reading.

"Besides," Cates added as an afterthought, "we—the S.O.—run the local jails, and we're so overcrowded that if we held her, we'd have to kick out a robber or rapist. Day's coming when all we'll have room for is multiple-ax multiple murderers, unless the county does something about more jail space."

BY NINE-FIFTEEN Friday morning, the two men were sitting in the front row of the spectator portion of Municipal Court Department 16. As Cates explained it, "first thing in the morning" was a relative term, and nine-fifteen was that as far as the courts were concerned.

Actually, he reflected, they should have gotten there earlier.

Court was already in session when they arrived. Judge Kenneth Kennling was conducting a preliminary hearing on some sort of dope case. He was a small, bald, gnomelike man with a toothy grin and a falsetto voice.

He also looked bored. Finally, he began reading something on the bench in front of him, pausing to look up from time to time.

"Probably this month's *Playboy*," Cates whispered to Winston.

"How can you tell?"

"He's looking at pictures, instead of reading."

"How can you tell that?"

"His lips aren't moving."

"Oh."

A preliminary hearing, or prelim in the jargon of the law, was a sort of minitrial that was held in all felony cases. The purpose was to require the prosecution to put on a bare-bones

1199

case in open court, to prove the matter warranted a full trial in Superior Court.

It featured a judge, court reporter, defense attorney, defendant, prosecutor and prosecution witnesses—the only difference between a prelim and a trial was there was no jury, and the burden of proof on the prosecution was less than that required for a conviction.

Watching it, Cates gathered that the case involved a cultivation of marijuana case of some sort that must have occurred the previous week.

That puzzled him. Under usual procedures, the prelim wouldn't have been held so soon—ten days was typical. As the testimony progressed, however, Cates realized that one of the crooks already had another case in the system, and an accelerated time frame had been adopted for this one to combine the two.

As Cates and Winston sat down, the witness met his glance and winked. He was a burly, muscular deputy with a ponytail that looked out of place with the suit he was wearing, his "court suit," as the cops sometimes called it.

The defense attorney, a florid, portly man named Tom Erdmann, who wore a pin-striped suit and a perpetual sneer, was in the middle of cross-examination. His technique combined a highly variable voice with the so-called leading questions the law allowed on cross.

"Now, Detective English," he said, then stopped.

Sheriff's Deputy Larry English didn't respond, but waited patiently for the onslaught to continue.

Erdmann gave him a hard look. "Are you with us, Detective English?"

Larry looked impassive. "I wasn't aware there was a question pending."

The attorney colored slightly. "Have you ever told a lie, Detective?" he demanded.

"Objection, argumentative."

The prosecutor was a woman deputy D.A. whom Cates hadn't seen before. At Erdmann's question, she had come in right on cue.

She was tall and young and had thick red hair. Cates guessed she was right out of law school, the ink barely dry on her certificate of admission to the bar. Still, it looked as if she had the right spirit, which was the important thing. The experience would come with time.

Judge Kennling looked up from whatever he was reading, or whatever pictures he was examining, if Cates's theory were correct.

"Overruled."

"Have you ever told a lie, Detective English?" Erdmann pressed.

Larry sighed. "Yes."

"In fact, you're a habitual liar, aren't you, Detective?"

"No. I'm not."

"You're a professional liar, then?"

"No."

"In fact, you are a paid, professional liar, aren't you, Mr. English?"

"No, that is not a fact."

Erdmann made a disgusted face. He walked across the courtroom to the empty jury box and leaned against the railing that separated it from the rest of the courtroom. He folded his arms across his chest and looked at English for several moments before continuing.

When he began again, the disgust was gone from his voice. Instead, he spoke in a studiedly patient tone, as if tired of the witness's intractability but willing to outlast him at it. All for the sake of the truth, of course.

"I believe you testified you're a narcotics detective, isn't that true?"

"Yes."

"And you often work undercover?" Again, the same patient tone of voice.

"Yes, sir."

"And when you work undercover, you frequently pose as a user of illicit narcotics yourself, isn't that correct, Detective?" Erdmann's voice dripped patience.

"Yes, it is."

"And you do that to attempt to purchase drugs from persons who don't realize you're a police officer in order to arrest them. Am I correct?"

"Sometimes, yes."

"And if one of those unsuspecting individuals should ask if you're a policeman, you'd deny it. Isn't that true?"

"Objection. Calls for speculation and conjecture," interjected the D.A. sharply.

"I'll rephrase the question," snapped Erdmann before the judge could rule on the objection. "*If* it pleases counsel for the prosecution, *when* one of those unsuspecting persons asks if you're a policeman, you in fact deny it. Don't speculate about what you might do; just tell us what you do do. Now, you deny it, isn't that true?"

"Objection. Irrelevant and argumentative."

Good lady, thought Cates.

"Overruled. You may answer."

Cates could see English grimace. Though every cop who had ever worked an undercover assignment and then had to testify about it later had experienced some variation of this dog-and-pony show, it was still a wearing and demeaning game to play.

"Yes. To further the investigation, I would deny it," English responded.

Erdmann pressed on. "Even though it was true, you'd deny it. Correct?"

"Yes."

"And you would be aware, you'd know, that you were a law officer at the very time you would tell them you weren't?"

"Of course."

"On those occasions, you haven't momentarily *forgotten* that you were a policeman, then?"

"No."

"So you consciously, knowingly said something, knowing that it was not true. Am I correct?"

"I suppose so."

"You lie to them, in other words?"

"If you call it that, yes."

The attorney affected a look of incredulity. "If I call it that!" he thundered. "Well, Detective, do tell us, what do *you* call it?"

English shrugged. "I call it doing what's necessary to further the investigation and buy from a dealer."

If this response was a setback for Erdmann, he didn't appear to show it. "You do this regularly. Correct, Detective? On a regular basis?"

"Whenever the job demands it."

"And you get paid for doing that job, of course?"

"Yes."

"It's your chosen profession to do this, correct?"

"Yes."

"And yet you don't regard yourself as a paid professional liar. Is that what you're saying?"

"That's what I'm saying."

The attorney gave a little shake of his head, thereby communicating his lack of belief to anybody who happened to be watching. Judge Kennling wasn't paying attention, so the tactics were wasted on him. In Cates's experience, however, juries were often swayed and misled by such tactics.

After a suitable pause, Erdmann continued his cross-examination. "All right, Detective English, on those occasions where you're acting undercover and lying and getting paid for it—but not as a paid professional liar, of course—" he paused to let his sarcasm sink in "—do you have a single undercover name, or do you just use whatever strikes your fancy for the current assignment?"

"Basically the latter."

Erdmann suddenly smiled. Even to Cates it had the appearance of a genuine smile. "Must be tough to keep the different covers straight," the attorney observed.

English didn't respond.

"Did you find that to be true, Deputy? That at first you sometimes had trouble keeping it straight?"

"At first," English replied cautiously.

"Not so much anymore, I take it?"

"Not really."

"You became a better liar with practice?"

"Objection, argumentative," snapped the deputy district attorney. "Really, Your Honor," she began, rising to her feet, "if Mr. Erdmann is going to go through his entire routine, perhaps we can save some time. I'll just stipulate that he asked his standard Narc Cross-examination Charade, and everybody who knows him will know what questions he asked."

The judge looked up. "Calm yourself, Ms Tiffany." He moved his mouth in a toothy display that Cates supposed was intended as a smile. "If you'll quit making frivolous objections, we can get on with this. This doesn't have to take all day. Let's get it over with, and maybe Mr. Erdmann can take you to a movie or something."

Cates could see the color in the young woman's cheeks. "Your Honor—" she retorted angrily.

Erdmann cut her off. "I'll withdraw the question, Your Honor," he oiled ingratiatingly.

Judge Kennling looked at him. "Thank you, Counsel. Now proceed, and let's not take all day."

"Of course not, Your Honor," replied Erdmann, by his tone managing somehow to align himself with the judge's condescending, we-men-have-to-humor-this-twit manner, as if the prosecutor were responsible for the delay. She stood for a moment longer, started to speak, then hesitated and sat down.

Cates, who himself had been on the receiving end of demeaning courtroom tactics, felt a pang of sympathy for her.

He glanced over at Winston. For once the black man's impassive look was bordered with grimness, as though he, too, could sympathize. Winston's eyes flickered to meet his.

"Judge needs to have his attitude adjusted," the FBI man muttered.

As if somehow in response, Judge Kennling looked up and made a vague wave with his hand at the court reporter. "The record should reflect my remarks were made in a humorous tone," he directed.

"So stipulated," affirmed Erdmann in an unctuous tone, though no stipulation was called for.

"I will *not* so stipulate," snapped the young deputy D.A.

"At any rate, Detective English," continued the defense attorney smoothly, "you frequently state as true things that are not true in order to further your investigations, and you used to make mistakes in doing it but you don't as much anymore. One final question, Deputy."

English didn't speak.

The attorney continued. "Despite all this, you of course wouldn't *think* of lying in court, would you?" Erdmann's voice was heavily sarcastic, the clear implication of his tone directly contradictory to the words.

"I've taken an oath not to, and I wouldn't even lie without the oath, that's correct," said English with awkward directness, which to Cates was as good an answer as could be given to this sort of meaningless bullshit verbal abuse.

The judge called a recess in the proceedings. As he rose to leave the bench, he looked at Cates and Winston. "I'll see you in my chambers in ten minutes," he announced.

"Thank you."

Robes flowing around him, the judge disappeared through a door behind the bench. Winston looked at Cates. "Why no 'Your Honor,' Cates?" he chided sarcastically.

"He isn't."

"Isn't what?"

"Isn't anything approaching honor. His, your, mine or anybody's."

Winston shook his head. "You're right," he murmured. "And so were they."

"Who's they?"

"The people who told me you were intractable."

English, meantime, had gotten down off the witness stand and approached them, a grin spreading over his features.

"Morning, Steve," the stocky narc greeted, extending his hand. "How'd you like the show?"

Cates made the introductions before responding to the question. If English was surprised to see him working with a Fed, he didn't demonstrate it.

"What a farce," Cates observed finally.

"That's Kennling," said English with a shrug. "And Erdmann, too, of course, though actually I don't blame him as much as I do the judge."

"How so?" inquired Winston.

English grinned. "Defense attorneys have to do that. It's in their nature, like whores have to give blow jobs and dogs piss on telephone poles. But the judge is supposed to set some bounds for this bullshit, and Kennling couldn't care less. Fortunately, most judges aren't like that."

Winston nodded in the direction of the prosecutor. "Who's the D.A.?"

"Name's Tiffany. Sandra Tiffany. She's new, but she's going to be good. If the Kennlings of the world don't wear her down first, of course." He turned to Cates. "What brings you guys here, anyway?"

Cates explained he was returning a search warrant, and briefly described the case.

English nodded. "I know the case," he said. "At least, I recall seeing it in the papers." He grinned at the two bikers, one of them in jail clothes, the other—apparently out of custody—in his grubby biker colors.

"I'm glad somebody knows the case," Cates observed in a wry tone, "because I sure don't."

English nodded. "In fact, when the story about the disappearance came out in the papers, I remember thinking back on it—Karchut and I were arresting these two dipshits about the same time, just across the canyon."

"You didn't happen to see the killer, did you?" Cates inquired facetiously.

"What, you want pictures or something? Jeez, you have to earn your cases, man. Like the rest of us do." He snickered at some private amusement.

"Pictures would be nice. Maybe a few shots with a long-range, telephoto, high-resolution camera of some sort." Cates grinned. "I mean, we've got an airtight case already, of course, but pictures are always nice."

"Pictures are nice," English agreed.

"Especially if they're color."

The muscular narc affected to shrug indifferently. "Matter of fact, I got the whole thing on video. I would have called you sooner, but I been busy. Plus, I didn't figure you'd need it anyway, seeing as how you're the hotshot, hot-shit homicide dick."

"Not to mention that I'm being helped out by the Feds," Cates pointed out.

"That, too."

"You see, we handle the real crimes, not this victimless, recreational drug stuff like crack and rock cocaine and crystal meth and angel dust."

"Yeah. Well, anyway, the color didn't come out too good on the videotape. You can see their faces real well, but the flesh tones are a little off."

"Well, we wouldn't want it then," Cates replied. "Only the best for us."

English made a good-natured gesture toward Winston. "Hell, Cates, you're already startin' to sound like a Fed."

"A great compliment," Winston said solemnly. "Detective Cates, I'm sure, understands that."

"Besides," the narc continued, "I think I already taped over it anyway."

"Over what?"

"My video of your homicide."

"What'd you tape? Something X-rated?"

"Nah. Cartoons. Which reminds me . . ." He proceeded to give a brief description of the nine-plant caper, including how the two defendants—English spoke just loudly enough for them to hear their actions recited—insisted on climbing up the line and leaping into the net.

"Tough case," Cates observed in mock sympathy. "And you're preaching to me about having to earn my cases?"

"It's a bitch. Anyway, you can plainly see I would have been way too busy crushing crime and dispensing justice to observe what was going on across the canyon." He paused and reflected on the events of the preceding Friday. "Actually, I remember it was real peaceful out there. Until these two dipshits barged into the picture, that is."

"Peaceful?"

"Yeah. One of those warm spring afternoons when everything seems sorta far away."

"Sounds nice."

"Yeah, it was. Not like today. Like the background noise—the freeways and all—were all kind of distant. You could see the cars in the distance; I remember a Caro's ambulance cruising around in that area. And you could hear the sounds. But it all seemed...removed, somehow. Like a TV that's in the next room."

Cates rolled his eyes. "Very poetic, Lar."

"Positively Homeric," agreed Winston.

The narc shrugged. "I just remember wanting to lie down on the side of the canyon and snooze for a while. And then Sneezy and Grumpy here came charging into my life and the rest is history."

At that moment, Judge Kennling appeared in the doorway. "Any time you gentlemen are ready, why don't you come on back," he said. The statement was addressed to Cates, and managed to convey a peculiar mixture of being accommodating and an inference that the judge had been waiting for them rather than the other way around.

Cates nodded goodbye to English, then headed back toward the Judge's chambers, wondering as he did so if by any stretch of luck the burly narcotics deputy had given him a clue after all.

20

Micah Harris

ON THAT SAME FRIDAY, Martie Griffin worked from seven to three out of LGS.

Working seven to three meant she reported to the substation at six-thirty in the morning and got back to her La Mesa apartment not long after three that afternoon. The city of La Mesa bordered on the south with Lemon Grove, and the distance was less than five miles. The day had been uneventful by law enforcement standards, at least for LGS, and, in sharp contrast to the weather earlier in the week, it had been cloudy and cool, with dark gray skies that threatened rain.

A bleak day, by San Diego standards.

Martie's schedule gave her Tuesdays and Wednesdays off, so this day was actually her Tuesday in terms of a normal work week. Though usually pretty adaptable, she felt strangely out of kilter now. Schedule lag, somebody once termed it.

An unusual mind fatigue beset her.

She felt drained of energy, but without any reason to be really tired. It was far too early to go to sleep; though she could easily have done so, that would have meant waking up in the middle of the night and further disrupting her biological clock. She rarely went to bars, unless it was with friends, and besides it was too early for that anyway.

It was too early, even, for good TV. Or dinner.

What the hell.

Probably, she thought, the best thing to do would be to go to the gym and work out.

An athletic woman anyway, Martie made it a point to work out with weights as well as run. She did so partly because it made her look better, though she still struggled with the physiological truism that a given volume of muscle weighed more than the same volume of fat. The result was that despite how trim she might be, the scale said a bigger number than it would have if she didn't lift, especially if she maintained the same relatively small percentage of body fat.

No way around it.

But she kept in shape for another reason, as well. This was to offset to some degree the hard, cold biological and physical fact that the average man was stronger than the average woman, and law enforcement was a profession where physical strength could make a difference. She didn't have any illusions that she could become stronger than a strong man, but she could at least climb a few notches above the average.

Alternatively, Martie thought, if she didn't feel like lifting weights, she could ride an exercise bike. Or maybe do an aerobics session; the gym normally held a four o'clock intermediate class.

Another possibility existed, however, a different approach to attacking the doldrums. She could crack a bottle of wine, draw a bath just as hot as she could stand it, toss in some bath oil, soak for about fifteen minutes, then paint her nails, watch TV and flip through the latest issue of *Vogue* or *Cosmopolitan*. There was that bottle of white zinfandel—admittedly, a foo-foo wine as wines went, but she liked it—in the fridge; with some sourdough bread, it could make a nice combination.

She really should work out, though.

Who the hell was it who said usually what you don't want to do is what you should do? Probably Brother Edgar, when she was in the seventh grade at St. Anne's.

With a sigh, she cast about for her workout tights, then remembered they were in her gym bag in her car.

With a crisp, hollow pop the cork came free of the bottle. A mild roaring sound issued from the bathroom as the water rushed into the tub. Martie switched on the radio; appropriately, the sounds of Billy Idol doing "Dancing with Myself" filled the apartment.

Good.

She liked Billy Idol's music and in a perverse way liked his bad-boy image, all the more so because she was a cop. Bubbles foamed as she measured in the oil; just as quickly, they vanished, leaving the water hot and slippery and clear. As she lowered herself into the tub, wineglass close at hand, Martie knew she'd made the right call.

Besides, she had run two miles on Tuesday anyway, after the autopsy on her first eleven-forty-four. There would be time enough to work out tomorrow.

The water was so hot it gave her goose bumps. She always thought of that as somehow backward, something that was supposed to happen when you were cold, not when you were hot.

Martie held her breath as she lay back in the tub, then let it out in something between a hiss and a sigh as the heat stung her flesh. In a drowsy and detached manner, she watched her pubic hair gently waving in the water, and her nipples, erect and taut from the initial gooseflesh reaction.

Her mind drifted over the events of the past few days.

She was troubled by Cates's angry reaction to her inquiry about Slaman and the Braxton caper following the autopsy. Was that only three days ago? She decided that it was.

Steve Cates was a mixed bag, all right.

No, make that multifaceted. The term sounded better and didn't carry as strong a suggestion that part of the mixture might not be all good.

All right, he was multifaceted. Physically imposing, the tall detective looked powerful and strong. She had heard he played college football somewhere, which fit. Yet even his ruggedness seemed somehow refined, not rough like most ball players or other tough cops.

Obviously, he was a reader and a thinker. His discourse on honor and chivalry showed that. But he was more than simply a theoretician, an abstract reasoner. Plainly, he sought to apply what he read to his world—their world, she amended, for after all, she was a cop, too—bridging the gap between philosophical principles and actual practice.

Applied epistemology. Hands-on philosophy. Where-the-rubber-hits-the-road metaphysics.

Multifaceted described him, all right. Martie doubted that many other people recognized it. Certainly she herself hadn't and probably wouldn't have, but for their discussion outside the morgue.

But there was something more to him as well, just as there was something more to her observations about him. She had been trying to put her finger on it, but it eluded her. Then, like the proverbial light bulb going on, it came to her. And, like most such things, it was simplicity itself once she saw it.

It had to do with precisely the fact that she wouldn't have guessed he had those interests and abilities.

The man seemed to enjoy understatement; at least, he understated his own qualities. He was sort of a chameleon, though in a deceptively subtle way. Yet she strongly suspected—no, she knew—that he would always manage to preserve his own personality. The changes would be in appearance only, not in any way altering his honesty and individuality.

Changeable he was, maybe even slippery, but a yes-man—or a Slaman—he was definitely not.

She shook her head at the thought of the fat deputy coroner. What a sleaze, she thought. And clearly what bad blood between him and Cates.

Odd that it would be that way. Martie had a strong aversion to oily, unctuous slimeballs of the sort Slaman seemed to exemplify. She remembered his patently lewd appraisal of her, the glitter of his eyes as he gazed at her, up and down. But even given all that, Cates's reaction had seemed disproportionately strong. To her, Slaman seemed more of an unpleasant nuisance than anything else. He might be a Slime-man, but he hadn't shown anything to warrant the kind of anger Cates had displayed.

She had heard about the Braxton incident, of course. Still, in retrospect what she had heard was only the tip of the iceberg.

The Braxton case had been talked about at the academy. Not officially, of course, but in that sotto voce manner in which a lot of the practical aspects of police work were taught—"how it really is, never mind about what the book says." It was one of those things that would afford a minor status to the trainee who might recognize Cates and be able to point him out to others and whisper, "That's Cates, the guy in the Braxton caper they were talking about."

Now she knew about it. And she knew as well that the rumors were hopelessly inadequate, and superficial and misleading, and she wished they would stop. For Cates's sake.

From the kitchen, the telephone rang in a sharp jangle, jarring her out of her thoughts.

She frowned. Her number wasn't listed, so casual callers were rare. It had to be going on four; who would be calling at this time? Perhaps the D.A.'s office, saying they'd forgotten to subpoena her on some case or another, and could she please come to court first thing in the morning?

Martie considered not answering it, then carefully pushed herself to her feet in the slippery water. Wrapping a towel around herself, she made her way to the telephone on the kitchen wall.

"Hello?"

A hard, Brooklyn-accented voice greeted her. "Martie, this is Lieutenant Patrick."

Apprehension jolted her. Lieutenant Patrick was the acting commander of LGS.

The day-to-day workings of each substation were normally the charge of a captain, running the law enforcement for the areas served by the station. In the case of LGS, it was Captain Blakely, widely respected as one of the grand old men of the department. Captain Blakely was on vacation, however, and Lieutenant Patrick was the acting man in charge.

Patrick was a tall, lanky man with sandy hair and an accent that Martie thought of as Brooklyn/Bronx/New Jersey, "one of those, anyway." He was a hard-charger and fair to his people, but he was also tough.

"Yes, Lieutenant?"

"I need to see you. Right away."

"In person, Lieutenant?"

"In person. Be in my office in . . . twenty minutes."

Martie glanced at the clock. Five minutes before four. "May I make that four-thirty, sir? I mean, I'll come sooner, but I'd like to get presentable, if that's all right."

There was a hesitation, then Patrick's strong voice came back over the line. "Make it four-thirty then."

"Yes, sir."

"Very well. Goodbye." The connection was broken before she had a chance to rejoin.

The apprehension expanded inside her. It made a knot in her stomach and ran down her limbs in little shivers. She respected Lieutenant Patrick. He was a good supervisor, and he believed in good police work, regardless of whose toes it stepped on. Still, whatever he wanted, the fact that he wanted to communicate it in person, under these circumstances, was definitely a strong indication that it was not good news.

What could she have done wrong?

She thought over the events of the past two days. They'd been slow days. A few tickets, several crime reports and two family 415s—domestic disturbances or husband and wife fights; arrests in both instances. One probable child abuse case as well, which she got involved with through a social worker with Child Protective Services and ultimately turned over to the Child Abuse Unit of the S.O.

Sudden visions of the child victim in that case swam before her.

Little Micah Harris, age seven, his back and the backs of his legs mottled with purple bruises turning saffron from the beatings inflicted by the dirtbag, drug-addict boyfriend of his dirtbag, drug-addict mother because the child wouldn't stop coughing. But those beatings had stopped several days previously, the investigators determined, because the two adults had found it more practical to simply lock him in an old steamer trunk with four holes drilled in it for air.

When the trunk was in the closet and the closet doors were shut, his mother explained with a thin, nasal whine, they couldn't hear him, "leastways not if'n the TV was on."

"Little bastard's a goddamn pain in the ass," the boy-friend had muttered when he was arrested.

"Jeez, what's the big deal?" had been the mother's only comment.

Martie had experienced a momentary sort of insanity, in which she nearly lost it. She had come too close to letting go and committing a frenzied assault with her nightstick on whichever of the two suspects had been handy at the time. Preferably on both of them. This was the first time in four years she had come so near to losing it, and it frightened her a little.

The child had been catatonic when the investigators found him, and, the hospital determined, in an advanced stage of pneumonia. Thanks to modern medicine, he was saved, though for what kind of a future Martie wasn't sure.

Martie had had nightmares about the case the following night, last night, in fact. The dreams disturbed her, and the fact they had occurred disturbed her as well. Maybe she wasn't as tough as she'd like to think she was. Angrily, she thrust the images from her mind and concentrated on the possible reasons for the lieutenant's call.

Had somebody complained about her?

Then she realized that the incident that triggered this didn't have to be something in the past two days. It could have been anytime, but with the heat just now surfacing. Had a ten-million-dollar lawsuit just been filed over something she had done? Had somebody she'd arrested turned out to be the wrong guy?

It was possible, of course—it was always possible—but she couldn't think what it could be.

There'd been a hanging in the jail about eight months back, before she came to patrol. The family of the deceased had initially made a lot of noise that somebody in the jail, possibly even a deputy, had killed him, and the hanging was a cover-up. But the noise had died down, especially when an independent pathologist hired by the family reviewed the autopsy and confirmed the only cause of death was the strangulation caused by the man's belt, with which he had hanged himself.

A longtime street wino had been found dead in the drunk tank one night she was working. The man was forty-seven but looked sixty-seven, she recalled. The autopsy had shown his er to be completely destroyed and his blood alcohol level at the time of death was probably in excess of .30.

The problem came when allegations were raised that the man had actually died before being booked. That meant the arresting officers—not from the S.O., though that didn't necessarily mean anything—had realized he was dead but booked him anyway so they wouldn't have to deal with the corpse. Regardless of how blameless the officers might be with respect to the death, it was considered bad form to photograph and print and process a dead man.

Martie had been interviewed by both the Jail Investigations Unit detectives and by San Diego Police Internal Affairs, she recalled. Beyond that, however, she had heard only that the results of the investigation were inconclusive.

Could that matter have surfaced again?

She hurriedly toweled herself, hit the ends of her hair with the hair dryer and gave minimal attention to her lips and eyes. She brushed her teeth, and by four-twenty was outside Lieutenant Patrick's office at LGS.

He was speaking into the telephone when she checked by his office. He glanced up at her, then brought the conversation to an end and hung up the phone.

"Come in, Martie." His voice sounded tense, and a little awkward, which surprised her. "Thanks for comin' down."

She hadn't been under the impression that she'd had an option, Martie thought. His earlier telephone call certainly hadn't suggested it. And somehow his words made things all the more ominous now.

She sat down in one of the chairs. The lieutenant walked around and closed the door, then returned to his position behind the desk.

"Assistant Sheriff Tisdale called this afternoon. Right about three, shortly after you left, apparently."

Fear seized her.

Lieutenant Patrick continued speaking. "I want to get your side of it, but I'll tell you right now that he's really pissed off. So just listen to me, hear me out, then give me your response."

"Yes, Lieutenant."

Patrick's brow was furrowed, his expression troubled. "You've got a good record, Martie. An excellent one, in fact. That's why I'm doin' it this way. Normally, I'd cross-examine you, so to speak, try to pin you down along the way." He took a deep breath. "I hope I'm not makin' a mistake to do it this other way now."

Lieutenant Patrick's speech had a halting, somehow slightly uncoordinated quality that was, however, by no means a sign of timidity. Even his everyday speaking voice was hard and strong, though he had a tendency to drop his g's.

Martie waited for him to continue.

"That body you found last Monday. The woman that disappeared—Fisher. That's developed into an extremely sensitive case. You read the papers, I'm sure, so you know the media loves it, but I'm not talkin' about that.

"For some reason, the sheriff himself is very interested in this case." He pronounced it in-ter-es-ted, four syllables, with the accent equal on all syllables. "Way beyond the stuff in the papers. The FBI is involved in it, and there may be some national security ramifications to it. Or so Tisdale told me, but he didn't tell me why this was so."

He hesitated, and Martie wondered if she should speak. Patrick continued, however.

"Now, he says you've continued to involve yourself in the case, beyond what you should apart from you were the one that found the body. Before I get your side, you should know that somebody at the coroner's office told him you were at the autopsy."

Slaman! she thought instantly.

That bastard! Her insides contracted into a cold knot of fear.

Lieutenant Patrick's face was hard, but beneath it he looked concerned. "I guess Tisdale had his secretary call out there to get a copy of the autopsy report. To put the rush on it. And they talked to somebody in the coroner's office, who said copies had already been sent to the investigating officer—Detective Cates—and to you. Which of course was not typical, because the patrol deputy who finds the body just never gets sent those reports.

"Anyway the assistant sheriff gets on the phone and reams the guy out for sending a confidential report on such a sensitive case to anybody except the homicide detective. And the guy tells him you were at the autopsy so he figured you were one of the investigators, on temporary assignment to Homicide."

Bastard! she thought. That bastard, bastard, bastard.

He knew goddamn well I wasn't assigned to it. Cates had been convincing when he passed it off that she was just following up on the autopsy of her first dead body. And Slaman's appraisal of the situation had been so patently sexual that she didn't have any doubt that he believed it, undoubtedly thinking that Cates was letting her tag along because they were lovers.

Or because Cates was screwing her, she amended with a certain disgust, which was how Slaman would put it.

Lieutenant Patrick was speaking again. "Did you go to the autopsy, Martie?"

"Yes."

"Now think it over before you answer me. Why did you go?"

For a microsecond, she froze. Then the decision was made. "A couple of reasons, actually. Mainly because it was my first 11-44, and I was curious to follow it through a little. See the autopsy."

"And the other reason?"

She shrugged. "I . . . liked Detective Cates. I was attracted to him. That plus the fact it was my first dead body made me want to follow it a little."

Lieutenant Patrick looked surprised. He thought for a few moments, then spoke again, evidently trying to choose his words carefully. "I'm probably not permitted to ask this, but are you two...involved with each other?"

She had hoped he would ask, because she wanted to clear the air. "No. And we're not sleeping together, either."

Patrick sighed. "Tisdale wanted you moved to jail duty."

Oh, God, Martie thought, back to square one. Only it would be worse, because now she would actually be in the hole. She'd have two strikes against her, a black mark to work off.

"I told him he couldn't do that, not without following the personnel procedures of giving you notice and a hearing and all that. There's nothing against the rules about punitive transfers, but you have a right to contest them. Not like the old days."

Christ, Martie was thinking, my career.

Patrick took a deep breath and continued. "He directed me to transfer you to midnights. I think he figured that was the worst he could do without having it considered a punitive action. Which is true—night patrol is considered equal to day patrol, so the fact he was pissed off when he did it doesn't make it a punitive decision."

He waited, and she sat there, numbed by the enormity of it all.

In the past four years or so, since she'd been on the department, she felt as if she'd become pretty tough, something of a take-charge person. And now, it seemed as if her assertiveness, her strength, had vanished, were all for naught. She'd almost lost control about little Micah, and now this.

Moreover, she felt as if she'd let somebody—many bodies—down. Cates. Even Lieutenant Patrick, who was being far more considerate than she felt she deserved. Herself.

Then the ship righted itself a little, and she managed to speak. "Will this go in my jacket?" she inquired.

"No. It's just a reassignment as far as your records are concerned."

"What about outside my jacket?"

"What do you mean?"

"Will this be something that follows me forever, or until Tisdale dies or leaves the department? Does the sheriff now think of me as a . . . whatever I am?"

Lieutenant Patrick thought about it. "I doubt it. This sounds more like one of those snap decisions, reflexive actions, that somebody like Tisdale makes when he's pissed off. And I wouldn't be surprised if he didn't tell the sheriff, because it might make him look bad to the sheriff. So unless the whole case really blows sky-high for some unforeseen reason, my guess is you'll be okay."

Martie didn't respond.

"Other people in the department have stepped on their—" Lieutenant Patrick caught himself and rephrased his description "—have stepped on themselves a lot worse than this, and have overcome it. Cates is one of them, in fact." He paused. "And, speakin' of Cates, he no way should have let you do this. Not on this kind of a case."

"Is he in trouble?"

"That remains to be seen. I have no knowledge of what will happen there. But I bet something will." Lieutenant Patrick grimaced. "He may be on midnight patrol next week, too."

She listened numbly.

"Now," the lieutenant said in a businesslike tone, "today's Friday, and you already worked. Seven to three, if I recall. Tomorrow, you'll work three to eleven, working one of the L.G. City cars. And Sunday, you'll start mids, eleven to seven. No reason not to keep the same days off, so that won't change. Any questions?"

Martie made a wry smile. "You don't have to break me in easy to mids, if that's what you're doing. Hell, I'll be there tonight if you want."

Patrick nodded. "I believe you would. And that's all to your credit. But that's not why I'm doin' this. It's for unrelated reasons, havin' to do with other manpower problems."

"I see."

"You've got a good reputation, Griffin. And you've earned it. Don't take this too hard. Chances are, it'll blow over."

"Thanks, Lieutenant." She got up to leave, then turned to speak with him again. "It's probably not my place to say, but I appreciate the way you went about all this."

He waved her out of the office. "Don't mention it. Good luck."

Outside, as Martie crossed the parking lot to her car, the skies glowered a dark gray and the breeze actually felt cold. She felt awful to the very marrow of her bones.

THE FOLLOWING DAY proved to be just as cloudy and bleak as Friday had been. The gray weather made it seem as if the twilight came earlier, and by seven-thirty that evening it was gathering and waiting.

Martie had slept erratically on Friday night. She tried to go to bed at eleven, but after tossing for an hour, had gotten up shortly after midnight. She made some hot cocoa and watched the *David Letterman Show*, which on the West Coast came on at 12:30 a.m.

At one-thirty, she gave it another try, and slipped into a fitful sleep.

Sometime before four, she dreamed little Micah Harris was in her bathroom, pleading for help. Hearing his muffled cries, she started to open the bathroom door, only to discover it was locked.

She stood back from the door to kick it in, cop-style. It refused to yield to her repeated attempts, so she abandoned proper police procedure and took out her gun to shoot off the lock, as in the movies.

And somehow Cates was there, telling her not to shoot the lock because a round might go through and hit Micah. She began shooting anyway, only somehow the bathroom became the blue Taurus and when she got the door open, there was Beth Fisher, already eviscerated by the autopsy....

With a sharp cry, Martie sat bolt upright in bed, her throat dry and her shoulders hunched as if against an anticipated blow.

She turned on the lights, then got up and made another cup of hot chocolate. She read for an hour, and finally fell into a deep, dreamless sleep that lasted until almost ten Saturday morning.

At two-thirty that afternoon, Martie reported for work at LGS. She flatly refused to respond to the inevitable questions as to why she had been reassigned. It was her practice to look for the bright side of everything, but on this day, it wasn't coming easily.

She was grateful that Saturday nights in the Grove had a lot of activity, plenty to divert her mind.

Lieutenant Patrick had assigned Martie for that one shift to a car whose primary area of responsibility was the city itself. Her unit designation was 61-Paul-1, and from the time the shift began, it seemed as if 61-Paul-1 was coming over the air every few minutes.

Never one to shirk her duties, Martie threw herself into the job, despite the fact that it was going to be a one-night stand as far as three-to-eleven was concerned. By six she actually felt pretty good, despite the gloomy weather and the circumstances of her being there. By seven she'd temporarily forgotten the mess that caused her to be there.

Shortly after seven-thirty—the homicide investigators would later determine it to be 7:34—Martie heard her unit designation come over the air yet again.

"61-Paul-1 and 61-Paul-2, check a report of an 11-7, possibly armed with an unknown type of handgun, in the area of 7112 North Street."

A hiss of static had accompanied the transmission. Martie thought she had heard it correctly, but decided to ask for a repeat. Maneuvering the patrol car with her left hand, she keyed the microphone with her right.

"61-Paul-1," she acknowledged. "Would you 10-9 that last transmission?"

The dispatcher's voice came immediately back. "Roger, 61-Paul. That's a report of an 11-7, possibly armed with a handgun, in the vicinity of 7112 North Street."

Martie's heart beat faster. Prowler calls were common on patrol, and in the vast majority of cases, either proved to be somebody's cat or else the suspect was GOA, gone on arrival of the deputy. This one, however, had a different ring to it, and she had yet to encounter a cat with a handgun.

"61-Paul-1," she responded, "10-4. I'm en route from Massachusetts and San Miguel. ETA is a couple." Dropping the mike in her lap, Martie made a sharp U-turn and accelerated quickly. She drove rapidly, without, however, pulling out all the stops and running full Code 3.

"Roger, 61-Paul-1," came the dispatcher's voice. "I'm getting no response from 61-Paul-2."

Martie thought quickly. "61-Paul-1, any further details?"

"Reporting party is an elderly woman, semi-invalid. Says a male subject s .e believes with a gun was in alley behind her house, cut through between houses and is possibly adjacent or in rear of 7112."

"61-Paul-1, do we have an address on the R/P?"

"Affirmative. R/P is at 7110 North."

"61-Paul-1, 10-4."

Martie dropped the mike back into her lap and hit the overhead flashing lights to go through the intersection at Broadway, then keyed the mike again.

"61-Paul-1. Any indication the R/P is acquainted with the suspect? Ex-husband or neighbor?"

"Negative, 61-Paul-1."

The headlights picked up North Street, intersecting from the left. The threatening gray clouds combined with the dusk of twilight to make a not-quite-darkness that was somehow more deceptive than full nighttime.

As she approached it, Martie could see that North Street appeared deserted. She switched off the headlights and hit the blackout switch, which also deactivated the brake lights as well. Window down, she rolled slowly along, scanning the sides of the street for an address.

7186. 7180. And across the street, 7177.

Good. The numbers were descending. She was going in the right direction. 7110 and 7112 would be on the right.

Even as she looked for the numbers, on another level her mind was formulating what to do. She hadn't heard anything regarding the second unit dispatched to the scene, 61-Paul-2.

Still, it was always conceivable that he was responding as well, something to be kept in mind in case she saw a sudden movement. And, she decided, the best approach would be to stay blacked out, and move in slowly. 7112 would come up first; if there was no sign of the 11-7, Martie would contact the R/P at 7110.

On the left, she caught another number. 7143. And up ahead to the right, 7138.

A duplex with 7132.

After that the numbers took a jump, dropping clear off to 7120, a small apartment complex with cars jammed around it. Then, as nearly as she could make out in the darkness, a string of four small frame houses, all similar.

No 7118.

There was 7116, which had a yellow porch light burning.

The next two were dark; the one beyond that also had a light. Probably the R/P, she thought, some poor old lady trying to live on social security and maybe her husband's pension. Frightened to death, so she's turned on all the lights to scare the suspect away.

Tires screeched and an engine roared, but that came from a block over, and receded into the distance. Somewhere a radio was playing, the song in Spanish. Mexican radio, she thought.

For no real reason, this didn't feel like a routine 11-7. Where is 61-Paul-goddamn-2?

Something moved in the shadows to the right, next to what should be 7114.

Martie looked sharply over, but it was gone.

She picked up the mike, keyed it and spoke softly. "61-Paul-1, 10-97. I'll be on foot for a few."

Having thus advised the dispatcher she was on the scene, Martie slid the idling patrol car into an open space in front of a fire hydrant, switched off the engine and got quietly out, not shutting the door because of the noise.

For an instant, she thought of taking the shotgun, a vastly superior weapon to the .357 Magnum Smith & Wesson Model 66 service revolver. Still, all the heart-pounding aside, the odds were that the call would be a dud. Besides, she wanted to be out faster and to be more mobile once she was out.

As she reached the sidewalk, she heard it.

Two things, actually.

Ahead, between 7112 and 7110, came a slight thud followed by a dry rattling noise. To Martie's ear, it sounded as if somebody had inadvertently kicked an empty cardboard box and sent it scraping over hard-packed dry earth.

The second sound seemed to come from farther back, to the rear of the house. It sounded like the peculiar thud of a toe against a wooden fence. The image it created in her mind was of somebody trying to go over by putting hands on the top, then jumping up and pressing down, in the course of which the toe of one shoe had clunked a board in the fence.

Martie crouched and moved forward.

She slid the gun out of its basket-weave leather holster, the hard rubber grips she had installed in place of the walnut factory stocks making a comfortable presence in her sweating palm.

A large, scraggly tree—a California pepper, she guessed—grew in the front yard, just to the left of where the property line would be. It had a thick, rough trunk and long, drooping green tendrils that brushed at her face and uniform as she slipped ahead.

Another sound, something being kicked. It was followed by a sharp intake of breath and utter silence, as if somebody had frozen to see if anybody else had heard it.

Martie froze as well. Her eyes strained in the near darkness, probing the shadows for any sign of the person, friend or foe.

For a minute that seemed like an hour there was no sound. Finally, to break the stalemate and because she had to do something, she moved quickly forward, hoping by instinct to avoid kicking the same box that the suspect had but not caring too much if she did. Then she was between the two shabby houses, and now toward the rear, and suddenly she saw him.

Her mind instantly assimilated the data. Male, probably. Caucasian; the face made a pale spot in the darkness. Medium height, say five-eight or -nine. Dark clothing.

Standing motionless in the backyard, almost straight ahead of her, looking off to her left, somewhere behind the house.

Something in his hand.

Something dark.

Then he moved slightly, and the something glinted briefly from some reflected light from somewhere. The something was a gun and it looked as if he was starting to raise it.

"Police—freeze!" she screamed, raising her own pistol at arm's length, flexing her knees slightly into a quarter squat and gripping the weapon in a two-handed bipod position.

Everything happened instantly.

The figure spun toward her, raising the gun and screaming "Die, fucker!" and for once in her life Martie reacted properly, knew she was reacting properly, didn't stop to think or analyze but fired instantly. She fired three times, just as fast as she could, a quick *boom! boom! boom!*

Martie was vaguely aware of at least one shot coming from the suspect, a quick, flat *crack!* accompanied by a white flash, probably of a .22 short or maybe a low-power .25 caliber. And then the suspect was falling and there was another noise off to the left by the fence and she was scrabbling for her hand-held radio in the leather holder on her belt.

She keyed the radio and screamed "11-99!" but before she could identify herself something ran into the wooden fence at the back of the yard.

She dropped the radio and swung the gun. It was another figure but he seemed to be trying to run away. It was dark and she couldn't see him very well, and she wasn't sure if he had a gun or not, so she hesitated. In that moment's hesitation he was over the fence and gone.

She stooped and picked up the handy-talkie, wondering if it would still work, but it had to be working because she could hear the dispatcher saying, "Unit calling? Identify yourself, unit calling on the 11-99? Identify yourself." So with shaking hands and voice she did that, "11-99, 61-Paul-1, at 7112

North. Shots fired, 11-8, 11-41," using the codes for person down, ambulance needed, while a weird part of her mind marveled that she still remembered those codes, which didn't get used that often. But they had taught her well at the academy, and after all, she was a diligent student who always tried to do the right thing, didn't she?

Then, the revolver still thrust out in front of her, clutched in both fists, she went over to the still form. Gun in her right hand, she crouched and gripped the barrel of the gun in the outstretched hand.

Even as she pulled it away, she realized that it wasn't one, not a real one, anyway.

Horror flooded over her, and she struggled to maintain control. She looked at the object in her hand and saw that it was a toy, not a cap gun but a toy gun nonetheless. Still, she set it behind her, off to one side, out of reach, then reached shakily for her flashlight with her left hand.

She shone it on the man she had shot.

The man was a teenager. Maybe fourteen, she guessed.

He was dead.

hot water

IT WAS HOMICIDE DETECTIVE Ben Grummon who got the call-out on Deputy Martie Griffin's shooting incident.

A written policy and procedure set the protocol to be followed for such cases. The P and P required that for every deputy-involved shooting, a command-level official and the Homicide Detail be advised. Apart from obtaining medical assistance for the injured and notifying the coroner for deceased persons, the patrol personnel did no more than preserve the scene for those investigators.

Grummon's regular partner was, of course, Steve Cates, who had been working the special assignment to the Beth Fisher matter. During the past week, however, Grummon had been teamed with Alberto Dejesus—pronounced *day-hay-soos*, though often the sounds became run together, the result being closer to *day-yay-soos*. Alberto was on loan from the Special Investigations Detail, which included both Vice and Intelligence, and was believed to be first in line for the next opening in Homicide. Obviously of pure Hispanic origin, he was a good-looking, athletic deputy with a dark complexion, a ready smile and soulful brown eyes.

For no real reason other than a hunch, Grummon had telephoned Cates after getting the call-out at seven-forty.

The interdepartmental grapevine traveled fast, and he had already heard something of Martie's reassignment to midnights. He had also heard that it had something to do with Cates taking her along on the Fisher homicide. Grummon recognized that action—assuming it were true—to be highly unusual. He speculated that it might be that Cates and Martie had something going between them. But he knew that was only one possible explanation for Cates doing so.

Cates answered the telephone midway through the first ring. Grummon told him what little he knew—that Martie had been involved in a shooting out of LGS. Cates sounded concerned, and requested Ben call when more details were known. He didn't share the reasons for his concern, and Grummon didn't ask.

Grummon was on the scene in ten minutes. This was exactly ten minutes before the news cameras got there, and fifteen minutes before the newsmen were concluding that the shooting was probably yet another example of law enforcement's attitude toward the minority community.

A few minutes after eight, Grummon telephoned Cates again, strictly unofficially, of course.

ALL THINGS CONSIDERED, it had not been the best of evenings for Steve Cates. Or the best of days either, for that matter.

He had awakened that morning, ill. It wasn't a hangover, exactly. A former girlfriend had aptly described the condition as *hont i haret*. The phrase was a Swedish idiom that literally meant "pain in the roots of my hair," and it seemed to fit exactly what Cates was experiencing.

The condition was caused in this instance, he suspected, by an unhappy combination of too many adult beverages, as he liked to put it, and too much food. Since he hadn't really had an inordinate amount to drink, Cates assumed the latter was as much or more to blame as the former.

Maybe.

Apart from the way his head—and hair—were feeling, his teeth felt as if they had sweaters on them. He brushed them long and hard, and followed the brushing with a chaser of two glasses of orange juice.

Then he turned on the shower, only to find there was no hot water. He lived in a small house just south of the city of El Cajon, east of both La Mesa and Lemon Grove and, of course, the city of San Diego itself.

After the water ran from the supposedly hot tap for five minutes without getting warm, Cates surmised something might be amiss.

Brilliant deduction, he thought, especially for one suffering from *hont i haret*. Perhaps the pilot light to the gas heater had gone out. The deduction pleased him; only a trained investigator would have found a solution so quickly.

The hot water heater was located in the garage.

He opened the door that led there from his dining area, and found his deduction to be correct. The pilot light had indeed gone out. The bottom of the not-quite-antique hot water heater that had come with the house when he bought it had gone out as well, and the entire garage was flooded.

Cates stared at the water in disbelief, then dismay and finally weary acceptance.

He shut the door and poured another glass of orange juice. And, though the thought of it was just a step or two shy of nauseating, he went to the cupboard and took out a fistful of desiccated liver tablets, a massive multivitamin and four lecithin capsules that somebody told him might help reverse the effect on his arteries of the six eggs he used to eat every day when he was playing college football. He gulped them down with the orange juice, and debated his next move.

It was not an easy task.

Homicide detectives should not replace hot water heaters. He knew that for a certainty. The whole concept of comparative advantage, upon which much of the science of economics was based, said that specialists were more efficient from the system perspective than amateurs. And plumbers were specialists.

It was Saturday. Between the cost of a new heater, a call-out fee and the hourly rate, he estimated the job could be done for a mere . . . what, four hundred dollars?

Or he could buy his own hot water heater through a contractor friend, and put it in himself. It would cost less than a couple of hundred.

Besides, if he did that, he could take the difference between what it cost and what he estimated the specialist would charge—a saving of, say, a couple of hundred—and put it into the Frivolous Fund.

The Frivolous Fund was an old steel ammo box into which went all varieties of found money and unexpected bonuses—not too many of those came around, these days—gifts from family, tax refunds and monies he saved by doing things himself. The only rule that governed the periodic expenditures from the fund was that it had to be something self-indulgent, something he didn't need and certainly couldn't justify spending "good money" on.

Like flying first class, which for somebody his size was a material benefit just in terms of seat room, but which he couldn't otherwise bring himself to do. Or buying an occasional case of expensive wine. Or even taking an extra, spur-of-the-moment vacation or trip from time to time.

As a younger man, he had put in his share of hours on the business end of a pipe wrench and blowtorch and solder, to say nothing of picks and shovels and hammers and nails. He could do it himself, though granted not as efficiently as a specialist.

A hell of a lot cheaper, though. But probably not as good for the economy. And it would somehow be better in the cosmic scheme of things—after all, he wouldn't like it if the plumbers started trying to solve homicides, would he?

Right. He didn't really like the thought of doing it himself, but there was always the Frivolous Fund to consider....

He spent the day replacing the heater.

The house was what real estate agents like to call "an older home," which in that area meant it had probably been built around the time of World War II. It was solid and well-built—overbuilt by modern standards—but it still had the original plumbing, which consisted of galvanized pipes, copper not having been in vogue at the time. The pipe was so corroded that he ended up replacing about fifteen feet of it, clear to the bathroom, as well as the hot water heater.

By the time he finished, it was late afternoon.

He was tired; he had scrapes and burns on knuckles of both hands; his back hurt from crouching in the crawl space beneath the house where some of the corroded pipes were; and oily grime had penetrated every pore of his hands. He did, however, have hot water. Or would soon have it, anyway, as soon as the new unit did its job. He would have it in unprecedented volume, thanks to the new copper piping he had installed.

Still, it seemed a hell of a way to spend Saturday after a tough week.

He had been holding forth the promise of a beer upon successful completion of the job.

He scrubbed the grime off his hands as best he could with Ajax and the now warm water, and replaced his grimy work clothes with a sweat suit. Later, when the water was really hot, he'd christen the whole job with a long, hot shower. In the meantime, he took a mug out of the freezer and opened a bottle of Dos Equis.

The dark, bitter Mexican beer was as good as he had anticipated. When it was gone, he rummaged through the refrigerator and found a block of smoked cheese and some whole wheat crackers. He took those and Dos Equis *numero dos* into the living room. It was a dark, cloudy evening, but the house was warm and he stretched out on the couch in appreciation of the day's labors.

At the end of beer number two—along with a half pound of the cheese and most of the crackers—Cates debated whether to have a third.

The affirmative side of the debate prevailed without much difficulty. After all, at his body weight it was equivalent to a petite 110-pound woman having one and a half beers, and he certainly wouldn't criticize her for that.

At the conclusion of that one, he wondered if he should at least test the quality control at the Dos Equis brewery by having a fourth. Thus far, he had to admit, the quality control had been quite good, but four was after all a more representative sampling than merely three. And still only two beers in almost an hour for the 110-pounder.

At that moment the telephone rang.

It was Grummon. As they talked, all concern over the quality control of Dos Equis vanished.

"Cates." The gruff voice of his erstwhile partner was immediately recognizable.

"Yeah, Ben. What's up?"

"I just got a call-out on a deputy-involved shooting out of LGS. The deputy is, ah, the same one who found the body in the Fisher caper. Griffin. I thought you might like to know."

"Is she all right?" Cates asked quickly. He liked Martie, and he still didn't feel right about having her involved in the Fisher case.

"Yeah. As far as I know."

"Details?"

"All I know is it was some kid, a teenager."

"The kid hit?"

"Dead."

"Jesus."

Grummon spoke again. "She was responding to a prowler call of some kind. She thought he pulled a gun on her, and she dumped him. What the kid was doing, or if he even had a gun or not, I don't know yet."

"He might not have had a gun?"

"I don't know yet. I was just calling you to let you know."

"Jesus," Cates repeated reverently.

Martie hadn't seemed to be possessed of the avenging-angel mentality some cops had. She looked like the type to take any shooting seriously. If it turned out to be a teenager, it would be that much harder to deal with. And if, God forbid, it turned out to be one of those cases where he didn't even have a gun...

For an instant, visions of Braxton surged before him. Angrily, he thrust them away.

Most cops he knew didn't go around on a day-to-day basis worrying about getting killed. The exception, he knew, was when you were actually involved in something really dangerous, like walking into a shoot-out, an armed robbery or a hostage situation. At those times, the pucker-factor was pretty high.

It was more common to worry about getting the hell kicked out of you on a traffic stop or responding to a bar fight or a family disturbance call. And when the barriers were really down, a surprising number of officers would admit that one of the things that would really be tough to handle was blowing away somebody who turned out not to be a crook, or even a crook who turned out not to have been armed.

It might be legally justified, or excused, in the sense the deputy wouldn't be punished for it. But emotionally, it would take some handling.

Cates, of all people, was aware of that.

Officers were entitled to base their use of deadly force on what the law called "reasonable appearances." In legal theory, if it reasonably appeared the person was a suspect who was about to inflict death or great bodily injury on you or somebody else, it was justifiable to blow him or her away.

But when it turned out that the suspect at whom you screamed "Freeze!" only had a screwdriver in his hand when he spun around and you shot him—your heart pounding and blood roaring in your ears and the adrenaline in your system leaving you tingly and wired for a half hour afterward—what appeared "reasonable" became a very iffy matter indeed. At those times, the Monday-morning quarterbacks came out in full force, from the ACLU to the media. Especially the media. And God help you if the person you shot happened to be black or Mexican or some other minority.

Cates knew all this.

He could imagine how hard it would be on Martie if something like this were the case. Then something else occurred to him, something that had been bothering him from the moment Ben told him what had happened.

"I thought she worked seven to three," Cates observed. "What's she doing on midnights?"

Grummon was silent for a moment. "Didn't you know?" he asked at last.

"Know what?"

"She got transferred to mids. Starting tomorrow. This is just some sort of interim thing."

Apprehension beset him. "Why'd she get transferred?"

Again, Grummon hesitated. "It's not my business, Steve-o, and I'm not asking for details. But the word is she got in some hot water over being involved in the Fisher 187 when she wasn't supposed to."

"I didn't know that," Cates said after a moment.

"Well, that's the grapevine."

Cates was silent as he digested the information. Finally, he addressed Grummon again. "Will you call me back when you find out more about the shooting?"

"You gonna be there?"

"Yes."

"Will do."

The telephone made a sharp click, and Grummon was gone. Cates replaced the receiver and stared moodily across the living room at the empty fireplace. Somehow, the idea of another beer didn't seem so appealing anymore.

Grummon called about twenty-five minutes later. If a voice could grimace, Cates thought, his was.

"Well, she's in the clear, but there's going to be a stink."

"Tell me."

Grummon did.

It seemed the person Martie had shot was named Pablo Cruz. He was Mexican, fourteen years old. He had seven brothers and sisters, and lived in Lomita Village, a district just south of Lemon Grove. In the moment of crisis, Martie's survival skills had not failed her. She'd fired three rounds— "popped three caps," as Grummon put it—and two of them had struck the youth in the chest, in the area of the sternum. Excellent shooting, Grummon observed. The third round had evidently missed entirely, and the slug was never found.

"Was he armed?"

"That's the thing. He had a gun, but it wasn't a real one. It was one of these toy things that fires a beam of light."

To Cates, recalling the laser-shoot scenario eight days and a lifetime ago, the world suddenly took on a slightly unreal aspect. Christ, was anything what it seemed? he wondered.

Grummon's voice broke in. "You there, Steve?"

"I'm here."

"You know the things I'm talking about. They're kind of like the laser vests Training Division uses. Your buddy wears a device that picks up the light beams—it's only the head or chest, so it's not anywhere near as sophisticated as the laser rigs.''

''What the hell was this idiot doing that for?'' Cates was pretty sure he knew, but he felt an unreasonable anger that Martie was going through this because of something so silly.

Grummon's voice was tight. ''The idea is you a... your buddy each get one and then sneak around and try to blast each other. Play war.''

''Or cops and robbers,'' Cates observed grimly.

''That, too. All part of the Rambo craze.''

''Is this—was the dead guy, Cruz, doing that when she killed him? Sneaking around after a buddy?''

''Yep. We found the buddy. Seems they had this thing going where they put on dark clothes and snuck around the area after each other.'' Grummon gave a grim, sarcastic snort. ''From what I can piece together, the buddy came real close to being dumped, too.''

''How so?''

''After she identified herself and told the first one, Cruz, to freeze, and he turned on her and she dumped him, Griffin heard a noise off to the left. She saw something there, but couldn't see what it was, so she didn't shoot. Turns out it was Cruz's playmate.'' Grummon made a sound that could have been a chuckle, only there was no humor in it whatsoever. ''Hell, the first unit on the scene was a La Mesa unit, because it's right on the boundaries. And the La Mesa cop came close to dumping the guy's buddy. Now, that would have been a mess.''

Cates thought it over. He had a good deal of respect for the La Mesa officers. He regarded most of them as conscientious and professional, not given to quick tempers. If one of them was as spooked as Grummon indicated, it spoke well for Martie's situation also.

Of course, no La Mesa officer could come out and publicly say that, however.

''You say it went out as a prowler call?'' he asked at last.

''Yep. I haven't run all that down, but it looks pretty good that they were what the R/P was reporting.''

"So she's responding to a prowler call, and the prowler turns on her with a gun that turns out to be a toy and she dumps him?"

"Something like that."

Cates breathed a sigh of relief. "Well, she's in the clear, at least. I can't imagine a clearer case of justification without it actually being a real gun."

"Yeah. Try telling the press that, though."

"What do you mean? What's the problem?"

Grummon's voice was bitter. "Hell, the least hostile of 'em are asking why we can't just wound or shoot the guns out of their hands, instead of hitting them in the chest. And a Channel 10 reporter already threw 'police oppression of minorities' at me."

"Why, for Christ's sake? We haven't had any major incidents along those lines. At least, not for a while. A long while, actually. Things have been pretty good, I thought."

"Shit," Grummon snorted angrily. "We haven't, but the P.D. has, and to the news bastards it's all one and the same. The sheriff has been notified, and he's gonna personally make a statement." Grummon's voice sounded hurried. "Look. I gotta go. Things are coming unglued here."

"Sure. I understand. Thanks for the call." Cates hesitated. "When are you going to be through with her?" he inquired at last.

"The deputy? Griffin?"

"Yes."

Cates could hear a long slow intake of breath on the other end of the line. "Probably nine-thirty or ten. Ten, more likely. No, a case like this one, I'd say ten-thirty or eleven. We'll process the scene, talk to her on a preliminary basis. Then the last thing tonight will be to completely debrief her."

"You going to do that at the Grove or down at Homicide?"

"Probably the Grove. No reason to go downtown."

"I might drift by there sometime after ten."

"I thought you might. See you."

"Thanks, Ben."

Cates hung up the telephone. For several minutes, he continued to gaze at the empty fireplace. Then with a sigh, he got up and made his way into the bathroom. There was plenty of hot water now. He turned on the telephone answering machine—and turned off the audible ringer and turned down the volume, so it would save messages but that was all—and he took a long, steaming shower. It felt okay, but somehow not as good as he had been anticipating.

AT A QUARTER AFTER TEN, Cates appeared at LGS. Though closed, the substation had its usual quota of Saturday night police business going on—deputies coming and going with prisoners, picking up equipment, writing reports. He did not see any news cameras outside, however, nor did he see any sign of Grummon or Martie.

"They went down to Homicide," one of the deputies informed him.

"Why down there?"

"Hell, Steve, you should have seen this place. Crawling with news crews. The sheriff even came out here and made a statement."

"What'd he say?"

"Usual stuff. It was pretty good, actually. 'We have to wait for the investigation to be completed before all the facts are known, but it initially appears that the deputy shot in self-defense, believing she was being attacked, et cetera, et cetera. Deepest sympathies to the family of the dead guy,' that sort of thing."

"Did he back up our deputy?"

"Seemed to."

"What was the tenor of the newspeople?"

The deputy gave a bitter grin. "What do you think? We murdered an unarmed young Mexican boy out of racial prejudice and because it's fun for us to do that."

Cates called Homicide and Grummon answered. "How's she doing?"

Grummon sounded tired. "Outside, she's holding up pretty well. Inside—" he hesitated "—I think she's taking it real hard."

"How so?"

"The cameras were there in full force at LGS when we got back there, along with a pretty good crowd of citizens. A couple of people in the crowd were yellin' that she was a murderer, that sort of shit."

"How did a crowd form up so fast?"

Grummon grunted. "Who knows? One of the Chicano activist groups was there, though, and the family of the deceased. Probably the media tipped them off so it would make better footage for the eleven o'clock news."

Cates thought it over for a moment.

Grummon, however, spoke again. "We'll be through in about fifteen. She rode down with one of us, so if you wanted to come pick her up, she might like that."

"She say that?"

"No. But at one point she asked if I knew how to get hold of you, then changed her mind." If Grummon was curious about the situation he didn't let it show.

"She did?"

"Yeah."

Cates sighed. "Yeah," he repeated. "Yeah. I think I'll do just that."

"I thought you might."

shelter

NEITHER OF THEM spoke during the ride back to the Lemon Grove substation.

Martie hadn't seemed particularly surprised when Cates walked into the Homicide offices. She appeared composed but strangely mechanical in her expressions, like a very good robot but not a human. Cates had offered to give her a ride back to her car at LGS, and she had accepted with a distant, "That would be nice. Thank you."

None of the things he had thought of telling her—none of his words of wisdom—seemed particularly useful, so he refrained from trying to impart them.

When they arrived at her car, Martie reached into her purse for her keys. "Damn."

Cates looked at her. The epithet didn't sound angry, just unbearably weary. It also contained a hint of defeat.

"What is it?"

"My keys."

"What about them?"

"I can't find it—them."

"Think they're lost?"

She shook her head. "I don't know. They must be back at Homicide. I must have left them at Grummon's desk."

"Do you have another set?"

"Not here."

"I'll take you home," Cates said gently. "To your house. Maybe you could use the company for a few more minutes, anyway." Although I doubt I'm much company, he added mentally.

She looked at him. "It isn't like that, you know. This isn't some ploy...."

"I know it isn't."

"You don't mind?"

"Not at all. Where do you live?"

"A few miles. La Mesa. Not too far from where all this went down, in fact."

The city of La Mesa lay just east of San Diego and north of Lemon Grove, and butted up against both. Cates made the drive on surface streets. Neither of them spoke except regarding directions.

Martie's apartment was about midway up the northeast face of a steep hill. He turned off Spring Street where she indicated, and then drove up a twisting two-lane road, the headlights cutting a bright slash in the darkness.

For some vague reason, Cates had expected her to live in something on the order of the complex where Beth Fisher had lived, a fairly new, good-size place with a pool and the other amenities.

Instead, when she said a quiet "right here" after ten minutes of climbing and turning, it was in front of an older building, the outlines of which were all but hidden behind a tangle of hedges and bougainvillea beneath towering eucalyptus trees. He estimated it probably comprised no more than four units, and he doubted there was room for a pool.

The building was situated on the downhill side of the street. From the back of it, he guessed, there would be a commanding view of the city to the north and east, out toward El Cajon. Cates guided the sedan to a stop on the shoulder behind a van and switched off the engine.

"You all right?" he asked.

"Yes. Thank you." Her voice was polite, formal. Actually, thought Cates, he liked it better when she sounded weary, because at least that was an indicator of genuine feeling. By contrast, the formality bespoke emotions held in tight rein.

"Will you be able to get inside?"

"There's an extra key in the planter."

"I'll walk you to the door." Christ, this is more awkward than a date, he thought.

"Thank you."

"You're welcome."

Even to Cates, the night seemed to have taken on a character all its own. No moon was visible in the overcast sky. Behind them crouched the mountain with its trees and bushes and houses and apartments, a strangely dark presence in contrast to the blanket of lights he could glimpse between the buildings ahead.

A chilling breeze stirred the leaves of the trees. A train whistle made its long, mournful sound from the tracks down by Spring Street. Cates hated train whistles, they were so utterly lonely. He wondered how many people, hovering on the brink of suicide from whatever circumstances faced them, had been pushed over the edge by that desolate, drawn-out sound.

Their feet made hollow clopping sounds as they crossed a short wooden bridge. Soon they stood on a redwood deck that evidently served as the front porch to three adjoining dwellings.

A low-wattage bulb was burning inside an amber glass globe adjacent to the door at the far end. It cast a pale glow across the deck. Beyond the door stood a wooden half barrel—one end of a wine keg that had been sawed in half—that held a dwarf citrus tree.

Cates trailed behind Martie as she walked over to the keg, bent and dug around in the soil. He could smell the strong, sweet scent of lemon blossoms against the somehow more distant presence of eucalyptus. To smell lemon flowers when the night was so cool somehow added to the feeling of disorientation.

Martie straightened up and stood still, facing the small lemon tree, her back to him.

He could see the rigidity in her spine, the pinched quality to her shoulders. For several long moments, she remained that way, motionless. He knew what she must be going through and felt powerless to help.

"Steve."

Her voice had a strangely conversational sound, almost matter-of-fact except for the tension.

He spoke as gently as possible. "Yeah, Griff."

"That boy's dead, isn't he?"

"Yes."

"Right now he's probably in the morgue, isn't he?"

"Probably." He sensed if he tried to shift the subject she would shut down entirely. Best just to see where it led.

"He'll be in the same cold room where . . . she was."

Cates knew she was referring to Beth Fisher's body. He didn't speak.

"And tomorrow," she said in the same bright, brittle tone, "Dr. Hastings or some other doctor will cut him open, just like they did to her. And Grummon and somebody else will be there watching, just like we were."

"That's true."

"They'll crunch through his ribs and slice through his heart and his lungs and his liver, and take out his brain, and do a report and go on to the next one, won't they, Steve?"

"They have to, Martie."

"I'm sorry I killed him."

"I'm sorry it happened," he said, wondering if she would understand the difference.

"I didn't want to kill him, Steve." Her voice sounded small and plaintive, as though trying carefully to explain a point that was somehow difficult to understand.

"I know."

"I didn't want to kill anybody. Ever."

"Me, either."

"But you did, didn't you, Steve? And now, so did I. How did it feel?"

"Not too good."

" 'Not too good,' " she repeated. "It didn't feel too good when I did it, either."

"I believe it," he said gently.

"And you know what, Steve?"

"What?"

"You know why I killed him?"

"I think so," he began, but she was continuing speaking, not waiting for him to answer.

"I killed him because I was scared. I thought he was going to shoot me, and I was afraid of being shot. I was afraid it would hurt. And it was all over in an instant, no more than that. But it flashed through my mind, 'My God, he's going to kill me,' and I was afraid it would hurt and I shot him first."

"That's the best reason there is, Martie."

"No, it isn't." Her voice was imploring. "It would have hurt if he had shot me, wouldn't it, Steve? It would have hurt, wouldn't it?"

"Yes. You didn't have any choice, Martie. You did the right thing."

"I killed a kid."

"I understand how you feel," he said.

Her voice turned suddenly harsh. "No, you don't. It's my fault he's dead. If I hadn't been afraid like that he wouldn't be."

Tell me I'm wrong, her tone begged. Argue with me. Make me believe it.

He moved to where she was standing, stood behind her and put his hand on her shoulder. "Martie," he said quietly, forcefully. "You did what was right. You did what you had to do. It was dark. You were told there were prowlers. He was as big as a man; he was practically a man. You identified yourself and he spun around with a gun in his hand and it looked like a real gun and you shot him. You reacted properly. You did what you had to do, based on the appearances and your training and what was reasonable."

"I shouldn't have fired."

"It would have been a mistake if you hadn't fired. And if you are confronted with the same circumstances tomorrow or the next day or next year and you don't shoot, that will be a mistake, too."

"I blew away a high school kid."

"And you didn't blow away his fleeing buddy," Cates pointed out. "Besides, *you* didn't kill this kid."

"What do you mean?"

"You just didn't. Fate did. God did. The universe did. His number was up, Martie. You were just one of the circumstances involved in it."

"Swell. The great cosmic-fortune-karma-roulette-wheel strikes," she said bitterly.

Cates didn't respond.

A few moments passed, then Martie gave a short laugh. "Tell me about honor, Steve."

"What about it?"

She didn't appear to have heard. "Tell me about reasonable force. And not punking somebody off. Tell me about chivalry. Tell me about all those things you said worked for you."

He didn't respond. She continued speaking, anger and sarcasm permeating her voice. "You know, I just keep trying to put them onto this situation. Like clothes. And you know what, Steve? They just don't seem to want to fit, somehow. How about that? Why is that, Steve?"

He ignored her last question. "The honor and chivalry and reasonable force come from making the best, good-faith choice you can under the circumstances," he responded.

"And killing a kid," she rejoined.

He sighed. "There's a lesson in all this," he said at last.

"What is it? This I can hardly wait to hear. It must be one hell of a lesson. Probably going to make me one smart son of a bitch, I guess."

"I don't know what it is," he said simply.

"Thanks a hell of a lot. You've been incredibly helpful." She shrugged his hand away from her shoulder.

"The thing is, Martie, you have to find it. Not me. You."

"Sure. Tell me where it is."

"I can't. It won't be given to you. You'll have to work on it. Look inside yourself. Take this whole incident out and look at it, a little at a time. Study it. Study your feelings about it. Someday, the lesson will emerge."

He paused. When she didn't make any response, he took a breath and continued.

"And there's no telling what it will be. Maybe you'll decide you don't want to be a cop—"

"I don't," she interrupted sharply. "I've already decided that one."

"And maybe you'll see that you do," he continued patiently.

"I don't," she snapped. "I just told you that. I've already decided."

"Shut up, Martie," he said gently but firmly. "Hear me out. Maybe you'll find out you're made of sterner stuff than you thought. Maybe you're destined for greatness, or it's your lot to follow the hard road through this veil of tears. Maybe this will act as a toughener for you. Maybe you'll help others in ways you don't know about, because this happened to you." He paused. "On the other hand, maybe this will take you under. But I don't think so."

She was silent.

"Look, Martie. The hardest thing about being a cop is the difference between appearance and reality. And you got caught smack-dab in the middle of it."

"What do you mean?" she asked. Her voice was still bitter, but less so.

"What's reality? How do you tell when something's real? You can't. A shadowy form spins around and pulls a gun on you. That's real. The reality is that you think you're about to get killed. So you dump him. That's the reality you have to deal with, the reality you have to react to when you pull the trigger.

"Then it turns out he's not a crook, but a kid with a toy gun. That's a new reality. But the point is it doesn't destroy the old one that you acted under, that you reacted to." He hesitated. "Martie?"

"Yes?"

"When you pulled the trigger, you knew he was about to shoot you, right? And if somebody could yell 'cut!' right then, you'd have passed a lie detector test on it. So it was the right thing to do, based on the evidence at the time."

"I guess so."

"Hell, I don't want to sink to the level of a defense attorney, but they have a saying—'we deal in evidence, proof, not truth.' Well, in this area, you're entitled to rely on what the evidence, the facts, reasonably show. You're after the truth, lady, and you're in for a hell of a long hunt."

She didn't respond. A half mile below them, on Spring Street, sirens wailed. Cates stepped forward and put his hands on Martie's shoulders in the darkness.

"Listen to that, Martie."

"What?"

"The sirens."

"What about them?"

"Some cop, La Mesa or San Diego, I guess, somebody you and I maybe don't even know, is going after a crook or going to the scene of a tragedy. He—or she—reached forward and hit the switches for the light bar and the sirens and is en route. Going to help somebody, or catch a dirtbag. That's what we do. And we do it because it's the right thing to do, and in a very real way it helps out."

She didn't respond.

"Martie?"

"Yes?"

"You're one of the good ones, Martie. You'll get through it."

"And what about them?" she asked sadly.

"Who?"

"His family. What's their lesson? Where's the benefit to them? Apart from more room at the dining table at holidays, thanks to me." Her voice was filled with self-hate.

Cates took hold of her upper arms and turned her toward him. She resisted. He turned her anyway, but she stretched her neck away from him, keeping her face in the darkness. He gripped her shoulder with one hand and turned her face toward him with the other.

"I don't know what it is, Martie, but it's there. Believe me, it's there."

Suddenly, convulsively, she began to sob.

Cates put his arm around her like a buddy and marched her to the door. He fumbled in her hand for the key, took it and inserted it grittily in the lock. He marched her inside and pushed the door shut with his foot.

A night-light glowed in the kitchen off to the left. He could see that they were in the living room, thickly padded carpeting beneath his feet, a sofa and other furniture ahead of them and to the right.

Martie turned and seized him.

She clutched him to her with amazing strength, her body jerking in spasms of grief. He held her and suddenly his need was as great as hers, or even greater. She must have sensed it, for her face turned upward and his lips found her cheek. He kissed it strongly, sucking at her skin, tasting her tears, then smearing and mingling them with his own as their mouths slid together.

They kissed, deeply, intensely.

His hands slid to her hips, her buttocks, clenching and gathering the fabric of her skirt in fistfuls so that it traveled up her backside. He felt the jab of a fingernail in the hard flesh of his abdomen as her hands fumbled at his belt, at the button and clasp of his waistband, and then at his fly. Then her skirt was above his wrists and his hands slid to the smooth flesh beneath it, beneath her panties, stroking her, squeezing her, pulling her against him.

He broke the kiss and knelt suddenly, sliding his hands around inside her panties to the sides of her hips.

Her own hands dropped and held the skirt in bunches on either side. Swiftly, he peeled the undergarment down to her feet. She stepped out of it, and he drove his own clothing down in a single motion as she sat down and lay back on the carpeting. Then he was on top of her, and their mouths met again. Their bodies joined with an urgency that was frightening in its intensity, a desperate affirmation of life and denial of death.

She was slippery and heavily lubricated, and he drove into her repeatedly, driven by their mutual need. A short time later, he felt the explosion would be too near, too soon. He sought to slow down, to hold back and change the pace, but she whispered in his ear, "No, don't stop," and then it was too late and there would be no stopping it, anyway.

For several minutes, they lay together, still joined, her inner muscles gripping him closely.

He could feel the rapid thudding of her heart against his, could hear her heavy breathing. The carpeting felt thick and rough on his forearms and knees, and he held her tightly.

Finally, he spoke. "Anything I can do for you?" he asked gently.

"You just did."

"I worry that I maybe left you up in the air."

He felt her shake her head.

"No," she replied softly. "I needed that. I needed to...feel." Her voice took on a speculative quality. "Yes, that's it. To feel. To be made to feel, to sense things. And to be needed. To realize I was still alive, and that it wasn't all just bodies and autopsies and guns and death."

She suddenly began to weep.

It was a soft, gentle flow of emotion, unlike the earlier violent, purgative sobbing. "Hold me," she pleaded, even though he already was holding her. So he wrapped his arms more firmly around her, and they lay together and made damp spots on the carpet with their tears.

He felt himself begin to grow ready again. Correspondingly, her crying lessened.

He sensed a slight catch to the rhythm of her breathing, a hitch as she inhaled. He disengaged himself and got to his knees, knelt beside her and picked her up, cradling her in his arms like a child. Then he rose effortlessly to his feet. For a moment he stood, using one foot to work his trousers and shorts off over the other foot, then repeating the process.

"Which way?" he said softly.

She pointed, and he carried her into the bedroom.

There was a double bed. It hadn't been made up, and for some reason he liked that. She offered no apology or excuse, and he liked that still more.

He set her on the bed and touched her cheek with the back of his hand, then tenderly removed her clothing. Her skin was

satinlike and hot, but became like gooseflesh as he caressed the
sides of her breasts and her flanks, barely grazing the surface
of her flesh with the back of his hand. He could hear her
breath catch in her throat; for his own part, it didn't seem as
if there were enough air to fill his lungs.

He removed his shirt and then he lay next to her, propping
himself on his elbow. He kissed her cheek and neck and breasts
and belly and downward, kissing and touching with exquisite
tenderness. Then the tenderness became firm, insistent, and
she came swiftly to a gasping, shuddering climax. As it sub-
sided, he moved up and entered her again with a single, easy
motion, and held her—no movement, no thrusting, just held
her and kissed her damp hair and sheltered her with his body
and his strength.

She went to sleep beneath him, in his arms, their bodies still
connected. He shut his eyes to doze also. At some indetermi-
nate time later, he awoke and discovered he had been sleeping
soundly. He found he was lying with most of his 220 pounds
pressing down on her. He started to move off, but she made a
little protesting sound in her sleep and pulled him back down.
He smiled and let himself drift away once more.

Then the Braxton dream returned.

He hadn't had this nightmare for over a year, but here it
was, back again, in living Technicolor and Cinemascope, with
one essential difference—it didn't stop. The film didn't break,
it played right through to the end. . . .

*Cates's eyes sweep the room. The entry men, Harris and
Ellington, are there, crouched, as far apart as they can be in the
confined area. That's good, he notes approvingly, because it
means two separate target areas instead of one, as far as the
bad guys are concerned.*

*Both men have their pistols in their outstretched arms, and
shots are still echoing in the room. The sour chemical smell of
gunpowder hangs everywhere. Where their arms and guns are
pointing are two men, sprawled on and around a shabby
couch. One is draped over it; the other lies on his back in front
and to one side. His back is arched and his left leg is kicking
in a peculiar, frantic motion, kicking downward, bending at*

the knee and then sharply extending, as if trying to kick off his shoe.

Cates is aware that Braxton is beside him, gun in hand. He seems excited; his face is shiny and his eyes glittering. Cates scans the area and there are no guns anywhere, and now Harris is scuttling forward, toward the kicking man.

Something goes thump behind them.

It is a purposeful thump, the kind that isn't a cat or something falling over, but is somebody hurrying into position in order to do something.

Cates spins around and so does Braxton.

In vivid slow motion Cates sees two people. One is clearly a hood, a dirtbag with prison tattoos. He has his arm around the neck of the other one, a kid of about fifteen or sixteen. And in his other hand he has a gun.

Cates starts to shoot. It's a dangerous shot but it has to be done and he knows he can do it. But the dirtbag is saying something, his mouth opening in a dark circle, he's yelling No! Brax, nooo! And then Cates's bullets are striking right where he knows they will, right in the dirtbag's body, to the left of the hostage. And Braxton is firing, too, in a wild and panicky way, once, twice, a third and fourth time. And he hits the dirtbag and he hits the kid and God knows what else, but why did the dirtbag know Braxton's name, why was he calling on him to stop...?

Cates's eyes opened, wide and staring in the darkness. For several moments, he tried to remember where he was. Then he realized it was Martie's apartment, that they had made urgent, need-filled love, and that right that moment she was deeply asleep next to him.

He lay there and replayed the film in his mind, marveling at the discovery that he had been right all along, that Braxton had murdered the dirtbag and had falsely accused Cates of reckless misconduct to discredit him.

Ballistics didn't matter, now. Slaman didn't really matter. Even Braxton didn't matter too much, though if the opportunity to add up the score ever presented itself, Cates might avail himself of it. In a world of illusion and pseudoreality, where hostages sometimes died and teenagers with toy guns got themselves killed, Cates knew the truth about one thing, at least.

And it was a wonderful, mind-freeing truth to know.

washing machine

THE NEXT MORNING, he had awakened about nine. Martie's bed was empty; he could hear water running in the bathroom.

Soon the door opened and she peeked out, saw that he was awake and then walked shyly toward him. She wore jeans and a sweatshirt. Her face was washed and her hair pulled back, and she looked nervous.

"Hi."

"Good morning, Martie."

After a moment, she inquired, "You sleep okay last night?"

He smiled what he hoped was a kindly smile and wouldn't be misinterpreted as a smirk. "Yeah, Martie, I slept fine. Are you okay?"

She nodded. Her discomfort was palpable. Cates sat up in bed among the covers and extended his hand. "Come over here, Martie," he said softly.

She did.

"Sit down."

She complied, sitting on the edge of the bed, her back straight and hands folded in her lap. Cates reached forward and pried one of her hands loose and held it in his.

"You worried, upset, about last night?"

She nodded.

"Which part?"

"All of it."

"Feel bad about it?"

She shrugged angrily. Then she nodded.

"Martie, listen to me. I'm not too smooth at saying all this, but I'll just blunder my way ahead and hope on balance it comes out okay."

She didn't say anything.

"The shooting—I told you how I feel last night. You acted on the best reality you had at the time."

She interrupted him. "I understand that. It will be a while before it all sorts out, I guess, but . . ."

"But that's not what's bothering you right now?"

"Not really."

Cates nodded. "I don't think you're the type who sleeps around a lot, even if you are a trendy young woman and all that crap. I think it's got to mean more than . . . rubbing an itch for you. And, at the risk of sounding old-fashioned, that's the way it is for me, too."

She looked up at him, her eyes wide and solemn and her face somehow vulnerable without any makeup and with her hair pulled back.

"Now, what happened last night was not just rubbing some kind of sexual itch. You know that. I know that. You were hurting a lot and you had crawled into yourself. Do you remember what you said to me, Martie? You said you needed to feel, thanks for making you feel."

Her face was pink. "Thanks for the instant replay."

He shook his head. "It wasn't meant to be that. It was meant as evidence that this wasn't some simple tumble in the sack, or on the living room floor where at first we didn't even get undressed other than to get to the vital parts."

He said it as softly and as gently as he could, and with a hint of humor. And her face pink, Martie smiled.

"Yeah," he said in response to the smile, "talk about urgent. Well, we were urgent last night. That wasn't exactly my best performance, I guess. Not initially, anyway." He winked. "To which you are of course going to say, yeah, but after that was stupendous, and I'll shrug and say twarn't nothing, and since we both know you were going to say it, you don't have to, now."

This time she laughed out loud. It was a good laugh, a genuine laugh. "It was good," she said.

"Twarn't nothing."

"I knew you'd say that," she said, still smiling.

"Yeah."

Martie suddenly got a mischievous look on her face. "Anyway, talk about charging where the brush is thickest..." With a stylized lewdness, she deliberately let the sentence trail off.

Cates looked at her in frank amazement, then it was his turn to laugh. "Hush your naughty mouth, Griffin." It occurred to him that if she could make a crack like that, she was okay.

"I don't know what you mean," she said with feigned innocence.

"Yeah." He turned serious. "Look. It was good for me in ways you can't even begin to understand. It—you helped me through a lot of stuff." He debated about telling her how it had unlocked the part of his subconscious where the truth on Braxton was stored. Then he decided it might make her own situation seem worse, because there was no corresponding neat truth for her to find.

He hesitated, then continued.

"I'd like to help you through all this, in any way I can. And I don't just mean some kind of bullshit Dr.-Cates-hands-on-physical-therapy, either. But in a sense, I've been there, and if it would ever help to talk, let's talk. And if it wouldn't, okay." He grinned. "And if the other, uh, approach, is ever indicated, feel free. Hell, I'll even make house calls."

She looked at him, her face solemn. Then she looked down at her hands, then back at him.

"You know..." The sentence trailed off.

"Yeah, Martie?"

"I can't say it any better than you did. And you're right, about all of it. I needed...what happened, for most of the right reasons. And just because it was in a context that could make it look like it was random and...shallow, doesn't mean it was that."

"I know."

There didn't seem to be much more to say. She probably wanted to be alone, and he sure as hell did.

Martie got up and left the room. Cates got up and dressed. He gave her a sisterly hug at the door, told her to hang tough and made his way back to the car. He felt edgy and restless. Partly it was due to his discovery—or rediscovery—of the truth in the Braxton matter, and partly it was because of the emotions brought forth by Martie's situation, the dead youth and their having made love the previous evening.

He got into his car and sat still, trying to let the turmoil dissipate, trying to get some sense of direction, of what to do.

It was then that he remembered he was supposed to go out with Joyce last night.

It was one of those things that just couldn't be. He couldn't have done it. Period.

It was just that simple. Somehow, he was mistaken, and he had not missed the date with Joyce because he was busy playing Galahad to Martie. It just hadn't happened.

Except that it had.

He felt guilty, he felt angry at himself, and he felt a sort of despair at having missed the chance to go out with her.

He reviewed the events of the preceding two days to try to figure out if in some way this were not the case. Today was Sunday. That meant yesterday was supposed to be Saturday. And it was, indeed, on Saturday night that he had agreed to go out with Joyce.

Face it, Stevie, you blew it. Oh, well, to hell with it. With a sigh, he started the engine.

His telephone answering machine was blinking with what he thought looked like a certain fury when he got home. He rewound it.

It had four messages. Three were from Joyce. The first one was one of the three.

"Steve, it's Joyce. It's about eight-thirty. I'm calling on the off chance that you got held up, and haven't left yet. Or if you have been here and gone, so that you'll know what happened and I didn't stand you up. Look. My day has been a total disaster. I helped my friend move all day, and his car got hit by another car, and I just got home and if by *any* chance you hadn't left I wanted to catch you, or if you've already tried my place and come back I wanted to let you know what happened. Call me when you get this. Thanks. Bye."

Cates stared at his answering machine.

Then he gaped at it. It just sat there, looking impassive. He switched it off before the next message began and then rewound the tape and listened to it again. It said the same thing the second time.

He was off the hook for forgetting the date. She hadn't been there, either. So his blowing it had been a no-harm-no-foul situation.

Not only was he off the hook, but he had been right about the friend. Not that he cared, not that he even had a right to care, especially after how he had conducted himself the previous evening, but chalk another up for the deductive abilities.

There is a great temptation, he reflected, to overuse lucky breaks like this.

However, he was determined not to do that. There was a kind of luck that should be pushed to the max, and a kind that should just be gratefully accepted for what it was.

Cates believed in streaks. He believed in streaks of good luck and streaks of bad. And when he had a good streak going, he believed in riding it out to the max. Conversely, when a bad streak was developing, it was time to draw in and try another way. Be flexible. T'ai chi-it, as it were.

Assuming it was possible. Sometimes, it might not be, and then you did the best you could.

He believed in chance, and in antichance, the odds stacking up the more fate was tempted. In a simple analogy, he didn't accept that the odds on the eleventh toss of a coin were still fifty-fifty if the first ten had all been heads. Never mind what the statisticians said.

It was part of the chance–antichance concept, he felt, that said when luck provides you with something out of the blue you accept it and use it but don't overuse it.

Overusing it would be if he called her up and said that he had been there to pick her up and where the hell was she, anyway? Oh, your *friend*'s car broke down? Sure. That's original.... Or at least use some variation of that, even if not so offensive.

Put her on the defensive, never mind his own foul-up. And
there was a time in his life when he might have done that, or
at least the minor version of it.

That was asking for trouble, he knew, because it wasn't the
truth. And he believed that such a misuse of the facts distorted the chance and dramatically increased the antichance.

Best to cop out to it, part of it, at least, maybe with a "No
sweat, I got called out on a homicide, anyway," which in a
sense was true.

The next message was from Joyce also.

"Steve, this is Joyce. It's about, oh, nine-thirty or so. I just
wanted to see if you were home. So I could explain things. I'll
talk to you later. Thanks. Bye."

The third one was from Grummon, saying they were not
going to interview Martie at LGS, but at Homicide.

The last one was Joyce again. She sounded dispirited.

"Steve, Joyce. Give me a call on Monday. Sorry we didn't
hook up this evening. Talk to you later. Thanks. Bye."

He leaned back and looked at the answering machine
thoughtfully. Maybe it was all some part of the grand scheme,
part of the fabric of things. He'd traveled far last night. The
events of Martie's shooting and of her grief had unlocked in
some strange, psychological way the events of his past, and
had freed him.

All that would have been well worthwhile even if he'd blown
the date with Joyce entirely. But now, somehow, even that had
been resolved in a way that should make him realize he was a
very lucky fellow indeed.

Maybe his luck was changing. Maybe he was going to get
somewhere with this Fisher mess. And maybe—just maybe—
it was the beginning of a streak.

He sent out brief thanks to the universe, or God, or whatever was out there. Then he went to the gym and came home
and went to bed, because he had something important to do
that evening.

IT WAS SHORTLY before midnight on Sunday night when Cates
got there.

The headlights of the sedan cut a vivid slash in the darkness. When he looked off to the side, however, Cates could see that the foothills were far from pitch-black. The clouds had blown away and the moon, an orange-yellow disk just past full, bathed the desert landscape in its glow. A glittering blanket of stars assisted, adding their own blue-white light. Far off to the west—his left as he ascended this particular stretch of road—the brighter glare of city lights looked coarse and somehow tawdry by comparison, like rhinestones compared to diamonds.

Part of him—the pragmatic and the skeptic—made him embarrassed, and glad nobody else was there to see him. But another part reassured him that it was right. Ironically, it had been the hard-bitten Ben Grummon who years before had lent much support to what he was doing.

Cates had been in Homicide about eighteen months at the time.

The veteran detective had noticed Cates's habit of returning to the scene of a 187, well after the initial processing of the scene had occurred. In a high percentage of cases, this was at night, because most killings occurred at night.

In the manner that men—and particularly cops—tend to adopt when talking about matters of sensitivity or of the "finer feelings," Grummon had approached the subject awkwardly and with unusual—even for him—gruffness.

"Forget somethin' out there, Cates?" he growled.

Cates looked at him for just a fraction longer than he would have taken to respond to most such gibes. "What do you mean?" he finally countered.

"You know what I mean."

"No, I don't. What?"

"The St. Germaine caper, that's what."

The late John St. Germaine had come to their attention—and caseload—after six-year-old Bunni Price's Scottie terrier was found to be chewing on a small rubbery cylindrical object that turned out to be a dried-out but still flesh-covered human finger. In the ensuing investigation, the deputies found John's desiccated remains covered with powdered lime and buried in a shallow grave, now partly uncovered by the Scottie, in the crawl space beneath an old frame house in the county area of Mount Helix.

"What about it?"

Grummon shrugged. "Just wondered what you was doin' out there half the night, that's all."

Cates glanced casually around to see if anybody was around to overhear the conversation. Nobody was. Then he gave Grummon a long, level look. "What evidence is there that I was even out there in the first place?"

"I got my sources."

"To hell with your sources. Show me some evidence."

"Evidence? You look like shit, like you didn't get much sleep last night."

"There are a lot of reasons why I might not have gotten any sleep," said Cates with an easy grin that managed, he hoped, to be both conspiratorial and salacious.

"Uh-uh," his partner grunted. "I ain't buyin' it. You been grousing around here about how your little dolly left you a while back, so I know that's not the reason you're tired."

"What makes you think she's the only one?"

"Shove it, Cates. I ain't buyin'," Grummon repeated.

The younger detective considered his reply for a moment. "I was just giving the place a last look-over, I guess."

"In the middle of the night."

Cates shrugged.

"Find anything?" Grummon asked.

"Maybe. Nothing specific, really."

"Yeah. I know what you mean."

Cates looked at him. "No, you don't."

"Yeah, I do."

"If you knew, why'd you ask?"

"I wanted to make you come out with it." Grummon furrowed his heavy brow. "Look, Steve. I'll tell you something, and if you tell anybody else about it, I'll deny it and I'll kick your ass all over the county."

"That might be a tall order, old man," Cates needled.

"I'll give it one hell of a try, at least." He paused and continued. "Look. If you're doin' what I think you're doin', I understand it. I've done it, myself."

Cates decided to give a little, but still hold back the real reason. "All right. So I was out there. I just decided to make a last run by to orient myself with respect to the layout, where the light comes from at night, that sort of thing."

"Bullshit."

"What do you mean, bullshit?"

"Just what I said. Bullshit."

"Okay, smart guy. If it's bullshit, then what do you think I'm doing instead of that?"

"Oh, I think that's part of it, maybe," the veteran acknowledged.

"Why, thank you."

"Stow the sarcasm, partner. Like I said, that might be part of it. But the real reason you were out there is to soak up the vibes." Cates started to reply, but Grummon shut him off. "The look on your face tells me I'm real close. I am close, aren't I, Steve? Go on. Tell me I'm wrong."

"Maybe." Cates deliberately did not specify if the reply referred to being close or being wrong.

Grummon looked irritated.

"For Christ's sake, Cates, stop being so goddamn coy. This isn't the press talking. It's me. Your partner. I ain't gonna go around blabbin' that you're tuning in to UFOs or something, for God's sake."

After a few moments, Cates nodded. "All right," he said, more to himself than to his partner. "All right. You're right. I was soaking up the vibes, as you put it. What's it to you?"

Grummon ignored the question. "How do you do it?"

"What's it to you?" Cates repeated. Then, seeing Grummon's look, he continued with his explanation.

He spoke in terms that sounded clumsy even as he said them, partly because the concepts were difficult to express precisely but also for the same reason that Grummon had been uncharacteristically curt when he approached the subject—it sounded less unmanly to put it that way.

"I don't know, exactly," he said. "It just seems to help, that's all. I go out there about the same time—even the same day of the week—as we figure the victim was killed, and I just sit there and sort of...well, just sit there." He was going to say "sit there and sort of gestalt it," but thought better of it.

"Soak up the vibes." The veteran detective nodded.

"Yeah, I guess that's pretty accurate," Cates acknowledged.

"Look." Grummon sounded patient but exasperated. "I told you. I do it, too, though it's nothing I'd admit to another person in the world." After an awkward pause, he added, "Does it help?"

Cates struggled to put his reply into the right words.

"Sometimes. Sometimes not. Sometimes, I don't get anything at all. Other times, I just get a strange feeling. It's as if I'm receiving a bunch of signals, energy waves, but I can't decipher them. Almost like radio signals but I'm tuned to the wrong freq and they're all scrambled anyway."

"What about the other times?"

"What other times?"

"The times when it works, for Chrissakes!"

Cates sighed. "Once in a while, I get a real strong...sense of what happened." He hesitated. "Yeah, sense is the right word. Sort of just experience the fabric of things, so to speak."

Embarrassed, he didn't try to explain how on very rare occasions it worked so well that he could almost tell what had happened, could sense how the killing had occurred, as if the psychic energy of a violent death were still there.

It wasn't what he thought of as clairvoyance, exactly. He couldn't go back in time, or actually see the killing again in terms of images, as if he were actually there. He doubted that could really be done. But more than once he had gotten such a strong sense of what had gone down that when he had happened to be in the presence of the killer—who wasn't even a suspect at the time—he had known it.

One time, he had even somehow learned—sensed? divined?—a pet phrase the killer had used just before striking the fatal blow.

Grummon nodded. "Yeah. I know what you mean."

"You do?"

"I told you. I've done it myself. Kinda gives me a feel for what went down." He gave Cates a penetrating look, his heavy brow furrowed. "Only thing is, I never went so far as to go back on the same day of the week."

"If you're asking why I do that, it's because of the cycles."

"Cycles?"

"Yeah. I kind of believe that everything is a circle. Or at least a cycle of some sort. A loop. It's like a washing machine that's on Spin. Your clothes are strung around the inside of it, around the drum or barrel or whatever you call it. Socks and shirts and jockey shorts. The barrel is going around and around, real fast. You want to find the one blue sock. With me so far?"

Grummon nodded. Cates went on.

"So, if you're inside it, looking for the blue sock, it doesn't do any good to look until the cycle is right. You have to wait until the right amount of time has passed so that the blue sock is going to cycle around again. Then you look for it."

"No kiddin'," Grummon commented.

Cates shrugged. "Who knows if it's true? But it makes sense." He thought for a moment. "In a way, it's the same as going back at the same time of day as the incident went down. That's one cycle. Trying to get back on the same day of the week is just carrying that one step further."

"You're assumin' these...cycles happen to coincide with our calendar periods," his partner pointed out.

"That's true. I am," Cates admitted. "And with no good reason, except it's at least possible the calendar cycles were adopted the way they are because we were subconsciously influenced by forces that repeated in those same periods of time."

The veteran detective considered that point for a few moments. "I don't get it. I'm not sure the...energy, or whatever the hell it is, works on those cycles," he said at last.

"Me, neither," Cates agreed. "What I'm trying to say, though, is that *people* work on them, so maybe they exist in nature, too."

"What do you mean?"

"Look at it this way. We humans divide things into weeks and months and years. Cycles. Maybe unconsciously we chose seven days for a week because that fits with some natural pattern, some cycle we aren't even aware exists."

Grummon appeared to consider that.

"Yeah," he said at last. "I see what you mean. Then again, it could be we use seven-day weeks because of history, or accident. Or maybe because that's what the Bible says, rather than because it fits some pattern. If you believe in that stuff," he added hastily, in what Cates interpreted as a reference to the Bible. Grummon went on. "The key word seems to be maybe."

"It's all 'maybe,'" Cates agreed. "Maybe it's because the men who wrote the Bible felt the influence of a cycle of nature, too. Maybe, if you want to look at it in those terms, if you believe in it, God created that cycle."

"Huh," grunted his partner noncommittally.

"Or, hell, maybe it's the other way around. Maybe because we humans act in those cycles, we create energy patterns that follow the same cycles, like a machine making waves in a pool." Suddenly, Cates felt foolish. "And maybe it's all bullshit, but it doesn't hurt to give it a try."

Grummon was silent.

For a moment, Cates wondered if his partner had been stringing him along, trying to sucker him into such a revelation that sounded ludicrous when verbalized and examined in the cold light of day. However, Grummon's next words dispelled his fears.

"I guess I'd worry that if I waited too long the crime scene would kinda lose its energy," he said thoughtfully.

Cates nodded. "I wonder about that, too. So I just try to make it the next week or the week after if it's a fresh killing. If it's one where the guy's been dead for a while, I figure some of the energy's probably dissipated anyway, so it's not going to hurt to wait a couple more days to at least hit the same spot on the seven-day cycle."

The two men fell silent. Then, with a crooked smile, Cates turned to his partner. "And if you ever breathe a word of this to anybody else, I'll kick *your* ass all over the county."

"I won't tell a soul," promised Grummon. "'Cept maybe Tisdale, next time me and him are having a beer together."

Cates grinned. He didn't know which was more farfetched, the assistant sheriff—a confirmed teetotaler—having a beer at all, or socializing with Grummon.

"Besides," his partner went on, "there's not a man on the department, any of them who've pitched in and really worked a killing, who hasn't had the same feeling. They just don't admit it, that's all."

Now Cates found the spot on the canyon road and pulled his car to the shoulder. He switched off the headlights, but sat there for a few moments with the engine running. Then he turned that off and continued to sit before getting out of the car. Part of him thought the process was somehow akin to easing into this mystical world a step at a time, and another part of him thought the first part was a damn fool.

He got out of the car and surveyed the empty landscape.

Far away in the distance a coyote howled. Somewhere a semi was taking a steep grade; he could hear the throaty hammering of the diesel as the tractor was downshifted and ground upward.

As his eyes adjusted to the darkness, the slope took on features. He could see the clumps of scraggly brush, the occasional granite boulders and the deep gouges made by the Taurus's wheels as the car was winched up the sandy hillside.

Cates sat on the shoulder of the road and waited, relaxing, *feeling*, for several minutes. He wore a leather jacket similar to a flight jacket, but a lighter-weight imitation. At last he rose and, hands in the pockets of the coat, started down the slope.

He reached the spot where the car had been, wedged into the scraggly brush that was backed up by the boulders. He scanned the area carefully, then sat down, hands still in his pockets, his back hunched against the cold and against . . .

Against what?

A vague uneasiness beset him, then seemed to subside.

He concentrated on trying to relax because to force it never worked. His eyes felt heavy, and he allowed them to close. He concentrated on the darkness of his eyelids, and tried to project himself out into the darkness, not searching for but ready to see the blue sock if it came around on the washing machine drum again.

He must have dozed, then fallen asleep as he sat there on the slope in the chilly moonlight. Suddenly he gave a start, aware that his body had actually jerked in sympathetic reaction to a terrifying blow, a blow that was both paralyzing and shockingly painful, a blow that seemed to begin inside the chest and explode outward. Then a large, dark shape was bearing down on him, slewing and sliding down the canyon, and he knew he had to get out of the way because it looked as if it were going to run right over him.

He twisted and scrambled to one side, looking upward in his sleep, straining to see the road, barely able to make out the short, dark, shadowy figure up there looking down at the plunging shape. The legs looked disproportionately big, doubtless foreshortened by the distance and the angle. And now a car was approaching the figure—a low, sleek Porsche, white—and then Cates was awake and realizing he was somehow on all fours, looking up at the empty hillside at his D-unit and more afraid than he had ever been in his life.

ambulance!

WINSTON WAS ALREADY at the Homicide Division when Cates arrived on Monday morning. The tall agent looked even more dapper than ever—if a six-foot-six-inch man can be dapper—in contrast to how Cates knew he himself must look, at least if he looked anything close to how he felt.

"Cates," Winston greeted him with cheerful if not effusive good humor.

"Winston," Cates grunted.

"A good-morning to you."

"And also to you." Christ, we sound like a church service, he thought.

Winston evidently thought so, too. "Let us pray?"

"Go to hell," Cates grunted, though he didn't say it with very much spirit.

"I hope you had a good weekend."

"Why's that?"

"Because, if I may be so bold as to say, you look like hell."

"Thanks." Cates filled a Styrofoam cup with coffee from the urn that stood at one end of the bull pen, than sat at his desk and put his feet on the surface. "I didn't sleep so well last night, is all."

"How'd you and Joyce get along?"

Winston said it so casually that it was perfectly ambiguous—it might have been in oblique reference to Cates's statement about not having slept much, or it might not have been. Cates couldn't tell which.

"We didn't," he said shortly.

"Oh?"

"No."

"If I may be permitted to inquire," said Winston courteously, a twinkle in his eye, "why not?"

"I forgot about it."

"You forgot about your dinner engagement?"

Cates looked at him in exasperation. "Yes, for Christ's sake. I forgot." He sat down and took a sip of coffee. Then, with a sigh, he began to explain. When he finished, Winston nodded solemnly, but didn't say anything.

"Well?" Cates said after a moment.

"Well what?"

"Well, aren't you going to offer any commentary? Or advice? Or anything of the sort?"

Winston chuckled. "As far as advice is concerned, you obviously don't need any."

"Thank you."

"You, at least, experienced, ah, some intimate female companionship. Not that it was simply some cheap roll in the hay," he added hastily. "I was merely alluding to the fact that unlike yourself, I spent the weekend alone. Trying to see the sights of San Diego, to be exact."

Cates didn't speak.

"Now, as far as commentary is concerned," Winston continued.

"Yes?"

"In the law there is a phrase, *res ipsa loquitur*, meaning roughly speaking 'the thing speaks for itself.' 'Thing' in the sense of event or act. In other words, it is plain no commentary is necessary."

"Yeah. Well, none would be appreciated, too." Cates sipped his coffee and wondered what the hell to do next.

"I'm sure. The last thing you want to hear is an opinion about your clear lack of intelligence, not to mention unutterable discourtesy, at forgetting a dinner engagement with somebody as attractive and charming as—"

Cates held up his hand sharply. "Enough!"

"So," said Winston at last, "what's on the investigative agenda for today?"

"You're the smart one, the Harvard lawyer and Fed—don't you have any bright ideas?"

"Ah, but as I recall you impressed upon me with considerable vigor when we first met, investigating homicides is your forte, not mine. I bow to your leadership—accepting all its occasional foibles and fumbles—and await your suggestion."

Cates had, in fact, been going through the imaginary notes he had scrawled on the imaginary scraps of paper and chucked into his imaginary in-tray.

That was it.

"Winston."

The black agent looked up. "Yes?"

"You ever kidnapped anybody?"

White teeth made a bright, brilliant slash across his companion's shiny black face. "Not lately," the Fed said, looking amused. "Why do you ask?"

"You ever thought about kidnapping somebody?"

Again, the grin. "Several times."

"You ever thought about how you'd do it in broad daylight, assuming you were trying to be sneaky and surreptitious and not just 'brute force' the thing?"

Winston looked at him. "What's your point, Steve?"

Cates swung around and put his feet on the floor, then leaned forward, forearms on his knees like a ball player on the bench. In some ways, he reflected wryly, the analogy was apt, at least as far as the case was concerned.

"Look. Suppose you wanted to do that? What might be one way to go about it? What type of vehicle might you use?"

The black man furrowed his brow. "Something nondescript, I suppose. Commonplace. Something that nobody would look too hard at."

"Right. And how about if it were something that could easily transport another person—the victim. And not cause any particular interest if it did. Something like—"

Winston's face lit up. "An ambulance," he said in wonderment.

"Right! Damn right, in fact. An ambulance. A one-each-by-God-standard-department-issue-goddamn-ambulance."

"Like your friend, Larry what's-his-name—the narc—said he saw across the canyon on the day she disappeared," Winston said softly.

Cates looked at him in surprise. For somebody who hadn't been there, Winston was quick, exceptionally quick.

"Exactly like that."

"He even saw what kind it was, didn't he?" Winston said after a moment.

Cates nodded. "Caro's. It's a private firm that contracts for paramedic services. We've got a couple of them here." He fell silent for several moments.

When he spoke, Cates's voice sounded optimistic, hopeful, affirmative, in a half-joking, half-serious way. The adrenaline boost from getting a possible lead in the case had done what the coffee couldn't.

"An ambulance would work," he said.

"An ambulance would work," Winston repeated in the same tone.

"It would do it."

"Yes. It would."

"We're reaching, though," Cates acknowledged.

"Indeed we are," agreed Winston.

"You got a better idea?" inquired Cates.

"None whatever," responded Winston.

"Why don't we speak with the friendly folk at Caro's Emergency Care?"

"Why don't we, indeed?"

CARO'S EMERGENCY CARE had several offices, including one in Lemon Grove. They decided to start with the one that was closest to where Beth had been kidnapped. It turned out to be a home that had been converted to an office. A large cement pad had been poured in what had originally been the back yard, and four ambulances were parked there.

The woman in charge of the facility looked about forty years old and quite indisposed to discuss Caro's policies and practices with them. She wore a severe business suit, and her hair was pulled back and rolled into a tight bun. A wood-grain laminated nameplate was mounted in a clear Lucite base on her desk, and proclaimed her name to be Ms O'Connor.

On the initial approach, Cates was his disarming best. Ms O'Connor was unimpressed.

"You come here with a search warrant, and I'll tell you," she stated flatly, in response to his query about how many ambulances they had and how they kept records on them.

With the same grace he had shown in his maneuver with the chair when Cates was handcuffing The Bush, Winston came in to back Cates's play.

"Actually, as a matter of law, a warrant is not required, Ms O'Connor. As Detective Cates indicated, this is a federal investigation as well. The FBI and the sheriff's office are cooperating in this inquiry."

He said it with the hushed formality—just a hint of awe— that he might have used if his words had been, "As Detective Cates indicated, it is God who is making this inquiry."

"What's the purpose of your inquiry?" demanded Ms O'Connor, but her eyes showed she was wavering.

"That, I'm afraid, is classified information," responded Winston. "Off-the-record, however, I will, ah, suggest to you that the matter concerns the possible theft of government secrets."

Cates put on his most solemn and earnest expression.

Ms O'Connor looked shocked. "By one of our people?"

Winston shook his head, and Cates answered the question.

"We have reason to believe that one of your ambulances may have been involved. It could well have been without the company's knowledge. At this point, we're interested in any possible...unauthorized usages that may have occurred regarding your equipment." He hoped the implication was that the focus could well become more specific if she didn't cooperate.

Winston nodded and took up the thread, speaking in his most professional tones.

"You could continue to insist we get a search warrant, of course. In that case, I might arrest you for obstructing an investigation, though frankly I probably wouldn't. Instead, we would simply leave and return with a subpoena from the United States Grand Jury for you and the records, something I should think would not be desirable to explain the next time Caro's contract with the city comes up for review."

Ms O'Connor gave him a hard look, then said, "Wait here."

She went over to the telephone, punched in a number, waited and then held a hushed conversation with somebody on the other end. At one point Cates was able to make out the words "grand jury." As she spoke, she looked over at them. She did not seem happy.

Finally, she hung up and returned to the counter.

"Mr. Caro requests that if possible we be kept out of the investigation." Her tone implied she would answer their questions, but that she couldn't bring herself to say so. She even made the statement as if it hurt.

"We will be glad to do what we can, of course," Winston assured her in his best Fed-side manner.

Ms O'Connor appeared to thaw slightly. "As a matter of fact," she said with a note of apology in her voice, "our records aren't—we've discovered some . . . inconsistencies in the records for some of the ambulance units. Mr. Caro was—is—quite upset about it, and steps are being taken to remedy the problem."

"What sort of inconsistencies?" Cates asked.

"Is there any particular time frame you're interested in?" she countered.

He nodded, and gave her the dates of the week Beth disappeared. She jotted them down on a slip of paper and said she'd be right back.

When she returned, Ms O'Connor was bearing a vinyl notebook.

"These are the originals of the log sheets for the four pieces of equipment that operate out of this facility," she explained. "Each time a machine is taken on a call-out, the time and mileage is to be logged. Well, actually the mileage is the only thing logged by the driver; the times are taken from our dispatch records. We use the information for billing the city or county or other appropriate party."

She opened the binder and removed four sheets of paper. "We post the information to our central ledgers on a weekly basis. Each unit has its own log, of course. We collect them each Monday morning for the preceding week, and furnish new ones for the upcoming week." She slid the papers over to them. "These are the four for the week you mentioned."

Cates and Winston studied them, one at a time, beginning in each instance with the top entries—Monday morning—and going through to the bottom of the page, which ended the following Monday at 8:00 a.m.

For each call-out, the figures for the beginning mileage reading seemed to be exactly the same as the figures recorded at the conclusion of the preceding call-out.

"These are good records," Winston commented to nobody in particular. From the corner of his eye, Cates saw Ms O'Connor react to the remark with, he thought, a hint of pride. It was just possible she might thaw out yet.

Cates paused for a moment midway through the second sheet. "What about personal usage?" he inquired of her. "Code sevens or code eights, that sort of thing?"

"What do you mean?"

He made an exaggerated grimace, as though she had asked something embarrassing, then hooked his finger in his collar and tugged on it in a passable parody of the famous Rodney Dangerfield move.

"Well, just between us friends—" he paused and made a show of clearing his throat "—on the department, we sometimes, ah, employ an official unit for, oh, a quick trip to lunch or the bank or whatever, even though strictly speaking it's not kosher."

Winston came in on cue. "Is that what you mean by a code seven?"

"Ah, yes, as a matter of fact."

"And code eight is?"

"Well, that really doesn't apply," Cates admitted. "I just threw it in. It's an unofficial designation for a, uh, pit stop."

"Pit stop?"

"To use the rest room, damn it." He continued the awkward look. "What I'm getting at is, strictly off-the-record, is it unheard of for somebody to grab one of these units and shoot down for a Big Mac or something? And if so, how is it recorded on the logs?"

Ms O'Connor smiled, evidently enjoying his apparent discomfort at the subject. "We used to allow that," she said. "But one of the machines was in a minor accident, so the rule is very strict that it must not occur. Mr. Caro specifies that one of the nonemergency company vehicles—mine usually, or even his if he's on this site—be used for that, and no need to be sneaky about it. He's really an excellent boss," she added.

"How about service calls?" Winston inquired. "Servicing of the equipment, I mean."

"Or going to the gas station, even," Cates added.

"Those get recorded on the logs just like any emergency usage, except under the Destination column we just write the number 94. That designates it was a maintenance or refueling usage."

Cates shrugged. "Sounds like you have a damn diary on each vehicle."

She beamed. "We try to."

"Hmm." It was Winston who made the sound as he studied one of the columns.

"Yes?"

"What about something like this?" He pointed.

Cates looked where the black agent was indicating, and his heart leaped. Externally, he showed no emotion.

"What is it?" Ms O'Connor asked.

"Well, here, for example. Last Friday. On all the other entries, the numbers match up. Starting mileage for one call-out is the ending mileage of the one before. But there's a gap here, it looks like."

Ms O'Connor moved her head in a strange circular, diagonal motion, as if she were trying to both nod and shake her head at the same time. "You *would* find the only glitch in my entire records," she said. Her voice had a tone of mock exasperation, intended—Cates was sure—to be friendly. Next thing, she'd be flirting with them.

He played dumb. "What is it?"

Winston pointed. "Right here."

"What about it? What are you driving at?" The question was directed at his partner; as he had hoped, Ms O'Connor came in with the answer.

"Don't you see, Detective? The FBI has found the one glitch in our *entire* records." She grinned in conspiratorial good humor, and pointed with her index finger. "The ending mileage from the last emergency usage at 10:23 a.m. on Friday is 44,184, and the beginning mileage for the next one is 44,257. There's an unaccounted-for usage of, what, sixty-three miles."

"Seventy-three," corrected Winston.

"Seventy-three," agreed Ms O'Connor. "I'd hate to be a spy if you two would be coming after me."

Cates, his heart racing, scanned the sheet. That was it! It had to be; the coincidence was overwhelming. Aloud he said casually, "well, seventy-three, schmeventy-three. I wish my own mileage logs looked this good. If they did, I'd be a captain by now."

Even while speaking he debated the merits of actively pursuing the inquiry.

For reasons he couldn't precisely articulate but that probably had their roots in nothing more than basic, close-to-the-vest cop paranoia, Cates didn't want to alert Ms O'Connor to the significance of the discovery. By now, any physical evidence would have been lost or dissipated from the ambulance itself. Thus, there was no foreseeable benefit to searching the unit, and that would have required demonstrating their interest to Ms O'Connor.

Winston evidently picked up on his thread. "You wouldn't be a captain if they asked for my input." He continued scanning the sheet, and casually—almost as an afterthought—inquired of Ms O'Connor, "What do you make of that, anyway?"

She shook her head. "It beats me, frankly. The most likely thing is that the figures had been misrecorded at some time in

1199

the past. I just can't figure it out, actually. Unless some space-
man came down and took a seventy-three-mile joyride sometime between—'' she consulted the sheet ''—between 10:23
a.m. and 7:12 p.m.''

Cates shrugged and turned his attention to the fourth sheet.
''Stranger things have happened, I guess.''

Twenty minutes later, they thanked Ms O'Connor warmly
and departed.

They had received a tour of the facility, and had admired all
four ambulances—specially equipped Chevrolet vans, roughly
comparable in size to one-ton pickup trucks—both inside and
out. Ms O'Connor said she was sorry they hadn't found what
they were after, but in a way she was glad because that meant
Caro's didn't have anything to do with whatever it was they
were investigating. Cates had reiterated that they had never
believed for a moment that anybody at Caro's had knowingly
been involved, but now it didn't look like any connection at all.

As they were leaving, almost as an afterthought, Cates inquired casually, ''Where are these logs kept? In the particular
vehicles, I assume?''

Ms O'Connor shook her head. ''No. As a matter of fact, we
keep them here in the office.'' She pointed to a wooden shelf,
over which hung four hooks. ''The keys to each unit are kept
there, and the corresponding logs right beneath them. When
a unit is dispatched, the driver takes both the keys and the
logbook. When he gets back, both are replaced there.''

''Why do you do it that way?''

She smiled warmly. ''It helps ensure that the correct figures
are logged into the book after each trip.''

Cates nodded approvingly. ''If you ever get tired of this, the
sheriff's office could sure use you.''

He waved to her, then unlocked the passenger door of the
pastel vehicle for Winston before walking around to his own
side. As he did, he heard the tall black agent mutter something under his breath.

It sounded like ''goddamn chameleon.''

25

FI

JOYCE ANSWERED the telephone and was pleased to hear the voice of Steve Cates.

Since the fiasco Saturday, she had been wondering if he would call again. More precisely, she had thought he might not, but had hoped he would. And here he was, in all his non-macho, quiet confidence.

She took a deep breath and plunged in. "I'm sorry about last Saturday."

He was silent for a moment. "No sweat," he said at last.

"It was for me," she replied awkwardly. "I wanted—I was looking forward to our dinner."

Another silence. "Well, it happened that I got called out to work anyway. So if you hadn't gotten hung up, I would have. We're equal."

"You're kidding."

"Nope."

"I thought you'd be really angry."

"I'm not in much of a position to do that, am I?" he said mildly. "Joyce?"

"Yes, Steve."

"There's something I need to discuss with you. A couple of questions, actually."

She frowned. This sounded like something to do with the case. That was fine, of course, but not what she had wanted.

"Is it something we . . . can discuss over the telephone?"

"Part of it is."

"Well, shoot." Then it occurred to her that this might not be an entirely fortunate choice of words, speaking to a cop. She said as much.

She heard him chuckle. "Actually," he replied, "the first question's simple, only a yes or no, no explanations required or expected." He hesitated. "Can we try for dinner again?"

Joyce caught herself smiling into the telephone, though of course he couldn't see her. "That can be arranged."

"Great. When?"

"When did you have in mind?"

"Tonight."

"Tonight?"

"Yes."

"Just a second. Let me check. Not to be coy, but I think I have other plans."

"No problem if you did."

She frowned. She was indeed not trying to be coy. The hell of it was, she thought there was something going on that evening. Cocking her head to one side to hold the telephone against her shoulder, she bent forward and retrieved her purse. She rummaged through it and found her personal calendar.

Monday night.

She had planned to go to dinner with Beverly Teal, a friend from college who was now an attorney in San Diego. Damn. This was the second time she and Bev had planned to get together. She didn't want it not to come off again.

"Yes," she said into the receiver.

"Yes, what? Yes, you already have something going, or yes, you can do it?"

"Yes, I'll do it."

After all, she thought defensively, Bev was the one who had caused the last postponement. Or "continuance," as Bev put it, explaining that was the phrase that attorneys and judges used. And Bev, who was also single and understanding of social conflicts, would understand.

To her surprise, he responded, "If this isn't a good night for you, we could continue it to another date."

She smiled into the receiver again. "No continuance is necessary, thank you."

"Seven o'clock?"

"Seven's fine."

Quite unreasonably, she suddenly didn't want to end the conversation. "So, have you solved any homicides today?"

He chuckled. "What's today, anyway? Monday?"

"Yes. Last time I checked, anyway. Why?"

"Well, Mondays and Tuesdays we crush crime. Wednesdays and Thursdays we dispense justice. On Fridays, we solve homicides. So don't expect anything before then."

"Oh, is that how it goes?"

Joyce heard him sigh. "I wish." He hesitated. "Actually, I've been learning about ambulances all morning."

"Ambulances?"

"Yeah. You know, those specially equipped things they carry sick people to the hospital in."

"I know what they are. What's the big deal about them?" He didn't answer right away. "If it's not confidential, or something?" she added hastily.

"Nothing of the sort," he responded. "It just occurred to me that one way to kidnap somebody in broad daylight would be to use an ambulance."

Joyce frowned, again forgetting he couldn't see her.

Something tugged at her memory, something urgent, something related to what he had just said. She reached for it, grasped at it, but it eluded her.

"You still there?" His voice brought her back to the present.

Then she had it. "I saw an ambulance when I was going to pick up Beth that night," she said excitedly.

"Are you sure?" His voice was suddenly urgent, intense.

"Sure I'm sure. An ambulance passed me while I was driving around looking for her street, MarVista."

"Where? When?"

She thought back.

She'd been late, and frustrated, looking for MarVista, the *right* MarVista—Court, not Street or Avenue or Way or Road. And there had been an ambulance, coming toward her. No red lights or siren; she'd thought grimly that the driver must be lost, too.

1199

"Steve, I can't be sure, but I think..." She hesitated, checking it in her mind. "I think they were coming...I believe maybe even from her street."

"Whose?" he demanded. "Beth's?"

"Yes."

"Jesus." He breathed the word.

Joyce normally didn't like it—hated it, in fact—when people said that, though she wasn't a zealously religious person. Probably something from her upbringing, she thought fleetingly. But Cates said it in such a tone of awe and reverence and disbelief all mixed together that somehow it didn't seem so bad.

"You're sure about this?" he said at last.

"Yes. I'm sure I saw one, anyway. I'm ninety percent sure on the part that it came from that street."

Joyce heard him make a long, controlled exhalation of breath. She started to make a quip about was he trying to make this into an obscene phone call, heavy breathing and all, only it didn't seem to fit. Instead, she waited.

"Is this important?" she asked at last.

"It could be very important." His voice became controlled once again. "You don't happen to recall what it looked like? What kind it was?"

"What do you mean, what kind? It was an ambulance. An ambulance-ambulance. What kinds are there?"

"Do you recall what color it was?"

"Mainly white. Or tan, something light. It had a name, but I don't recall what it was."

His voice sounded careful. "You know how some ambulances are sort of like motor homes? I mean, bigger, blocky sort of things?"

"Oh. I see what you mean. No. This wasn't like that. This was a van. Like a Chevy van or an Econoline or something of the sort."

"You said 'they.' Were there two people?"

She frowned. "What do you mean?"

"A moment ago, you said 'they were coming maybe from her street,' or something like that. Not 'it,' or not 'he.' Was there more than one person in it?"

"Did I say 'they'?"

"Think, Joyce." His voice was urgent. "Think."

She thought, but it didn't come. "I'm sorry. If I said that, it may have been because I saw two people, but I just can't remember if I did. Or it may have been because ambulances usually have two people."

"Or kidnappers using an ambulance would have two people," he mused. Then, abruptly, he seemed to put the subject aside. "Seven tonight?"

"Seven it is."

Joyce hung up the telephone and sat for a moment, racking her memory about the incident. Cates's obvious appraisal of its significance, and his resulting intensity, were infectious.

What makes him tick, she wondered, this tall detective who could so easily have lied to her about last Saturday?

He could have said that he came out to pick her up but she hadn't been home. Or, more acceptably, he could have just kept quiet when she had confessed error, so to speak, not actually lying but letting her think she owed him one. He could have put the burden, so to speak, on her.

He hadn't, however. She liked that.

Of course, it was remotely possible he was trying to make her jealous. Or, it could be a really sophisticated macho trip, to see if she would go out with him in spite of his missing their date, in effect, even if it were work-related.

She had read the papers about the shooting incident. The deputy involved in the shooting was a woman, she recalled. Was that what he had been called out on? she wondered. Was she an old girlfriend of his? Had he slept with her?

She felt a pang of jealousy at the thought, and anger at herself for having it. Her relationship with Cates—if one developed—hadn't even begun, and she had no right to have those feelings. After all, it wasn't as though she had exactly been a cloistered nun in the past.

Not my business, she said, and then realized how that sounded like something Steve Cates would say.

Still, rightly or wrongly, she couldn't help wishing she hadn't gotten hung up by the traffic accident on Saturday. Then the burden would definitely have been on *him*.

To hell with it.

With a start, she looked up and saw The Bush standing next to her desk, a sheaf of papers in her hand.

Startled, Joyce felt conflicting emotions. Anger at The Bush for somehow intruding and, on a more general level, for being who—and what—she was. Dismay, because it was never pleasant dealing with Pam. Embarrassment, a sense of being flustered, as though she, Joyce, were somehow doing something wrong by dating—as part of her own personal life on her own time, no less—the cop who had arrested Pam. And, overriding it all, irritation at herself for so thinking, for being on the defensive.

"Uh—hi, Pam." She had no idea how long The Bush had been standing there.

"Hello, Joyce. How are you?"

Gee, she sounds almost civil, Joyce thought. Could it be by any stretch of the imagination that Pam had, well, if not learned a lesson then at least been humbled a little?

"I'm fine, Pam. How... about you?"

The Bush looked a trifle embarrassed. "I'm all right. I...I made kind of a spectacle of myself the other day, I guess."

Was that an apology? wondered Joyce. Aloud she said offhandedly, "Are they... is anything going to happen to you as far as the company is concerned?"

"I don't know. It has caused a big flap, of course. And I got chewed on by Foster." Foster was the administrative VP, Joyce knew. More significantly, he was the vice chairman of the board of directors. Pam spoke of him bitterly, as though the incident weren't her fault. For some reason, that was reassuring to Joyce, as if it validated that the leopard was not, in fact, about to completely change its spots. "I guess they're going to wait and see how the court case comes out," she added sulkily.

Joyce didn't say anything. After a moment, The Bush spoke again. "Was that the cop? Cates?"

"What are you talking about?" Joyce demanded, thunder-struck that Pam could have known.

"Come on, Joyce. Don't be a prig about it. I mean, you and he did start this whole thing. You were together when it all started. And anybody could see that you were following him around like you were in heat when he and Kareem Super-spook were out here?" As an after gibe, she added, "Or was it Kareem you were after?"

"Look, Pam," Joyce flared angrily. "What I do on my own time, and with whom, is none of your damn business. Now, if you have something to do here, something that involves me, tell me—or do it—and leave. And if you don't, then just leave. I don't want to argue with you."

Abruptly, The Bush did an about-face. "I'm sorry, Joyce. I—I don't know what's wrong with me. Whatever happened last week, I was . . . I shouldn't have said that to you."

Joyce looked at her, still angry but also pitying. The Bush seemed truly stressed.

It was unnerving, in a way, because it showed she was hu-man, and had feelings, instead of being the unmitigated bitch that she appeared. It somehow made her more difficult to de-spise, Joyce realized with some chagrin.

"Forget it," she said irritably. "Just forget it, Pam. Yes, that was the detective. And yes, I'm going to meet him for dinner. Let's just leave it at that. All right?"

The Bush still looked curiously human. "What was that about ambulances?"

"What? Oh, nothing. He's just got some theory that whoever kidnapped Beth used an ambulance to get away with it, that's all. Look, I really don't want to talk about it any-more. What can I do for you? Work-wise," she added hastily, to make it clear the personal talk was over.

"I just—nothing. It's nothing that can't wait. I'll talk to you later. So long, Joyce."

The Bush turned on her heel and strode away. Joyce stared after her, fuming and wondering if maybe The Bush were human, after all. An unpleasant human, to be sure, but a person nonetheless.

After all, everybody was human.

Joyce did not know, of course, what Pam did after that. She couldn't know how Pam returned to her desk, picked up the telephone and dialed a certain number.

And she certainly had no way of knowing that the number was to a telephone ostensibly located in an empty garage behind a house in Pacific Beach. The garage did not actually have a telephone in it, because it was only a front to fool a casual, first-level trace, and the call was actually forwarded back to La Jolla, to a house on the hill above the Pacific Ocean, where it rang and rang and a man finally answered it....

CATES TURNED to Winston after he hung up the telephone. The black agent had been watching him, his shiny pate gleaming under the fluorescent lights of the Homicide Division.

Predictably, Winston didn't address the real issue first.

"So, Cates, you're going to try for two with the lady." He said it as a statement, an observation, rather than a question.

Cates nodded. "Thought I might."

"It sounded like it."

"Yeah."

The phone rang. Cates was vaguely aware that one of the other detectives answered it, then called his name. "Cates!"

"Yeah?"

"Line three. It's the lab."

It was Gina Takahashi. She told him that she had analyzed the dope in the bindles he brought over. It was cocaine.

She read off the gross and net weights. She said that the stuff in the bindles, including the one he had brought over separately from the others, appeared chemically identical. She said that for what it was worth the paper used to make the bindles themselves was the same, probably from the same page or ream, but she hadn't been able to match the edges up to be able to conclude they were definitely cut from the same sheet. Still, it did seem likely they came from the same dealer.

Cates thanked her and hung up. He related the information to Winston, then sat and took another sip of his coffee.

"So," Winston said finally.

"Yes," Cates responded.

"Do you see what I see?"

"Yes, Counselor."

"Spell it out."

Inwardly, Cates was elated by the information, slim as it was. Outwardly, he affected to be bored. He shrugged. "Beth Fisher and the Hotch woman got their coke from the same source."

"Yes, indeed."

Cates looked at Winston thoughtfully. "You know, I always did like the Hotch woman as being involved in this somehow," he said ruminatively.

"Like her?"

"Yeah. You know. Liked her as a suspect. Meaning, thought it looked pretty good she was involved."

"Oh."

Cates thought some more. "I still like her as being involved. And now we know there's a connection between her and the dead woman."

"It is a connection," Winston admitted.

"Not much of one, though."

"Thin."

"Real thin."

"Gossamer." The black man was silent for a few moments. "So what do we do with it?"

"Think on it."

Winston smiled. "You're holding back on me, Cates."

"What do you mean?"

"What else did Joyce tell you? Something having to do with an ambulance?"

"And how!" Cates broke into a jubilant grin and slapped his palm against the desktop. "And how, brother!" He related the conversation to Winston, who nodded sagely.

"I'd say it's definitely looking pretty good," the black Fed agreed. "Still thin. But at least we put the ambulance leaving right after she—the Fisher woman—could have disappeared.''

"You got it," Cates rejoined enthusiastically, wondering how these new pieces of information fit together and trying not to think that each could turn out to be nothing more than a coincidence.

Winston was speaking again. "There's only one minor problem with all this."

"Yeah." Cates knew what he was going to say.

"Where do we go from here?"

"Yeah."

"Check every licensed ambulance driver in the state of California? Or every licensed kidnapper?"

"Beats me." Cates felt the euphoria begin to evaporate.

"We've practically got it solved, haven't we?" Winston said with heavy sarcasm.

Cates sighed. "Look, Mr. F. B. of I. man, I know what you're saying. But we're a hell of a lot farther than we were last week, at least if this ambulance thing pans out. And even more important than what we learned—more important for now, anyway—is the fact that we learned something. Anything. It's gotten us started. Like pushing a car, it has overcome the inertia. We've got a little momentum, damn little, but at least some, and I'm not going to piss it away."

" 'Win this one for the Gipper,' " Winston commented.

"Go to hell."

Winston grinned. "You're right, of course. I didn't mean to be so negative."

Cates waved that away. "The hell of it is, you're right. And now, having made my brave speech, I'm damned if I know what to do with it, either."

"But we'll do something."

"We'll do something."

"What?"

Cates sighed. "I don't know. But—" suddenly his eyes lit up and he made his voice melodramatic and strong, like John Wayne at the Alamo "—failing all else, when everything else fails . . .''

Winston raised one cultured eyebrow at him. "Yes?"

"When it looks like all the doors have slammed shut in your face..."

By this time a couple of other homicide dicks who were in the bull pen had stopped whatever they were doing and were regarding Cates curiously.

"Who wound him up?" a visiting area detective, not assigned to Homicide, muttered to one of them.

"He gets that way sometimes," was the amused response.

"When the odds against you are overwhelming, when there's no way out except to sell your life dearly and maybe take a few of the bastards with you..." Cates continued, now going full steam.

"Yes?" came Winston's prompt.

"You check the FIs. You check the one each, by God, standard department issue FIs."

"The FIs?"

"Sure. The field interview slips. See who's been contacted in the area. See if maybe—just maybe—the jerk got shaken down by a patrol jockey."

For once, Winston's face showed he was surprised. Whatever dramatic finale he had expected, this was clearly not it.

"That's it?" he queried in amazement.

"That's the trouble with you Feds. You don't have it on videotape, you ain't interested. Preferably color video at that."

"Talk about thin," Winston rejoined. "You know what a long shot is, Cates?"

"You got a better idea?"

Winston got to his feet. "As he said, you check the FIs."

The two men turned and headed toward the computer terminal.

The information on the field interview slips was routinely input into the computers. The hard copies such as those Cates had been perusing at the LGS that Friday when Joyce—and ultimately Beth Fisher—had walked into his life and his caseload were then destroyed. The information was maintained for a certain period of time in the computer, then purged altogether.

Cates and Winston sat at the computer terminal in the Homicide Division.

"Where to begin?" Cates muttered as they sat down.

Winston didn't say anything.

"What the hell? Let's go for it."

"What do you mean?"

"Let's start with the Friday she disappeared. Who knows? We might get lucky. Find some cop wrote them a cite in the ambulance." His grin said that he didn't really expect that to be the case.

And, indeed, it wasn't.

"So we go back a day," Cates muttered.

They started perusing the FIs for Thursday, the day before Beth's kidnapping. Nothing. Ditto for Wednesday.

Cates turned in the chair and looked at Winston. "We better come up with something pretty quick, or we might have to look elsewhere for our clues. Do some real police work, or something." He winked as he said it, but he didn't feel too jolly.

Nothing for Tuesday.

Cates scrolled the computer screen to Monday. Suddenly, he paused and stared at the screen. "Jackpot!" he breathed.

Several of the FIs had looked familiar to him, largely because he had been leafing through the hard copies for this same period out of the Grove the day Joyce came to the counter. And this was one of them, but he had forgotten it completely, on a conscious level, at least.

"What is it?" Winston bent forward to look over his shoulder.

Cates scrolled the information to center screen.

"Well, what do you know?" Winston murmured.

Cates was staring at the FI. A deputy had contacted a subject sitting in a car in the middle of the afternoon, 4:00 p.m., to be exact.

And the car was a white Porsche.

It wasn't possible. His dream, or vision, or vibes or whatever the hell it was out at the scene had included a white Porsche.

But that couldn't be. He had believed in the vibes, or the washing machine theory, enough to go out there, sure. But the dream—it had to have been just that, a dream. Vivid, sure. But probably just the result of stress and wishful thinking.

But here was an FI with a white Porsche.

Coincidence.

Wait. The FI would have a physical description of the person involved.

His eyes scanned the screen. There it was. Male. Five-seven. Two hundred. Build stocky/muscular. Eyes brown. Hair black. The deputy's note said "possibly Oriental?"

Good work by the deputy, he thought, and checked the bottom of the screen to see who it was. Griffin, M. Christ, he wondered, why do the same names come up again and again on this case?

The description fit. It would be a short, stocky powerful man, the man he had seen in his dream at the top of the embankment as Beth's car had come plunging down. It fit the man who could kill by the death touch, the *noi cun*, a man who was possibly Oriental according to Deputy Griffin. . . .

As Winston had said in another context, gossamer. And yet, Cates knew it was so.

Something was bothering him. Why was Winston so interested in this FI?

Cates hadn't told him about the preceding evening's visit to the canyon. He certainly had not mentioned what happened out there. So the Porsche and the driver's description couldn't mean anything to the Fed. Why had Winston keyed in on the FI, too?

The black agent spoke. "That's too close to be just a coincidence, Steve."

"What do you mean?"

"The address, man. Look at it. It's right across the street from the ambulance place."

Cates had been so absorbed in the other aspects of the FI that he hadn't seen the significance of the rest of the information. Heart racing, he checked it.

Sure enough, it was directly across the street from the Caro's Emergency Care facility.

Jackpot! he thought exultantly. We have a guy casing the place, scoping out the ambulance activity, in preparation for "borrowing" one later on in the week. And, though this would never find its way into any paperwork, the guy was the guy from Cates's vision or dream or whatever the hell you called it.

He read the rest of the form. Deputy M. Griffin had responded to a citizen call of a suspicious person sitting in a car. She'd made contact and had FIed the guy. And, because there wasn't anything else she could do, she had filed the report and gone back to whatever else she was doing.

The man's name was Cecil Andrews. He'd given an address in Encinitas and a telephone number.

Cates wondered if it could be that easy.

Winston was looking at Cates. "That's what you were thinking, isn't it? Or is there something else on there I'm missing?"

"No," Cates lied, "that's it, all right."

His partner seemed unconvinced. "Why did you ask me what I meant when I said it was too close for coincidence?"

Cates pushed back from the table and winked. "Just testing you."

pen register

IT WASN'T THAT EASY.

First, Cates and Winston went to Encinitas to check out the address.

The address wasn't. It didn't exist. Or, to be more precise, the street existed but the number didn't.

Next, the two men returned to Homicide and ran the driver's license number from the FI through the DMV to see if they got a "hit," or match, on either the number or the name. In the middle of the search request, the computers went down, and they waited a frustrating hour and a half for them to go on-line again.

No hit on the number. That meant no record of that license. On the name search, the results were no better—there were a few Cecil Andrewses, but none of them lived south of L.A.

The plate on the white Porsche was no help, either. The DMV records showed only that it was owned by a leasing company in Oakland. No individual person was named.

Cates tossed the DMV printouts on his desk disgustedly.

"That was fun," he muttered, thinking *we drive down the goddamn field and at last have an opportunity to score, and it gets intercepted or something.*

Winston didn't respond. He, too, seemed dispirited.

Cates walked over to the coffee machine and filled a Styrofoam cup with coffee. He sipped it, grimaced and poured it out before returning to his desk. Winston was sitting in the chair next to the desk, his huge body giving the illusion of a normal man sitting in a child's chair.

"There is one thing," Cates said at last.

Winston looked up at him. "What's that?"

"It would have been too easy."

The black agent considered it. "Yes. I suppose that's so."

"This guy's a pro," Cates went on. "We've got to face it. Hell, a guy like this could have ten driver's licenses all so genuine looking that the DMV couldn't tell they were fakes. Made in Russia, maybe. This isn't some ordinary one eighty-seven."

"Why Russia?" Winston asked quickly.

Cates let it pass. "We're not talking about some jealous boyfriend or ex-husband or some triangle type of case. This isn't somebody she picked up in a bar who killed her. It's something completely different."

"I agree," Winston responded. "But why not?"

"Too smooth," Cates said promptly. "The whole thing was too smooth. The bit about using an ambulance for the kidnapping, for one thing. Too bold. Too sophisticated."

"*If* he did it that way," Winston reminded him. "*If* that is in fact what happened. We don't even know that."

"It is. He did. It has to be. It feels right for this case. But no boyfriend or girlfriend or ordinary killer would do it. Or could pull it off, for that matter." He hesitated a moment, realizing that he was putting an awful lot of weight on what was essentially a dream. Maybe, he thought, I'm stressing out.

"There's another aspect as well," Cates went on.

"Yes?"

"Why?"

"Why?" Winston echoed.

"Yeah. Why. You must have asked yourself why? Why go to all the trouble unless you have some reason? Something like wanting to take her alive."

The black agent considered the point. "You mean so he could talk to her, maybe? Something like that?"

Cates nodded. "Yep. He had to have her alive. He had to question her or find out something from her. Maybe find out what she knew. And then he could kill her. It's the only way it makes sense. It's too elaborate, otherwise."

"There were no signs of torture," Winston reminded him.

"It doesn't necessarily leave marks."

"True enough."

Cates thought it over some more. He could feel the anger begin to swell. Anger at the lack of leads. Anger at having the Cecil Andrews connection turn up a dead end, and to hell with whether it would have been too easy. Anger at the heat from Assistant Sheriff Tisdale and with having to work with a Fed who was playing hide the ball, regardless of how much he liked Winston.

But there was another reason for the strength of his emotions. He knew what it was, and he didn't like it.

It was born of his own qualms—he refused to call them fears—at the possibility of ultimately confronting the killer, a powerful, bull-like man who paradoxically would possess the martial skills of the far East.

And that was the paradox, he thought—there were powerful, bull-like guys and there were martial arts guys, who usually tended to be lean little bastards regardless of how skilled they were. But there weren't supposed to be guys who were both. It brought out memories from when he was a kid, and he and the other kids would read action comics and body-building magazines and watch Superman on TV. Back then they all thought that bodybuilders were as strong as they looked, and they would wonder, *What if there was a Mr. America who also knew karate?*

Now, of course, he knew that it was the powerful, stocky men who were the strongest. Here was one who would also be skilled in martial arts to a degree that was unimaginable. And, because the guy was a pro, he probably wouldn't be limited to the unarmed combative arts—hell, he could be just as good with edged weapons or firearms as with the death touch.

It scared him. He remembered the Fisher autopsy and the ruined heart tissue. Don't try to take him alone, Chan had said.

Angrily, Cates pushed the fears from his mind.

"Whatever it is, it's big," he said. "Sophisticated as hell. This is pro league all the way, and that makes me wonder how somebody like Beth Fisher could possibly be involved in something of that size." He thought for a moment and offered an answer to his own question. "Drugs, maybe."

"Maybe," Winston agreed.

Cates hardly heard him. "Or spies."

"Spies?"

"Yeah. Spies. She worked at a place that did hotshot government defense stuff. Hell, you saw the security up there. Maybe she was a spy. Or the agent for a spy. The mole or whatever you call it." He looked at Winston.

The black agent returned his look impassively.

"It would explain a few things," Cates went on, his voice hard.

"Such as?"

"Such as why the U.S. Attorney was all over the sheriff, who in turn was all over me. Or the assistant sheriff was, anyway." Cates's eyes narrowed. "Such as why you're here," he added, his jaw jutting grimly.

Winston looked at him levelly. "Look, Cates, I know how you feel about that. And I'm sorry. Our differences aside, I like working with you. Sure, there's some stuff I'm not telling you. But that's the way it is."

"Hell, I like working with you, Winston," Cates said irritably. "But you're holding out on me, goddamn it."

"A little. But it has to be."

"Maybe. Maybe not."

"What are you saying?"

"I could beat the hell out of you."

"Or try," Winston said evenly.

"I'd do more than try."

The two men stared at each other. And in the back of his mind Cates knew what kind of trouble he'd be in if he did beat the hell out of Winston . . . if he wasn't fired, he'd be working the jail for an eternity. And besides, this was Winston, and he mainly liked Winston. The tension broke and Cates felt the anger evaporate. He let out a breath of air and shook his head. Winston smiled a big white smile, beneath which Cates thought he looked just a little relieved.

"Ah, what the hell," Cates muttered.

"What, indeed," echoed Winston.

"Got any bright ideas on what we do next?"

"One."

"Shoot."

The black agent nodded. "We've already established that the Fisher woman and Pam Hotch got their coke from the same person."

"At least the bindles were the same," Cates agreed.

"So let's see if there's any other connection."

"Great. How?"

"Remember the speed dialer you took from the Fisher woman's place?"

"Yeah."

"I got a call from the local field office. The lab has the results of the decoding. Who knows? There might be something there."

Cates considered it. "There might, indeed," he said. If Winston realized Cates was mimicking him, however, he didn't show it.

THE SAN DIEGO FIELD OFFICE of the FBI was located in the sprawling, rust-colored Federal Building downtown. Cates and Winston checked in at the lobby, and Cates was given a visitor's pass.

The main work area was an open bull pen affair with clusters of metal desks butted up against one another. Agents, most of them wearing handguns in high-riding waist holsters, perused files or spoke into telephones. Cates followed Winston as he threaded his way among the desks.

Minutes later they were in an interview room with a large brown envelope and a box that contained bundles of long strips of paper, like cash-register tapes. The paper had a sort of silvery coating, and Cates could see numbers printed on the visible surfaces.

Cates recognized the tapes as coming from a pen register, a machine that could trace and record numbers called from a particular telephone. The numbers were printed out on the tapes. It was a mechanical device only, however, and did not record any of the actual conversation.

You bastard, Winston, he thought, you've been holding out on me.

Winston evidently saw him looking at the tapes. "Pen register," the agent said. Cates thought he looked a trifle embarrassed.

"Winston, Winston," said Cates, shaking his head. "You've been holding out on me, Winston." His voice was all mock surprise.

"A little," Winston responded for the second time on that subject.

"What's it to?"

"Which telephone, you mean?" And here Winston looked even more embarrassed. "Pam Hotch."

Cates nodded. "You liked her for being involved, too?"

"I liked her."

"How long has the register been in place?"

"Since she got out of jail."

With a grimace that was real, Cates shook his head. "Annoys me that you zeroed in on her before I did. Maybe I was too pumped up from making a grandstand play in front of all those little yuppies that I didn't see what was there," he added ruefully.

Winston grinned. "It did make an impression, didn't it?"

"That it did."

"Anyway, Cates, I can't take any credit for getting to her as a suspect first. As you have repeatedly observed, I've been privy to some information that you weren't."

"Holding out on me, you mean."

"Exactly."

"Anything you'd care to share with me now that we can be so free and open and all?" Cates inquired.

Winston shook his head. "Actually, there's not much there. No smoking gun, that's for sure. We had just run a background on the Hotch woman, and found that she had a few surprising things—and friends—in her past for somebody who ended up working in a sensitive position. Given the, ah, exigencies of the case, it seemed appropriate to throw a register on her phones."

Cates remembered Joyce's comment about Pam's being an unlikely type to be working at DRT. Aloud he observed, "I thought she would have had a pretty thorough background check to get the clearances she had as part of the work."

"That's true. But there are background checks and there are background checks, if you understand my meaning."

"I take it you're not the only Fed who's been working on this," Cates said casually. Of course not, he thought with a savage satisfaction, this thing is a hell of a lot bigger and you probably have fifty Feds running all over the place while you play street cop with me.

"No, I'm not. There are a few select agents performing certain specific tasks that have a bearing on this case."

"Swell."

"Swell, indeed."

Cates gestured at the pen register tapes. "Shall we, uh, see if there's a clue or something buried in here? Or is that for your eyes only, too?"

"I asked that somebody analyze the numbers already. Hopefully, that has been done for us." Winston was opening the large envelope as he spoke. He removed a sheaf of what appeared to be computer papers. He scanned them briefly. "Yes. This will save us considerable time."

The first sheet was a breakdown of the numbers decoded from Beth Fisher's speed dialer. A second column identified the subscriber of the respective number.

Cates scanned the column. Several obvious family members, obvious because the last name was Fisher. A few people that would probably be friends, though they would have to be interviewed to determine if that were in fact the case.

One of the names leaped out at him from the page. Pam Hotch.

Winston must have seen it, too, for he spoke immediately, his soft voice heavily laced with irony. "Well, would you look at that? Among the numbers that Beth would presumably call frequently enough to put it in a speed dialer is none other than one belonging to the much-beloved Pam Hotch."

"*Ms* Hotch to you, asshole," Cates quoted.

"Surprise you?"

"Not now. It would have earlier, I guess. Hell, Beth was only at the company for a week or two. And pretty much kept to herself, from what I understand."

Winston was turning his attention to the other computer printouts.

The first was an analysis of numbers called from Pam Hotch's telephone. Each number was listed, along with the number of times it had been dialed. A separate document reported the subscriber of each of the numbers.

The analysis sheet contained several numbers that had been called repeatedly. Friends, family probably. And it also listed six different numbers that had only been called one time each.

Cates looked over at the subscriber listing. The six numbers were all public telephones. Four of the pay phones were located in La Jolla, two in San Diego.

"Interesting," Cates commented.

"Very," Winston agreed.

"I doubt if most people place calls *to* pay phones six times a year. Let alone in a few days."

"True enough."

"Makes you think she's calling somebody at prearranged times and prearranged numbers. Somebody who doesn't want the calls going to his house. That sound about right, Winston?"

The black man nodded.

Cates was elated. Here was a lead that confirmed what he had recently decided about Pam Hotch. Now they could focus on her, and see where it took them. Keeping his voice calm and his words deliberately understated, he continued. "Looks like the Hotch woman might be involved."

"It does, indeed."

"I always did like her for this case, Winston."

Winston grinned. "So you've told me."

"Could be drugs, Winston. Could be a dealer she's calling."

"Could be drugs," Winston agreed, but he didn't sound very convinced.

Cates suddenly remembered how Winston had come to the point when he had tossed out the possibility that the suspect's fake driver's license could have been made in Russia.

"Or spies," he said casually.

"Or spies," Winston agreed, but he wasn't smiling anymore.

the inside man

THE DINNER HAD BEEN about as good as those things can be.

The restaurant was up the coast a ways. It was on the ocean, quite near the water—Cates had the feeling that at high tide the waves would be hitting the vast windows. It was short on decor and long on service and cuisine. Joyce had shrimp and Cates had swordfish, and between them a bottle of fine, oaky Guenoc chardonnay disappeared so quickly that they said what the hell and had another. They had talked and listened to each other talk and enjoyed both.

By the time they left, Cates driving, he had enjoyed himself so much that the decidedly negative aspects of the afternoon were completely forgotten.

When they arrived at her condo, Joyce said, "Would you like to come in for a drink?"

She said it a trifle awkwardly. Cates wondered if the awkwardness came from the fact that the offer included other things besides a drink, or because it didn't.

He said, "Yes, that'd be nice."

It was a town house in a complex of other town houses. Cates parked his car in a space toward the rear of the complex, on the opposite side from where he had parked when he arrived. Joyce led the way. They passed through an iron gate, down a path, around a pool and down a path some more.

She unlocked the door and let him in. She asked him what he'd like to drink, and Cates said a martini if she had it, but he realized martinis weren't fashionable these days, so gin and tonic otherwise. Joyce said she had surmised he meant a gin martini, and she didn't have any vermouth anyway but would he like gin and tonic. He said yes, so she made a g and t for him and poured a glass of wine for herself.

His drink in one hand and hers in the other, Joyce made her way toward him when the telephone rang.

Or, more accurately, it made a funny electronic chirping from its position on the end of the barlike affair that separated one wall of the kitchen from the living room.

Joyce frowned and glanced at a clock—an old-fashioned, art deco affair on the bookcase in the living room. Nine-fifty, not quite ten, perfectly acceptable for a work night.

Her action in looking at the time appeared reflexive, and Cates wondered fleetingly if this were the *friend* whom she had helped move earlier. He hoped not, because he didn't want the jerk to interrupt them, whoever he might be. He didn't want it because he just wanted them to be alone and continue the good talking and the fun.

Aloud, he said, "Go ahead and answer it, if you like."

She shook her head and smiled. "I *don't* like."

"I don't mind. It could be family or something, this time of night."

"Don't worry about it."

The fourth chirp was only a half chirp, and suddenly the vague electronic background noise of an answering machine came on. She evidently had the volume turned up, perhaps so she could monitor the caller's message and then grab the telephone midway through it if she felt like talking to whoever was calling.

Joyce was still bringing him his drink, and Cates thought with mild amusement that it put her on the spot—either she would have to make a fairly obvious—and hurried—approach to the machine and turn down the volume or answer the phone, or the caller's message would be played at full volume for the edification of both of them.

Her own outgoing message was a noncutesy, no-nonsense one. Cates liked that.

"Hi. This is Joyce. Please leave your message and the time of your call at the tone. Thanks for calling."

The answering machine made its tone, and the caller's voice came into the room.

It was The Bush.

Unlike a lot of people who left messages, she didn't use any pauses or "uhs" or "er-uhms" in her diction. Well, that figured, thought Cates.

"Joyce, this is Pam Hotch. It's about ten minutes to ten in the evening. I'm at work. The reason I'm calling is that Mike Stevens from Security called me and said there's some classified material that was left out in your area. As a favor, off-the-record, he agreed to not write up you or your group if you can come down and get it put away. He—"

With a beep the machine cut off.

Joyce looked at Cates. "Oh, god*damn*," she said wearily. "Damn it, damn it, damn it." The third damn it had more anger than weariness, as though she were working up steam.

Cates started to speak, when the telephone chirped again. Angrily, Joyce set the drinks on the table and strode over and answered it on the third ring.

"Hi, Pam," she said after the hello and some unintelligible—to Cates—statement from the caller. "Yeah, I heard it. Or the last part of it anyway—I was just coming in when the message clicked off." She turned toward Cates and rolled her eyes in silent acknowledgment of her white lie.

Joyce was speaking again.

Cates listened as hard as he could without actually cupping his hand around his ear or walking over, trying to catch Pam's end of the conversation. However, all he could make out—apart from Joyce's words—was some faint electronic squibble when Pam was speaking.

"What material?"

Squibble.

"How could that be? I don't know about that. I mean, I know about it, but it's been on hold for two months at least. It hasn't been out, not that I know of."

More squibble.

"Yeah, I know." She sounded weary. "I know. Look, can't, couldn't you—"

Sharp squibble this time.

"Yeah, you're right. It was cool of Mike to do that. I wouldn't want anybody in the group to get written."

Short squibble.

"All right. Yeah, I'll come down. I'll be there in about twenty minutes or so."

Squibble.

"Yeah. I understand."

Squibble.

"I know. Thanks, Pam. Bye."

Joyce hung up the phone and leaned against the counter, tilting her head back in a gesture that was both weary and exasperated. Cates looked at her in sympathy, and at the same time tried to figure out what was bothering him about all this.

She took a sip of her wine, then another, before she spoke.

"You heard that, I guess?"

He shrugged. "Some of it."

"Some idiot in my group must've left some classified documents out. The government people who handle the clearances are real strict about that. We get written up for violations."

"Written up?"

"A record is kept. Too many of them and somebody—or the company—loses a clearance."

Cates grinned. "Like points on your driving record with the DMV," he suggested.

Joyce grimaced. "Yeah. Something like that." She set down the glass of wine and looked around for her purse.

"Joyce?"

"Yes?"

"Why did Pam call you?"

"What do you mean? Because of the classified—"

He interrupted her. "I know why she *said* she called you. I'm asking why she really called you."

Joyce stared at him. "What are you saying?"

"She's hardly your best friend, is she?"

"No."

"Do you guys, you two, go way back? Old sorority sisters or something?"

"What on earth do you mean?"

He spoke patiently. "What I'm driving at is this—is there something in your and her past, some common factor that might cause her to have some minimal loyalty to you, even though you two hate each other's guts now?"

"I never met the woman until I came to DRT."

"Not members of the same secret sisterhood, or something?"

"Go to hell." Joyce said it with more than a little snap in her voice. Cates caught it—he could scarcely have missed it—and it bothered him, but only a little.

"And, from what you said earlier, she obviously knew we were going out. You and I. And that we were going out tonight, for that matter."

"I told her," Joyce responded, her voice defensive and angry. "I'm sorry if you're upset—"

"I'm not upset about it. But you have to concede that I'm probably not too high on Pam's list of favorites, either."

Joyce stared at him. "What are you trying to say?"

Cates wasn't sure what he was trying to say, yet. Not exactly, anyway. But he knew he was on the right track. A light had come on in his mind, and the light said Hazard.

Finally, he opted for the easy way out. "I'm trying to say what I said a couple of minutes ago. Why is she calling you?"

"Damn it, I don't know!" Joyce sounded truly angry now. "Maybe she's afraid we'll all get in trouble if we get written up. Maybe she got written herself, and she's afraid some of the heat will come over onto her. Maybe . . . hell, maybe she was supposed to circulate a memorandum about it, and she forgot it."

"Maybe," Cates admitted.

"And maybe—" Joyce raised her voice "—just maybe she wants to make amends to me, in some way. Maybe she wants me to owe her one. And why can't you leave your cop suspicions behind when we go out on a . . . a date!"

She turned abruptly and grabbed her purse and keys. Cates didn't respond.

"You—it makes me mad. Hurts my feelings, actually, Steve." Her voice was softer. "I like you. And I know that going out to dinner was not just part of the investigation, or whatever you call it. Part of the case. But it feels a little like that's what it is."

"Sorry." He barely glanced at her as he said it. He was lost in thought. "The dope was the same," he mused.

"Steve."

He looked at her. "The bindles found on her were the same type—cut from the same paper and therefore probably made by the same person—as the one in Beth's locker. So, one of them must have been furnishing the other, or else they had a common supplier."

Joyce lapsed into something between a hurt and a sullen silence.

"She has all the right clearances," he said speculatively.

"All the right clearances for what?" Joyce asked sulkily.

"For being a hell of a good mole, an inside man, informant, snitch, whatever, for a spy."

"Oh, come *on*! The Bush a spy? You've got to be kidding. Or crazy."

"It makes sense. It's one possible—just possible mind you— explanation, anyway."

"But you're talking about . . . about . . ." Joyce fumbled for the right word. "About treason. Betraying the country. What possible gain would she get from that?"

He shrugged. "Coke, for one."

"Coke?"

"Yeah. You know, drugs."

"She could get drugs anyway."

"Sure. But she'd have to pay for it."

"I still don't think she's that much of a user."

"She's thin enough, lean enough, to be one. And certainly temperamental enough. And, it's a pretty common way to pay off spies, I'm told. For the real spies to pay off their inside men, I mean."

Cates started sifting and sorting the evidence in his mind. It certainly seemed . . . if not exactly convincing, not enough for probable cause, then at least consistent. And intriguing as hell. It felt as if it fit.

It felt right.

He thought back to his arrest of The Bush in the DRT facility. She had been strangely subdued when he put the cuffs on her. At the time, in his anger and his ego, he had attributed it to the suddenness of his actions. Their unexpectedness. And her embarrassment. Maybe even the force of his own character.

Still, it had fleetingly entered his mind that he was a little surprised she hadn't turned into a real 148, a screaming, biting, clawing, groin-kneeing, eye-gouging resistance case. And yet she hadn't. She obviously had suddenly, frighteningly realized she had gone too far.

But it obviously wasn't the law she was afraid of. Her contempt for that was crystal clear.

And Joyce had told him that even her security clearance was probably not in real jeopardy. Certainly not in immediate, imminent jeopardy.

Maybe it was something else that had made her seem so chastened. Maybe she realized—or thought—that somebody else would be unhappy at her having called official attention to herself in such a dramatic and visible way. Somebody who had a lot to lose. Somebody who wouldn't give her a lot of due process rights in dealing with her for screwing up.

Somebody who "ran" her. A case agent, or intelligence officer, or spymaster or whatever the current jargon was.

It was a weak reed. But it was a reed. Added to the rest of the factors . . .

Joyce had evidently been thinking about his earlier arguments. "Steve, I see what you're saying. But I just can't believe Pam would . . . I just don't believe it."

"Why not?"

"I just don't. She's unpleasant, sure. She's even a . . . uh, bitch. But—look. Are you saying she killed Beth? Or even that she kidnapped her? It just can't be. I just don't believe it."

Cates shook his head. "No. I'm not saying she killed Beth. Remember, she would only be the inside man. Somebody else would run her."

Somebody who could kill with the death touch, the *noi cun*, he thought silently.

He turned to Joyce. "Have you ever seen Pam's car?"

The non sequitur caught her off guard. "Her car?"

"Yes. What does she drive?"

"Why, lately she drives a Porsche. Leased, I gather. Before that—"

Cates interrupted her. "It's white?"

Joyce looked surprised. "Yes. How'd you know?"

At that moment, the telephone chirped again. Before it could ring again, Joyce wheeled and grabbed it.

"Hello!" Her voice was sharp, angry.

Cates could hear the squibble, somehow different than before. Then Joyce was speaking again.

"Oh. Uh, of course I remember you. Sorry I sounded abrupt."

More squibble.

"Uh, sure. He's right here. Hang on."

She extended the telephone to Cates. "It's for you."

"Me? Who the hell knows I'm here?"

She shrugged. "It's Winston Keith."

illusions

"CATES, THIS IS Winston."

"Yeah, Winston."

"Cates. Listen to me. Things are starting to come apart. I'll meet you at the company."

"What are you talking about?"

"At Data Research. Joyce just got a call to go there—"

"How the hell did you know about that?" Cates demanded.

"Listen." Winston's voice was urgent. "There's no time to talk about it. We've had her line tapped. I know about the call."

"Whose line? Joyce's?"

"No. Pam's line at work."

"Who's 'we'?"

"The people working with me. Look. It's a long story. We don't have time to go into it now."

Anger welled in Cates, anger directed at Winston for holding out on him, and anger at himself for not seeing it before now. After all, the signs had been there.

Stubbornly—knowing he was being stubborn—he refused to give in.

"Who's 'we'?" he repeated. "How'd you get a wiretap? The federal judges don't just hand them out like blank bonus coupons. What the hell is going on here?"

Winston's reply came with such tight control that Cates could feel his tension. Perhaps he, too, was angry. "Steve, damn it, listen to me. We've had a wiretap on Pam for some time. And on several other people at Data Research. I'm sorry I couldn't let you in on it, but I just couldn't before now."

Instinctively, Cates knew that this wasn't the time or the place. Of course Winston had been holding back on him. Just as he had held back a little on Winston. And of course this wasn't simply a joint federal-state operation; wiretaps and Winston's mysterious calls and all the other signs pointed to it being much more than that.

And of course that meant Winston wasn't what he seemed, a cultured, educated FBI agent trying to get the best possible case for court....

The erstwhile Fed was speaking again. "Pam wasn't the only one. We got a wiretap on several people at Data Research. But hers was the best bet. And this call to Joyce—it's a ruse to get her down there to the company."

"Joyce?"

"Yes."

"Why?" Cates demanded.

"I don't know, but I don't like it." He took a breath, then continued hurriedly. "I've been doing some more work since you left for your date. I got through on the records on the Porsche that showed up on the FI we were looking at."

"The white one? The one FIed across from the ambulance place?" The one in that vision or dream or whatever it was up on the hillside, he thought, the one next to the short thick bastard who broke Beth Fisher's neck—figuratively speaking—and sent her down the hill in a Ford coffin? But he kept his thought to himself.

"That one," Winston responded. "And it's leased to Pam Hotch."

At least now we have concrete evidence, thought Cates, evidence that would be admissible in court, assuming the wiretap hadn't hopelessly screwed things up. More admissible than a dream or a vision anyway. Aloud, he simply said, "No kidding?"

"Yes, indeed."

A thousand questions ran through Cates's mind. A lot of them had to do with theories about the case, but a lot of them had to do with Winston.

Who the hell was he to order wiretaps like that? And who were the people he was working with?

To get a legal wiretap—a Title Three, as they were known in the investigative jargon—required something just short of an act of God, Cates knew. It was a hundred times tougher than getting a search warrant. In California, only federal agents could get them. You had to convince a judge that all other investigative leads were hopeless; and a very strong showing of probable cause was required. And even then, they had to be strictly monitored under a judge's orders.

And if it were an unauthorized wiretap?

Highly illegal, but possible.

He dismissed the idea; popular fiction and movies to the contrary, the FBI didn't go in for unauthorized wiretaps, period. The Bureau was too clean for that, at least in recent years.

Unless Winston weren't really FBI, but that was too fanciful to be even worth following up on, wasn't it . . . ?

And how the hell had he gotten the information about the rented car?

"Cates?"

It was Winston's voice on the telephone.

All the questions could wait, Cates thought. He looked at Joyce, who wore an expression of fear.

"I'm on my way," he said grimly. "ETA about ten."

JOYCE WALKED WITH HIM out to the car.

She looked on in silence as Cates went around to the trunk. He took out a high-riding belt holster that held his Smith & Wesson .357 Magnum revolver. He unfastened his belt at the buckle and pulled the leather strap back through the first two belt loops of his trousers on the right side. Then he threaded it through the slots in the holster, and ran it back through the trouser loops and refastened it.

She watched as he made a little hitching motion, to settle the weapon against his side. She noticed it rode high on his waist with the mass of the flat-metallic weapon above his hip, and only the barrel extending down below the belt.

I'm afraid, she thought. I'm afraid, Steve. I don't know what's going on, but I wish you'd tell me it's all right.

He didn't tell her it was all right.

Instead, he reached into the interior of the trunk and took out two dark-colored blocky objects like big spools for thread. Each looked perhaps an inch across by an inch and a half long. He dropped them into the outside right pocket of his blazer. They must have been heavy, for they pulled down and distorted the fabric and the pocket more than she would have expected.

Evidently, he caught her intent gaze. He looked at her for several moments, his face expressionless, so much so it looked frightening.

"Speed-loaders," he said simply.

She shivered.

"Spoils the drape of the clothing, wouldn't you say?" His mouth made the shape of a smile as he spoke, but his eyes were cold.

He put a small flashlight in the other coat pocket, and slammed down the trunk lid, then opened it again almost immediately. He reached in and took out a pair of handcuffs. These he put over his belt toward the center of the back, looping them over the leather strap so the center links were at the top and the two wrist cuffs hung down on either side, flat against his body.

Then he turned to her and spoke.

"Don't go to your office, Joyce." It sounded like an order.

"Why not?"

"I'm not sure it's safe. There's something going on there, and Pam's involved in it."

"Is that what Winston told you on the telephone?" she inquired, but for a response he simply shook his head. "What's going on, Steve?" she persisted. "Where are you going?"

He looked at her, and his eyes were intense, his features grim. Then he took her by the shoulders and spoke in a low, forceful voice.

"Joyce, I can't tell you all that right now. There isn't time."

There's enough time to argue with me, she thought, but didn't say.

"I'm going to meet Winston. He's got a break in this case. It may involve Pam. And it may be something at the DRT facility. That call could have been a ruse to get you down there. And even if it wasn't, it could be dangerous."

Joyce looked at him. "A ruse? Are you crazy? What could be going on—"

He cut her off, his voice hard. "Don't argue. Just don't go there." Then his tone became softer, but still insistent, and with a certain impatience that Joyce resented. "Please. I'll tell you all about it later."

Joyce felt her face redden. She felt left out. It was as if this man whom she wanted as a friend and something more were excluding her, or didn't trust her. Or perhaps was pulling some sort of macho number on her. It hurt her feelings.

She swallowed. "All right, Steve."

His eyes searched her face. "If you're here, I'll call you as soon as I know anything."

"Yes. I'd like that."

He looked at her for a few moments, then abruptly nodded, more to himself, she thought, than to her.

"Good." He strode to the driver's side of the car, then looked back at her. A crooked grin crossed his features.

"I had a good time, Joyce. At dinner."

She nodded. "Me, too." She felt a little better. "Call me, okay?"

"Yeah."

Then he got in the car and was gone.

revelations

A FOG HAD DESCENDED to blanket the coastal area.

It turned the lights into fuzzy yellow blobs, and made the May night chill seem even chillier. Cates drove fast considering the conditions, but it was still closer to fifteen minutes before he came up on Winston's car, parked at the access road to the several facilities in this part of the Golden Triangle.

Winston's car was a rented Cadillac, dark blue. Under other conditions, Cates would have made a comment based on ethnic stereotype, but this didn't seem like the time or place.

Cates guided his car up next to the Caddie and got out.

The coastal fog enveloped him like a chilly damp blanket. He took a deep breath, filling his lungs and using the action to muffle the emotions he felt. He strode around to the passenger door of the Caddie and got inside.

"Winston."

"Cates," the black agent responded.

He was dressed in one of his dark suits. As the interior light came on, Cates caught a glimpse of an Uzi submachine gun in the back seat of the car, along with what looked like a .45-caliber Colt Gold Cup automatic.

Cates took it all in with a single glance. He felt angry. He was tired of games, and there was a cold spot of fear in the pit of his stomach. Squarely on top of that nice dinner, he thought grimly.

"What's going on, Winston?" he demanded.

The black agent answered him directly. "I think this Pam Hotch is working as a spy inside the company."

Cates nodded.

So the bullshit was over, the foxy games and footwork behind them. It was time to get down to bullets and brass tacks. And now that Winston had said it, it was obvious.

"I think so, too," he responded.

He'd blown it, Cates knew, when he underestimated Pam and her potential role in what was going on. She had the clearances—the tickets, as Joyce called them—to have access to the sensitive material. And what had Joyce said about her, that Pam had always seemed to be philosophically aligned more against the establishment than with a government contracting company?

All the easier to recruit, to corrupt.

Winston was speaking again. "I thought you were headed along those lines."

"Yeah." The pieces fell into place even as he spoke; the cards filled his hand like those of a gambler on a roll who keeps drawing the suits he needs. "My guess is that Beth Fisher saw something she wasn't supposed to see. Maybe she even tried to use it, trade on it, for dope from Pam."

The tall black agent considered this. "When Pam told her intelligence officer what had happened—what Beth had seen—he kidnapped her, questioned her and killed her."

"Intelligence officer?" Cates asked. "You mean the spy?"

"Yes."

"So call him a spy."

Winston shrugged. "The mole inside the company is usually called the agent, the person who runs him or her is the case officer or intelligence officer. Usually—almost always—the intelligence officer works for some country, some national power."

"What about free-lance?" Cates asked. "Could he be working for himself, acting as some kind of middleman to buy from the . . . agent and sell to the Russians?"

"Rare. It could happen, but rarely."

"Not enough money in it?"

"No, that's not necessarily it. If you knew what you were doing, and were a tough bargainer, the money could be there. The Russians—choosing them by way of example—are not particularly altruistic folk, of course, so you'd have to be pretty hard-nosed yourself. You could have the key to the entire U.S. national defense, something they might pay a hundred million dollars for, and if you demanded five thousand, they certainly wouldn't offer to pay you more."

"Like us," Cates commented dryly.

"Precisely. And, of course, a major hurdle is convincing them the stuff is genuine, and not a plant by us to mislead them." Winston hesitated and took a breath. "We may be dealing with a free-lance type in this case, however."

"Why so?"

"Little things, here and there. The pattern fits." He declined to elaborate further. "Which makes him all the more dangerous," he added.

Cates thought of the *noi cun*, and of violent, bruising destruction of a heart the pathologist had carved from the body of a dead young woman.

He remembered Henry Chan's words, an inner power so strong and so concentrated it can kill a person without actually touching him. The death touch. Don't try to take the dude by yourself, Henry had said. Don't try to take him at all. Shoot him.

And Cates had quipped about how he had done the eleven reps at 315, so the *noi cun* would be no problem.

Somehow, eleven at 315 didn't seem like so much, now, when the man with the death touch was probably waiting for him in the DRT facility.

Well, as a matter of fact, eleven at 315 wasn't that much, actually, Cates realized. Hell, the 165-pounders are lifting that these days.

Best not to think that way, Steve, he thought.

He looked at Winston. "You seem to know a lot about the spy business."

"Yes. But what I don't know is why he's getting Pam to lure Joyce down here at this time of night."

Cates shrugged. "I think I know."

"Why?"

"Find out what she knew, or had told me, maybe. You see, Joyce told me that Pam knew we—Joyce and I—were getting together tonight."

Winston arched an eyebrow. "Really?"

"Yeah. I guess Pam was standing there when we were talking on the phone, and they got into a minor four-fifteen about it."

"Four-fifteen?"

"Fight. Disturbance. Dispute."

"If Pam Hotch knows you and Joyce were getting together, I'd say the chances are about ninety-five percent he's planning to do the same to her that he did to Beth."

"Yeah." After a moment Cates spoke again. "You know who the spy is? Know anything about him?"

The black agent shook his head. "No. I would have told you if I did."

"No," Cates said simply.

"No?"

"There's a lot of stuff you know that you aren't telling me. Haven't told me. And haven't told me all along."

Winston considered the statement for several moments, then nodded. "Yes. I suppose that's correct. But those things have concerned operational details, not substantive knowledge about what was going on or who we were up against."

"I'll bet."

"Well, it's true." He shrugged.

Cates considered Winston's statement in silence. Maybe Winston knew who they were after, and maybe he didn't. But Cates knew. Or at least he knew what, if not who.

They were after a master of the death touch. A shadowy figure with a stocky, oddly powerful physique who could destroy the tissue within but not leave a mark on the surface—a man who could strike without hitting.

Nothing seemed real anymore.

Cates had lost the ability to distinguish between appearance and reality. Or maybe there was no difference between the two concepts.

The more he thought about it, the more it seemed to be so. Maybe in the short run, appearance is reality. Or appearance is reality in the short run.

He had the sort of letdown that in his experience sometimes accompanied the breakthrough. Triumph, sure. But with it a sense of loss. And of sadness. And, in a strange way, of fate.

He'd come close to finding it on Martie's front porch.

Maybe the whole world was an 11-99; maybe nothing was. The truth about it was there was no truth, and this was especially so in police work. All that existed were reflections of the truth, images of the truth, things from which certain features of the truth could be deduced. Sometimes the deductions were accurate; sometimes they weren't. And always it depended on one's perspective.

Circumstantial evidence, in other words.

Damn.

Through his peripheral vision, he became aware that Winston was gazing, staring, out the windshield with the same meditative look that Cates knew he himself wore.

"Cates."

It was Winston, his voice still rich and cultured but strangely subdued.

Now Cates felt himself possessed of the same feelings he had experienced when he knelt at the open door of the blue Taurus at the bottom of the canyon, looking at a dead woman in whose body rigor mortis had come and gone. It had been a feeling of, well, destiny, of the game having begun, the antes made, the cards dealt at last.

Now, it was the same game, except much farther along.

Most of the cards had been played. The bets had been laid, round after round. This was the big table, the high rollers. And, with each round, somebody had folded, and the textures and tensions of the game had altered and become more clear.

The game constantly changes, Stevie, he chided himself.

Don't get in a snit because it doesn't change the way you want it to, or the way you guessed it would. Those earlier theories that were wrong were mirages; don't defend past mistakes, and don't pout because it doesn't unfold to suit you.

He knew what Winston was going to say. "Yeah, Winston."

"Cates, you know why I'm here, don't you?"

Of course I do, he thought. It's been there all along. I just didn't see it at first.

Aloud, he responded, "Yeah, I know."

"How long have you known?"

It depends on what you mean by *know*, Winston. I think I've known it for quite a while, but I just now admitted that I knew it. "A while, I guess."

"How'd you know, Cates? How did I give myself away?"

Several things, he thought. Things that showed you weren't an FBI agent, at least not in the sense of somebody who investigates crimes. You didn't know what returning a search warrant was. Then, too, you didn't know that the FBI—the real FBI—had already been to DRT before we got there; you'd have known that if you were one of them.

And, in a strange way, you weren't cynical enough when The Bush got released so easily. You reacted to that just like a common, ordinary citizen who expects justice and for the system to work right. For what you were supposed to be, Winston, you were too damn naive in too many aspects of the cop business.

"Oh, no one thing," he responded at last. "Just a few things here and there."

Winston spoke carefully. "Listen. Trials and arrests don't work for guys like this, Cates. You know that. In a trial, the guy gets to have discovery of the government's case. You know what discovery is, Cates?"

Of course, I know, asshole. I'm a cop, remember? Discovery is where the crook gets to know everything about the prosecution case, gets all the reports, sometimes even gets to read the D.A.'s notes, so he can fabricate the best possible defense.

"Yeah, Winston, I know."

"Well, if a guy gets discovery when he's charged with spying, that means we have to give him and his lawyer all the stuff he was spying about, so he can try to prove it wasn't harmful. Or contrary to the interests of the United States. So he gets access to all the secret stuff in the guise of preparing his defense to the charge of spying. It doesn't work."

Yeah, I guess it doesn't, Cates thought.

"Yeah, I guess it doesn't, Winston."

"So they sent me to shortstop the trial, Cates."

"Shortstop?"

"Shortstop. It's as good a term as any."

"Yeah, I guess it is, Winston. You're a killer."

"I'm a killer."

"An assassin. A government hit man. That's what you are."

"If you put it that way."

"You're here to kill this guy. Among the guys I hang out with, that's called first-degree murder. Premeditation and deliberation. Malice aforethought."

"I prefer shortstop."

"Yeah. I see why you might."

"Besides, I'll only kill him if it becomes necessary."

Cates looked at him disgustedly. "What do you mean? If you don't want him being tried, how could it not be necessary?"

Winston shrugged. "Well, a number of ways. It might be that he would—or will—die anyway, in the ordinary course of events. It might be that you will have killed him, for instance, completely independent of my presence. Maybe he will take his own life to avoid capture. I'm here, ah, as backup to ensure that he does not survive the arrest. To shortstop a trial, as I said."

"Shortstop," Cates repeated.

"Does that bother you?"

"Yeah, I guess it does. You see, Winston, it's kind of like my job to prevent that kind of thing if I can. It's what I get paid those big bucks for. Usually I can't prevent it, of course, so I just have to arrest the guys afterward." He paused. "Hell, yes, it bothers me!"

"I'm sorry about that, Cates. I mean it."

Cates looked at the big man thoughtfully. "You do this often?"

"Here and there. Rarely, actually."

"Do other people do this often? Is it done often in other cases?"

Out of the corner of his eye, Cates could see Winston's mouth move in the shape of a sardonic smile. There wasn't much humor to it. "Isn't this where I'm supposed to begin my answer with something like '*often* is such a difficult term to define,' or something like that?"

Cates didn't respond. Winston continued. "Anyway, the answer is no. It's pretty damn rare, actually."

"Huh," Cates grunted.

Cates thought it over for several moments before speaking again. "Winston."

"Yes."

"Why are you telling me this?"

"I don't know. Because I owe it to you, maybe."

"Why would you owe it to me?"

"Maybe because you're my friend, and I didn't want you to get hurt. This guy's a heavyweight. I didn't want you reacting in a way that would jeopardize yourself because you thought I wanted to arrest the guy instead of kill him."

"That makes sense."

"I thought so. I doubt that the people I work for would think so, however."

They were silent for several moments. Finally, Cates spoke. "One more thing, Winston."

"Yes."

"Are you really with the FBI?"

"Sometimes. I actually work for another, ah, group within the government, though from time to time it is convenient to be an FBI agent assigned to a special strike force. Makes a good cover. And, usually the FBI is in no position to object, as long as I don't embarrass them."

"Did you really go to Harvard, at least?"

"Yes."

"You're really a lawyer, then?"

"Yes."

For some reason that pleased Cates. "Good."

JOYCE'S TELEPHONE made its little electronic chirp.

The sound made her jump, causing her to splash wine from her glass onto the kitchen floor. She had morosely poured a small glass after Steve left, and was standing at the counter gazing out the kitchen window when the call came through.

She made some quick calculations.

Steve had left only ten minutes ago. That meant it couldn't be he—it was too soon. Unless, of course, it was all a false alarm, and now he was calling her up to ruefully explain what was going on.

More likely it was Pam Hotch, calling her up to ask where she was.

Damn, but it made her feel guilty. Guilty about not going down to the company. It just seemed too incredible, too unbelievable, that there could be anything dangerous out there. Steve had it all out of proportion. He was overreacting. Pam was a bitch, but she couldn't be a spy. And here she was, trying at last to be decent, to extend the olive branch and help prevent a security violation, and Joyce was turning it down.

A ruse? Preposterous.

Damn him. It was his fault. She didn't know why this could be so, but that was how she felt.

She decided not to answer the phone. The answering machine would allow her to monitor it. If it was Steve, she could grab it. And, when he told her how he had been mistaken, there might still be time to hurry down to Dirt and give some excuse to Pam about why it had taken her so long to get there.

It wasn't Steve. It wasn't Pam, either.

A familiar masculine voice came over the speaker.

"Ah, Joyce? This is Mike Stevens at Data Security. Ah, there's a, ah, file that's been left out—did Pam Hotch call you about this? She says she did, and I just wanted to, ah, to call—you weren't here yet, and—"

Joyce snatched the telephone up.

"Hello? Mike? This is Joyce."

"Ah, hello, Joyce."

He sounds worried, Joyce thought. She felt a rush of appreciation that he would call her, as stolid and conscientious about his job as he was.

"Of course, Mike. Hi." Joyce made her decision instantly. "I...I was just on my way out to go down there. I got held up a little, that's all."

Jesus, that sounds weak, she thought.

The man on the other end of the telephone hesitated. "Well, Joyce..."

He's having second thoughts, she realized. He's changing his mind. He's going to write it up anyway. Which is what he should do, of course, but here he was willing to let us slide, and somebody in my unit will get a violation out of it. And all because Steve thought...

What did Steve think?

Steve thought it would be dangerous. That something bad was going on at DRT. That it was maybe a ruse to get her down there.

Well, this proved he was wrong.

He had to be. Even if Pam was mixed up in something—drugs, maybe—she wasn't a spy. That would require Mike Stevens to be involved, too, and that was unthinkable. It just wouldn't happen.

"Mike. Look. I'm on my way down. I'll be there in twenty minutes. Fifteen. I really appreciate your call. I just got hung up, that's all."

"Okay, Joyce. Ah, I'll see you—"

The line clicked off.

Joyce frowned at the receiver.

That was odd, she thought. Still, he's so straight arrow, this must have been a tough call for him to make. Real nice of him, however.

She found her keys and purse and headed toward the door.

case closed

THEY WENT IN through a utility door at the rear of the DRT building.

Winston, Cates learned, had obtained a ring of keys and a small slip of paper with combinations to the cipher automatic locks at DRT. As if in anticipation of Cates's question, the tall agent remarked simply that the people he worked with had gotten them for him.

Cates didn't reply.

Moving cautiously, they made their way through the bowels of the building toward the lobby. Most likely the killer would either be on the floor where Joyce worked—where the documents that purportedly had been left out would be—or someplace between the entrance to the building and her floor, waiting to grab her. Without any real reason why, Cates believed it would be the former.

To get there, they had to go through a back hallway. The hallway was unfinished, in the sense that it was Sheetrock or drywall that had never been coated or painted, and there was no carpet or other covering over the cement floor. It was cold in this part of the building. A dry, musty smell emanated from the bare cement and the gypsum in the Sheetrock. Evidently, thought Cates, neither the corporate big shots nor the public used this hall.

Only cops and killers used it, and Cates wondered which category he belonged to.

The stainless-steel revolver with the black rubber grips made a comforting weight in his hand. Its flat finish was dully visible in the bad light.

Winston wore an expensive-looking, tan knee-length trench coat, which made a curious contrast to the unfinished surroundings. Cates noted the cut of the coat, how the upper third of it was styled in a capelike fashion, so that it hung down over the lower two-thirds at about his waist.

Very dashing, he thought sarcastically. But practical—he knew to a certainty that beneath the coat would be the short Uzi and the .45, and that there was some tricky way of getting to them fast.

They passed some storage rooms, some utility rooms, a door marked Electrical and Authorized Personnel Only. The building felt ominously, heavily empty.

Cates looked down the hall. Ahead, the corridor dead-ended into a T with another that ran right and left. A low-wattage bulb glowed from a metal fixture on the ceiling.

Where are you, bastard? Cates thought, forcing his fears to become anger, changing the shape of his emotions to work for him rather than against him. Come out, come out, wherever you are.

For a microsecond he thought, Christ, what if he can dodge bullets? But that was the stuff of ninja fantasy, and anyway it was bullshit.

Forget it.

Forget Beth Fisher's ruined heart. What matters is that you're doing your job, the job the sheriff and the laws of the state of California have commissioned you to do. You're the one people call when something goes bump in the night. Never mind that you might feel a pang or two of uncertainty or mortality.

No sweat. It goes with the territory.

Still, he wished to hell this guy didn't know the *noi cun*.

He glanced at Winston.

The tall black man had taken out a stubby automatic weapon, half carbine, half pistol, from beneath the coat. A strap was looped over his right shoulder, like a purse, and he gripped the weapon close to his body. He moved slowly, with the same tall grace he normally displayed, only somehow it seemed more careful, deliberate, even ponderous. In spite of the cold, his face was shiny with sweat and, Cates realized, anticipation and fear.

They reached the T in the corridor.

"It's to the left," Winston whispered.

Cates nodded and moved forward. He held his revolver in his right hand and supported it with his left, the weapon near his head, muzzle pointed upward.

Come on, killer.

Thank God Joyce hadn't come down.

Noi cun.

He drove the thoughts from his mind, and gripped the gun and smelled the musty hallway to bring him back to reality.

When they got to where the wall ended as the hallway led off to the left, Cates stopped. He looked carefully behind them, and saw the coast was clear, then crouched down on his hands and knees. Putting his head a few inches off the cement floor, he peeked around the corner.

Nothing.

Nothing but the dusty, musty cement odor and a dark-colored door in the dim light and a strange, dark shape crumpled on the floor.

With infinite caution, Cates turned his head 180 degrees and looked down the hallway to the right.

He held his breath in apprehension, knowing that if the killer was there, waiting to scramble his brains with the death touch, it probably would have already happened. Still, he turned his head slowly as if trying not to spook a wild animal.

Nothing there, either.

The hallway was completely empty.

On one side of the corridor, about fifteen feet down, was a steel door marked No Entry. About ten feet beyond that the corridor dead-ended with a set of double doors, both steel with reinforced glass in the top portions. The other side of the glass had evidently been painted white, and the reinforcing wires sandwiched into the glass made a pattern of little diamonds against its background. The two doors were controlled with panic bars on each; Cates could see a chain and padlock looped between them.

No threat there.

Still moving his head slowly, he checked left again.

1199

Everything was the same. The shape on the floor had not moved. It was about the size of a man, and Cates assumed it was what was left of Mike Stevens or one of the other security people. That probably meant the quarry had chosen the lobby or a spot close to it as his ambush site—otherwise, the absence of the guard might have alerted Joyce when, according to the killer's plan, she arrived, unsuspecting, to replace the documents....

He took out his flashlight and shone it down the hall. Its brilliant quartz-generated beam made the ceiling bulb seem dim by contrast.

It illuminated a steel door painted a reddish-brown color that Cates thought of as industrial iron red. The word Lobby appeared on the door, not as a neat placard or professional sign but in a handwritten scrawl with a grease pen or marker of some sort.

The beam also illuminated the shape on the floor.

Cates got to his feet. "Clear," he whispered.

They slipped into the hallway and started toward the lobby door. The flashlight beam had revealed the sprawled form of an elderly man in a blue security guard's uniform. The silver name tag on his uniform shirt said simply Phil. The flesh of his face had been blasted into shredded meat.

No *noi cun* there, Cates thought.

No sirree-bob, that looks like your garden-variety shotgun blast to the face at close range. Double-ought buckshot, by the looks of it. And more than just a few minutes ago; the blood had begun to coagulate into jellylike beads and rivulets.

Cates felt a strange sense of exhilaration.

Partly this was because any lingering doubts as to his and Winston's theories had vanished. More than that, it was because at last the battle was joined, or very soon would be. The cards had been dealt and the hand would be played. Whatever was going to happen would happen. And soon.

But to Cates the pitiful sight of old Phil's ruined body and the ghastly damage to his face did something else as well. It somehow made their quarry seem less superhuman, more mortal, to find that he had used such a common killer's weapon. True, it could mean that he had somebody else with him, but that wasn't likely. This guy was a loner. And equally true, it could mean he was even more dangerous, because he had a weapon in addition to the terrible art of the death touch.

But none of that mattered.

Gut-level emotions, not logic, were at work. And those emotions reclassified the killer, restored him to the status of what he was, not a martial arts superman but a dirtbag criminal murderer, albeit a highly dangerous one.

Cates realized he was nodding to himself. He could deal with people like that. After all, it was his job. It went with the territory.

He glanced at Winston. Fear was evident on the tall agent's face as he surveyed the guard's body.

Cates made a minute gesture with his head toward the lobby door. He wanted to press forward, to finish the deadly game now, to ride the exhilaration before it faded.

For a moment, Winston didn't respond. Then he nodded slightly.

The door was designed to open toward them. Cates gathered himself and gripped the knob with his left hand, his weapon held muzzle pointing upward by his right shoulder. Gently, ever so slowly, he applied pressure to turn the knob.

Not locked. And soundless.

He glanced at Winston. All ready.

Cates took a deep breath and let half of it out. He yanked the door open and dived into the lobby to the left, rolled and came up in a crouch with the revolver gripped in both hands at arm's length before him, his balance a little forward from long habit, so that if he took a hit maybe he wouldn't go over backward but could instead stay on his feet and get off a couple of shots in return.

The lobby was dark and expensive looking. Dim lights glowed in the corners and from recesses in the walls, revealing the shapes of furniture and large indoor plants and trees.

Nothing moved.

Where are you, you bastard? his mind screamed.

Nothing moved.

His eyes swept the darkened room and the blood pounded in his ears, and then suddenly one of the plant shapes flew toward him faster than the eye could follow, except the plant was a man, and somehow he knew the man's feet were coming at him in a terrifying kick, a kick that could kill.

He knew there was no time for the gun.

As the killer's foot flashed toward his chest some instinct or training, perhaps from the t'ai chi ch'uan, allowed him to instantaneously relax, exhale and turn a degree or two away from the direct vector of the blow. And still it knocked him backward, and he went spinning across a low coffee table, both hands still clenched around his gun and a terrible, paralyzing pain building and growing inside his body.

He had a flash from the autopsy and what the heart had looked like. Then his pain grew and spread, and his consciousness seemed to dwindle and narrow down into a tunnel, through which he could watch with a curious detachment the events at the other end of it. It was like looking through a kid's telescope from the wrong end.

He watched the tiny figures through the telescope.

There was Winston, turning toward Cates and his assailant. He had gone to the right side when he and Cates came through the door, as Cates had gone left. He was bringing his automatic weapon toward the man, and through the tunnel Cates was able to see that it was okay for Winston to shoot because the kick had knocked Cates out of the line of fire. Not safe, maybe, but okay, though all that really didn't seem to matter much.

But the man was bringing out a gun of his own.

It was a short, sawed-off shotgun, a bastard weapon, the type of gun used by ordinary killers, and through the telescope Cates could see that he would fire before Winston could.

Too bad, he thought distractedly.

Then he realized his own gun was still in his hands at the end of his outstretched arms as he lay on the carpet, and it would be nice if he could shoot, too. He concentrated really hard, trying to tell his hands to point the gun at the man and pull the trigger, but nothing seemed to work anymore and he felt all cold and dead inside.

The tunnel narrowed a little.

His mind screamed orders at him. *Fight it, Steve, fight it, don't give in, you won't die unless you want to....*

He could still see Winston through the tunnel. You're not going to make it in time, Winston, he thought. Then for an instant it appeared that maybe Winston was going to make it—he was fast for such a big man.

But at that moment an orange flame leaped a foot out of the man's bastard weapon, and the twin blasts, a sort of hollow *bomb-bomb!* And Winston was flying backward, hurled by the impact of the buckshot or whatever bastard ammunition the man was using. Winston's own weapon was firing aimlessly and no doubt chewing up the paneling on the far wall of the lobby. Through the tunnel Cates could smell the sharp, dry, chemical smell of the burned gunpowder.

Curiously, the tunnel seemed to open up a little. Cates heard some more gunshots, slower and evenly spaced, almost deliberate. Belatedly he realized they came from his own gun.

Good. The signals he had given his hands must have gotten through.

He counted the shots. One, two, three, four. Then for some reason they stopped, something he didn't really remember but might have to do with training, something about always saving a couple in case there was another threat somewhere else.

One and two missed, he knew.

Three and four didn't. The man turned to look at him, and the dim light illuminated his face and his form for the first time.

He looked short, and even with the bad lighting Cates could see he was massively muscular. His shoulders were thick and deep, and his legs bulged at the thighs, like a speed skater's. His thick dark hair was straight, and he had cleanly chiseled features that wore a puzzled expression, as if he didn't know what had happened.

He looked at Cates and then down at the stomach area of his own body, where presumably the bullets had struck, but Cates couldn't see any marks because it was dark and the man had on dark clothing as well.

Then the tunnel was gone and Cates realized he was able to move.

He rolled himself onto all fours, and Christ his chest hurt, but the hurt felt wonderful because he could move and it seemed to energize him. The man was probing his abdominal area with his left hand and the sawed-off shotgun dangled down in his right. Cates pushed himself to his feet and took a deep breath, which also hurt and also felt good.

From somewhere beyond the stocky killer came the sound of a key in a lock, followed by two sharp metallic clicks. The main door to the lobby opened and somebody came in.

Cates froze, stunned.

No!

It was Joyce.

Her purse hung from her left arm, and she was trying to re-move her keys with her right hand, and both Cates and the killer swiveled toward her at the same moment.

Instantly, the man with the death touch sprang at her.

He was there even before she turned around. He snatched her away from the door and whipped her like a doll around in front of him, his left arm like an iron bar around not her neck but across the front of her shoulders. With his right hand he broke open the breech of the sawed-off shotgun to reload it.

Hostage!

"No!"

The word tore from Cates's throat in a terrible roar. No fear. No uncertainty. It was a bellowed order, a command of how things would be.

Cates swept his revolver up toward them.

His senses felt so alert and attuned that things appeared to enter a dimension of superslow motion. He could see it all, microsecond by microsecond; microframe by microframe in the high-speed camera of his eye and his brain.

He saw the man reloading his common killer's shotgun, this man who had murdered a young woman with some incredible ability from his bare hands and the *noi cun*, but who was really nothing more than a dirtbag murderer. He could see Joyce, shocked and uncomprehending, a human shield for half the man's body, a shield who would feel pain and bleed and maybe die if Cates missed.

If he missed.

And without hesitation, Cates swept his weapon around, the Smith & Wesson revolver, a cop's weapon in a cop's hands, and at precisely the right microsecond he fired.

He fired not once but twice, snapping off the last rounds in his weapon, two quick booms that sounded different and not as loud as the earlier blasts from the stocky man's brute weapon.

And now the brute killer was staggering back, and Cates was making a headlong football charge, a linebacker filling the hole, slamming into the dying man with his shoulder, knocking him away from Joyce and into the wall.

As the killer bounced off the wall toward him, Cates stepped to one side and clubbed him on the back of the head with his empty revolver as he fell.

Noi cun, my ass, he thought in a strange, wild exultation.

He grabbed Joyce as she staggered, apparently about to faint, and hauled her out of reach of the fallen killer. She collapsed against him, and he caught her and held her to keep her from falling, never taking his eyes off the man he had shot and then body-blocked into the wall.

The man lay sprawled on his back, his chest working painfully. There was no bright frothy blood from his mouth, so maybe the lungs hadn't been hit. If that was so, the tough bastard just might make it.

Not likely, but possible. Fascinated, Cates studied him, the thick legs discernible even through his trousers, the incredible development in the arms and neck clearly visible above his clothing.

Behind him, at the other end of the hall, something moved.

Cates took a quick glance over his shoulder, and saw Winston struggling to his feet.

"Winston!"

Even as he spoke, Cates realized the tall black agent must have been wearing body armor.

Winston got to his feet in evident pain. A dark trickle of blood ran from the corner of his mouth. He shed the Uzi, the strap of which was still over his shoulder. And he took off the trench coat, revealing the bulletproof body armor beneath it.

The center of the vest had been chewed and mangled as the high-tech synthetic fabric and backing had absorbed the projectiles from the sawed-off shotgun. A dark stain showed above the vest, near the neck, proof that some of the pellets had struck him above the armor.

But he was alive.

Winston's face was contorted in pain and anger. "Anybody ever tell you it doesn't hurt, he's lyin'. It just doesn't kill you, that's all."

"How bad?" Cates demanded.

"I'll live. What about him?"

"Let's take a look."

It suddenly occurred to Cates that if Winston could have body armor on, so could the killer. But the dark stain of blood soaking into the carpet said otherwise.

Cates let go of Joyce. She could stand. He dumped the six empties from his revolver and expertly reloaded, using one of the speed-loaders and never taking his eyes off the fallen man. He tossed the speed-loader aside, and looked closely at the man's chest, and yes, it was still moving. Then, too, the blood was still flowing from his side, which was some indication of life.

To be still alive, with four high-velocity .357 rounds in him, meant he was a tough man indeed.

"I think he's still alive," Cates said.

"I'll take care of that," Winston said, his expression ugly.

"No, you won't."

Before Winston could respond, Cates holstered his weapon and took out a set of handcuffs. Every nerve taut, alert for any sudden resistance and ready to react with ultimate physical force if any occurred, he rolled the wounded man over onto his stomach and cuffed him with practiced ease. The wrists were so thick in bone and muscle they almost didn't take the cuffs.

"Cates."

He looked at Winston. The man was holding a small case in his hand, something like an eyeglasses case. "Yeah?"

"Why don't you go for a short walk?"

Cates glanced at the case and shook his head. "No."

"Do it, Cates."

"What's in that little case, Winston?"

Winston's voice was an angry snarl. "For God's sake, Cates! This is my job. Now you take Joyce and you two go find a telephone and call for an ambulance and for the cops, and I'll watch the prisoner here."

Cates looked at him for a moment, then shook his head. "No."

"Don't worry, I won't shoot him. Now, take a walk!"

"And when we come back he'll look just the same, with my bullet holes in him, only he'll be dead and there'll be a little tiny needle track somewhere? And some medically undetectable drug in his system? Is that it, Winston?"

"For Christ's sake, Cates, he's probably gonna die anyway!"

"Maybe."

Their eyes met and locked. Cates could feel the will and the fury in the black man's determination.

"Go make the telephone call, Cates."

Cates looked at Winston grimly. "You're a friend, Winston. And you're one of the best partners I ever had."

"Go make the call."

"But he's my ten-sixteen. He might live and he might die. But the fight's over. I won it. I'm taking him in, assuming he doesn't bleed to death while we're arguing."

Cates could hear the rasping of breath, Winston's or the wounded man's, he couldn't be sure which. He must be one tough dude, thought Cates with a certain grudging admiration. Both of them, actually.

"Go make the call, Cates."

Winston's eyes glittered dangerously. There was no banter in his voice. He was giving an order, and he expected it to be obeyed. Cates suddenly knew that Winston was every bit as dangerous as the man on the floor.

It was now-or-never time.

Deliberately, he drew his revolver and pointed it at the tall black man. His hand was steady, his voice deadly. "You go make the call, Winston."

"Cates!"

"I'll shoot you if you come any closer, Winston."

For long seconds, they stared at each other, eyes locked in a mortal contest of wills. Then, finally, Winston let out the air in his lungs in a long sigh. He nodded slightly, more to himself than to Cates, and took a step backward, lifting his hands slightly to the sides in a gesture of submission.

After several seconds, he spoke. "Cates."

"Winston."

"They were right about one thing, you know." The voice sounded more normal, more in control, and even had a little of the cultured sound of the old Winston to it.

"What's that?"

"You are indeed intractable."

Cates nodded and lowered his weapon. "That I am, Winston."

Old spies never die.
They return with a vengeance.

R O B E R T   P R I C K E T T

Trans Continental Airlines is paying a cool million every month to terrorists threatening to blow up their planes. The CIA is baffled, and in desperation it contacts the one man prepared to stop them—Cantrell, a top agent before his breakdown....

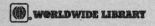

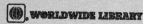

Dan Fortune is back—neck-deep in murder

MINNESOTA Strip

Private investigator Dan Fortune is up against one of his gris-
liest cases ever! Hired to locate a missing boy who is determined to avenge the brutal murder of a Vietnamese refugee,
Fortune finds himself deep in a nasty network of white slav-
ery, narcotics, prostitution and . . . hired killers.

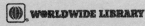